A Switch in Times

The Clash of Timelines: Volume II
Blaine McCants

Antimacassar Books

Cover Art by Lance Buckley

ISBN 978-1-957754-08-6

This is a work of fiction. All of the events and characters portrayed in this novel are either products of the author's imagination or are historical figures portrayed fictitiously.

Contents

Introduction

I started reading science fiction when I was twelve. Indeed, I retain my dog-eared, softcover copy of H. Beam Piper's *Lord Kalvan of Other-when* from that era. I always wanted to write something akin to Piper's *Paratime* series, but naturally life got in the way.

I graduated from college in 1975, became an US Air Force officer, and left active duty after four years to get a PhD in economics. Subsequently, I collected paychecks as a federal government civilian employee. I am now completely retired, both as a civilian and from the USAF Reserves.

I feel I owe a debt to the US Navy, which, back in the day, put up with me for a year as I attended their War College in Newport, Rhode Island. I enjoyed my year on Aquidneck Island. Except for all those lobster rolls; it turns out they play heck with one's cholesterol.

Finally, a special thanks to all those who put on the uniform, got up at zero dark whenever, and then got orders to hurry up and wait.

Dramatis Personae

The Sherwood Family
John "Hotshot" Smith (born Robin Fletcher Sherwood)
Maude (maternal aunt to Robin Sherwood)
Max (husband of Maude; retired Ft. Detroit City mob enforcer)
The Bala Cynwyd Women's College Rifle Team and Associates
Katherine Green (Wife of John Smith)
Melinda Charlotte Arnold Burr (Wife of Joseph Sammartino)
Penelope Bartholomew Cabot
Ruth Brittany
The Green Family
Sally Elizabeth Shaw Green (mother to Katherine Green)
Joseph "Tiny" Franklin Sammartino (cousin-in-law to Kathy Green)
Rhonda Green Cameron (twin sister to Katherine Green)
The Lafitte Clan
Jean Lafitte (patriarch)
Wendell Honoré (nephew; brother of Delilah; deceased)
Delilah Honoré (niece; sister of Wendell; psychiatrically confined)
Jules Thibodeaux (nephew; brother of Victoria; restaurateur)
Victoria Thibodeaux (niece; sister of Jules; historian; businesswoman)
The Burr Family
Sir Charles Burr
Lady Charlotte Cabot Burr
Royal Confederated Colonies Royal Marines
Master Sergeant Lucius (Scarbutt) Oglethorpe
Major Stuart
Captain Franks

RFC Army

Major General Sir Randolf Bartholomew (uncle of Penelope and godfather of Melinda)

Brigadier Madeline Hamilton, Chief, WASP Legal Affairs

Warrant Officer First Class Glynda Smith, Senior Admin for Brig Hamilton

Sir Rupert, Permanent Senior Secretary, Department of the Army

RFC Navy

Vice Admiral Francis, Deputy Chief of Naval Operations

Senior Rear Admiral Frazier, Head of Navy Legal

Commander Woodson, XO to Admiral Frazier

Rhode Island and Providence Plantations Colony Militia, Women's Auxiliary Service Program, 1st Mounted Dragoons, Troop "A," "The Valkyries"

Anne

Barbara

Beth

Connie

Francine

Jennifer

Susan

Assorted Other Characters

Eduardo (purveyor of illicit drugs, in a coma)

Miss Eva Braun (alleged actress)

Ferret Phil (thug from Ft. Pitt City)

Herr Doctor Professor I. Ron Cross (actor)

Jasmine, aka Miss Annabelle Lee (former secretary to Delilah Honoré)

Ratso Jimmy (thug from Ft. Pitt City)

The Visitors from a Different Earth

Major Paul Drake, Intelligence Operative

Senior Sergeant Llywelyn, bodyguard

Major Lycus, cross-earth-travel air-sea craft pilot

Major Marcus, cross-earth-travel air-sea craft navigator

Sergeant Julius, communications technician

Dr. Astrid Martingale, surgeon
Nurse Mary Potter, Senior Sister of Healing
Nurse Theodora Karras, Senior Sister of Healing
Members of the Irish Fraternal Organizations
The Widow Bridget O'Shaughnessy
Elizabet O'Conner (personal secretary to Bridget O'Shaughnessy)
Slab (bodyguard to Bridget O'Shaughnessy)
Wires (bodyguard to Bridget O'Shaughnessy)
'Fingers' Malone (Safecracker)

Part One

Visitors

The Unexpectedly Cordial Cajun

Fiddlers Green Restaurant, Philadelphia, Commonwealth of Pennsylvania Colony, Royal Federated Colonies, Greater British Empire

"Uh, Tiny, don't flinch, but the guy who just walked into your restaurant, well, your gorgeous and homicidally insane new bride gut-shot his cousin."

Tiny, whose actual name was Joseph Franklin Sammartino, was obviously not used to dealing with such subtle hints; he flinched.

I was born Robin Fletcher Sherwood and I still have issues when a conversation turns to green leggings, feathered hats, and bows and arrows. When I was eighteen years old, I enlisted in the marines under an assumed name even dumber than Robin Sherwood.

My first name change actually didn't last very long. The marines sent my boot camp graduation picture and a standard blurb to my hometown newspaper. The newspaper wrote back and provided the marines my real name. That event precipitated the first occasion I got yelled at by officers instead of sergeants. It wasn't the last such occasion; not by a boatload.

My legal name got changed again, this time to John Smith, when I joined an ultra-elite unit for my third and final hitch in the corps. Of course, everyone in that unit was named John Smith, so my colleagues nicknamed me Hotshot. I had a talent for pushing lead downrange.

Well, sometimes I also have responded, reluctantly, to "Hey, stupid." It's a sad fact many marines have suffered similar indignities due to the company we are often forced to keep. Squids often give vent to their well-deserved inferiority complex by insulting their betters. But I digress.

Life happened, my hitch ran out, and I left active duty. I became a security consultant for a couple of years and was soon up to my ears in murders, drugs, and spies. Almost a year ago, I married a former client after an Imperial Russian Spetsnaz platoon attacked her and her best friend forever. You'd have thought things couldn't get worse than that, but two months ago Wendell Honoré, a legitimately insane and totally drugged-out flicker producer, kidnapped my wife and her best friend, albeit briefly.

In the wake of those adventures, my new wife, the former Miss Katherine Green, her extended family, her friends, and I were all trying to restore our lives back to a semblance of normalcy. Kathy's best friend, fellow alum from Bala Cynwyd Women's College, Melinda Charlotte Arnold Burr Sammartino, had talked the Green family into expanding *Fiddlers Green*, Kathy's family's restaurant. Melinda envisioned adding a combination cocktail lounge and nightclub featuring exotic drinks, the finest wines, light dining, dancing and a cigar bar annex. To that end, Melinda had purchased the building due south of *Fiddlers Green* and was planning how to renovate it.

Penelope Bartholomew Cabot, women's college classmate and rifle-team bosom buddy of both Melinda and Kathy, was the alleged financier of this operation. Kathy and I both knew better. Melinda was worth about sixty million pounds sterling, despite her father publicly disinheriting her three weeks ago, the day she married Tiny. Melinda swore us to secrecy and kept Tiny in the dark about her personal wealth. I thought her secrecy obsession was a stupid idea, but I hadn't been permitted to voice an opinion.

Melinda wanted the annex, in part, as an excuse to keep seven of her surviving lady bodyguards employed and on her payroll. They were all veterans of the now disbanded Rhode Island and Providence Plantations Colony Militia's Women's Auxiliary Service Program, 1st Squadron Mounted Dragoons, the Valkyries, for which Melinda had served as Colonel Commanding.

Melinda had established the unit, on a whim, back when she was still on speaking terms with her father. He was a multi-billionaire who basically owned the governor of Rhode Island and Providence Plantations Colony and controlled a baker's dozen Members of Parliament of the Royal Federated Colonies.

One former Valkyrie, Barbara, was no longer mobile enough to serve as part of Melinda's first-line security team. She had her legs chewed up by shrapnel when Wendell Honoré, the aforementioned crazed flicker producer, kidnapped Kathy and Melinda. Barbara was now studying to acquire her sommelier's certification. Her nickname from when she served in the Royal Federated Colonies' WASP Military Police was "*Grape Juice.*" We expected her job switch would work out well.

The other six Valkyries would serve as waitresses and hostesses in the wine bar while simultaneously providing security for Melinda and the club. We expected Anne, Beth, Connie, Francine, Jennifer and Susan to arrive any day.

These ladies already had Pennsylvania Colony security guard accreditation. They were also licensed in Rhode Island and North Carolina, but Melinda wouldn't return to Rhode Island and I couldn't envision circumstances under which we again would visit North Carolina Colony, down in the Royal Crown Colonies.

Right now Melinda and Kathy were in a back office mushing around and trying to design attractive waitress and hostess uniforms which would enable the Valkyries to carry concealed weapons. They had nothing better to do because Melinda's architect was again reworking his remodeling design to better fit with Melinda's evolving ideas for creating a swank appearance.

Meanwhile, Tiny, the former maître d' of *Fiddlers Green*, was instructing me on how to replace him in that function at the main restaurant. I acquired a lot of experience in both launching and dodging lead projectiles during my three tours in the marines; having opportunities to not dodge big wads of cash seemed like a decidedly pleasant career move.

I discovered the most important part of my new job was palming gratuities deftly enough to neither call excessive attention to the customer's generosity nor deprecate his largess. It's tougher than it sounds;

Tiny's hands were almost twice the size of mine, so he was much better than I was at hiding or displaying the right amount of cash.

It was still early evening when the door opened and a well-dressed man of thirty years old walked in. He had dark hair, blue eyes, was a tad overweight, and had an incipient case of male-pattern baldness. He was carrying two formal stationery envelopes, smothered with gilt and closed with wax seals. Tiny had not reacted to him in the slightest when he had first entered the restaurant. I gave Tiny the prompt which made him flinch.

The man fluttered his envelopes. "I am not a process server, Mr. Smith. One of these is for you and the former Miss Katherine Green. Could you tell me how to find Mr. Joseph Sammartino? The other one is for him and his new wife, the former Miss Melinda Burr."

"Tiny," said I, "this is Mr. Jules Thibodeaux. He was a first cousin to the now justly deceased Mr. Wendell Honoré.

"Jules, the massive mountain of muscle standing beside me in his overpriced threads is Mr. Joseph Sammartino, known to his family as Tiny. Joey, meet Jules. Jules, meet Joey. Do you plan to expand your dine and dance operations into the Commonwealth of Pennsylvania Colony, Jules?"

"No, my uncle took your advice. He sold all of those gentlemen's clubs to an ostensibly legitimate, closely held corporation, albeit one controlled by the widow of a previous chairman of one of the New York Fraternal Organizations. I no longer have to work with the hard guys. While I am grateful to you for that, I am here because my sister, Vicki, and I would like to extend our personal thanks to your wives."

"That's decent of you, Jules. Not many people would thank the folks responsible for getting your other cousin, Delilah Honoré, stuffed into a rubber room."

"She deserved it, Mr. Smith. My uncle's not dumb. He has sources of his own. Moreover, after you reported back to him on the official how's and why's of Wendell getting his just deserts, Uncle Jean thinks he figured out some parts of the story you left out. He shared his thoughts with Vicki and me."

Jules took a deep breath; then locked eyes with me.

"So I would like to thank Mrs. Smith for shooting Sidney Parker before he could kill me, and Vicki definitely would like to thank Mrs. Sammartino for perforating Cousin Wendell. Vicki never forgave Wendell for what he did to poor Snowball; she loved the mutt. Also, it's now clear Wendell wanted to be Uncle Jean's only heir, so he would have murdered Vicki eventually. We feel obliged to you all; we don't like to leave our debts unpaid."

I had met Jules and Victoria Thibodeaux separately, almost two years ago, when his uncle, Jean Lafitte, had hired me to find out why two of Lafitte's top executives had been killed and, in another instance, turned into a vegetable. I thought I had cracked that case, but realized, almost too late, that I had missed the guilty tree hidden in an entire forest full of red herrings.

Back then, Jules was managing a string of his uncle's semi-sleazy roadside strip-clubs slash restaurants slash mob-adjacent money-laundering operations in New York, Connecticut and Rhode Island Colonies. Jules's sister, Miss Victoria Thibodeaux, a raven-haired beauty, had fronted for her Uncle Jean's accounting firm down in North Carolina Colony. I suspected her of being an accessory before the fact to murder, but not, I told myself, merely because she had looks to kill for.

Two months ago, Jules' Cousin Wendell had kidnapped Kathy and Melinda. Wendell had planned a full menu of torture and rape for the ladies. Wendell was about to finish with the hors d'oeuvres and proceed to the entrée when Melinda managed to plug Wendell five times in the gut with her hide-out gun. And then she plugged him a few more times, just a bit lower, for what she believed were good and sufficient reasons. The constabulary declared, officially, that Wendell and his chauffeur had killed each other during a pinochle game gone badly wrong.

I reviewed my interactions with Jules and Vicki. Neither, personally, had ever wronged me, my kith, nor kin, though Vicki had been a tad abrupt during her interactions with me. Still, given the criminal history of one of my relatives, not to mention many of Kathy's, who was I to cast such aspersions on anyone? I figured I would listen to his pitch.

Jules continued, "Open the invitations, Mr. Smith, Mr. Sammartino."

Miss Victoria Thibodeaux and Mr. Jules Thibodeaux
Request the pleasure of your presence for an extended stay at
Chateau Pirates' Paradise, Outer Banks, North Carolina Colony.
Please respond in person to Mr. Jules Thibodeaux
At your earliest convenience

"Vicki and I are joint owners. It's a modest little thing compared to what the former Miss Burr is used to; only twelve rooms, but it has a gorgeous ocean view. It's in a semi-private community. The only access to it is through a North Carolina Colony park and the park closes to the public every day at dusk."

Tiny shook his head a fraction, "I don't know. Thanks, I guess, but money looks tight for a while. Melinda swears the numbers work out, but the loan she took from Penelope was huge."

Jules started to speak, but I stepped back a half step so that Tiny couldn't see my face and I shook my head a fraction. Then I said, "Tiny, why don't you go upstairs where the ladies are working so we can bring them in on this? I'll keep Jules occupied."

Tiny headed upstairs; I signaled the senior waiter to take over at the maître d's station. Jules and I grabbed an isolated, vacant table.

Jules blurted out, "Vicki says Melinda is still worth mid- to high-eight figures. Vicki's employees create and analyze dodgy financial statements involving multiple shell corporations for a living. What is going on with Joey?"

"Melinda doesn't want Tiny to feel like a kept man. Don't breathe a word. She's still looking for the right way to tell him she's still wealthy as sin. Also, if we go, we will take a security detail of a half dozen lady bodyguards. Melinda is still paranoid after two dozen Imperial Russian Spetsnaz troopers took potshots at her. And of course your late Cousin

Wendell made two kidnapping attempts on her, the second of which briefly succeeded."

Jules looked up at me; he had been glancing idly at a dinner menu. "Imperial Spetsnaz, wow; your authorities sure smothered that story. I heard there was a massive burglary attempt gone badly wrong at the Burr mansion, but had no clue there had been an earlier kidnapping attempt. I guess every family has secrets."

He paused; then continued, "Speaking of secrets, Uncle Jean told me if I thought you folks might accept our invitation to coastal Carolina, I should tell you the full story about Vicki. He didn't want you to set her off, inadvertently. She's sort of fragile."

Jules gave me a look; then he took a deep breath. I guess it wasn't easy for him to share family secrets.

"Well, I always thought Sidney Parker scored on his charm alone; he had me fooled for sure. Memory wiping drugs followed by rape! He deserved what your angels of vengeance gave him.

"Yeah, you never came right out and said which of your ladies shot Sidney, but my uncle's not dumb. Kathy and Melinda qualified for Olympic rifle team slots and their pal Penelope is no slouch. Still, Melinda was in Europe and Kathy is a better shot than Mrs. Cabot, so I know who the smart money would pick to take the kill shot on Sidney."

"No comment. What's this to do with Vicki?"

"I'm sort of sneaking up on that. The official story about Wendell and his driver, Robert, killing each other over a card game is pure bull. As next of kin, Uncle Jean saw Wendell's body. Only a badly wronged lady would take those particular shots. I figure Wendell didn't kidnap your ladies merely to grab some ransom."

That kidnapping never happened, officially, because Kathy's former RFC Army Reserve boss had intervened. Brigadier Madeline Hamilton, Women's Army Service Program Chief of Legal Affairs, somehow had leaned on the New York Provincial Constabulary. The latter quickly went public with their idiotic alternative explanation for Wendell's death.

I blinked, and Jules was staring at me. "I believe it means they each have something sort of in common with Vicki."

"What are you implying, Jules?"

Jules responded. "Do you remember what I said about the late Gallant Captain Freddy to whom Vicki was engaged, albeit briefly? I sort of lied to you; that was the cover story Uncle Jean and I came up with once we found out what actually happened.

"Vicki had been saving herself for her wedding night; she wanted to live that whole faux aristo thing which was her public persona. Gallant Captain Freddy tired of waiting. So one night he got plastered and beat the crap out of Vicki. You can figure out the rest. She had to wear pancake makeup for a month. I guess Captain Freddy thought he was connected enough to get away with it."

I nodded slightly. Our RFC aristocrats are not known for an atrophied sense of entitlement, but the aristos in the Royal Crown Colonies usually make our own nobs look like St. Francis of Assisi.

Jules continued. "My sister's no shrinking violet. She didn't inform Uncle Jean or me about this until after she steamrolled Captain Freddy into prison on bogus charges. We still don't know how she set that up, not that she'll ever say.

"One thing I still don't know is whether Captain Freddy getting himself scragged while in prison was premeditated or not. I don't think Vicki arranged his death, and I wouldn't begin to know how to organize such a thing, but Uncle Jules might have. He knows a lot of folks on the dark side.

"That episode left Vicki with a lot of emotional scars. She didn't always wear her resting bitch face twenty-four seven. I think it would be good for her to be with normal folks for a while."

He gave me an expansive grin. "I have a roomy definition of normal."

Tiny returned with the ladies and they joined us at the table. Jules explained it was a sincere invitation to visit *Chateau Pirates' Paradise*. The two of them rented it out summers and then Vicki stayed there when she took her own mandatory two-week out of office stint every late September. Right now, their rental management firm was oversee-ing the chateau's top-to-bottom, end-of-season housecleaning.

Jules then hit us with his best shot. "We don't keep servants at the beach house. That means we have to cook all our own meals and all of us will pitch in on the cleaning up. John knows I managed restaurants of a sort for Uncle Jean; I planned to earn enough to start my own high-end restaurant. I don't hate managing, but I loathe working for other people, so my goal is to become an owner-chef. I had heard you folks don't have any actual cuisine here *Fiddlers Green* and my quick glance at your menu confirmed that."

Kathy went rigid. "We have the finest steaks and chops, and we serve both Provence and Northern Italian cuisine of extraordinary quality. Our head chef, Leonardo, is a Philadelphia legend. I am close to getting my intermediate chef's certification as well."

Talk about a home girl. That's my Kathy. Then Jules gave her a laughing semi-sneer and zeroed in on her weak point. He obviously had done his homework.

"You haven't tasted actual food until you have tasted Cajun and Cre-ole. I was the third best Cajun chef in New Orleans and I know I can improve my skills further. I only worked for Uncle Jean to earn enough money to start a place of my own. I've now saved enough money to open a restaurant, but I want to brush up on my cooking.

"I figure preparing meals three times a day for a dozen folks would help me return to something close to professional competence. Also, Mrs. Smith, if you ever wish to learn how to cook zesty food and not just stuff smothered in cream sauces, I guess this could be your golden opportunity."

I glanced back at Kathy. She looked like a laryngitis-stricken turkey trying to make gobble-gobble noises. I was so not going to share that description with her. Jules kept talking.

"Tell you what; let me go back in your kitchen for half an hour. I figured out how to prepare *Lobster Thibodeaux* suitable for white bread and mayonnaise northern palates. Then you folks think about it for a day or two and decide if you wish to learn what real cuisine tastes like."

Kathy composed herself, led Jules back to the kitchen, and introduced him to the kitchen staff. She returned, and I spent the next half hour warning everybody their taste buds would lock down in shock while their hearts gave up the ghost. I cautioned the ladies this had to be a convoluted, devious plot to kill us all. Jules emerged from the kitchen with a lobster salad of some sort.

Kathy took one bite of *Lobster Thibodeaux*. She then signaled for Melinda to take a bite. Melinda did and nodded. Kathy spoke.

"Pay no attention to my idiot husband, Jules. Is there anything we can bring when we come down to visit?"

Well, that was a whole different kettle of *étouffée*.

Interlude: The Dirigible of Deadly Deceit

Somewhere over far Western Canada

The door at the top of the circular staircase opened just as I reached for the handle. I had tired of all the adulation coming my way every time I wandered into the first-class passenger lounge, so I decided I would work on my tan. The tanning deck on our super-luxurious transcontinental dirigible was topside, naturally. It was restricted to premier-class passengers, so I was surprised to discover it already occupied.

I stepped onto the deck. Two very healthy young ladies, dressed in much less-than-regulation navy lady lieutenant's white uniforms, snapped salutes at me. I returned their salutes automatically.

I regarded them carefully. They appeared to be twins, both of them blonde, though one of them wore an exceptional amount of mascara and eye shadow. I guess the goop was to help me tell them apart.

Their abbreviated uniforms consisted only of translucent short sleeve blouses with shoulder board rank tabs, similarly translucent form-fitting, mid-thigh skirts, white suspenders and tights and white deck shoes. It was exactly the same uniform my marine recruiter had sworn all navy stewardesses wore. Until this moment I figured he had been lying to me about such uniforms; he certainly had lied to me about everything else.

"Ladies; I'm off duty and all I'm wearing is a pair of swim trunks. What's with the salutes?"

The blonde sans the eye-shadow responded.

"Major Muffin, Sir! The Pride of Provincetown is also a Navy Reserves Auxiliary dirigible. We are both detailed as navy stewardesses for *special passengers. We are thrilled to meet you. Our orders are to provide you with anything you need to ensure your journey from Victoria to New York City is both relaxing and personally pleasurable.*

"My call sign is 'Blondie.' My sister's call sign is 'Angel Eyes.' Your whim is our desire. We can't believe we were fortunate enough to meet you, especially after you saved the Emperor of the Chrysanthemum Empire from a fate worse than death, and he offered you the hand of his eldest daughter in marriage. We saw her picture in the papers. She's a total knockout."

"That's the problem, girls; marriage. This here magnificently chiseled stud-muffin marine just ain't quite ready to settle down. Besides, I figured the cheapskate emperor should have at least offered the hand of one of his many nieces to Captain Smedley. Smedley deserves some credit for saving world civilization."

Both blonde babes grimaced and shuddered visibly. Angel Eyes spoke. "We met the socially challenged Captain Smedley earlier today. He inquired whether the two of us would like to join him for some exotic recreation. We declined his disgusting offer, with prejudice. Right now he is bothering the first officer about the Mark XIX auto-pilot system newly installed on our dirigible."

"Yeah, Smedley never changes. All he cares about are dirigibles, golf, and beautiful dolls of sufficiently low moral character. Speaking of which, girls, what's with the almost see-through uniforms?"

"Oh, it's because we're on a dirigible. Weight savings, you know. But that's not important. Right now we have to make you comfortable, with a nice tall drink, so you can enjoy the midday sunshine."

"Pull the other one, ladies. It has bells on it. You and I both know the moment Professors Franken and Furter discovered how polarized negatronic rays interacted with confined helium atoms to give the latter negative atomic mass, weight hasn't been an issue for any dirigible."

They both grinned. Then Blondie pouted. "The VADM in charge of BURNAVPER held an auction for all the young single ladies at HQ the moment he discovered you would be booked on this dirigible. You wouldn't believe what we had to promise to do with that lecherous old goat to get this gig. He is more disgusting than is Captain Smedley. Still, it will be worth it, even if all we do is to bask briefly in the aura of your incredible masculinity."

"You got that right, ladies. Still, you might try to have his wife show up right before things become too intimate. I've heard that usually works to dampen his badly aging ardor."

I shooed them away, then spread out, face down, on one of the six chaise lounges on the otherwise empty tanning deck. About a minute passed before I felt delicate hands rubbing something onto my back.

"Please relax, Major Muffin. It's tanning oil."

I glanced at her. "What happened to your uniform, Angel Eyes?"

"Oh, the tanning oil leaves such terrible stains if it gets on our uniforms. We couldn't take the risk. Besides, it's only the three of us, Major Muffin. Is there any other service you desire? And just so you're aware, neither my sister nor I aspire to marriage, though we would both be honored to bear you many, many children."

I sighed, inwardly. Such offers were a recurring hazard of being the most famous marine on the globe and saving the world on a more or less weekly basis.

Suddenly, another voice rang out from the entrance hatchway. It was a feminine, authoritative, and stentorian voice. "I have come for tanning and libations. To where have disappeared the overly indolent domestic servants in charge of administering such?"

Angel Eyes whispered, "That must be Miss Trapp. Well, one of them, anyhow. Nobody knows anything about them, and they have kept to their room so far, but she and her twin sister paid, in gold, for the ultra-premier service, right before we departed from Victoria."

A red-headed vision strode onto the tanning deck. She was stunning. She was dressed in a green and periwinkle diagonally striped silk cocktail dress. It was way too tight. She glanced at the two naked stewardesses and then casually took off her own clothes. Miss Trapp was not wearing any lingerie under her cocktail dress, other than silk suspenders and silk tights. That seemed eccentric even for an ultra-rich passenger. She lay down on the chaise lounge beside me, naked, shame-

less, unconcerned, and far beyond merely gorgeous. I wondered what her game was.

Angel Eyes and Blondie dashed into the adjoining kitchenette only to return moments later wearing regulation summer khaki uniforms. This time they each appeared to be sporting a full set of lingerie and their now opaque skirts' hems fell to their top of their kneecaps. It was crystal clear those mischievous scamps had been lying to me about the weight savings.

Miss Trapp snarled at them when they reappeared. "I require the application of fragrant oils to assist in the epidermal absorption of solar rays. You two scullery drudges! Begin to apply such! When I am well-oiled and glistening, you will bring me a large flute of alcohol-imbued sparkling muscatel."

Angel Eyes and Blondie stood, stunned. Carrot-top ignored them. She focused on me instead. "You would be Major 'Stud' Muffin. I recently read of your adventures in the popular press. Tell me, Major Muffin, why is it those two self-evident, lower-strata female domestics may use the entirety of their bodies to absorb your primary star's ultra-violet rays while you must wear mid-thigh-length breeches which hide your manhood?"

"Where are you from, Miss? And it's my massive manhood. I learned from bitter experience if ladies are unprepared to see too much of me in the altogether, they tend to faint. The navy medical and legal types tired of dealing with all the resulting concussions and lawsuits.

"Oh, and I'm not sure the girls have access to any sparkling muscatel. Maybe, though, they can pour you a generous slug of top-notch Champagne. I know we have oodles onboard."

"I am Miss Honey Trapp, a scientist from Chronos, a small town in, uh, France. What is Champagne? I am subject neither to swooning nor other types of erratic, involuntary autonomic behavior. Why did you ask? Have somehow I made you suspicious? Already?"

"Perish the thought, toots. I was merely wondering if you were from around here. Being French is no big deal. I mean, you French folks are

usually our allies, at least those times when you're not gleefully stabbing us in the back."

The blondes were still looking stunned. I decided to spur them into action. "Hey, Blondie or Angel Eyes; one of you go rustle up a lady's swim outfit for Miss Trapp while the other helps Miss Trapp with her tanning oils and Champagne."

Blondie beat feet. Angel Eyes stared at Miss Trapp, dumbfounded. Miss Trapp ignored her.

I refocused on the scarlet menace. "You being from 'France' and all, I guess I should tell you a few more things about our amazing country."

"There is no need to do so, Major Muffin. My sister and I already researched your, uh, country extensively before we embarked on our journey. But why do I require a garment to swim? It would only increase my body's coefficient of hydrodynamic friction."

Miss Trapp glared at Angel Eyes. "You there, scullery wench; begin rubbing the fragrant tanning oils onto my prominent mammary glands. Do so immediately or I shall have you flogged!"

Miss Trapp next looked at me quizzically. "Or is 'spanked' the correct word in English?"

"In this context it's spanked, Miss Trapp. And don't worry about it, I promise you when the time is right, I will spank her myself. Perhaps you know the old saying, 'If she didn't enjoy being spanked, she never would have let herself be caught by a press gang and forced to join the Royal Navy.'"

I winked at Angel Eyes. "Better do like she says, sweetie. Still, once you're done slathering goop, you and your twin should go track down the charming Captain Smedley. I might be busy with Miss Trapp for a while."

Miss Honey Trapp reeked of mystery; I wondered if I should bring Smedley in on this case. Nah, I had better not. He was always way too over-eager when smoking hot babes were involved. He would rouse her suspicions too quickly. I had a better chance of unearthing her secrets if I handled things all by myself.

I turned my head to examine Miss Trapp more carefully. She packed plenty of assets, and none of those were in any way hidden, but I had growing suspicions she might be from somewhere farther away than Chronos, France. Perhaps from much, much farther away.

Once Upon a Dark and Stormy Night

Outer Banks, North Carolina Colony

"John, remove your nose from that inane book and do not so much as think about taking it with you. Jules and Vicki are expecting us on the upper veranda for casual cocktails. At the least, I expect you to pretend to engage in civilized conversation."

That was my wife Kathy, emerging from our attached dressing room whence she had gone to remove her makeup and day clothes. She emerged wearing a peignoir, evening robe, and slippers. Even sans makeup she looked far better than any somewhat weathered marine ever deserved.

It was nine-thirty at *Chateau Pirates' Paradise*. It had been two weeks since Jules Thibodeaux had tracked us down at Kathy's family's restaurant. Melinda and Tiny had already retired for the evening and would skip the digestifs. Ah, newlyweds.

I had been re-reading, for the gazillionth time, *"Major 'Stud' Versus the Curvaceous Commandos from Contra-Chronos,"* while Kathy changed out of her day clothes. I had been stewing about Wendell Honoré's deathbed warning about aliens from other earths ever since Jules visited *Fiddlers Green*. Alas, Brigadier Madeline Hamilton, the RFC government, and even Kathy and her lady friends seemed oblivious to the prospect of an imminent or extant invasion of underdressed, busty babes from outer space.

Curvaceous Commandos was the premier sciencey fiction novel I owned regarding that subject, albeit the pickings in my travel library were slim. Still, I hoped it might provide me a clue, or at least an inspiration. Someone had to be prepared to thwart an insidious incursion of insufficiently clad ingénues and I figured I was just the marine for the job.

Jules and Vicki were waiting for us, one floor up, on their screened-in, roof-top veranda. Jules poured Kathy a white wine, and the three of them started chatting about stuff.

I grabbed a sparkling mineral water instead of a glass of wine because I was still basking in the spicy afterglow of Jules' Cajun dinner cuisine. Well, I thought it was spicy. Nobody else thought so.

Then I couldn't help myself. Since I had left my novel downstairs, I started playing with my new field glasses. I had left them on the veranda earlier in the day. Vicki had presented them to me when I arrived, figuring I would enjoy them.

Did I ever! They were Jena Optical Products *GmbH*, two-and-a-half-inch in diameter lenses. They were Jena's top of the line and had to have cost a thousand pounds sterling. Vicki must have loathed her late cousin Wendell Honoré with a passion. I only wished there was more to see besides Atlantic waves lapping up on the beach or distant pop-up storms with occasional small bolts of lightning.

I could see the shoreline and parts of the beach because *Chateau Pirates' Paradise* was on a slight rise about fifty yards west of the outer dune. Like all the beach houses in this semi-private community, what should have been the first floor was largely open to the elements. It consisted of twenty-one massive steel and concrete foundation pillars, two stairwells, three small storage rooms for expendables, and paved parking spaces for vehicles. The veranda was placed on the roof like a widow's walk, above the third floor. It faced the Atlantic, so the low outer dune only blocked about half of the wide, sandy beach from my line-of-sight.

So there I was, staring out into the ocean, when a bolt of lightning illuminated a flying ship. I immediately realized it wasn't a lighter-than-air ship like a blimp or a dirigible, because it flew at blazing speed just off the water, roughly parallel to the shoreline. No dirigible would ever go so low over water intentionally. I could sense it was decelerating slowly.

It was also enormous. I didn't have a range finder on the field glasses, but I had my sniper's training and instincts for judging distances. I would have bet my late parents' cherry farm the craft was three hundred feet long. The flying monster prominently displayed a distinctive insignia on its vertical tail. Had it not been for that insignia, the fortuitous lightning, and my new field glasses, I never would have spotted it.

I started jumping up and down and yelling, "It's true; it's true!"

Everyone else stared at me like I had gone crazy. I barked instructions.

"Kathy, warn everybody to go to battle positions. Bring Connie and Susan inside, douse most of the upstairs lights and alert Melinda and Tiny. Tell the Valkyries to grab their carbines. Whatever that thing offshore is, it screams military."

Jules cut the veranda's lights and those in the descending stairway behind us. Vicki grabbed a pair of field glasses for herself. I showed her where the strange craft had come to a stop, about a mile offshore.

I kept scanning the waves. Ten minutes passed before I spotted a large rubber raft heading towards the beach. It landed. Eight figures emerged from the raft, four of them set up a perimeter; they appeared to be armed with some sort of rifles. Two others lifted a smaller rubber raft from the larger raft and carried it a couple dozen yards up the shore, leaving it just past the high tide line.

Then those two returned to the large raft, grabbed what I figured was a large sea bag, carried it a yard or two past the small raft, and dropped it. The final two figures walked up to the smaller raft. They were both wearing dark hoods. One figure took off his hood to expose a mass of white. The other figure slowly unwrapped bandages from the first figure's head and stuffed the bandages into a side pouch.

Half a minute passed and all eight figures gathered. I relaxed just a little; at least they all appeared to be normal human men. The guy who had been wearing the bandage faced the other seven who were lined up with one guy in front and the other six standing in a perpendicular line formation behind him. The seven men pounded their left chests with their right fists and stuck their right hands out straight and level while still making fists. The other man returned the gesture. Then the seven guys got back into the large raft.

The lone guy watched them go. Ten minutes later, the strange monster craft started moving again. It rose about fifteen feet above the ocean, accelerating to an enormous speed. The craft suddenly was engulfed in a ball of flickering energy. I was reminded of St. Elmo's fire. It flickered and vanished. Beside me Vicki muttered, "By the Virgin, what a sight!"

The guy on the beach stared for a bit out towards where the strange craft had vanished. Then he walked a few more yards past his seabag and sprawled out. I kept my glasses focused on him for another five minutes. He didn't move.

I turned to talk to Kathy and Jules; I realized Francine and Jennifer had joined us. I gave my field glasses to Jennifer and said, "We can stand down, sort of. We'll run an indoor guard detail for the rest of the night. I want Anne and Beth up here. They can take turns monitoring the guy lying on the beach. Have them wake me up if he moves or someone else shows up and might discover him.

"I doubt he'll move before dawn. He'll probably stay there for an hour or two after it gets light, just to give somebody a chance to find him seemingly washed up on shore. All the rest of us should try to sleep for a couple of hours. We want to be fresh when dawn arrives and we 'accidentally' find him washed up from his fake mishap."

"I don't have a clue what you're talking about, John; you need to explain." That was Jules.

"It's an infiltration. He will pretend to be shipwrecked or something similar. I don't know how sheltered you are, but no country on earth has the technology to build such a flying craft. Heck, no country has so much as dreamed of having such advanced technology. It's the stuff of two-for-a-half-crown pulp magazines, of which I used to read occasionally, in my early teenage years."

Kathy glared at me. She next raised an eyebrow.

"Okay, I still read the stuff; heck, I've wallowed in it all my life."

Kathy raised her other eyebrow. I had met no one else with such precise eyebrow control.

"Right; I read this stuff every waking hour where I don't positively have to do something else. I am completely insane over these types of books and I have lived for this moment to find out they're all true. Trust me on this; I know every possible plot permutation our most cunning authors have ever imagined. That guy is not from this earth. I just hope he is a genuine human and not a lizard man in deep disguise."

I got a lot of strange looks in response to my concern. I felt sorry for my companions; it probably wasn't their fault that they reached adulthood while remaining functionally illiterate regarding cutting-edge sciencey fiction. Still, I sensed I needed to reestablish my shattered credibility.

"Should I wave a dead rat in front of him to test him?"

That was my beloved spouse, disrupting my thoughts. She clearly had been gossiping about me with my old marine corps buddy, Gunnery Sergeant Lucius Oglethorpe, aka Sergeant Scarbutt.

"*Thanks, Kathy*," I thought *very* silently to myself. "*Way to be supportive.*"

"I need to be among the folks who find him," said Vicki. "I suspect our stranger has some connection with ancient Greece or Rome. Did you recognize the Rod of Asclepius insignia on the flying craft? It was used by the Greeks and Romans to signify medicine and healing.

"Moreover, those salutes were Roman legionary salutes. I was working on my doctorate in classical studies when Uncle Jean asked me to front for his accounting firm. I suspect I know more about ancient Greek and Roman history than anyone in this room."

Kathy chimed in. "I should join you. One can't graduate law school without knowing some Latin. I took two years of it at good old BCWC besides the four years of Latin I studied at the M. C. Thomas School for Occasionally Wayward Girls. '*Castitas, Humilitas, Sobrietas.*'"

Kathy shuddered slightly. "I was re-living some memories. I had to wear a pleated skirt every day of girls' school for eleven whole years. And wear a white blouse, white gloves, white tights and saddle shoes."

Melinda nodded in sympathetic agreement. Then Kathy and Melinda turned towards Vicki.

Vicki winced. "Luxury. Yeah, we wore the white blouse, gloves, tights and the saddle shoes while attending St. Joan the Martyr of Rouen, my parochial girls' school. But when we knelt for prayers in our pleated skirts the sisters would also check if our skirts touched the kneelers attached to the pews in front of us. If our skirts weren't long enough, Sister Martine applied her ruler of unusual size. Vigorously. Growth spurts could be painful."

Francine and Jennifer locked eyes, and then simultaneously rolled their eyeballs skyward while shaking their heads in disbelief. Oh yeah. They had each done ladies' boot camp and three tours as army lady MPs—the cowards never started, the weak died along the way and they darn sure weren't wearing cute little pleated skirts and white tights when they croaked.

The metaphorical cricket-bat of enlightenment suddenly conked me on the noggin. I realized I needed to add a little more real world experience into the group which would make our initial contact.

"You and Vicki will work fine, Kathy. You two look harmless and gorgeous. But just to be safe, Francine and Jennifer, you trail about twenty yards behind them and carry carbines. Right now grab all the sleep you can. Come dawn I will be on overlook from up here. Tiny, grab your medical kit and be ready to examine the undoubtedly phony bump on his head. Jules, prepare to cook an early breakfast with an extra chair."

We all got up a half hour before dawn and met in the kitchen to grab some coffee. Kathy had put on a moderate weight beach dress. Francine and Jennifer wore their mounted infantry uniforms. Vicki showed up last and was wearing only flip-flop sandals, thin cotton clam-diggers and a tight, thin cotton undershirt tied in an even tighter knot under her breasts. It was clear there was nothing underneath either garment.

Being guys, Tiny and I spotted Vicki's abbreviated wardrobe right away. Both of us immediately stared at the ceiling. Call that the recently married men's survival instincts in action. Francine and Jennifer reacted to us and started to smirk.

Jules shook his head. "Vicki, Vicki; do you plan to give that poor spy a heart attack? Or do you intend to drown these married guys in matrimonial hot water? And isn't the weather this morning a little cool for that outfit?"

"I thought about this overnight, Jules, and I have a plan. I had field glasses last night, you didn't, so you didn't see how incredibly handsome the stranger is. I was looking right at his face using the field glasses when there was a flash of lightning. I'll give you fifty-to-one odds he has an ego to match his looks. That concerns me.

"John is convinced our potential guest-to-be is from another world. If so, this could be the most important moment in our earth's history."

Her voice dropped a couple of tones. I could see from my peripheral vision she now was looking at me. "John, look directly at me."

I stopped staring at the ceiling and turned towards her, but focused my eyes beyond her. I realized I was reacting as if she was my old drill sergeant who was in the process of sharing words of profane encouragement with me.

"Understand this, John. Your stranger may be important, but should he conduct himself as less than a perfect gentleman I will toss him out of my house, instantly. If he is a viper, I intend to provide him an irresistible opportunity to reveal himself as such."

She spun to present her profile. She had plenty of profile to present. "I think my nipples will harden nicely in the cool morning weather and concentrate our spy's attention. I expect to take his true measure before the day is through."

Vicki turned back to face me straight on and graced me with a basilisk glare. "However, John, if your visitor is not from outer space and I have dressed up and acted as a floozy for nothing, then I will demand of Jules that he poison you."

She looked next at Kathy. "Do you speak any French?"

Kathy shook her head. "Not really. Only the Latin."

"Then wave your hands and grunt occasionally, while I do the initial talking. French is known as the language of *l'amour*. I will test that proposition. It's almost true dawn. Shall we proceed?"

The four ladies walked down the front road for a bit and then, as I had instructed, walked over to the beach to approach the stranger from the direction we could see his face had turned. I figured he would sneak the occasional peek, so I didn't want the girls to surprise him. I also wanted him to be aware he was being approached by young ladies so he wouldn't feel threatened.

As Vicky and Kathy approached the figure, Vicki raised her voice to say, *"Blessent mon cœur d'une langueur monotone."* Then she paused, then cried, *"S'il te plait, mon Dieu!"* before she ran up to the prone figure, cupped her right hand around the stranger's head and gently lifted it. Consequently, her barely covered breasts were about four inches from the guys' eyes when he opened them.

Vicki asked, *"Quel est votre nom; Quelle est votre quête?"*

He blinked his eyes several times and replied in a strangely accented version of French.

"My name is Paul Drake; I seek that which is lost. *Parlez-vous Anglais, Mademoiselle?*"

Then he groaned. Kathy later said he groaned rather theatrically. She would know.

Vicki replied, "I am from New Orleans, originally, so of course I also speak English. I am Miss Thibodeaux. And who are you, sir? Why are you here?"

"My head hurts. Have you seen my sea bag? I need to travel to Washington, District of Columbia."

Vicki turned to Kathy. "My companion is Mrs. Smith. Do you know of this place, Kathy?"

Kathy said, "I have never heard of a Columbia, per se. The largest Columbus is the capitol of Ohio Province, and of course there is a Washington Town in my own Commonwealth of Pennsylvania Colony, some thirty miles southwest of Ft. Pitt City. There are also smaller towns and villages named Washington scattered throughout the various Crown

Colonies. I have never heard of a Washington, District of Columbia, though."

The stranger examined Kathy and then Vicki. He grimaced and said, "*Stultus sum!*"

Kathy muttered, "I very much doubt that."

Vicki spoke again, "We have a friend whose husband was a medic. You appear to have a head injury; it will need examined. My house is over the dune. Let us help you walk. We will send someone to fetch your sea bag; it looks too heavy for us to carry. Kathy, you are stronger than I am; could you and Francine will help this gentleman walk? Jennifer, you bring up the rear. I will carry Francine's carbine."

They got him back to the house where Tiny examined him. Anne and Beth left to collect his sea bag before any beachcombers swiped it.

I glanced at him as he passed. I hated him on sight. Vicki had been correct about his looks; nobody should be so handsome. His physique might have been chiseled out of granite by Michelangelo. He appeared youngish, but I sensed he aged slowly and would bet a case of beer he was in his mid-thirties.

Tiny finished giving the guy a quick exam, snorted and grabbed an unopened bottle of non-narcotic pain killers. Tiny next reached into his medical box and pulled out the *RFC Army Field Guide to Emergency Medicine* book. It was written in English and French and had the Latin words for all the medications contained in the standard army first-aid kit. Tiny turned to the page listing pain killers and gave the manual and the medicine to Paul who glanced at them and took two pills.

I had examined the stranger's sea bag while Kathy told me what had happened so far and Tiny was making with the exam. I couldn't find any identity papers, but his sea bag contained a huge medical kit. Heck, he could have diagnosed himself. The names of his medications were in English, but the medication brand names and the names of their manufacturing companies were unfamiliar.

His bag also contained a large handful of small, nearly pure gold and silver ingots. I guesstimated their aggregate value at over a thousand pounds sterling.

Tiny said, "Come grab some coffee, you slacker."

"Slacker?" said Paul, in a definite accent. It took him almost four months of continuous conversation and study to become respectably fluent in our version of English.

"A slacker is somebody who fakes an injury to avoid work. I was a field medic in the army. I have a few other skills, as well. You think I can't tell that lump was professionally done? Somebody hit you barely hard enough to give you a bit of a lump, but not nearly hard enough to rattle your skull. Maybe he should get together and compare notes with Kathy's cousin Benny. Anyhow, it looks like you're going to need a better sob-story than the one you were planning to tell us.

"In the meantime, let's grab a bite to eat. I bet you can use it. We will get a proper breakfast going in an hour. Jules' food is sort of strange, but his coffee is excellent. I know you can walk on your own."

I glanced through the doorway. Paul appeared grim. "I can use some coffee." He walked with Tiny into the informal kitchen-breakfast room where Jules and the first course of an early breakfast were waiting. I followed.

Breakfast at Thibodeaux's

We all slurped liquid wake-up. Vicki showed up a few minutes later, having changed into a short, sleeveless, strapless, white sundress. At least it wasn't nearly transparent. Vicki squeezed Francine out of the way and sat on a high stool next to Paul.

Vicki purposefully showed a lot of excellent leg. She was throwing herself into the overly distracting, femme fatale role more convincingly than I had expected. Granted, that was a trope in many of my favorite sciencey fiction novels, but I didn't think she was much of a fan. I kept my thoughts about feminine wiles to myself because I neither wanted to give her game away in front of Paul nor give her an excuse to poison me.

After everyone was close to being finished with coffee and Cajun donuts, Melinda shooed the Valkyries from the kitchen. "Need to know, ladies. I learned that much back when I was your Colonel Commanding."

I added, "Emergency is over for the moment. Back to regular shifts and duties. Anne, Beth; get some solid sleep or come back for proper breakfast in an hour or so. Thanks, ladies."

Kathy turned to Paul. "Given your means of arrival I was hoping you were from another planet, Mr. Drake. My husband is fascinated by other planets; at least I believe that to be true based upon his teenage and current reading choices.

"He still has shelves full of imaginative novels at his uncle's house in Michigan, almost all of which assume the women of Venus wear only skimpy loincloths and the women of Mars wear only leather straps. Also, the latter ride eight-legged horses and shoot atomic-ray rifles. I am sure he would like to know the truth of the matter if you are indeed from outer space."

Paul gave her a look; then he said, "The surface temperature of Venus is like the inside of a blast furnace. Mars doesn't have much of an atmosphere. Any women dressed as you describe would die almost instantaneously on either planet."

"Since you are far too human to be from a different planet, Mr. Drake, are you perhaps a solicitor or a language professor? I, myself, am a solicitor and I had to study a fair amount of Latin to prepare to pass the bar. It's rare these days to find those who speak English, French and Latin. As for the latter, I suspect you are not actually much of a fool."

Vicki said, "Let him suck his coffee, Kathy. I will be back in a moment; there is an easy way to get some answers."

She waggled her butt as she walked out. Kathy noticed me noticing that, so I had to stare at the ceiling yet again. Somehow I was already in trouble on the spousal front and the day had barely begun. Well, same old, same old. Vicki returned with a two-foot in diameter political globe.

She put it down on the table in front of Paul and said, "This globe reflects political boundaries from about five years ago. There have been a couple of changes in Africa and I think one border in the Balkans has shifted, but give it a slow spin and decide if there is anything you wish to share with us."

Paul slowly turned the globe. He took a deep breath and said, "I had hoped it wasn't the case, but I may have been switched in times. My folks may look for me in the wrong location. Not geographically, but on a different version of earth. If that's what happened, I'm at risk of being stuck here."

I had a stray thought; heck, it happens. "About that, Paul; what's so special about this place, geographically? Of all the beach houses on all the shores in the world, why did you walk in here?"

"Tactically, this house was showing more lights than were its neighbors and I wanted to be discovered this morning." He waved at the globe. "Geographically, it is located within a couple of hundred yards of the eastern-most point in Carolina."

He ran his finger longitudinally up and down the globe, starting from our location on a North Carolina barrier island.

"You'll notice if you head north, the next landfall is almost two hundred miles away, on the Delmarva Peninsula. Go due south and there is nothing but a couple of Bahamian islands of no particular import until you hit the Cuban east coast due north of Guantanamo Bay. It's easy to find this location again."

I nodded. His story seemed logical and was consistent with the contents of his seabag. The companies which made his medicines and such all had names like Jones and Jones, Inc.; I guessed "Inc." stood for "Incorporated." The standard for all the members of the Greater Britannic Empire is Ltd.; for Limited Liability Corporation. Still, I thought the yarn he spun was a trifle too pat and he seemed a little too blasé. I sensed a faint reek of a deceased rodent.

I addressed his original point. "Yeah, it could be tough, Paul, getting home and all. We sure as heck can't give you a ride. Our politicians, globally, tend not only to be crooked, but cheap. Well, at least they're darn thrifty when they dole out stuff to the tax-paying public.

"We have lighter-than-air rigid airships and we have a few gliders, but not powered aircraft, except a handful of suicidal toys for a couple gonzo gazillionaires. We could build more of them, I guess, for some military applications. The costs would be enormous though, and then all the major powers would be forced to do the same thing.

"That's not going to happen; it would mean wasting a lot of money on expensive military kit which could be used personally by our politicians on real essentials like gambling, mistresses and champagne. Anyhow, I don't think we could build a monster like the beast you arrived in anytime in the next century."

I decided to unleash my inner snark. "Speaking of return journeys and such, how much effort will your folks expend trying to find you? I mean, who the heck are you? Really?"

He shrugged. "No one of consequence. Well, at least I don't count all that much in the grand scheme of things. Let me think of how to best describe what I do."

Paul paused about ten seconds and said, "If I ever return home my mission debriefings will be disastrous. I guess you folks have already figured out most of my story. Fine, I'll give you the short version because looking around this house it is clear it will take your earth a century or two to develop the technology to take advantage of what I am about to say."

He pointed at Devon in England on the globe. "I was born here. I rank in the fringes of the minor nobility. I am the second son, so I always expected to be an academic. Since you already mentioned you are members of the Greater Britannic Empire, it is clear on your earth the American Revolution either never occurred or it was unsuccessful. I make this assumption based on my two doctorates in history. I have done some postdoctoral work in philology as well."

Vicki suddenly smiled like she was the cat who had fallen into a saucer of fresh Devon cream.

Paul continued, "The first doctorate is in world history, my world's history, but focused on how technological developments affected historical political choices. My thesis examined the interaction between public health issues and political and economic power; stuff like sewer systems good, lead pipes for water delivery, bad.

"My second doctorate is in comparative histories, the histories of other versions of earth. Those we know of. I had to write a lot of case studies for that one. The doctorate is a highly classified degree and only a couple of hundred civilians know the degree program exists. Then I had to learn a lot more about languages.

"We are learning our way around the multiverse; we only have been exploring other versions of earth for eighteen years. I am also a military officer, but that's mostly so they can court martial me if I screw up too badly. I take it you're an officer as well?" He looked directly at me.

He paused. I responded, "Second lieutenant, marines, now in the reserves. I did nine years active duty."

He nodded. "I never dreamed I would wind up in the military, but they pay the bills. Anyhow, we researchers investigate other worlds to see if we can acquire different technologies to help end our competition with the Ming Empire, or at least keep it from going out of control. Our Ming's correspond to the Manchu's of your world if I read the globe correctly."

He shuddered, slightly. "I have been to a version of earth where all conflicts ended in a cloud of radioactive dust and a subsequent nuclear winter. We suspect that occurred about fifty years ago and ended sentient life on that earth. We are desperate to avoid such a fate.

"The folks who dropped me off are supposed to come back for me in exactly one year." He frowned, "Assuming, optimistically, that they can figure out the version of earth on which they left me."

Vicki spaced out on us for a moment and intoned, pretentiously, "There are more histories in Heaven and Earth, Horatio, than are dreamt of in your philosophy."

Paul looked at her querulously. "I sense I should recognize the reference, but it is obscure to me."

I spoke up. "It refers to a famous theater play. A lot of people talk pointlessly for a while; then they do nothing and consequently most of them die. Real militaries use the play to illustrate that a good plan executed violently now normally works out better than a perfect plan executed a couple of weeks too late. Ignore the over-educated strumpet. She's trying to show off her misspent years at some fancy and stuck-up girls' school."

Kathy, Melinda and Vicki yelled at me simultaneously, "Women's College!" but they all added different insults as to my lack of looks, intelligence or ancestry, so that latter part was a little jumbled. I waved them off so Paul could continue.

Paul continued, "My craft caught some lightning as we transitioned away from our own version of earth. It's a hazard of how we are forced to operate. We are based out of what you call Bermuda. My craft got here and spotted large houses and electric lights, but we didn't pick up radio broadcasts on the frequencies we expected. I suspected our reconstruction of a primitive radio might have been damaged by the lightning.

"I had to make a choice, and these trips are enormously expensive, so I said, what the heck, it's only a research trip; let me out. You guys go back home, figure out where you dropped me off, and come back in a year."

I thought about that; I sympathized. I remembered a couple instances where I spent time in foreign realms hoping the airship service would show up as promised and haul my overly exposed keister home.

"So what were you planning on doing here for an entire year, Paul?"

"My mission is to learn, or at least collect information on, advanced technologies. I guess what I wind up doing depends on what technologies you folks have that we don't. I doubt you have many.

"I had prepared to go to a version of earth where George Washington led the thirteen colonies to independence from Great Britain under George III. The war lasted from 1775 to 1783. George III was furious to lose, but his treasury was drained and his options were constrained after the French, and later the Spanish, jumped into the war on the side of the Colonies. In the 1860s, the northern colonies fought the southern colonies over the slavery issue.

"In 1864 a general named George McClellan won the election in the North. The war was already over, with the northern side victorious, and McClellan got credit for an overwhelming victory at a place called Antietam Creek in Maryland. Historians later determined he had a severe concussion during the entire battle, and a General Hooker took effective charge and led the Federal forces to victory. Hooker was killed in the closing minutes of the battle, though, enabling McClellan to grab credit in victory's aftermath. That world is a little behind us in technology, overall, but has taken some interesting paths."

"That sounds like you paid attention to your courses on military strategy and policy, Paul. Most officers I knew spent more time and effort trying to suck up to their superiors."

He eyeballed me intently.

"For how long were you a sergeant, Lieutenant Smith? And while your officers were sucking up to their bosses, were you engaging in tavern brawls?"

Darn, he nailed me on both counts; he clearly realized there are not too many second lieutenants with nine years plus time-in-grade. Kathy already knew all about the fight in the *Pickled Herring* down near the Philadelphia Navy Yards. Heck, that incident still merited a full boxed-text page in the most recent army JAG training manual. Actually, the Brigadier had mentioned another bar brawl in Kathy's presence once, but I think I got away with it.

I had elided over the details of another fight, the one in the *Sozzled Sturgeon*, St. Petersburg, Russia, back in the day. Let's just say if Kathy ever had a notion to travel to Imperial Russia to check out their ballet, then I would have to bail on her. I glared at Paul; then I decided to shut up, listen, and stop underestimating the dude.

Melinda interjected before I could respond to Paul. "In our history George III had a fit during a banquet and choked to death on an oyster in 1767. His widow Charlotte was a marvelous regent for the very young George IV. Charlotte was my great-to-the-ninth grandmother."

Paul eyeballed Melinda a little more closely. "That means the version of English which I studied diverged from yours some 225 years ago."

Paul's response meant he missed Vicki sticking her tongue out at Melinda. I didn't want things going off on a tangent so I signaled Jules to get up with me and we made sure everybody had fresh coffee.

Who Ever Loved Who Loved Not at First Sight?

Paul resumed his tale. "My earth diverged from your own path around 35 AD. Gemmellus succeeded Emperor Tiberius, followed by Emperors Claudius and Britannicus. Rome itself lasted as a political power a couple hundred more years than it did in your world. By the time Rome itself was crippled by plagues and lead poisoning, the heart of the Western Empire had moved to Britannia.

"We remained unified and were better able to stave off pagan barbarian invasions than on your version of earth and we maintained the bulk of Greek and Roman learning intact. Our average technological development rate was, on balance, less than that occasionally achieved by other worlds we have found, but it began from a much higher base and was far steadier."

"Finally, my Christian name is Paul, my senatorial name, representing the leadership qualities to which I am supposed to aspire, is Tiberius and my family name is Drake. I hail from the Greater Britannic Roman Empire. I am an officer by fate; I didn't grow up planning to join the military, but I will do my duty."

"I suspect your nearest equivalent to my actual rank would be a lieutenant commander in the navy or a major in the marines, though your world has no equivalent to the military service to which I belong."

Paul turned to Melinda. "Did I hear correctly that you were a colonel? Would you be the one in charge? Also, should I address you as Your Highness?"

Vicky, Tiny and Jules said, "What?"

Melinda said, "Obviously."

Kathy laughed. I said, "Heck no!"

I got up and pointed fingers appropriately. "Former military does not count. Melinda used to be about two thousand folks back in the line of succession. That's before she gave her birthright up for true love. I'll explain later, maybe. Important stuff next; that is, military rank since this has now turned national security secret squirrel.

I pointed around the table. "So, civilian, civilian, civilian, civilian, lieutenant commander, RFC Navy Reserve Judge Advocate Service. That means Kathy is not in the line of command during actual military-related festivities. I am a second lieutenant in the RFC Royal Marine Corps Reserve. If I put on my dress uniform, though, you're obliged to salute me first. I will be wearing the Wolfe-Montcalm Cross."

Paul responded. "I am unaware of this decoration, but I studied their battle. They both died bravely."

Paul could be tactful when he tried. One might argue stupidity was a contributing cause of death for both men.

"I take it, Lt. Smith, the decoration is seldom awarded?"

"Four other living men currently wear the decoration. I would salute all four of them first in a heartbeat."

Then I pointed around the table again.

"Husband and wife. Husband and wife. Brother and sister."

"Victoria Thibodeaux is the first one you met. She is the co-owner of this residence, so if it not a security matter or a matter of operational urgency, you should consider yourself her guest and behave with all appropriate courtesy."

Vicki had tensed up the moment Paul mentioned his theoretical marine-equivalent rank. She un-tensed a little when he stood up, bowed at the waist with a flourish, and said, "The honor is all mine, Miss Thibodeaux. I will do my best to be the soul of courtesy. I thank you for your hospitality, especially as I entered your house under false pretenses."

Then he said, "Though apparently you were all aware I intended to do, so I am not sure that all I promised should apply fully."

Paul turned to Jules. "Sir, I am not yet aware of the customs prevalent in your world, so I ask this question in all earnestness and out of ignorance, with no intent to offend."

Then Paul smiled broadly and shared his smile with all around the table.

"Regarding your little sister; is she dressing so provocatively for a reason? She can be most distracting. It is almost as if I have entered into a spy farce of some sort."

Jules started laughing and choking on his coffee. Vicki grabbed a beignet and threw it at Paul. Then she grabbed another one and threw it at Jules. Then she started laughing as well.

Kathy turned to me and said, "I am surprised you didn't notice Vicki's outfit, John. I guess it's just because you find Jules' and Vicki's breakfast room ceiling so utterly fascinating. Really, dear, you could at least have been paying more attention to me. Perhaps you might do so if I wore nothing but stiletto heels, a skimpy loincloth, and a short cape like all those ladies in your favorite novels wear? Or do you think my figure is insufficiently attractive to carry off either such look?"

Where the heck did that come from? Kathy had been correct earlier. In my favorite books, only ladies who lived on Venus wore those outfits and I refused to believe that Paul was telling the truth about Venus.

All my books agreed; Venus was cloud-covered and Venusian temperatures were always in the mid-nineties, with matching humidity. Consequently, most Venusian women wore only mere wisps of silken loincloths to preserve their modesty, and only wore capes if they were outside during the evening. The rains on Venus never fell till after sundown. Compared to some of my previous deployments, Venus was a pretty congenial spot.

Ladies on Venus wore other stuff besides clothes, of course. Venus didn't have banks or mutual savings societies, so most Venusian women also carried their wealth on their bodies in the form expensive jewelry. And they sported twin holsters filled with rayguns to ensure their jewelry remained safe.

I knew for sure that Kathy had read a couple of my books which took place on Mars, but she had never read my all-time favorite book. In it, Morgaine, the Malevolent Marquesa of the Martian Mountains, wore only a leather harness and riding boots. She couldn't wear stiletto heels because that would be ridiculous given the saddle and stir-rups of her faithful mount, her eight-legged Martian giant thylacine, "Bubbles." Morgaine didn't wear a loincloth because you can't strap a five-foot-long atomic death rifle to a loincloth. She couldn't wear a cape because it would become tangled with the rifle barrel.

It was a great adventure novel; but completely logical and sciencey. The other women in that book had made similar, and also scientifically constrained, wardrobe choices. When I thought about it, though, most women in almost all of my favorite books had some sort of wardrobe issues. That was probably a coincidence.

I missed that book; I had left it behind in our base-camp near La-gos. Most of us were off doing something else when a local gang in a five-sided civil war overran our nearly deserted base-camp in what was the single, stupidest, most pointless mission in which I had ever participated. What frosted my cake was I could never find another copy of that book.

I was about to tell my lovely wife she had more than enough figure to pull off the look and of course I would encourage her to strut around wearing nothing but high heels and a loincloth, but I somehow wised up first. I suddenly realized she had asked me a trick question.

Kathy had probably voiced her snarky comments about outer space wardrobes because she was jealous. Well, not jealous, jealous; just sort of annoyed. Vicki had spent the last hour successfully flaunting her own outstanding figure and Vicki's overly abbreviated outfits had indeed grabbed the bulk of Paul's visual attention.

Kathy and Melinda tended to wear knee-length or longer, fully lined, widely flared A-line skirts or dresses, with matching length slips, plus suspenders and tights even in socially casual situations. They wore that style the better to conceal the .25-caliber semiautomatics they habitually wore holstered on their outer right thighs.

Kathy had changed into that very look the moment she got back from her jaunt along the beach. I knew what I was looking for, so I could spot the faint bulge of her holster and weapon under the folds of her skirt.

Not that I would cast aspersions. I was wearing a sports coat to breakfast to conceal my shoulder-holstered .32-caliber semiautomatic.

I may have mentioned that the primary qualification to become an RFC Royal Marine is to be super-duper intelligent. And to have a magician's ability to distract. So the two primary characteristics of a marine are brains and dexterity. And rugged good looks. So the three primary characteristics of marines are intelligence, dexterity and charisma. Heck, the bards sing our praises. I may have come up a little short when these attributes were distributed because I blinked twice and Kathy was still glaring at me.

So I answered, "You know, Kathy, the autumn Premier League lacrosse season starts in a week. Do you think Philadelphia has a chance to make the playoffs this year?"

Kathy reached across the table and grabbed a beignet and threw it at me.

Vicki told everyone to calm down. Kathy bounced another beignet off my noggin before she signaled she had finished horsing around. Vicki then asked Paul, "What does the Rod of Asclepius insignia signify? We know it as a traditional sign of medicine and healing."

Paul paused a moment. "In for a penny, in for a pound, I guess. We have twelve huge, sea-skimming, wing-in-ground effect craft. They use air reflected from water's surface to reduce aerodynamic drag.

"Eight WiGs are operated by my Empire to assist the Sisters of Healing in responding to catastrophes such as hurricanes or earthquakes. The WiGs excel in that role because docks and shore facilities often are destroyed during natural disasters. Those eight craft also serve to camouflage the four special WiGs which can transit among the alternate worlds.

"Our ability to visit other earths is highly classified. We don't think our rival nations, such as the Ming and Persian Empires, know about it. We try to keep it that way by basing both types of WiGs in places like Ascension or Bermuda which are off limits to foreigners."

"Do you take passengers? Can I visit other worlds with you?"

Kathy glared at my interruption. Paul shook his head, no. I figured that would be his response. Still, you don't ask, you rarely get.

He continued. "When we want to visit another world, we send out a WiG in the middle of the night when we know we can find a storm or a heavy fog to hide in, and poof, we disappear. Then we drop folks off or pick folks up or both, and pop back home."

"We needed something like that monster airframe to travel across parallel worlds because the transition only works if we are airborne. Also, the ancillary battery arrays associated with the auxiliary power plant are massive. We needed an enormous craft to carry a useful number of people or supplies. Even so, I don't think our earth-hopping WiGs can carry comfortably over twenty passengers besides the standard eight-man crew and four-man security force."

Vicki said she was getting hungry and ordered the rest of us to help Jules whip up a proper breakfast, not merely coffee and beignets.

"We can stop off at the library room to drop off the globe and offer Paul a glimpse of the resources we have available for him at the moment. Next he will take a shower. You are still covered with beach sand and sea spray, Dr. Drake."

I said I would tag along to lay down the security rules.

We walked over to the library room, and Vicki put the globe back in its usual place. One corner of the library had a small shrine of sorts; Christ on the cross and pictures of The Virgin and a picture of St. Dismas, patron saint of reformed thieves. Vicki had mentioned earlier that Dismas was her Uncle Jean Lafitte's favorite saint, bar none.

Paul looked at the shrine and made the sign of the cross with his three middle fingers extended and his pinky finger and thumb curled and touching.

Vicki got Paul's attention and said, "I have dabbled in history myself. I spent two years at the Sorbonne in a doctoral program. Approximately one-fifth of my library is in French. Feel free to read my books to orient yourself."

Three sides of the room were covered with built-in bookshelves and they were all packed. I hadn't paid any attention to the room, hitherto, once I had learned Vicki disdained sciencey fiction. Paul immediately began paying more attention to the bookshelves than he did to Vicki.

Not being shy, she spoke again. "You appear to be religious, Major Drake. Are you Catholic?"

Paul refocused. "I guess you could say that; it's called the Holy Church back home. A handful of top theologians are aware of our world hopping capabilities. If you know what you are looking for, you can tell which folks they are, because they are the ones who wander around with their eyes crossed, walking into walls and mumbling to themselves.

"As you might imagine, the confirmation of multiple earths has a lot of theological implications. I figure it's too far above my paygrade for me to resolve what multiple earths mean in terms of religious doctrine. I guess the people tasked with figuring out these issues will let me know if and when they do."

I told Paul we needed to keep moving and showed him the nearest shower room. I explained I would post one of our lady security guards outside the room and he was to notify her before he left.

Fifteen minutes later, Francine led a scrubbed, clean, and freshly dressed Paul back into the kitchen and breakfast dining area. Jules, with Kathy's help, had outdone himself on the quantity front. We all tucked in.

Five minutes later I bit into something a bit spicier than the cuisine Jules had been whipping up the last several days. I made a couple, totally subtle, gestures to indicate my throat had been sliced open and fire peppers chosen by Satan himself had been poured into the gaping wound. I may have knocked over a chair while in my uncontrollable, pre-death throes.

Jules shook his head at me. "I merely bumped up the seasonings to medium low. Kathy; your husband's a total wimp."

Kathy only nodded in response while stuffing her traitoress face.

Jules shook his head, no. "Sorry, John. Get used to the heat. You're outnumbered by folks with actual palates. I cook stuff New Orleans style. The spice must flow."

I chugged some sweet iced tea. It seemed to help. I now understood why they had more cavities per capita in New Orleans than they did in England. I went back to stuffing my face.

Vicki jumpstarted the conversation just as we were all running out of places to stick additional food and coffee.

"Are you married, Major Drake?"

I again shooed the Valkyries away before Paul could answer. Francine grabbed coffee and grub to go, explaining she would give these to Connie and Jennifer who were outside on watch. Paul answered after the Valkyries had cleared out.

"They conscripted me into the secret program after I earned my first doctorate. If I understood your personal history correctly, Miss Thibodeaux, you must know, at least secondhand, how tough it is to juggle a marriage while working full time on a doctorate. Once they conscripted me, the powers that be said they doubted I would live long enough to enjoy being married. In any event, I would face being away from home for years at a time."

Vicki was now completely fixated on Paul. Both Melinda and Kathy were now staring intently at Vicki, though neither said anything. Paul didn't acknowledge Vicki's fascination.

"I am, after all, thirty-four years-old and I have had a handful of romances, some of which I regret. Oh, and I am still required to confess my sins when appropriate, but, given my job, the only two people in the Empire to whom I may confess are the Grand High Archbishop and his principal deputy. It's rather difficult to get on their schedule.

"Would you excuse me so I may examine some of your books? I feel I will be in a much better position to answer your questions once I have a better sense of how your world differs both from my own world and the earth I expected to visit."

Vicki gave a sniff of disgust, but she was smiling when she flounced out and led him back to the library. I followed, left the two of them there, and returned to help clean up the kitchen. I was scrubbing dishes when I realized Paul had deftly finessed answering whether he was married while implying he wasn't. That could have stemmed from how languages diverge over time; alternatively I suspected I would have to listen carefully to what he said to ensure I was not reading into his answers things I hoped were true.

I had a thought; heck, it happens. Neither our marines nor our airship service have professional intelligence cadres. The other two services often make snide, yet risibly unfunny, jokes about that. Paul exhibited a few too many behaviors similar to those of our very own and much beloved navy intelligence pukes.

Yeah, back in my relative youth I clearly had spent far too many post-mission hours being debriefed by navy intelligence. They were weasels, the lot of them, once you got past their public, fair-of-face personas. They were usually pretty bright, though.

I suddenly remembered the RFC Navy Intelligence Service's unofficial motto. They put the motto on all their coffee mugs and such, under the picture of an anthropomorphic weasel, rampant, and wearing dark glasses, a fedora, and holding a bloody knife. That motto is "*Cutelli in Tergis Aliorum.*" That's the shorthand Latin version of "*Knives in the Backs of Others Are the Rungs of Our Ladder to Success.*"

I figured it wouldn't hurt to maintain situational awareness. Still, I wasn't all that worried to find that other earths existed. I knew we couldn't be in any real trouble yet; there was no sign of a dame. Every book on the subject I had ever read had made the rules crystal clear. To wit, nothing spins out of control unless and until the dazzling but deadly dame makes her overly dramatic entrance. No dame, no trouble; QED.

Shipwrecked in Times

I interrupted Paul five hours later and said, "Lunch time. Jules has prepared oyster poor boys, gumbo, corn fritters and more sweet iced tea. Maybe you understand what our alleged and possibly homicidal chef is talking about; I'm clueless."

We all ate lunch and then I started grilling Paul again. "What have you got?"

"I have two conclusions, one good and one unfortunate. Prefacing the bad news first, the expression used on the earth I intended to visit is, and pardon my inadequate French, 'le oops.'

"I will be stuck on your earth for at least a year. I don't know how to assemble an emergency beacon from the equipment available in your timeline. I examined the radio in the study—it uses vacuum tubes. My earth hasn't used those commercially for centuries. My only hope to return to my earth is to wait for my folks to come looking for me.

"I next examined the books in your library pertaining to my academic specializations. I discovered your earth has only a handful of vaccines, such as for smallpox and rabies. I am surprised your scientists invented a tetanus vaccine. The good news is I believe you can develop vaccines for diseases such as polio, mumps, measles, and scarlet fever without a need to overcome serious technological bottlenecks to do so."

I turned towards Melinda and Tiny. "First things first; once we talk vaccines, we need to bring Ruth in on these discussions. Is that all right with the two of you?"

Tiny said, "Yeah, sure. I was a medic, remember. Saving lives is important. I know firsthand that scarlet fever sucks; it's a nasty way to go. Ruth will be fine with that."

Kathy locked eyes with Melinda, read something into Melinda's expression, and spoke for both of them. "Ruth is a living saint, in her own way. If we limit our avarice, she will throw her heart and soul into helping us."

Tiny turned to Melinda. "It looks like you need to start stroking some bank drafts. Well, the medicine business may be a step up from selling grossly overpriced plonk."

Melinda frowned at me. "If you blabbed even a single word to Joseph, I will baste you with Jules' spices and roast you over open flames."

Kathy glared at me, suspiciously. I shook my head no. Paul looked confused.

"Spill it, Joseph. Or else!" growled Melinda.

"Nah, John's innocent, for once. My Cousin Charlie, on my father's side of the family, is a chartered accountant in New York City. Not everybody he deals with is on the social register, if you know what I mean. Anyhow, when I evaluated the projected cash flow for the wine bar you're building, it didn't add up. I asked Charlie to check a few things to see if I needed to work an extra job to keep you happy. He owed me a favor after I fixed things for him regarding a couple dudes who thought Charlie owed them money."

"Charlie had to use some technically less-than-legal techniques to estimate your net worth. Well, he's good at such stuff. Anyway, he calculated you're worth sixty-five million pounds sterling, give or take ten million. I figured you would tell me about it in your own good time, but with millions of lives at stake, I don't think we have any time to play games about my not-so-hurt feelings. I've seen what polio does to kids."

Paul interjected, "I have a question for all of you. How much influence do you people have? None of you appear to be in your own country right now, based on the globe and the books in Victoria's library."

Jules answered, "Not one of us is a subject of the southeastern colonies, such as North Carolina, which comprise the Royal Crown Colonies of North America. Vicki and I are subjects of Louisiana Province of the Trans-Mississippi Territories. Everyone else, including

Melinda's lady bodyguards, is a subject of the various colonies within the Royal Federated Colonies.

"Legally, we are all subjects of His Majesty, Emperor of the Greater Britannic Empire, etc., though our actual obligations to our ruling sovereign are usually negligible. Movement restrictions amongst subjects of the various Greater Britannic Empire members are similarly minimal. The same currency is used throughout the Empire, so Mrs. Sammartino's pounds sterling spend exactly as well in Carolina as they do in Pennsylvania."

Vicki spoke up, "I also asked my people to do some research. Mrs. Smith's former boss, when Kathy was briefly in the RFC Army, is the RFC Foreign Minister's wife. Kathy now works directly for the Deputy Chief of Naval Operations the one month during the year she performs her navy reserve duties. If Melinda ever reconciles with her family, her father directly controls the governor of Rhode Island Colony as well as approximately ten members of the RFC parliament.

"My researchers think he bought five outright, three he blackmails, and five are related by blood. There is obviously some overlap. So despite their rather pedestrian previous and projected choices of employment; soldier, marine, waitress and barmaid, respectively, they have lots of influence and connections up in the RFC."

Melinda frowned at Vicki, but nodded agreement. "That's close to the exact count, Vicki; you employ competent folks. The actual number is fifteen, but that number includes four MPs who are not yet aware they will be blackmailed if my father truly needs their votes. Let me know if your research folks ever want to work in the RFC."

Vicki continued, "I, myself, have numerous interactions with the North Carolina Colony bureaucracy."

Jules started to sputter and choke.

Vicki barreled through his interruption. "Well, I do, Jules. Right now, back in Charlotte, half-a-dozen vindictive Crown flunkies are taking advantage of my absence to play bumper tag with my solicitors. They are trying to prove my firm engaged in financial malfeasance. Once those parasites leave empty-handed, I fully intend to have my solicitors sue the Colony for torturous interference, to teach them a lesson."

Vicki regarded Paul thoughtfully. "Speaking of lessons, Dr. Drake, would you consider becoming a scholar in residence here at the soon to be established Outer Banks Institute for the Evaluation of History?

"Consider, if you travel on your own, you may well miss your only chance for a ride back home. Also, if we keep you isolated here, we are less likely to start a panic over invasions by aliens from other worlds. In return, we will acquire every research resource you think you might need to determine which scientific breakthroughs our Empire might replicate relatively easily. We can bring in experts whom we can trust to evaluate which of your recommendations are feasible.

"You appear to have the historical expertise and judgment to know which technologies are likely to bring, on balance, improvements in the life of the average subject of our Empire. Lord knows our Empire doesn't need better ways of killing each other."

Jules sputtered, "But I was sort of counting on my rental income from this place."

Tiny took Melinda's hand. "This could spare a lot of kids a load of grief, Melinda."

Melinda said, "Done. Okay Jules, if you want in on this, I think you will make a mint. If you don't want to be involved and you want to be bought out, then name your price and I will double it. Victoria; do you think your Uncle Jean would sell your firm to one of the all-Empire accounting firms for a fair price?

"From what you just said, I suspect the North Carolina Colony authorities would trip over their own feet in the rush to grant approval for such a sale. Besides, if you are going to be heading up a research institute here, you can't be running all over the place. It's an eight-hour trip between here and Charlotte by motorcar. The rail connections are worse."

Vicki sighed. "Uncle Jean has already considered selling the firm. He is trying to clear the decks, so to speak. He has spoken to two different specialists in New York City the past few months and they suspect he has early stage lung cancer. If the doctors are correct, then Uncle has two years or fewer to live."

That stunned me. He wasn't that old and he appeared vigorous enough when I saw him last year.

"Victoria, Jules; do they know how that came about? Lung cancer is rare. Few doctors see many cases of it; other diseases usually kill you long before lung cancer or prostate cancer or things like that do."

Jules responded. "Not a clue, John. Some folks blame smoking. Uncle Jean never smoked."

We all turned towards Paul, almost simultaneously. He shook his head.

"I am not a physician." He shuddered. "I can help you folks develop a handful of new vaccines. These should protect against specific diseases, but I can't cure anyone who already caught something."

That comment pushed my brain back into gear. "That brings up a potential problem with Dr. Drake, here. Both the authorities and the existing pharmaceutical companies will investigate us the moment we announce inexplicable scientific breakthroughs, even if we use Ruth as a front.

"Heck, if the RCC finds out the truth about Dr. Drake they will snatch him in a second, and firms like Lavoisier Chemicals will certainly try to do so. I think we are stuck here until Paul's ride shows up. We will need a lot of eyes on watch to make sure we can contact his ride and get him on board if his ride for home ever arrives."

Paul commented, somewhat suspiciously. "Aren't you being more than just a little generous? I seem to be at your mercy."

I checked faces around the room and got various signals of acquiescence. "Paul, each one of us at this table has a personal reason to despise kidnappers. If we kept you here against your will, that's what we would be. If your folks want to grab you and go, that's fine, at least as far as we are concerned. Tell them how nice we are. You look like you will earn your keep over the next year.

"That's not to say that politicians in either the Royal Crown Colonies or the Royal Federated Colonies will feel the same way, especially if the wrong folks find out about you first. So I think we should inform a certain Brigadier Madeline Hamilton sooner rather than later. She's often a nasty piece of work, but she believes in justice. Sort of. Well, sometimes.

"Also, her husband is the RFC foreign minister and is the person with whom you will negotiate about anything official. So I think we first need to talk to Madeline. After that, we need some adjacent real estate, including a lab for Ruth."

Melinda corrected me. "No, John. We first need to set up an unbreakable legal basis for everything we do forthwith. Then, and only then, do we talk to Madeline. And yes, Madeline is exactly the person within RFC officialdom with whom we first need to talk. Trust me; Madeline has surprising connections."

I turned back to Paul. "I guess you heard the lady. She's the one who's going to stroke the bank drafts to pay for any ideas we come up with. Speaking of ideas, we might be able to conk two birds with one coconut.

"I think the new medical research firm is going to need a corporate symbol. Do you think if we flew some rather large flags featuring the Rod of Asclepius in front of our buildings that your folks would understand the message if they came looking for you and you were out?"

Vicki, Melinda and Tiny drove to Elizabeth City the next day to set events into motion. Jennifer and Francine rode with them to provide security.

Melinda first established an account with the largest local bank. When she returned to the bank after lunch, she had fifty thousand pounds sterling deposited there for her walking around money. That helped open a lot of other doors.

Melinda next contracted the most highly recommended local solicitor. Melinda wrote him a bank draft for five thousand pounds and told him to work with a local estate agent. She ordered him to purchase or lease any of the three combinations of two houses immediately adjacent to Vicki's beach house. Vicki figured the lease or purchase step should be easy; all the adjacent beach houses functioned primarily as summer rentals.

Melinda's solicitor's other task was to work with the solicitor for Vicki's homeowners' association. Vicki had warned Melinda about the petty tyrants running that organization. They would likely demand substantial proffers before they agreed to permit Melinda and Vicki to install the flagpoles and lights.

Vicki engaged a local construction firm to install three large flagpoles and associated floodlights the moment the HOA granted a variance. She also special-ordered six extra-large boat flags at the local marina supply and told them to search for a fast, ten- to twelve-passenger motor boat.

Jules had whipped up something called "Hurricane Cocktails" to greet the travelers on their return that evening. Melinda was well into her second before she stopped muttering, "Damn all homeowners associations to Hell and back, and then damn them again."

Ruth arrived late the next day. She monopolized Paul Drake for the rest of the evening; the conversation switched back and forth from being conducted in English, Latin and Greek. Ruth had studied both languages extensively as part of preparing both to become a genius level biochemist and to better understand scripture.

Ruth announced the news at breakfast. "I talked late into the night with Paul; there is no way around it. Some of us will need to relocate and conduct our initial medical research at Joint Base West Kingston, Rhode Island. It would take years to build a lab to my specifications here near the coast and there is no need to do so when there is an underutilized lab available at JBWK.

"Saving lives, and letting people live longer lives, will give more far people the opportunity to accept the Word than will my efforts to do so retail. Anyway, Sharon has a cousin who can fill the pulpit at the *Olde Cherokee* and do an excellent job. If your firms will underwrite his preaching, then I will work on vaccines."

Melinda fluttered her right fingers, signaling assent. The pulpit would be filled.

Ruth continued. "There is another reason for using an army or navy facility: security. Lavoisier runs an aggressive corporate espionage program. They have compromised every other major pharmaceutical research firm in the RCC and the RFC. The moment, or shortly thereafter, another firm is ready to apply for a patent on a potentially profitable drug, Lavoisier acts. They duplicate the drug and file for patents in France and Austria and Spain, at the least. Then they smother their rival with phony patent infringement lawsuits filed from abroad.

"Most firms discover it's less expensive to pay off Lavoisier in a settlement than to continue to fight bogus lawsuits. This happened to me twice back in Delaware, involving projects I worked on during my first job out of college. The blackmailed corporations inevitably jack up their prices still more to pay off Lavoisier. That practice is the main reason I quit the business.

"Lavoisier initiates all this lawfare from its corporate headquarters based in Cuba. Its North American subsidiary companies are uninvolved, so they can't be held responsible. If Lavoisier somehow strong-arms its way into becoming involved with the polio vaccine effort, they will figuratively rape every pocketbook in North America and the Empire."

Ruth took a deep breath. When she spoke next, she reminded me of the scene in that flicker where Joan of Arc was motivating the French troops.

"We cannot let that happen. Do you know how many children are killed or permanently crippled by polio each year? Not just here, but worldwide. Lavoisier executives are truly the spawn of Satan, and we must keep them at bay. I will do everything in my power to help smite their evil ways."

She turned to Paul. "I am certain your general knowledge of how technology can progress will lead to many breakthroughs. We will need a cover story to account for them. I am at a loss for what that might be. We have some time to work on the issue, though. Perhaps Madeline can help."

Paul nodded. "So who is this legendary Brigadier Madeline Hamilton, and how can she provide us access to a medical research facility in Rhode Island?"

Melinda fluttered her fingers again, this time to get Paul's attention. "She is a sister alumnus of mine. She's quite the charmer *and* well connected politically."

Auld Acquaintances Are Not Forgot

New York City

Kathy called the New York office of her former boss, Brigadier Madeline Hamilton. Kathy had a pleasant chat with the Brigadier's personal assistant, Warrant Officer First Class Glynda Smith. Glynda scheduled us to meet with the Brigadier in two days. Early the next morning Kathy, Paul, Ruth and I drove to Raleigh to catch a train to New York City. Jennifer and Francine rode along with us, saw us onboard the train, and drove back to the Outer Banks.

Glynda ushered us into the Brigadier's office at ten in the morning the next day. Madeline greeted the four of us, eyeballed Paul, and said, "He stays in better shape than you do, John. Which service?"

I replied, "Brigadier, is this room secure? I don't believe I should answer your question unless the answer to my question is a strong yes."

She scowled at me and said, "This better be worth it. I hate using that stupid room."

She hit her intercom and said, "Glynda, call downstairs and tell the guard I will need the secure room in five minutes. If anyone is using it now, have them kicked out."

The secure room in the Brigadier's office complex was a small conference room; at most ten people could fit in it. All six sides of the room were almost entirely lined with copper, cork and then another layer of copper, except for the forced air ventilation vents. The ductwork for the latter had multiple and otherwise unnecessary interior right angles and copper screens at every angle. Lighting came from portable lead-acid battery powered lamps. The five of us sat around the small conference table.

The Brigadier started things off in her usual jovial manner. She said to Kathy, "I don't know what you see in John. He seems more trouble than he is worth. Has he come clean yet with you regarding those adventures of his regarding the *Sozzled Sturgeon*? Or is he still invoking that state secret excuse?"

I took her question as a cue to change the subject before I had to give my wife a lengthy explanation about something which absolutely was not my fault. I will never understand why various Imperial Russian military units have so many types of ostentatious uniforms and why they could be so darn arrogant and touchy about trivial observations. Heck, if they didn't want to be mistaken for French sailors, then they should have designed a different uniform, perhaps one with a couple fewer visually jarring pastels incorporated into the color scheme.

"Brigadier," I said, "meet Major Paul Tiberius Drake, PhD, PhD and linguist. He's from the Greater Britannic Roman Empire, not of our world. We can help improve the odds he returns home. In return, he offers to share his knowledge about developing vaccines for diseases such as polio.

"We came to you, Brigadier, because I think you are one of the few people in a position of influence who would not throw Major Drake into a dark hole and suck him dry, merely out of expedience. I know you believe in justice for individuals; I hope you can convince our politicians to think similarly."

We talked. The Brigadier questioned Paul at length. Eventually she asked, "If we were to throw you in a dark hole and pump you dry, would your empire retaliate? Hypothetically?"

"I don't think so, Brigadier. My empire has a lot of other things to worry about. They would regret my loss, but might write it off as a business hazard. They may not know on which earth they left me. I can't guarantee their lack of response, of course. I have studied a lot of histories and sometimes politicians make inexplicable decisions."

I cleared my throat, preparatory to telling the Brigadier that throwing a not-yet-proven guilty person into a dark hole would occur over my dead body. I was not entirely sure whether the Brigadier would view my objection as an obstacle or an opportunity.

Fortunately, Ruth spoke up first. "I will not be party to any such injustice. You would have to silence me as well."

Madeline waved her off. "I know that, dear. I have no intention of advocating any such thing. I need a hypothetical stick to go along with the actual carrot when I talk to select politicians. I have evaluated thousands of constabulary interrogations in my professional life. A cooperating witness will let you know when you have asked the wrong questions and tell you what the right questions are. We do not know what questions we should ask of Major Drake. We will be far better off earning his cooperation.

"I have other questions, Major Drake. How many worlds are there and how worried about them should we be?"

"Good questions, Brigadier. The short answers are we don't know and not too much. We discovered cross-earth travel technology by sheer accident. After eighteen years of cross-earth exploration, we have discovered fifty-nine alternate earths. Not one of them realizes travel to other versions of earth is technically feasible, though several are sufficiently advanced to replicate the technology. We suspect there are more earths, perhaps billions, but I am sure will never know how the exact number.

"The first constraint we face is it is enormously expensive for us to send out our cross-earth exploration craft. They have tremendous maintenance needs, exacerbated because we have to operate delicate and sensitive equipment in a maritime environment."

"Why's that?" asked the Brigadier.

"That's part of my second point. We don't understand everything about our own technology. We know how it works, and we discovered we have to be airborne when we transition, but not why that is so. We also found that using Wing-in-Ground effect craft gives us the most punch for the pound in terms of payloads and stealth.

"Our navigation methods are seat-of-pants. Our navigators keep track of how long the craft has been moving in the energy bubble while their instruments look for a weak spot in the other-worlds continuum. We are constrained by how far we can travel by the food and chemical fuel we can carry on board.

"If our instruments detect a weakness in the force, we can try to pop in and explore. The process is like how your own world's Portuguese explorers charted the coast of sub-Saharan Africa some five or six hundred years ago. Geographically, much of sub-equatorial Africa is an enormous plateau. If you are sailing offshore, there are few places to land safely. Now and then you see a river emerging from the plateau, and you can head in and explore the local area. But you can only dash in when your lookouts spot a river."

"So you haven't yet met yourself in a world nearly identical to your own?" I had jumped in; I figured by virtue of my extensive reading of the relevant literature, I was the expert on trans-temporal travel. I also again thought about asking Paul whether the women of his world preferred to wear leather straps or loincloths, but I caught a glance of Brigadier Hamilton in my peripheral vision and put my question on hold.

Paul responded. "I haven't met a doppelgänger yet. The earths we have discovered thus far are distinct. Timelines seem to split, so to speak, in a discrete process rather than being on a continuum. We don't know why, but we're investigating.

"We are confident the Ming Empire, the other major power of our world, does not know about our program. We have also been on the lookout, hitherto without result, for signs other earths have visited our world. While absence of evidence is not proof of absence, our world has faced the risk of a global war for a hundred years and our internal security folks are renowned for their vigilance."

The Brigadier thought for a moment and decided.

"From now on, unless I tell you to the contrary in person, this affair is now way beyond top secret. Ruth, I agree you need to return to Joint Base West Kingston and start getting the lab in order. I will send Glynda with you. I want to ensure that you can reach me to resolve any urgent issues with any army or navy brass.

"Speaking of which, I will call General Bartholomew and Vice Admiral Francis. They trust me enough to vet a couple of doctors to help with your research, even without me telling them the entire story. I will wait until I see them in person before I do that. My husband will handle informing the Prime Minister and Prince Albert.

"Meanwhile, Ruth, do you need any financial assistance? I can cover some things out of my budget."

Ruth shook her head. "I only need permission to enter the Newport navy base and JBWK. I am now the chief scientist for Melinda's new corporation, '*Royal Asclepius Medical Research, Ltd.*' John is her chief of corporate security. Kathy is the chief legal officer. Melinda brought her lady bodyguards onboard as Asclepius security officers, increased their wages outrageously, and they all signed non-disclosure agreements.

"We brought along Kathy's proposed contract with the government to establish a legal framework for our research. You can look at the terms; we expect to do modestly well, but not extravagantly, because we want to make our discoveries affordable for as many people as possible."

I jumped into the conversation. "All our Valkyries will need full licenses to carry weapons and work as bodyguards in any East Coast colony. Someone needs to clear the paperwork with the RFC constabulary and make it so."

"I'll have Glynda add that to my list of tasks."

The brigadier smiled at Kathy. "Kathy, when you return to Carolina, you must tell Melinda to reconcile with her father. Or vice versa. Rhode Island isn't large enough for the two of them if they are not on speaking terms. I will talk to my husband tonight about starting the process."

Madeline mused aloud. "Back in my youth, I once attended a local carnival. A Han fortune teller told me I would live in interesting times; that's a Manchu expression meaning I was born cursed. I guess she was right; I had been planning to coast along until I retired. That's in less than two years."

She smiled as she said it, though.

Ruth traveled to Rhode Island accompanied by Glynda and two lady MPs. The rest of us returned to the Outer Banks. We walked into

Chateau Pirates' Paradise to find Melinda swearing like a sailor about homeowner associations in general and Victoria's association in particular. Fortunately for us, she was directing her venom at her high-priced solicitor on the other end of the telephone line.

"You tell that other bottom-feeding parasite if he doesn't come through with the variance, then I will see to it the entire homeowners' association board of directors is charged with animal cruelty, indecent exposure and aggravated mopery. And then I will get angry."

She slammed down the phone.

She saw us and smiled. "I think I have them on the ropes. Sometimes sweet reason alone is not enough to deal with moronic sub-humans. No offense intended, John. You know how I have to come to admire you crayon-eaters."

"None taken, Melinda. You have been the soul of courtesy on those occasions when I reverted to manners suited to a Royal Marine Corps mess-hall and began eating food with my toes and fingers. Oh, and Madeline informed me you and your father will have to make nice to each other within the fortnight. She is arranging something as we speak."

Melinda's jaw went slack. "It would take a *Royal Command* for my father to budge. That's impossible, even for Madeline."

I pointed at Paul Drake. "We live in a time of miracles. Who's to say?"

It took Melinda's solicitor another week to negotiate five-year leases for the two adjacent beachfront houses north of Vicki and Jules' house. They had ten rooms each and, like Vicki's house, were built on steel and concrete posts. Melinda said she had to pay well over market value. It took another three weeks to get a variance to fly the Rods of Asclepius flags on each house and illuminate them at night.

Meanwhile Vicki's uncle, Jean Lafitte, appointed an interim manager for Vicki's accounting firm and began negotiations for its sale to an all-Empire accounting mega-firm. The North Carolina Colony financial oversight authorities didn't bother to hide their jubilation.

Sergeant Scarbutt's Lonely Hearts Rugby Club

Outer Banks, North Carolina Colony

Sixteen semi-permanent additions joined our little group of insiders two weeks later. WOFC Glynda Smith accompanied Ruth when they returned from Rhode Island. The navy sent two captains, Chaplain Father Seamus O'Brien, doctorate of divinity, doctorate of Latin literature, etc., and Dr. Semmelweis, an infectious disease expert. They came accompanied by thirteen marines in civilian clothes who plussed-up our security detail.

The good Father wore his civilian priest outfit; the doctor looked like a doctor and Glynda looked like a middle-age matron. The marines all looked like marines uncomfortably wearing civilian clothes. God bless the corps.

We installed the two doctors and the marines in one of Melinda's newly leased houses. Kathy and I, Melinda and Tiny, plus Anne, Connie, and Jennifer, moved into the other. Vicki, Jules, Paul, and Ruth, together with Beth, Francine, Susan and Glynda, stayed in Vicki's house.

I ambled over and made nice to the marine detachment head.

"Gunny Scarbutt, I am sorry I had to ask for your much abused backside to be sent down here, but you are the best we've got. Also, those are the darnedest looking graduate seminary students I have ever seen. That fiction will never fly."

The Gunny rolled his eyes. "I thought I taught you better than that, Hotshot. Never apologize; it's a sign of weakness."

Then he grinned, "I'm fine with this job; it's about time I had a vacation. Anyhow, about these youngsters I brought along with me. Well, you know how close I am to the Deputy CNO. So Admiral Francis invites me over to his polo club for booze and cigars one afternoon and says, 'Gunny, you're the only one I can depend on to keep Father O'Brien and Doctor Semmelweis safe. Choose the nastiest twelve crayon-eaters you can trust to keep their mouths shut and not ask questions and keep the good Father and doctor undisturbed by heathens.'

"You're right about us leatherneck pigs not flying, but we have to pretend to be civilians of some type because the Admiral may have sort of forgotten to tell his RCC counterpart he has a bunch of RFC Marines running around on RCC territory. My marines don't know who Paul is and I told them not to think about asking. Anyhow, how's the grub around here? You got any beer? And it's Top now, not Gunny."

"Congratulations, it's about time you got promoted. But it's going to be tough calling you that. There's only one Top."

I stared at my old buddy. I paused.

It's the darnedest thing about sea-spray. Even if you spent years on or near the ocean, it can make you tear up at the oddest times. I felt it happening to me. I saw the same thing was happening to Scarbutt. Well, the moment those red and white flares lit off in the night sky above that Moroccan beach some five years ago, the then Staff Sergeant Scarbutt had been the one who had picked up Top's body and single-handedly carried it some three hundred yards back to the waiting trucks.

I figured I would change the subject. "Yeah, we have some beer on ice. But nobody is going to believe those guys are seminarians, Gunny. I mean, Top. Though I think they would make a fine-looking rugby team."

Scarbutt blinked away the effects of the sea-spray. "See, you are a genius, Hotshot. As of now, I am their coach and they are in secret training to win next year's RFC seminary rugby league championships. I guess we are forced to train down here to keep from being observed by our nefarious competitors. You know how unscrupulous those seminary rugby teams can be."

He grinned. "That means the doc can be our trainer and Father O'Brien can be our theology tutor. Heck, this cover story will give my marines a reason to keep in shape and give me an excuse to yell at them, not that I ever need much of one. We'll have to buy some rugby outfits and equipment, though. And we have to buy some more weights and weight benches and such.

"Oh yeah, the DCNO wanted me to pass this on. If Mr. and Mrs. Sammartino and Miss and Mr. Thibodeaux and the new guy would like to attend confession, Chaplain O'Brien is available. The Chaplain suggests they call upon him after breakfast tomorrow."

I doubt Vicki had many recent sins to confess. Once Paul had picked up our local customs, he told Vicki he was not the type to love and then leave a lady of quality. He said he would review his decision after a year had passed and, if it seemed to be the case, that he was stuck on this world. His decision depended, in turn, on whether the gracious Miss Thibodeaux was still interested in him. He believed such an outcome was unlikely, given how lovely and charming she was and considering how she probably constantly had to fend off countless potential suitors.

Vicki smiled and dressed less provocatively after that. She made a point of observing him every time he joined the rugby practices or hit the weight benches, though. She appointed herself his research assistant, acquiring books and professional journals on any topic where he needed to know where we stood in terms of technology.

When he was not studying to understand or help us, Paul worked hard to stay in shape. Tiny and I got embarrassed about Paul's physical work ethic, so we stepped up our own exercise programs. So did the Valkyries.

I realized, after seeing Francine and Jennifer lifting weights next to a couple of marines, we would have to work out some guidelines for both security and personal interactions between the marines and the Valkyries. The Valkyries averaged perhaps six or eight years older than Scarbutt's marines, but they were all single or divorced former army police, had decent looks, kept in shape, and had normal urges. I asked Top to consider the issue.

The next day, Top Sergeant Scarbutt had a motivational talk with his troops. Being good neighbors, Tiny and I came over to listen in and introduce ourselves.

Scarbutt bellowed at them. "At ease, you civilians."

I wasn't sure Scarbutt truly understood the whole civilian thing.

"By now you have observed that some of the local ladies walk around while wearing khaki uniforms and carrying light assault carbines. They are all former army police-ladies who are now licensed bodyguards.

"The great news for you clowns is because they are now civilians that normal fraternization rules do not apply if you are off duty. The other news is you will behave as gentlemen, so those ladies will be treated as ladies. Consensual is fine. Bruises are not. Also, it's ladies' choice. There are six of them and eleven of you mutts are not married. If any of you jealous horndogs decide to step out of line because you think your buddy is getting something on the side and you're not, then we'll have a serious conversation."

Top pointed in our directions, "Let me introduce your new neighbors, Mr. Smith and Mr. Sammartino. If I am somehow incapacitated, one of them will be your new commander until you hear otherwise from the corps. I'm not freelancing; the Deputy CNO has written orders to that effect; they each have previous military experience and will be recalled to active duty instantly if I become incapacitated. Mr. Smith is a second lieutenant in the marine reserves. Mr. Sammartino will be recalled to duty as a senior master chief petty officer.

"Let's talk about those lady security folks. Any of you mutts who ignore my fatherly advice and manage to hurt one of those ladies, well, you're going to regret it. Be aware Mr. Sammartino has offered to provide one-one-bare knuckles boxing instruction for any such individual. He was the bare knuckles champion for the *Invincibles*. I will serve as the referee. After he has beaten you senseless, if you still somehow wake up, I will prepare charges against you for 'Failure to Maintain.'"

A younger marine asked, "Top, what's the story about those phony combat infantry ribbons some of those broads wear on their khakis? Hell, Top; two of those babes are wearing combat wounded ribbons. I asked one of them about it and she pointed at her butt and said, 'You want to kiss it and make it better?'"

Top glared at the questioner and replied. "I suspect you talked to Miss Francine Miller. For your information, she served three hitches in the army military police, reaching the rank of staff sergeant. She then served as a brevet SWO in the Rhode Island women's militia unit. Now, two of you chowder-heads have sort of worked with these ladies before. I am proud you kept your yaps shut about that incident."

Top took a controlled breath. "The rest of you should be aware it was Major Stuart, the current XO of the 2nd of the 3rd, who wrote up the recommendations for these ladies to be awarded their CIBs and other awards. The reasons behind these awards are classified. One lady they used to work with also got herself a posthumous DSO during the incident. After this deployment is over, I will be delighted to arrange an in-person conversation with Major Stuart for any you morons dumb enough to think the Major would recommend phony awards.

"One last thing, my precious pretties. Mr. Smith is one of five living people who wear the Wolfe-Montcalm Cross. If I am not around, and he tells you to do something, then he has a damn good reason to do so.

"Okay, Schultzie, take over. You have twenty minutes to ready half of these goldbricks to take a little run, so grab civilian rucksacks and canteens. Head five miles up the beach, then five miles back. You fighting devil dogs are all going to get in shape for rugby. The rest of you lazy mutts have twenty minutes to goof off. Then I will review some changes to our security procedures. Don't become too used to the air service lifestyle, though. When Schultzie gets back, I'll take the rest of you for a little jaunt of our own.

"Get going." They got.

"What's the story with these guys?" I asked Top.

"The Deputy CNO had a chat with the Brigadier commanding the 3rd Regiment. Major Stuart and I could pick any twelve marines in the regiment for a year-long classified deployment. We went through a lot of records and chose three dozen guys to talk to. They had to volunteer. I could promise them sun, sand, and a personal guarantee we would be sent to a place where the natives spoke English. Our mission would be to protect a pair of navy captains from being interrupted in their work. Odds were, nobody would shoot at us, but we couldn't guarantee that.

"We would also work with some unusual civilians, but they couldn't ask the navy captains or the civilians about what they did or why they did it. I told them I would be in command. Anyone who broke these rules would find themselves in a navy brig for a long time. Major Stuart said he would owe a personal debt to any marine who volunteered.

"All these guys already served at least one tour. Schultzie is a staff sergeant and my second in the command. He was a corporal back at Casablanca. He's heard about you. He's a good man and he'll make gunny in another three, four years. Two of the guys I brought down here served in the two platoons Major Stuart brought over from Battery Park to hit the Spetsnaz from the rear. I bet that's why you didn't recognize them the way you would have remembered any guy holed up in Melinda's estate's garage complex."

Then Scarbutt grinned, "I am going to make so much money on this gig."

"You getting hazard pay for this vacation, Top, or are you planning to find some pirate treasure?"

"Nah, I think by the time this gig is over, these guys might provide the base for being the best rugby team in the corps. If I can keep the unit together, we have a decent chance of winning the Atlantic Coast Marine Corps Championships next year. I'm looking forward to sticking it to the bookies."

Brigadier Hamilton came down to visit us three weeks later. She wanted both to evaluate our progress and to pass on a message to Melinda.

"Children, you lead me into the strangest situations. The Governor General called in his one lifetime favor of Albert, his Majesty's younger brother. The Governor General and Albert attended Rugby together. Anyway, Prince Albert sent an informal letter to your father via first the governor and then my husband. My husband hand-delivered the letter to your father, Melinda. I know what was in the letter since I made a copy. Yes, I am shameless."

Dear Sir Charles,

Though I am not at liberty to explain my reasons, I urge you to reconcile with your daughter, who will be announced as Lady Melinda on the next honors list. I assure you I would not make this request absent a valid reason of state. Should my request fall on fallow ground, given the urgency of the situation, my older brother will pen the next request.
Albert, Duke of Cornwall, Etc.

"Honors list, Madeline? What are you talking about?" asked Melinda.

"It's about that incident last year involving the Spetsnaz. Surely you remember. You fearlessly refused to duck when the grenade was thrown into your room. The one the late MSgt Mutton jumped upon."

"I didn't know it was a grenade until it exploded underneath him. I shot the Spetsnaz trooper entirely by reflex."

"Minor details, Melinda, dear. Grace under enemy fire is what counts. Had not the Russians interfered, you would have inherited your father's title upon his passing. Prince Albert agreed that awarding you a title on your own merits would help your father reconsider past events in a new light."

Two weeks later Sir Charles Burr informed Melinda she had been reinstated into her family. It turned out his Majestic and Imperial Highness did not have to write his own letter. Probably a good thing; rumors that England might suffer a crayon shortage had hit the jarhead grapevine. Marines try to stay aware of such things.

A couple of months passed. We tried to minimize travel—Kathy and Melinda kept track of the renovations to *Chez Plonk of Fiddlers Green* by calling Barbara once a week. Barbara appeared to be keeping the workmen and architects under control.

Ruth and Dr. Semmelweis spent most of their time extracting knowledge from Paul. Once a month they went to Rhode Island to share new ideas to army and navy doctors and researchers. Paul, Ruth, and a couple of Valkyries traveled to the medical school library in Raleigh on alternate weekends.

When Paul wasn't helping with research, he was scanning the latest available leading newspapers from Raleigh, New Orleans, New York, London and Munich. He claimed he was trying to get a feel for our world. I figured he was looking for something more specific, but he never dropped a hint what that might be.

Developing vaccines is hard, but Ruth and Dr. Semmelweis claimed they were making progress. Paul shared other insights while the vaccine research percolated. Our navy had wondered for a decade why certain navy retirees exhibited an above average incidence of cancer. Suddenly navies all over the Empire started swapping out shipborne dials and such with instruments which did not use glow-in-the-dark paint.

Navy doctors began work on a publishable statistical study to argue for banning such paint for most civilian applications. That alone was enough to convince Vice Admiral Francis to discard any remaining doubts about our little project.

We were gathering for one of Jules' Cajun-fests when Vicki came in, streaming tears. She blubbered, just a little, sniffed and said, "Uncle Jean has been told he has only three to six months to live. It's definitely lung cancer and there is nothing the doctors can do. After I put down the phone, I realized Uncle Jean has been carrying his favorite glow-in-the-dark pocket-watch in his suit pocket every day for the last thirty years. I can't prevent him from dying."

Paul got up from his stool at the big center counter where we were eating family style, walked over to Vicki, and wordlessly hugged her for about five minutes until she settled down. As far as I know, that was the first time he ever touched her.

I quizzed Vicki about Paul several weeks later, while Paul, Chaplain O'Brien, and a pair of marines wearing mufti were taking a leisurely morning beach walk. Paul and the chaplain had planned to discuss comparative theology or something. I was finishing my last cup of morning coffee and I realized that Kathy and Vicki were the only other folks still hanging around the breakfast counter. It was as good a time as any to ask Vicki a couple of questions which had been noodling around inside my skull.

"Yo, Vick! What's with Paul? Is he the real deal?"

Kathy was rinsing out her coffee mug, but thoughtfully took the time to whack me hard on the back of my head with her open palm. "Talk like the hayseed you are, farm boy. You can't do Philly speak."

"Yeah, Boss, right! Well, Vicki, that's a real question. Do you have any thoughts you can share?"

"You mean aside from his Greek-god like physique and his unblemished face? He seems rather sheltered for an officer of any sort, and of course, he is much smarter than any officer I have known. He also turned out to be an absolutely perfect gentleman. I am surprised you ever had any doubts about that score, John."

She smiled, not so sweetly, at me. I gave her a phony smile in return. I didn't recall being the person who had those particular doubts.

Vicki continued, "I guess his intellect is understandable. His Empire commissioned him because of his academic knowledge and he wasn't brain-damaged by doing rough and tumble and hanging around with insensitive morons.

"I think you could take the three best history professors at the Sorbonne and add them together, and they wouldn't add up to someone as insightful as Paul. He can read through one of my books once and absorb completely everything in it. I would have killed, figuratively of course, to have had instructors like Paul at the Sorbonne. And I thought I had a gift for languages; he leaves me in the dust."

I grumbled. I may have scowled. "That's precisely the point, Vicki. Paul is polite, knowledgeable and educated, but I sense it's an act. If you scrape away a couple of coats of phony paint, he has every bit the self-assurance Melinda has, if not more.

"That's what worries me now; he is too much of a gentleman. His type of social polish and sense of self is not taught; it's acquired by osmosis while growing up in the nose-bleed ranks of an aristocracy. I mean, you could make me a gazillionaire tomorrow, but I would still be the same guy who grew up on a Michigan Province cherry farm. There's something way too phony about him."

Vicki sniffed at me haughtily. She turned to Kathy and said, "No real offense dear, but when your jealous husband grew up on that cherry farm, did he have indoor plumbing? Your gumbo-brained spouse could certainly take more than a few lessons from Paul about how a proper gentleman is supposed to act in the presence of ladies. It's amazing how quickly Paul has picked up on everyday courtesies."

"Oh, I know!" said Kathy, and began commiserating with Vicki while enumerating my multiple other failings. I bailed from the room to do something more pleasant than being the goat of the ensuing conversation. Maybe I could low crawl through a muddy, barbed wire covered field while being shot at. I wished more folks shared my paranoia, which, of course, it isn't, when they're genuinely out to get you.

Months passed.

Cry Havoc and Let Slip the Nuns of War

We threw an *"Ides of March"* party for Paul. He had read all of Shakespeare's plays by now and was amused by how badly the Bard had mangled the actual history. Jules did his best to prepare Roman delicacies. I doubt any of Caesar's contemporaries would have recognized the food, but it was outstanding. Everybody had a couple of drinks, except for the two marines and one Valkyrie on watch duty and Ruth and Doc Semmelweis and the two marines who had accompanied them to Rhode Island.

Then Francine, the Valkyrie standing watch at the widow's walk of the house next door, ran through our front door and grabbed me. "It's confirmed by Schultzie. There's a large, powered rubber raft heading right towards us. We counted four people in the raft; they are about a half mile offshore. We were lucky to spot them under a quarter moon."

"General Quarters!" I bellowed. "Top, grab the Chaplain. Assign two men to him and take him back to his house. He speaks Latin. If somebody knocks on the door nicely, direct them over here. If they are not nice, don't shoot first."

"Jennifer, take Kathy and two marines back to our house." I turned to Kathy, "Kathy, I hate to ask you to do this without me, but you have the next best Latin. It's the same deal as with the Chaplain. I need to coordinate from here. Paul, come with me to the upstairs veranda; we will work the phones from there. Susan, pass out the carbines. Top; keep your crayon-eaters from doing anything stupid. And appear to keep the party going; the folks coming to visit us will notice if the lights suddenly go out. Let's move, people."

We scattered.

Paul and I ran up to the veranda and grabbed field glasses. We watched the raft hit the beach, whereupon four people got out and then dragged the raft to just beyond the high tide line. All four figures stared at the Rod of Asclepius flags flying above all three buildings. One figure gave something shaped like a rifle to another figure and slowly walked towards Vicki's house. I picked up the phone on a private party line which connected Vicki's veranda with the observation posts at the other two beach houses. "They look like they are trying peaceful first. Everybody keep calm."

I turned to Paul. "Can you say something to the lone stranger when he gets close enough to the house?"

"Certainly," said Paul, "but I wasn't expecting anyone for another six months. Something's wrong."

The single approaching figure came close enough to Vicki's house for its outside lights to illuminate his features. Suddenly, Paul started yelling rapidly in his version of Latin. The guy answered back more rapidly, talking for about a minute.

Paul turned to face me. Just for an instant, he didn't look like he was shocked; rather, it was as if he was completely livid. He got it under control in a couple more heartbeats and said, "It's Senior Sergeant Llywelyn. We need to use your motorboat. There are thirteen ladies who need rescued. Our WiG is floating about two miles offshore. Technician Sergeant Julius will go with you on your boat to direct you to and communicate with our craft. The other two men will sail the rubber raft back to our craft.

"Sergeant Llywelyn will stay here and brief me on what happened. You can send your guard ladies and marines back to their quarters if you don't want them involved in tonight's adventures. You might also ask Jules to make some extra food. I don't think the just-arrived ladies have had much to eat the last half day."

I went downstairs, broke up the party and grabbed Top. "Tell Schultzie to tuck the marines out of the way. And bring back the Chaplain."

I sent a Valkyrie to locate Kathy. Paul went outside to talk with Sergeant Julius. Kathy returned. I explained the plan to her.

"Kathy, Vicki, Melinda; you girls are driving. We'll take all three motorcars up to the marina and grab our speedboat. Choose three Valkyries to serve as guards. Top and I, together with one newcomer, will take our boat out to that monster machine floating about two miles offshore. Paul says we will rescue thirteen ladies."

We scooted off to the association's private marina, about two miles north. Top, the stranger and I hopped into Melinda's motorboat, leaving the six ladies and our motorcars behind.

The other-earth technician didn't have any English; I had very little Latin and Top had less. The technician focused on the dials and screen of some handheld radio-like thing and got us to the WiG by pointing his arm in the direction he wanted us to go. Occasionally, he would talk into his radio thingy. We got there in about fifteen minutes.

Once we arrived at the enormous craft, the techie directed us to a hatchway in front of the massive overhead wing. The hatchway was about three feet above the waterline. We helped thirteen ladies into a boat meant for twelve, which already included the three of us, so it was a little crowded. Twelve ladies were wearing formal, white, ankle length vestments of some sort. Ten of them appeared to be in their early twenties, the other two were pushing forty years old. They all wore crosses hung around their necks and red Rods of Asclepius broaches pinned above their left breasts on their vestments.

The last lady, about thirty years old, wore a white, knee-length business skirt suit which was cut nearly identically to the blue outfit which Vicki had been wearing when I first met her about two-and-a-half years ago. The lady passed me an oversized briefcase to place in the boat; I figured it weighed twenty-plus pounds. No other lady had any luggage at all, which was just as well given how overcrowded we were already.

We returned to the marina and discovered there wasn't enough room in the three sedans for all of us. Top, Julius, Connie and I waited there at the marina for ten minutes until Susan returned.

We arrived to find Jules and Kathy cooking up a storm for the new-comers while Paul was talking rapidly with the lady in the white suit. He was clearly angry, but it was hard to tell what it was about because she was giving back as hard as she got and they were both using their version of Latin.

Minutes passed. Paul signaled Vicki, Melinda, Tiny, and Kathy and asked them to join him in the study. I brought Top along. We left Chaplain O'Brien and to serve as a translator for thirteen new ladies, Llywelyn and Julius.

Paul started talking English, but he was now was almost machine-like in his detachment. "I had a long talk with Senior Sergeant Llywelyn while you were rescuing the ladies. He was the security detail leader for the earths-hopping WiG on alert. The Ming launched. Our defenses didn't perform quiet as well as we had hoped. We retaliated. Our military HQ at Mount Snowden sent the general warning, which was picked up by Bermuda.

"Llywelyn kept up with the broadcasts from his monitoring station at his guard center. He ran to the ready room for the twelve man-duty crew for the alert WiG said prepare for an emergency launch. Then he saw the lights on at the little chapel about one-hundred yards outside the security perimeter for the WiG. He found these ladies at prayer. He told them the base was under attack and he needed to take them to safety."

"Twelve ladies are members of the Sisters of Healing; two are what you might call senior nuns, an anesthetist and a senior surgical assistant. Ten are novitiates; all are trained and just-licensed nurses getting field experience before deciding upon a specialization. The last lady is Dr. Astrid. That's her first name; she was born in what you might call the Kingdom of Scandinavia. I guess her last name would best translate as Martingale. She is a superlative general surgeon.

"She was once a novitiate of the Order before she became a medical doctor. She had, as you say in this world, stress issues. The Sisters always invite her to any important vigil services in the hope such will help Dr. Astrid overcome her issues."

Kathy interrupted at that point, "A doctor; a lady doctor? With stress issues? Let me guess; she has ego issues as well."

Kathy's mom, Sally Green, is a senior nurse who works the night shift at Philadelphia's premier hospital. Kathy's opinions of medical doctors had not fallen very far from the mommy tree.

Paul grimaced, gave Kathy a hint of a nod, but continued. "By the time Llywelyn got the ladies chivied to the sea skimmer, the eight-man duty flight crew had the craft warmed up and ready to leave. The four-man security guard squad got on board last, and the sea-skimmer scooted. They were about ten minutes out to sea when Sergeant Julius reported Mt. Snowden reported Londinium had been destroyed. Mt. Snowden went dead three minutes later. The pilot announced, 'Prepare for transition. We're going to go visit a friend of mine. If we're lucky.' They transitioned.

"I told you folks about radiation and nuclear winter. Those thirteen ladies, the four security men, the eight aircrew members, and I may be the only survivors of my home earth.

"You need to talk with your government folks and have them decide what to do with a 130 foot by 300 foot WiG from an alternate timeline. If they haven't decided by the day after tomorrow, we plan to scuttle the craft somewhere in deep water. The WiG pilot will keep it hidden until then. He will detect nearby ships before they can spot it. Our pilot is skilled enough to move the craft around without it being spotted, at least until he runs out of fuel. Julius will stay here and if we have to scuttle the WiG, he will direct your motor boat to their location so you can rescue the remaining crew."

He stopped talking and stared at a wall.

Vicki said, "He's in shock. Paul needs to process. I'm taking him to bed."

She took his arm and gently tugged him to the door leading to the hallway. Paul did seem to be in shock.

A House-Hunting We Will Go

I asked Top to contact Admiral Francis' office. The rest of us moved to the large combination breakfast room and kitchen to sort things out. We assigned the Sisters of Healing to my house. Tiny and Melinda moved back into Vicki's house, which is where we installed Llywelyn and Julius.

It took an hour to transfer everybody. Kathy and Father O'Brien got through to the newly arrived ladies our intent to purchase wardrobes for them tomorrow. Melinda appointed two Valkyries to head to the mainland the next morning to purchase additional clothing, food, women's toiletries, tooth polish and such. All our ladies donated some clothes for the interim.

Scarbutt tracked me down to apologize to me the next morning. I thought the world had come to an end.

"Damn it, Hotshot. You were right; I never thought I would say those three words. Women actually showed up from another earth. Of course, most of them aren't quite drop-dead gorgeous, and instead of wanting to conquer our earth and drain us men of our precious bodily essences, they spend most of their time in prayer. And they say they plan on devoting the rest of their time to the healing arts. But other than that, you hit the damn nail plumb on the head."

I shared a few self-improvement suggestions with Sergeant Scarbutt. Had my deceased mom been around to hear these suggestions, she would have washed my mouth out with soap.

Admiral Francis' office let us know that tomorrow a half dozen tugs would tow a navy floating drydock from the Philadelphia Naval Yards to Nova Scotia. Three nights from now, it would be well offshore and out of normal shipping lanes. It would carry a lot of tarps to keep outsiders from seeing what it might be hauling.

Technician Sergeant Julius contacted the WiG pilot and told him when and where to rendezvous with the drydock. The WiG pilot was not at all worried about being able to maneuver the WiG into the drydock while at sea in the dead of night. Actually, he was confident *he* could do it drunk and blindfolded.

Our navy next needed to choose an isolated place the WiG could call home. The navy bases at Halifax and Sidney had a handful of airship hangers which were large enough to hide the massive WiG. Navy civil engineers figured they could float the WiG onto some modified flatcars and use a locomotive to tow the WiG from the drydock into a hanger. To do that, they needed to lay railroad tracks from the nearest trunk line through a hanger out and past the shoreline.

Navy engineers were evaluating their terrain-constrained options. They would decide whether to choose Halifax or Sidney before the drydock reached Nova Scotian waters. The navy would billet the WiG's crew at the chosen base until at least such time as the navy safely hauled the WiG into a hanger. Technician Julius and Sergeant Llywelyn would rejoin the rest of WiG's crew after the latter were assigned quarters.

I wondered where Vicki and Paul had gotten to. They showed up around ten o'clock in the morning. Holding hands. Paul sat down and started sucking coffee. Kathy and Melinda grabbed Vicki and disappeared to somewhere private. All three girls came back in about ten minutes, smiling and giggling. They were joined in the smiles and giggles by various Valkyries as the day progressed. Kathy finally fessed up to me that evening.

"Vicki has picked up a lot of medical stuff the last few months, dear. The first thing one learns about people in shock is they need to be kept warm. Vicki thoughtfully took his clothes off, put him to bed, and piled on the covers. Then she took off her clothes, jumped under the covers next to him, and held him close. Body heat, you know. About three in the morning, he comes out of shock and realizes Vicki is intertwined with him. All of us girls could tell he liked her, but he was far too much of a gentleman to make the first move."

Meanwhile, we had to deal with our fifteen new arrivals. Melinda got with Father O'Brien to take advantage of his contacts within the Catholic Church. She spent the afternoon making a lot of calls. Of note, she arranged temporary housing for the newly arrived Sisters in a Newport guest lodge owned by Salve Sancto Virgo University, the college run by the Order of the Merciful Sisters.

We had to get them there first. The RFC navy promised to send a destroyer escort fifteen miles offshore, outside the RCC twelve-mile territorial limit, arriving early morning in three days' time. We would use our motor launch to take the twelve Sisters of Healing out to the ship, which would then sail for Newport. Once Melinda herself arrived in Newport, she planned to talk to her father to find a permanent residence for the Sisters of Healing.

I figured the authorities were going to go ballistic when they found out what else our own ladies had done. Kathy had sidetracked Chaplain O'Brien with a theological discussion during a long walk on the beach. Meanwhile, Vicki and Melinda via Paul told the newly arrived Sisters of Healing about the whys and wherefores of our version of earth.

They finally finished their discussions. Each of the ladies signed employment agreements with Vicki to become employees of the Outer Banks Institute for the Evaluation of History, a wholly owned subsidiary of Royal Asclepius Medical Research, Ltd, owned by Melinda.

It got sneakier. Melinda had her father tell his pet governor to reinstate the Rhode Island and Providence Plantations Militia Women's Auxiliary Service Program. All the newly arrived ladies also took commissions in the just-formed RIPPM/WASP Medical Corps.

The interlocking contracts guaranteed if the RFC authorities ever tried to take advantage of the ladies, then the Sisters would be represented by Melinda's hand-picked solicitors. Most of those guys made sharks and barracudas look cute and cuddly.

The process seemed dicey as all heck to me. Kathy assured me the actual point of the legal swaddling was to wrap the newcomers in so many layers of statutory entanglements our beloved bureaucracy could not figure where to start to untangle the Gordian knot.

Once Melinda got the RIPP/WASP legally reconstituted, she asked her Valkyries if they would like to rejoin. If so, she could offer substantial signing bonuses of twenty-five big ones up front, coming out of her own pocket until she was reimbursed by the Colony. Any lady who rejoined would be briefed fully on the mission details, after agreeing to certain security constraints. The ladies, already all Asclepius employees, would now be given stock options.

All six ladies agreed. Melinda took her Valkyries to a vacant room, read them back into the RIPPM/WASPs and Lt. Commander Kathy Green Smith, RFC Navy Reserves Judge Advocate Service, served as a witness.

Simultaneously, Top Sergeant Scarbutt told his marines they had come to a crossroads. They had a choice between getting a full security briefing or returning to normal duty. If they chose the latter option, he would cut travel orders for them. Some Valkyries then would drive them to Raleigh, where they could catch the next train heading north.

All the younger guys were having the time of their lives; they agreed instantly. Only Staff Sergeant Schultz balked, and only initially. He was from Lancaster, where his wife and children were staying while he was on this assignment. He wanted to know how long he would continue to be separated from his family.

Top talked to me, then Kathy. We then talked to Schultz. Kathy explained she wore a Lt. Commander's uniform one month per year when she worked directly for the DCNO, Admiral Francis.

She promised Schultzie she could ensure he got three-day passes twice a month and extra travel time so he could travel from Rhode Island to Pennsylvania. Also, as soon as this assignment was over, she promised to find for him or create a navy billet at Fort Benedict Arnold for his final three-year tour. He said that was the best deal he had been offered since he joined the marines.

Top Scarbutt then briefed all the marines on the real circumstances. The two navy captains and Kathy served as witnesses, though no one signed any paperwork. We explained the project was so secret squirrel we dare not put anything on paper. Top jovially assured them all that any jarhead who was less than discrete about anything he had learned would be hunted down like a rabid dog and dealt with similarly.

We ferried the Sisters of Healing out to the destroyer three days later. The rest of us spent two weeks plotting our future while Paul wrapped up his current research. Most of us then headed north. Jules stayed behind to oversee turning over the three houses to his rental management firm to be rented for the impending summer season. He would also supervise shipping whatever books and such Paul wished to retain.

Dr. Martingale also stayed behind because she wanted some peace and quiet to go review some of Paul's notes. She also planned to go through Vicki's library to become oriented on the general political and technical level of development on this version of earth. Chaplain O'Brien remained to help Astrid translate stuff and the two senior Valkyries, Jennifer and Francine, stayed on to provide security.

I couldn't help but observe that every time Paul and Astrid were in the same room, the temperature seemed to drop about twenty degrees. I hadn't a clue what they were talking about, but between their tones and their body language, they didn't exhibit any sexual tension between them.

I realized eventually their arguments had the same atmospherics as the ones I used to have when my two sisters, Marian and Olivia, both older, ganged up on me. I celebrated the bright side of their interplay; this was a rare time in my life that, whatever was going on, I knew there was no way I was to blame.

The rest of us set out separately to Rhode Island. Kathy and I first spent two weeks in Philadelphia at *Fiddlers Green*, as it had been almost seven months since she had visited her extended family. She spent most of her time reviewing the restaurant's financial books. She spent three evenings serving as the principal assistant chef to Leonardo because she was tired of Cajun and Creole and wanted to brush up on her Northern Italian cuisine. I spent those same evenings serving as the maître d'. I figured cooking was her way of dealing with stress. I wished I could have gone to a weapons range.

Sweet Doctor, You Shall Be My Bedfellow

Philadelphia

Jules, Astrid, Jennifer and Francine pulled into Philadelphia ten days after Kathy and I arrived, having driven up from the Outer Banks in Jules' sedan. Jules spent his first full day giving a lot of expert commentary and advice on the progress of the hooch part of Melinda's wine and cigar bar. Melinda no longer needed to operate such a place, now that she had admitted to Tiny how rich she was, but she was too good a businesswoman to abandon a business which projected a healthy cash flow.

Jules spent a lot of time with Barbara, who had finished her sommelier course. Their conversation quickly transitioned into discussing which brands of various high-end cognacs, brandies, ports, Sherries, and wines could be purchased to transform Melinda's vision into reality. That was a major bottleneck; Melinda insisted on high-quality plonk. It took much longer than Melinda had planned to acquire a sufficient inventory of these beverages. The charcuterie and cheeses were the simple part.

Kathy and I dined with Jules and his party in a private room at *Fiddlers Green* the evening after they arrived. Astrid had made measurable progress with her English, though Kathy occasionally had to translate Astrid's Latin. Astrid seemed, if not quite amused by the experience of bouncing between worlds, unconcerned. Astrid wasn't exceptionally fair of face, but had a sculpted physique. Tonight she was wearing the same white outfit which she wore the night of her arrival, only this time she wore a translucent-blue stone mounted on a silver broach. It was pinned immediately above her left breast.

Astrid turned slightly and the light hit her broach at precisely the right angle. I did a double take. On the back side of the stone, carved scrimshaw-like, was a double-headed puffin. Puffins brought back an unpleasant memory.

"I have never seen a broach like that, Dr. Martingale. What type of gemstone is it, may I ask?"

"It's not a gemstone; it's a type of antique glass, left over from a medieval Scandinavian iron-smelting process. Its unique coloration comes from the unusual composition of silicon in the local ores and the smelting techniques used to process them. We call this color Norwegian Blue. Lovely plumage details on the puffin, you'll notice. The carving itself is about six hundred years old. It was put on a sturdier mounting about fifty years ago. It's not terribly valuable on its own, but it's a family heirloom."

Astrid said all this exuding an unshakeable self-confidence which would do credit to a princess royal. One might even call her arrogant.

"Cream rises to the top, dear," she explained to Kathy later that evening. "I am an incredibly skilled surgeon and will remain so, even using the primitive instruments available to surgeons on your earth. Jules has explained I will need to be licensed to practice my profession and has explained passing the Rhode Island medical board exams should not be difficult. Jules has informed me I need to attend a funeral service first, though."

It wasn't clear to me whether she lacked the English to sound empathetic or whether she didn't care, but I know how I would have placed my bets. I could sense Kathy was about to respond with some scathing comment about conceited doctors, so I gave Jules a light elbow in the gut.

At that point Jules jumped in and said his uncle had only a week or two to live, and he and his party would have to travel to New York to make final arrangements. He asked Kathy if she could take Astrid, Francine, and Jennifer shopping the next day to help them acquire wardrobes suitable for the upcoming funeral and associated events. Kathy agreed, and Jules seemed vastly relieved.

The next morning, after the ladies left to be fitted for black funeral dresses and such, Jules cornered me while I was alone. "Astrid is this close to being nuts. What am I going to do? If she keeps up at this rate I am going to be dead before Uncle Jean."

"You're not making sense, Jules; settle down and explain."

"Six days ago, so we're still at the beach house. Towards the end of dinner, I was complaining about a splitting headache. Astrid, through the Chaplain, explains to me she might have something in her medical kit, that monster briefcase of hers. She tells the chaplain, Jennifer, and Francine to wash up the dinner dishes while she examines me.

"We head for my room; she takes my temperature and pulse. Then she looks at my eyes, nose, ears, checks the glands under the back of my jaw, all the usual doctor stuff. She offers me a pill; tells me it will cure my headache for sure, but warns me it might induce some harmless side effects. My head was splitting, so I shrug 'whatever' and take the pill. She tells me to lie down and says she will be back in an hour to see how I am doing.

"She comes back in an hour, having changed into a big fluffy robe. I realized then my headache was completely gone, but I was sporting wood like a lumberjack. I mean, massive. I couldn't have hidden it under a dirigible hanger. She says, haltingly, she warned me about potential side effects. She takes off her robe; she's wearing nothing else, and she says knows a sure way to reduce the swelling. She told me any additional treatment was entirely my choice. I thought to myself, 'What the hell?' Three hours it took to reduce the swelling."

I may have mentioned that I was a marine; marines always lie about stuff like that. I could sense Jules wasn't lying. Wow!

Jules continued, "I got the story out of her over the next couple of days. She's a surgeon, so she doesn't drink and she doesn't use drugs and she lasted only three weeks as a novitiate. So far, she has found only one surefire way to reduce the stress in her life. She understood Father O'Brien was precluded from reducing her stress. I was the only other male around and she said she was getting desperate for relief. Yeah, I thought it was a good idea at the time, but now I think she's going to kill me with her attention.

"I asked her how she survived in her own world. She said aircraft pilots. She said most of them aren't functionally literate, so they don't try to distract her by discussing philosophy or poetry or some such. In her medical judgment, most pilots are incapable of thinking with organs other than their genitals. She said, offhandedly, that Lycus, the pilot of their world hopper, was literate. If I ever meet Lycus, I'll ask him what that crack means.

"Anyhow, she's wearing me out; she has a more than healthy body and she insists on using it."

I was still staring at Jules; he was living the dream of every marine I ever knew.

Jules continued to whine. "Astrid may be unusual, even for her earth. For instance, it only took her about three or four days to recover from her grief of losing not only her world, but her entire stable of on-call pilots. She must be amazingly resilient.

"I needed to tell somebody who could help. Astrid made it clear she would not do squat for us unless she feels her physical needs will continue to be met. Since I am a minority stockholder in this mess, I felt I had to contribute, but not if it means my early death. You're the security consultant, so go secure someone suitable for her. Find some dashing, overly muscled navy or marine officer or perchance an airship pilot. Or better yet, three or four of them."

"Gee, Jules. My hearts bleed. You didn't have to buy the cow and now you're getting the milk for free. Well, I guess I can drop everything. I'll tell you what; I'll place an advert in the *Times* personal columns. 'Decent looking and incredibly horny lady doctor from outer space desires bevy of men. Inquire of Brigadier Hamilton, Department of the Army, to see if you qualify.'"

Jules glowered at me while wearing an expression like a puppy which had just been kicked. I, justifiably, have always prided myself on my incredible sensitivity, so I stared right at him and sneeringly said, "If you're going to be such a total wimp about this, you should have joined the airship service to have made it a twofer.

"I kid, I kid," I said. "Fine; I will try to free her aircrew as soon as I return to Newport. Then I'll start exploring other angles. Only don't complain too publicly about a decent-looking lady throwing herself at you; it sets a bad example for the real males of the species."

Jules and his ladies left for New York City two days later. Vicki, accompanied by two Valkyries, Connie and Susan, took the train down from Rhode Island to join them. Melinda insisted Paul stay behind, as we could not afford to place all our eggs in a non-secure basket.

Jean Lafitte died five days after Jules and Vicki arrived in New York. They had a small church service. Laffite's remains were cremated and shipped to New Orleans, where they would be placed to rest in a memorial park in the vault housing the urns of his predeceased, older sisters.

Laffite and his solicitors had been working to resolve his financial affairs for months. He had sold most of his former businesses to various closely held corporations in the greater New York City area and had the proceeds converted to cash. Vicki and Jules shared thirteen million pounds sterling after paying off the solicitors and putting aside sufficient funds to ensure the continuing medical supervision and lifelong rubber-room incarceration of their criminally insane cousin, Delilah Honoré.

Jules and Vicki split up after the service. Vicki and her two guards caught a train back to Kingston and were met there by one of Melinda's father's limos. Jules and his entourage drove first to Mystic. Jules owned a four-bedroom townhouse at the edge of the downtown area and had lived there the previous three years. He needed a couple of days to deal with the managing estate agent, his personal solicitor, and his banker.

All the to-ing and fro-ing meant Kathy and I arrived back in Newport before Jules and Dr. Martingale. They drove up two days later and Jules was looking a little frazzled; he appeared quite pale when he emerged from the car. I figured either he was not getting enough sun or he was being preyed upon by a vampire. I mentioned these possibilities to him; he cursed me thoroughly.

Astrid, sensitive to the emotions of others as ever, which meant not at all, started complaining that she needed a gymnasium. Melinda took her on a tour; the Burrs had two gyms on their estate. One was the original; a small facility in the basement, which the family, guests, and the Valkyries used. The other was a larger, temporary weight training facility in the garage complex, which was used primarily by Master Sergeant Scarbutt and his marines.

"What was that about, Jules?"

"She's taken up pole dancing as her new hobby. We stopped in at one of my old joints to chat with the chef; he was the only natural chef working that chain of dives. It was past the lunch hour and though the place was closed for business, some noon-shift dancers were still going through their cool-down routines. Astrid observed the girls and asked what the heck they were doing. I explained the old business model to her and checked with Antonio, the chef.

"He said the business model had not changed. The dancers still could not freelance. Moreover, the old bat controlling the business enforced those rules more strictly than I ever did. Then I talked with a couple of the dancers and they found a spare costume for Astrid. She changed into it and they worked her through some simpler routines. She's now interested in the idea of pole dancing as exercise."

"I could teach her how to crawl through mud, under barbed wire, while being shot at, if she wants to learn new ways to burn off calories."

"You're not helping, John. Anyhow, while Astrid was learning beginning pole dancing, I talked with Antonio and learned more about the new owner-in-truth. He explained the chain is now owned officially by *Queens' Celtic Cross and Shamrock Holdings, Ltd.* Its listed owner is a thirty-something Irish lady who lives in New York City. Antonio explained he had never met her and undoubtedly never would, as she was a cutout for her mother.

"Antonio told me the mom is something else. So this old bat of an Irish lady walked into his joint a couple of weeks after the chain got sold. You should remember the drill, John. I once told you about the hard guys who showed up on weekends and gave the girls the big tips; well, her two bodyguards cut the mold for those guys. Also, she brought some plain slip of a youngish private secretary with her.

"The four of them sat down at a table and every nearby table magically cleared. They ordered dinner. Antonio was working that night, so he was in the kitchen and didn't know what was going on out on the main floor except that everyone who walked back into the kitchen was tense."

"It was probably justifiable, Jules. I'd also be nervous if I thought I would be an accessory to murder by over-seasoning."

"You're an utter wimp, John. Maybe I've mentioned that before. Anyhow, an hour later, the old broad and her bodyguards and her secretary come back into the kitchen and tell Antonio that he is staying on. Then the old bat turns to one of the two ogres standing next to her and says, 'Slab, notify the dancers I will examine them in the changing room. They have two minutes to prepare for my inspection.'

"All the dancers take a break. The old bat and her entourage head to the changing rooms. The dancers strip down to bare-ass naked. She picks out three of them and says they have two weeks to lose the fat or lose the job. They all lost the weight.

"Antonio claimed his food and drink suppliers don't beef about anything anymore and the quality of their food has improved. The girls don't think about turning tricks on the side or failing to turn in their special tips. He told me their legitimate tips are larger than ever, maybe because the girls are in better shape than ever. I figure the pole dancers' sculpted shapes must have been what attracted Astrid's attention. Then Antonio whipped all of us up some lobster rolls, fritters, and coleslaw for a late lunch, and then we drove up here."

Ambush at Aquidneck Bay

Newport, Rhode Island and Providence Plantations Colony

I again took over supervising physical security once I returned to Melinda's cottage. I had less to do than I might have. Melinda's father, Sir Charles Burr, had already revised security procedures in the aftermath of the Spetsnaz incident. He pensioned off his older folks and brought in a half dozen recently retired army MPs recommended by Major General Bartholomew.

He had also worked a lot on his grounds. He hardened various positions to blend in with the gardening décor and vastly improved his internal phone systems. He rebuilt his three back-up generators inside rebar-reinforced high tensile strength concrete walls. Their air ducts and ventilation systems were screened by extra-tightly knit high strength steel screens. He had also expanded his basement facilities in the cottage in various ways. Last, he had purchased two more armored limousines and expanded his garage complex.

Simultaneously, the navy and constabulary had increased their awareness of what went on throughout Aquidneck Island. Once we arrived with Melinda's six Valkyries and Scarbutt and his twelve marines, I figured we were in an overkill situation regarding physical security. Better more than less, I figured.

Only two of the marines, plus Top Sergeant Scarbutt, had been involved with the original incident involving the Spetsnaz. Those two guys had been in the sleep-shift platoon over at Battery Park, so they had missed most of the fun. I scheduled two days to take the marines on a battlefield walk.

Scarbutt made a few calls and the next thing you know, we hosted RFC Marine Captain Franks, DSO, who had been the first lieutenant commanding the two squads of marines hidden on the Burr Estate when the Spetsnaz attacked us. One of General Bartholomew's staff captains from JBWK also joined the tour.

Franks, Scarbutt and I spent two days walking his twelve marines and the staff captain through each step of the Spetsnaz incident. We reviewed our planning, our reasoning, and our split-second decisions. We shared our thoughts on what we believed to be the Spetsnaz commander's decision-making process.

It's rare to be able to share the actual participants' insights of an actual battlefield with active duty marines. North America, except for Mexico and Texico, has only a handful of actual battlefields, none of recent vintage, so the usual walkthroughs are with academics or local amateur historians.

We took the time to do this for a couple reasons. First, I wanted our marine detail to know the terrain intimately, since they might have to defend it. I also wanted their input if they came up with a better insight on how to defend the estate should another battle occur.

Franks, Scarbutt and I pointed out each location where we took or gave casualties, finally winding up in the inner room where then RFC Army Staff Sergeant Mutton jumped on a French-manufactured grenade, albeit one tossed by a Russian. Melinda showed up at that point to describe what she went through when she killed the Spetsnaz as he jumped through the door.

All the younger marines were subdued by then and gave drop-dead gorgeous Melinda some strange looks. They all cheered up, though, when we took them to Providence and treated them to a couple of beers and dinner at the RIPP Militia's MSgt Ralph Mutton All Ranks Club. They all came away a little more aware that perhaps they hadn't all volunteered for the least hazardous duty in the corps.

Before he left us, Captain Franks grumbled to Scarbutt and me that the Spetsnaz incident was, in a way, the worst thing that ever happened to him. Yeah, he had already been on the Captain's list, and yeah, after the incident he was promoted with immediate effect. Yeah, they gave him a DSO. But they also made him a staff officer.

Now he worked directly for a brigadier who worked force planning at the Marine Corps Annex in Philadelphia. Franks was getting sick of being stuck at a headquarters and being at the beck and call of senior officers. He would far prefer to be riding around in a boat some place commanding an RFC Marine Corps company of his own. As it was, when he wasn't pointlessly warming a chair, he was the junior guy at staff meetings, the guy being told to "Grab us some coffee, Franks!" or "Push the button, Franks." He hated it.

I shared Franks' woes with Kathy. She grabbed me, and we tracked down Scarbutt, and she asked him if the captain was married.

"What's that got to do with anything, dearest beloved?" asked I.

"Some ladies enjoy being married to marines, dear. At least we do on those rare occasions where the marine in question is not being dense. I suspect a couple of good meals at a nice restaurant with a charming dining companion would cheer up the young captain.

"Fortunately, I know of an outstanding restaurant in Philadelphia. I also know several well-educated, delightful, still single dining companions for the handsome captain. They all graduated from the premier women's college in the RFC, providentially located just west of Philadelphia. That is only if the captain actually is a gentleman. Is that the case, Top Sergeant Oglethorpe?"

Kathy asked her last question in her lieutenant commander's voice. I had to keep her away from Brigadier Hamilton; Kathy was learning too many tricks. Scarbutt went to brace before he answered.

"Yes, Ma'am. Absolutely. Other than Major Stuart, I cannot think of a finer young officer in the corps."

Kathy turned to me. "I am so glad we can at last solve some problems."

"Dear," I asked, "don't you think we should ask Captain Franks his thoughts about all this?"

Kathy looked at me like I was some long dead creature a dog had just found and dropped at her feet. "There you go, being thick again. Still, to put your mind at ease, I will ask Melinda and Penelope if they have any recommendations they can offer. Do you feel better now?"

Top and I shrugged at each other. It's tough knowing one of your own is heading into an ambush and there is absolutely nothing you can do to prevent it.

The Farmer's Daughter

I realized I had never got to know the Valkyries. Back when Melinda created them, I sort of hoped they would keep out of the way. Once I got involved with Kathy, it didn't feel right nosing around other women. That motivation hadn't changed, but I figured if I didn't understand them better, I'd probably screw up and not use them correctly the next time the horse droppings hit the rotating blades.

The next day I had time to talk with, at length, Francine Miller. She was five foot, nine inches, thirty years old, brown hair, medium frame and athletic rather than curvy. Her breasts were between small and medium and her nose was a bit on the sharp side. I told her I understood marines, but there weren't any lady marines. Could she tell me about army lady MPs?

"I am asking, Francine, because when the real estate situation settles out, I'm planning to use the Valkyries to provide physical security for the Sisters of Healing. I'd like to hear from both you and Jennifer, as the two Valkyrie ranking members, if you think your ladies can handle that on their own.

"I think you can; I am about eighty percent certain you were the one who nailed that Spetsnaz on their far left flank. I tried to get you a medal for that, but I wasn't convincing enough. What's your story?"

"Thanks for the try on the medal, John. I keep telling myself I am only sixty percent certain myself. If you were keeping track, Priyanka was in full spray and pray mode. Since she acknowledged a couple of thousand divinities, she was doing her damnedest to fire off a bullet for each one of them. She might have hit someone more or less by accident before she went and got herself killed.

"Anyhow, I was wondering when you were going to focus on us and start doing your damn job. Lady Melinda is decent for a nob, but she knows she doesn't know squat about security. That's despite her being able to shoot the nose ring off a bull from two fields over. She didn't hire us just to be decorative, though we didn't mind appearing that way because might surprise potential hostiles. We all know what we're doing.

"You want to know about me in particular? Fine, I grew up on a farm in down-province Illinois. By the time I was eighteen, I could ride a horse, shoot for the pot, repair a fence line and castrate a hog. You grew up on a farm; so did you do anything like that?"

"My folks grew cherries, Francine. I could shoot for the pot and repair fences, but not the other stuff. Besides, horses are just plain evil."

Francine snorted; then said, "Wimp. Anyhow, I was the fourth and last daughter in my family. I saw my older sisters marry young and have kids. I wanted to see more of the world than down-province Illinois dirt, though, and my family was sure not going to send me on the grand tour of Europe or anything. Not that there's any doubt *I* would have fit right in, hobnobbing with royalty and such."

I clenched my jaw, but kept smiling. Now was not the time to mention a single word about that fight in the *Sozzled Sturgeon*.

"Heck, we were pretty well off, considering. My dad was even a reserve constable for the township, but unlike some ladies I might mention, I never got to wear white tights and cute little pleated skirts and saddle shoes in grade or high school. The first clothes I ever had which weren't hand-me-downs were the fatigues the army handed out in boot camp."

"Yeah, Francine, I feel your pain."

She inspected me closely. "You must have looked awfully darn cute, what with only having two older sisters. I guess that's why you had to join the marines. An army recruiter would have laughed himself silly, you showing up on his doorstep wearing a frilly frock or some such."

I glared daggers at her. "My folks traded clothes with families who had older sons and younger daughters."

Francine grinned back broadly. "I'm just joshing with you, Hotshot. I know the drill; a lot of farm families did the same. Anyhow, I realized I would never go to a real college or anything. I did earn a two-year criminal justice degree during my nine years in the army, but it's from a provincial school and half of that was by correspondence courses.

"So the day after I turned eighteen years old, I joined the army hoping to be more than another lady clerk typist or a staff driver. Lady MPs are the only ladies in the army allowed to carry weapons, so I was hoping I could wind up where I did."

"Ever been to Great Lakes Combined Training Center? Damnedest mix of lake-driven cold, humid winds and unrelenting heat you can imagine. And that's all in one day."

"I grew up a couple of miles from the Eastern Shore of Lake Michigan, Francine. I know all about the winds coming off that lake. You are lucky you trained on the easy-weather side of Lake Michigan."

Francine snorted but continued. "I got to meet Staff Sergeant Drill Instructor Bonnie Brown. She and two senior corporals had the pleasure of shepherding twenty-four of us, all of us eighteen- or nineteen-year-old girls, most of us wondering what we had gotten ourselves into. So there we were; standing in formation in ill-fitting fatigues. She had arrived to welcome us gently into the army's loving arms.

"Staff Sergeant Bonnie was explaining the facts of our new lives. 'Ladies,' she said. 'You look like the most pathetic collection of mama's girls I have ever had the misfortune to meet. It will be both my duty and my pleasure to wash your worthless asses out of basic to keep the army from having to feed you for the next three years. Not to mention the benefits which will accrue to the army when I keep you wretched excuses for would be soldiers from getting into the real army and screwing up our fine institution. Maybe, just once, I will get lucky and two or three of you little girls might amount to something.'"

I interrupted. "Heck, Francine, she sounds nice. My drill sergeant, at least when he was in a good mood, also called my whole training platoon a bunch of ladies while he was waking us up. Of course, what with his bashing the aluminum trash can with a cricket bat while using a lot of extraneous adjectives, it was clear he did not think we were of extraordinarily gentle birth."

"Let me finish, Hotshot. Back to Bonnie; she was on a roll saying all us baby girls would head home and cry our little eyes out within a week. Then we would use our momma's apron to dry the tears. She claimed we wouldn't be able to concentrate. She bellowed, 'Look around the Post, ladies. What do you see? You see men. Well, overgrown boys, anyhow. Marching around in formation. Showing off their muscles. Bragging about how good they are in the sack.'"

"There's a marine saying, Francine. 'Those who can't, brag. Those who can, do.'"

"Oh, please, Hotshot; enough with your trash-talking the army. So, are you going to keep telling your lies, or are you going to let me finish mine?"

I stood mute; I learned how to do that during Captains' Masts. A lot of Captains' Masts.

Francine made sure I was going to remain silent for a while, then continued. "Anyhow, so Bonnie's yelling at us. 'If any of you fools listened to them, you would think there are twelve miles of rock hard manhood on this base. I'd guess it's closer to three miles' worth, because men always lie about such things. But all their lies won't matter a bit to you ladies, because for the next twelve weeks, you aren't seeing so much as six inches of that stuff. The reason, you ask? It's simple; from this moment on, your pathetic, loser, weak, whiny, cotton-candy asses are all mine.'"

"Gosh, Francine. Do ladies really talk that way?"

"She was staff sergeant drill instructor, Hotshot. They're never ladies. So she continues, saying, 'When I say jump, you will be jumping while you say, 'Yes, Staff Sergeant.' When I tell you to do anything else, you will respond 'Yes, Staff Sergeant!' while you do it. Is that clear, ladies?'

"Some moron, of course, answered, 'Yes, Ma'am.' There is always at least one."

We both laughed and said in unison, "Don't call me Ma'am; I work for a living."

Francine continued. "At that point Staff Sergeant Bonnie said we were all dumb as dirt and she hoped a little exercise would focus our miniscule minds. She said she saw a horizon over there and we could all march in formation until we got there."

"Why did you quit, Francine? I mean, nine years. Another eleven years and you would have earned a pension."

"I got the crap end of the stick once too often. Lady MPs have to deal with all the kids on post and such. My last tour there was a rape accusation. Some eighteen-year-old little trollop in her senior year in high school set her sights on getting some from a nineteen-year-old private. She bragged to all her school pals about how she manipulated him.

"I pitied the dumb private; the poor kid was as hard as a rock but dumb as a stump. Don't know how he made it through basic. He convinced himself he loved the scheming little tramp. Her dad was a Lieutenant Colonel. Sweet Cheeks quickly got bored with him, but the private didn't realize at that point he was supposed to cry himself senseless and go away. So she whined to daddy.

"I talked to all her school friends. They admitted she had planned everything in advance. I nailed everything down. I shared everything with the private's defense counsel. We should have had her lying ass dead to rights, but she stood in the witness stand wearing a white Sunday dress with a lace collar, wearing silk tights and kid gloves and her Sunday go to service hat. Butter wouldn't have melted in her mouth as she lied through her teeth."

Francine paused, sighed, and continued.

"I don't think the panel bought her lies since they threw out all the major charges, but the poor, dumb sod still got three years breaking rocks. I guess all the officers on the court martial must have thought they had to make an example of the stupid mutt to protect their own horny daughters. My tour ran out; I didn't reenlist."

"Ouch, Francine, that's nasty. You're right about the dumb as dirt part; heck, most marines aren't stupid enough to go sniffing around a light colonel's daughter. What happened after that?"

THE FARMER'S DAUGHTER 103

"I spent about a year in New York City doing bodyguard work for a security agency. I wound up here when Lady Melinda put out the call to form a ladies' mounted infantry unit because I was getting damn tired of big city life. Also, how often can a girl get paid to ride show-quality horses?

"Then all of us Valkyries saw how Lady Melinda, and your own wife, cared about doing the right thing. Sergeant Mutton was nobody special, but all you folks did your damnedest to make sure he wouldn't be railroaded. Then you made sure we were equipped and armed and trained. Most guys I knew who went through advanced infantry training didn't have even half the range time we got."

"Thank Melinda for that, Francine. She wound up paying for the ammo. Though Brigadier Hamilton swears the army will reimburse Melinda, eventually."

Francine laughed in my face. "Damn, Hotshot; you should go into comedy with a deadpan delivery like that.

"Anyhow, our little skirmish with the Spetsnaz platoon was the first military action on RFC territory proper since the last battle with the Sioux Nation in 1882. And we are the only women in the RFC to have ever earned the Combat Infantry Badge. Hell, most guys in the regular army don't have those, unless they were in a battalion which rotated out for a tour in Kashmir or Kenya or some exciting place like that.

"What I am trying to say is that a lot of folks walk through their entire lives without ever working for somebody who gives more than a rat's ass about them. Thing is, if you want us to keep the Sisters safe, then we damn well will, or die trying."

Francine then shocked me. "I think it's my turn to ask a question. Is Master Sergeant Lucius Oglethorpe interested in women? Is he married? If the answers are yes and no respectively, I am calling dibs on him. That manipulative tramp Jennifer has her eyes set on him, but I saw him first, and from what I heard, he is the last person on earth who is going to complain about that small scar on my own butt."

It took me a moment to realize she was asking about Top Sergeant Scarbutt. "I can safely say that he is not adverse to women, but I believe he is married to the corps. I thought you and Jennifer were pals."

Francine gave me a strange look.

"Heck, I love her like she was another sister; I called dibs first, is all. Oh sure, even if I land him, he'll probably break my heart someday, just like every guy I ever met in the army did, but a girl's gotta have hope. Well, realistic hopes, anyhow. Not like Miss Thibodeaux's. Damn, that girl's gone and fallen for a guy harder than any girl I've ever seen. I doubt that's going to work well. Hell, I'll paint my ass purple and join a convent if your sneaky pal Paul's not hiding something super important."

I was glad someone shared my concerns about Paul. Mostly, though, I wondered what type of Irish blarney Scarbutt had been feeding Francine and Jennifer.

Scarbutt claimed descent from an impressive number of martial heroes. He had always maintained he was a direct descendent of The General Oglethorpe of Georgia colony fame, albeit not a legitimate one. He claimed Oglethorpe was a little too friendly with some of the Native tribes, if you get my drift. And on his great-to-the-whatever grandmother's side he claimed descent from a Creek war-chief who fought the Spanish to a standstill, though the name, alas, has been lost to history.

It got better. He also claimed to be descended both from the first Ashanti King and the Irish hero, *Cú Chulainn*; via Niall of the Nine Hostages. He had once explained an Irish great-to-the-whatever grandmother had been sixteen years-old when the Great Irish Rebellion of 1798 broke out. Spain left the Irish high and dry in 1799 when their own rebellion in what was then Spanish Mexico broke out. Spain's difficulties freed several West Indian regiments to be sent to help quell the Great Irish Rebellion.

When the 5th West Indian Native Light Regiment of Foot left Belfast to go back to Kingston in 1801, Scarbutt's great-etc., grandmother was the new bride of a Corporal Agamemnon, no last name, of that regiment. Many non-commissioned officers of the regiment found Irish wives during the campaign. At least she didn't starve to death like so many other Irish lasses in her situation. Then Sergeant Agamemnon was emancipated in 1809 like all the other folks in his predicament.

The way Scarbutt calculated things, he was plurality Irish. He claimed he had been raised Catholic. He admitted to having neglected religious services and confession since the day he turned eighteen. That was also the day he hopped a freighter in Kingston and headed to New York City to enlist in the RFC Royal marines. He could certainly sling the blarney; heck, some of it might contain a grain of truth. I hoped Francine and Jennifer had done their homework; still, neither woman was exactly a naïve young school girl nor was I, as I reminded myself, their mom.

When Irish Eyes Are Smiling

Once Melinda reconciled with her father and moved back into the ancestral home, possibly for the next several months, her father felt obligated to talk to his neighbors. He regretfully notified them the risks of "kidnapping attempts on Melinda" might be on the upswing again.

I had not met the next-door neighbors the first time I was guesting at Melinda's cozy little bungalow. Apparently, the patty cake games we played with the Spetsnaz had made a bit of an impression on the adjacent estates. I guess there is no way around being noticed when dozens of grenades explode and thousands of rounds of military grade ammunition make bang and boom noises in the middle of the night. Not to mention the two dirigibles and the light shows with the all the flares and the subsequent ambulances and coroner's wagons and such.

The neighbor immediately to the east, also named Burr and one of Melinda's many fourth or fifth or sixth cousins or something of the sort I could never keep straight, was easy. He took this as an opportunity to sell his estate for an impressive price. He was a retired career diplomat who had served in various garden spots in Asia, Africa and the Middle East, as well as two tours in St. Petersburg. I never did ask if he was stationed in St. Petersburg during my abruptly cut-short visit to the place.

The Honorable Ambassador Burr figured he had experienced enough gunfire in his life and felt the urge to retire from the *noblesse oblige* lifestyle for good. He planned to move to a place south of Raleigh to work on his golf game and scotch habit year round.

That solved our problem of where to establish the Sisters of Healing in long-term residence. Melinda would purchase his estate and convert it into a priory, loosely associated with Salve Sancto Virgo University and the Order of the Merciful Sisters. We would move the Sisters of Healing from their temporary quarters at the University within days of Melinda closing the transaction. Next up was dealing with the neighbor to the west. Melinda said she would initiate that particular bit of out-reach.

Said neighbor was Mrs. Bridget O'Shaughnessy. She had not been in residence when the Spetsnaz hit; she had wintered in Florida that year and had been taking a leisurely yacht trip back to Newport. She was in her middle or late fifties and had been widowed for five years.

Melinda dragged the lot of us to the next Sunday morning service at one of the three Catholic Churches in Newport, the church colloquially known as *St. Patrick the Smiter of Heretics*. It was a feast day, so the church was full to bursting, with barely standing room left. The entire first row, though, was occupied solely by a sort-of-elderly lady, a plainly dressed lady of in her mid-twenties, three overdressed, giggling young girls, two fidgeting young boys and two uniformed nannies. No one crowded them.

After the service, Melinda made her way alone to one of the chauf-feurs driving a trio of limousines parked about a half block from the church. She introduced herself as the former Miss Burr and current next-door neighbor to Mrs. O'Shaughnessy. Could the lady spare a few moments?

Meanwhile, Tiny and I closely eyeballed the drivers and other male members of her entourage and they eyeballed us back. One of them took out a six-inch blade and started cleaning under his nails. Did I mention two of them were built along the same lines as Tiny? Ten minutes passed until Bridget O'Shaughnessy emerged from the church. The nannies chivied and hustled the five children into two of the waiting limos.

The limo driver with whom Melinda had talked approached the older lady and spoke briefly. The lady waved at Melinda to come closer. They squeezed hands and pecked each other on the cheeks through their prayer shawls. They talked for a few minutes and parted ways.

Melinda tried to explain things when we got back to her estate.

"I first met Mrs. O'Shaughnessy when I was twelve or thirteen years old, I think. I met her seldom, as my mother refused to socialize with her. My father explained to me that Bridget is not from old money, as such things go. Most of her ancestors came over in the 1840s via Quebec when the potato blight struck the old sod.

"Most of Bridget's more recent ancestors were prominent Irish community leaders in the greater New York City area, providing a variety of community services, including emergency financial assistance, entertainment, mutual insurance services and community consulting of all sorts.

"She has one son, now a solicitor in private practice in New York City. Her four daughters are all happily married with lots of children, and all are married to leading members of the Irish community. Those dear, cute children you saw in the front row were some of her grandchildren sent from the city for the summer to enjoy fresh air and exercise."

I turned to Tiny and said, "Could you translate that into peasant-speak for me, Tiny? Please?"

Tiny processed his wife's line of bull for a moment and croaked, "That's not just any Mrs. O'Shaughnessy; she's the fracking Dowager Empress. Her husband got whacked five years ago. Nobody can prove anything, but everyone in New York suspects a New Spain or Cuban Organization. Her son's the chief consigliere of a New York Fraternal Organization. All her daughters are married to up-and-comers in the Fraternal Organizations. Well, one married into the Boston Irish Mob."

I must have reacted in some manner. Tiny addressed his next remarks directly to me.

"I guess you were sailing donuts in the South Atlantic when the drug war exploded. Some Cubans and their pals tried to muscle in on the New York City area's longshoremen's and teamsters' guilds in order to expand drug imports into the region. The Fraternal Organizations have a couple of hard and fast rules. One rule is nobody sells drugs in Irish-Catholic neighborhoods. The Cubans intended to break that rule. Bad choice.

"The FOs put aside their modest territorial differences until they dealt with the Cuban incursion. There were quite a few unexpected wakes within the FOs, but far more Cubans and their buddies got turned into fish food. Right now, Bridget O'Shaughnessy hates New Spain and Cuba more than she hates the English. And that's saying a bunch, in case it has escaped your notice how the English and most of our own aristocratic nobs treat Irish Catholics. Heck, because of that two-hundred-year-old grudge, they look down on the Irish as even lower forms of life than Italian Catholics."

Melinda got the discussion back on track. "When I mentioned our increased security concerns with dear Bridget, she said she would consult with her family. She said she knew nothing of such matters and would be guided by their recommendations. She has agreed to meet with me within the week and share her thoughts."

Tiny snorted. "That old bat is twice as tough as Brigadier Hamilton. On top of that, the rumor in Philly is she had her heart surgically removed, so emotions wouldn't interfere with the advice she gave her now late husband. Word on the street is her late hubby only made it to the top of the heap because she was the one who told him on whom to step and when to step on them."

Jules interjected. "That must be the lady who now controls my old chain of gentlemen's clubs. She gets more respect than my late uncle ever dreamed of."

Tiny thought for a moment more, then grinned. "If somebody tries to take yet another crack at us, I hope they screw up their reconnaissance and ring on Bridget's doorbell instead. If her security is ready to receive hostile intruders, I wouldn't want to hit them with anything less than a reinforced company of the *Invincibles*."

Tiny smiled at Melinda. "That also explains something which has been bothering me for a while—the hard guys in New York being willing to work with your family to prevent you from being kidnapped. I can't recall any such deal being offered to any other prominent family. Mrs. O'Shaughnessy must have received tons of kids and other visitors over the years, so I can see how she would have wanted to minimize stray shots in her immediate neighborhood."

I processed Tiny's revelations. Two years ago, the authorities were gobsmacked when they discovered an entire Imperial Russian Spetsnaz platoon was parked on Aquidneck Island. If the Russians hadn't attacked us, we might never have known about them. From my conversations with my Uncle Max, a retired Ft. Detroit City Purple Posse torpedo, I knew the large mobs had information sources beyond those which our only occasionally vigilant army, navy, and constabulary counter-intelligence types could tap.

"Melinda, Tiny; we need to give her a reason to help us so we aren't surprised again. Moreover, if she works with us, our physical security problems will be a lot easier."

Tiny and I were not the only folks working security issues. Two troops of armored cars from the 1st Armored Cavalry Brigade based at Ft. Lord Jeffrey Amherst in western Massachusetts Colony appeared at JBWK to provide a rapid reaction capability. Also out of the blue, the army began standing up a company-sized permanent opposition training force to be based at the Joint Base. It made sense, in a way, to locate it at JBWK. We already did most of our evaluation of potential enemies' land weapons there.

The latter move seemed, somehow, much too smart, if you knew the top army brass. They often made Labrador retrievers look like geniuses. It wasn't at all like those folks to be bright enough to establish a cadre of guys equipped with enemy weapons and who understood potential enemies' doctrines and tactics. If they set up such a force, it would give our regular forces a chance to practice against what they might face. I mentioned to Kathy I could not believe our brass had been so brilliant.

She smiled. "You owe it all to Top Sergeant Scarbutt. Well, indirectly, at least."

"Does the admirable Sergeant Scarbutt have any clue he is going to be blamed for this, dear?"

"Probably not, but it's still his fault. After our initial chat about Captain Franks, I talked to Penny and Melinda. Then I talked to Top again. I grilled him until he volunteered that Captain Franks had unusual tastes in religious literature."

"Say what, Kathy?"

"He reads the *Geneva Bible* rather than the *King James* version. Well, I immediately talked with Penny and Melinda and we made some calls, including a couple to Madeline. Oh, and extremely coincidentally, Captain Franks will be assigned to JBWK to observe how the army develops its opposition training force. He is going to be the officer in charge of developing an elite, platoon-size, marine version of the same and he will be that unit's first commanding officer."

I was stunned; coincidence my shot-at ass. Kathy kept talking.

"After all, he was the obvious choice. The Deputy CNO realized Captain Franks was the only officer in the corps who led outnumbered marines into battle against Imperial Russian Spetsnaz and they were equipped with French weaponry. And Major General Bartholomew's aide was quite impressed with the way Captain Franks conducted the battle analysis.

I thought for a bit. Sometimes that's tough for a burnt out marine.

"So, if I have this straight, you and your girls' school chums have manipulated the rankest of the army, navy and marine brass to set up a pair of opposition forces training programs. And you did all this only so you can dangle a potential husband in front of your other chum, Ruth Brittany?"

"I think that's a rather crude way of putting it, but I guess that's one way of describing it. I'm sure our top brass would have thought of it, eventually. We sort of greased the wheels."

Doctor, Doctor Give Me the News

Mrs. O'Shaughnessy paid a formal call upon Melinda seven days later. Melinda's mother left in a huff to visit the Bartholomews of Long Island the day prior rather than be forced to acknowledge her next-door neighbor. Sir Charles Burr perforce accompanied his wife. Mrs. O'Shaughnessy used a three-limo convoy to travel the vast distance from her estate next door, though two of her three limos parked at the gate and did not enter Melinda's estate.

Bridget had done her homework. After introductions and a few minutes of social pleasantries, she laid down the law to Melinda. "We need some truly private discussions to work this out. I suggest that only you, I, my ward Elizabet, and your arrogant lady doctor who's not of this earth and who likes pole-dancing, attend."

Kathy and Melinda went wide-eyed.

Bridget eyeballed Kathy. "Mrs. Smith, please take yourself, your husband, Mr. Sammartino, my two bodyguards and everyone else off someplace. Perhaps you could show off the new rec-room in the basement. The one Melinda's father put in between the newly constructed miniature emergency room and clinic and the newly built tunnel which leads to your garage complex."

Bridget turned towards Melinda and continued. "Your father used workmen from the carpenters', electricians' and laborers' guilds, as well as catering their lunches from various dining establishments in Newport. Some of which I own, at least in part."

Melinda, quicker than she might have been, asked, "The guilds or the restaurants?"

"A question worthy of your father, Mrs. Sammartino, though the answer is both. You don't give your father enough credit for foresight, dear. He has reasons to want the world to think he is the platonic ideal of a pompous aristocratic and he takes extraordinary steps to convince most of the world how ordinary his talents are. It's an act, of course. Your mother, contrarily, does not have to act. Bless her heart."

Melinda harrumphed but did not protest the slur.

Bridget continued. "I also control several restaurants in Kingston, close to the joint base. Additionally, I interrogated the dancers at my Waverly Gentlemen's club. The latter reported Astrid mentioned she was a doctor and an incredibly skilled surgeon nearly two dozen times while she was learning about pole dancing. Since there is no such person as a Dr. Astrid anybody listed as having a medical license anywhere in the RFC, I deduced she was not from around here."

Bridget signaled her own entourage, "Wires, Slab, you may each have one pint. Behave, we are guests."

"Mrs. Smith, I request you make yourself absent because you remain a member of the bar. Both professionally and personally, you are too close to Madeline Hamilton. While I will not be surprised if she hears of our discussions in short order, you should not be a direct witness to anything. It's actually for your own good."

Melinda nodded in understanding; most of us headed for the doors. Melinda ordered tea and coffee and pastries set up for four in the informal library room with the ocean view.

As we were walking out, Tiny said, "You guys have quite the reputation. How they hanging, Wires, Slab?"

Wires responded, "Usually by their necks, Wanker. Mrs. O'Shaughnessy doesn't pay me to be creative. I heard of you as well; word is you throw a decent punch. Is he really Detroit Max's nephew? My own uncle once ran into Detroit Max. Fortunately for both of them, it was the dead of night and they were both lousy shots back then. You guys got a dart board down in your rec-room? Want me to show you two how to toss stilettos?"

Tears of nostalgia blurred my vision; I was reminded of conversations around the campfire in the Upper Peninsula deep woods when Uncle Max would let me come on fishing and hunting trips with some of his beer-drinking buddies from work. Ah, the innocence of youth. It turned out I sucked at tossing stilettos. I lost five pounds sterling.

After our guests left, Melinda gathered us together and explained how she had experienced the strangest conversation of her life. She said, "You observed for yourself Bridget O'Shaughnessy's ward Elizabet was wearing one of the plainest, most colorless outfits which has ever existed. She wore absolutely no makeup. She is also seriously not normal. After my serving staff left off the tea service, Bridget said, 'Let's try to be informal. Call me Bridget; this is my ward, Elizabet. May I call you two, Melinda and Astrid?'

"You may not have noticed, John, but Astrid has an ego. She responded to Bridget's gracious offer by saying, 'I am the best damn surgeon on this benighted ball of dirt and I will damn well be called Dr. Martingale until I have decided differently.'

"Bridget smiled and said, 'If you are skilled enough to back up your arrogance, I will call you the Queen of Sheba if that's what you wish. Just make sure you know with whom you deal. Elizabet, share with these young ladies exactly how you met me.'

"Elizabet said, 'Yes, Mrs. O'Shaughnessy. Lady Melinda, Dr. Martingale; I first met Mrs. O'Shaughnessy when I was eleven years, three months, and seventeen days old. I am now twenty-four years, four months, and eighteen days old. I met her at approximately eight-thirty at night when my late stepfather had offered to pimp me to the late Mr. O'Shaughnessy for the price of a half-pint of whiskey.'"

I saw Kathy tense. Well, she had assassinated a man who had raped one, and probably more, of her college friends. She, herself, almost had been raped.

Melinda continued her narration. "Elizabeth described how she and her stepfather were outside a marginally reputable Irish pub in Queens where Mr. and Mrs. O'Shaughnessy and two bodyguards had emerged from a private meeting. The O'Shaughnessy's had a business interest in the establishment."

I looked back and forth at Kathy and Melinda. "Uh, not that I have ever experienced this firsthand, but every Top I ever knew told his marines, just before any shore leave north of New Jersey, how if we were stupid enough to injure one of the ladies working in a bordello controlled by an Irish Mob, we were way too stupid to wear a marine uniform."

Melinda responded to my unvoiced question. "Their operating model is, perhaps, unique in this business. I'll explain it to you someday, if you wish. To continue, though, Mrs. O'Shaughnessy told her husband to crush that swine's kneecaps.

"Mr. O'Shaughnessy instantly bounced the tip of his walking stick on the pavement, whereupon the walking stick rebounded about three feet into the air. He grabbed his walking stick near its lower end and swiftly lashed out twice. He crushed both of Elizabet's late stepfather's knee caps. She later discovered this walking stick had a two-and-a-half pound lead weight at the gripping end."

I stood up and pantomimed bouncing the barrel end of an imaginary Battle Enfield off the pavement and catching the barrel off the bounce. "He had to be strong as all blazes, Melinda."

"Elizabet said he was, John. Mrs. O'Shaughnessy next considered Elizabet for a moment and said, 'Come with me, child. Nobody pimps out children in front of my pubs.' They all walked away, leaving Elizabet's late stepfather screaming and lying crippled in the gutter."

"Bridget seems real nice, Melinda. What happened then?"

"Elizabet described how, when she was thirteen years, five months and five days old, Mrs. O'Shaughnessy took her to a paupers' hospital in Brooklyn where Elizabet's stepfather lay helpless and dying. Bridget gave Elizabet permission to spit in her late stepfather's face. He died two days later. Elizabet explained she remembered all of this because she recalls everything which has happened in her life since she was four years, seven months and six days old."

I was startled. I had read somewhere, maybe in the tabloids, that there was no such thing as a photographic memory.

"Really, Melinda? Elizabet can actually remember everything?"

"It seems so, John. During my grand tour of Europe, I met one of my sixth cousins, an Austro-Hungarian Countess. I learned a couple of simple phrases in Hungarian. Early on during our conversation, I said 'Thank you very much' in Hungarian. Thirty minutes later, I asked Elizabet to repeat what I had said. She pronounced the phrase precisely, mimicking even my own wretched accent.

"To continue; Bridget turned back to the two of us. 'Now that Elizabet has established what a sweetheart I am, we can all pretend to be civil and call each other by our first names. Elizabet will remain silent. There is no need to take notes. As you have discerned, Elizabet has a photographic memory and is scrupulously honest. So, Astrid, if you are indeed the best damn surgeon on this benighted ball of dirt, then we can come to an agreement. My only son needs his gall bladder removed. There is not a doctor or hospital in the colonies where I trust the staff not to murder him on the operating table via incompetence or malice.'

"Astrid responded there was no doubt about her skills, and a gall bladder removal was trivial, but if she were going to operate, then she would need a staff she could trust. That being the case, she was going to call upon some Sisters of Healing to help. Astrid also said, in the spirit of full disclosure, both she and her nurses were not yet licensed by Rhode Island Colony. However, if Bridget was willing to ignore unnecessary and petty bureaucratic dictates, then so was she."

What is Permitted for Jupiter is not Permitted for Cattle

Liam O'Shaughnessy, his wife, his son and three daughters visited Bridget the subsequent weekend. After attending Saturday night Mass, Liam stayed at Melinda's cottage where Astrid put him on a fast and imposed fluid restrictions. The operation was scheduled on Monday morning in the clinic in Melinda's mansion's basement.

Astrid was stunned by how few medicines our world had which met her standards. She explained we had discovered some antibiotics and antivirals, but we used them only because they seem to work. We did not yet understand their underlying causal mechanisms.

Astrid and Mary were pleasantly surprised to find they could acquire ultrapure samples of sulfanilamide, a chemical used to process textile dyes. Mary was absolutely amazed to discover we already used thiopental for an anesthetic; she had been worried we still relied on a half-pound of sand wrapped up in a couple of socks to put folks to sleep.

Astrid and Mary didn't use any of these chemicals; Astrid used supplies from her kit. She wanted to know what was available if she exhausted her kit.

Astrid had imposed an unusual condition as a prerequisite for the procedure, since this would be Astrid's first surgical operation under primitive conditions. Astrid said she wanted to record her impressions to be able to share her real-time observations with the medical folks of our world. Melinda explained to Astrid it would take a couple of months to build a sound studio like the record companies used. Astrid suggested asking Elizabet to observe the procedure and serve as a human recording device.

As Astrid was hacking and slashing and stitching, she was also usually talking loudly enough in English for Elizabet to hear what Astrid wanted Elizabet to hear. Some of what she said, though, was in her version of Latin to minimize misunderstandings with the two senior Sisters of Healing. There was also some Gaelic and what we later identified as Old Norse mixed in.

"Memorandum for the record. Conditions for the future use of antibiotics: Both the prescribing physicians and the issuing chemist should be criminally liable for any abuse. I recommend crucifixion as a deterrent to the overuse and over-prescription of any form of antibiotics. Is that his bowel? What's it doing up near his gall bladder? Theodora, stop rolling your eyes at me like that; you've worked with me before. I know damn well that's not his bowel. It may be his knee cap.

"Wipe my brow, please. If crucifixion is not permitted, then public flogging may be an acceptable alternative. Under no conditions should this earth's medical profession permit or contribute to developing any antibiotic-resistant bacteria. Number two thread. Get the topical disinfectant. Peroxide will suffice in the future, if that's all they have. Stupid primitives. Now Mary, stop muttering in Gaelic. I am not insensitive. I am quite ticklish, actually, under certain conditions. There, that's all tied up. Did I leave a scalpel in there again? Joking dears, just joking.

"Damn, I was good. That was the hard part. Speaking of which, somebody find me a young man, about twenty-two-years-old. He must be rock hard and stupid. Any of those marines stashed above the garage will do. Have one bathed and perfumed and sent naked to my room. Wipe that smile off your face, Mary; I know Tribune Paul would threaten to have me flogged for fraternization. It would be an empty threat; not even that assassin Llywelyn would dare lay a finger on me. '*Quod licet Iovi non licet bovi.*' He certainly refused to so much as touch me the first time Paul was visibly angry with me.

"When we return home, I will explain to Sigrun that Paul was still seething over the time she and I used our birch branch bundles to chase his eighteen-year-old naked ass out of the sauna and into the snow. Corporal Llywelyn was laughing so hard he teared up, saying, 'Tis clear they have no concealed, deadly weapons, your young lordship.' We made Paul beg for over a minute before the other guards insisted we let him back into the palace lodge before his princeling ass froze solid.

"Put your finger there; press. More of the smaller thread. Britannicus is still madly in love with Siggy; it's so rare arranged marriages work out so well. Don't snort at me like that, Theodora. Well, I suppose I could have killed the senile geezer, but then Siggy would be bereft of her favorite sister. It's probably better I'm hiding out here.

"Okay, I'm done. Move him to the recovery room. Hold Liam there for two days; if nothing goes wrong, have him sent back to Bridget's cottage. Schedule novitiate nurses to take shifts in attendance, first here and then there around the clock, and call me immediately if there is any sign of distress or infection. Has anyone chosen my marine yet?"

Elizabet reported first to Bridget O'Shaughnessy. Elizabet had little idea initially what the Gaelic or Old Norse words meant, but Bridget brought in language experts under her control. They worked out the gist of Astrid's monologue. Subsequently, Bridget invited Kathy, Tiny, Melinda, and me to review the amalgamated transcript. We had a lot to think about, given what Astrid had revealed.

I focused foremost on how our visitors were lying through their teeth about some things; Astrid clearly expected to go home, perhaps soon. What further tweaked my professional interest was Astrid calling Llywelyn an assassin. If she was serious, he might mean trouble.

My concerns grew once I realized Astrid and Paul had known each other for at least fifteen years. I figured any relationship wherein Astrid and somebody named Sigrun had chased a naked Paul out of a sauna had to have been close, at least at one time.

I recalled that the night Astrid arrived at *Chateau Pirates Paradise;* she and Paul had screamed at each other for a good couple of minutes. I wondered why Paul and Astrid ordinarily had avoided each other since that episode and why they now acted as if they did not know each other well. I kept most of those thoughts and suspicions to myself; our visitors had shown no sign of ill-intent yet and I did not want to appear paranoid.

Elizabet claimed, truthfully, when Astrid debriefed her, that she had understood only the English and Latin parts of Astrid's monologue. Astrid failed to ask whether Elizabet had talked to anyone who might have figured out the rest.

Astrid was appalled to discover we no longer used crucifixion as a punishment. She was somewhat mollified to learn every colony except Pennsylvania and Rhode Island still had flogging on the books, albeit the punishment had been unused for about 150 years. She suggested flogging be brought back with a vengeance and Rhode Island and Pennsylvania laws be changed accordingly.

Astrid sincerely was concerned about forestalling resistance to antibiotics. I figured one day Astrid would explain to the peasants what antibiotics were and why she was so concerned about their prospective misuse.

Four days later, two days after Liam had been transported back to his mother's cottage, Bridget, Elizabet, Slab, and Wires paid another visit. This one was far more cordial. Bridget brought up her own doctor from New York to evaluate Liam's recovery. Bridget explained to her doctor Liam had been camping in the woods alone when he had a gallstone attack. Fortunately, a hiking Boy Guide found him, heated his pen knife over an open flame, removed the gall bladder, stitched Liam up, but wandered off before he could be thanked. Bridget's doctor, of course, pretended to believe her story.

"My doctor told me to track down the Boy Guide and promised to pay the lad's way through medical school out of his own pocket. He said he had never seen such precise incisions. He was amazed at the delicate hand revealed by the stitching. He was more amazed at the utter lack of any sign of post-operative infections. Liam can go back to light desk work next week and should be almost normal within three to four weeks after that. I find myself more obligated to all of you than I expected. If there is any small favor within my ability to grant, please ask."

Astrid spoke first. "Get my damn air-crew out of prison. Your navy has them locked up like criminals, though they are supposed to be treated like the armed forces of a neutral nation who entered the country inadvertently. How convenient that they have no embassy to reach out to! They are all stuck at the tail end of nowhere near Sidney, Nova Scotia. Sidney is nothing but clapped out iron mines and a small base your navy forgot to close and my crew members have to be going out of their minds with boredom."

Astrid waved her hands around, gesturing to encompass all of us. "Your navy doesn't care two rat's asses about nurses or lady doctors and they already had an arrangement in place for Paul. But they somehow think a double handful of predominantly warrant and non-commissioned aircrew can show them how to build a sea-skimming aircraft well over a hundred years in advance of this world's stone-age technology. Melinda and Brigadier Hamilton have argued on their behalf, but the navy is adamant."

Bridget interrupted Astrid and turn towards me. "Speaking of the military, how many marines do you have stashed above the garage complex? I can count on the fingers of one hand how many times my own sources have failed to discover important details such as that."

"There are thirteen marines," I replied. "They're helping protect us for another five months. We are worried that either the Tsar's folks, or a more unscrupulous foreign pharmaceutical company, might hire some folks to interfere with our research. We want to vaccinate everyone in the Empire against polio as soon as possible. We also would prefer to make sufficient profits to ensure Paul and his folks are taken care of.

"Some pharmaceutical firms, like Lavoisier out of Cuba, would kidnap Ruth and Paul and Astrid in a heartbeat if we gave them an opportunity. Then Lavoisier would take over the vaccine trade and jack up vaccines prices into nosebleed territory. Given our connections, and your own gracious presence, any thugs they hired probably are from New Spain or Cuba."

Bridget smiled. It was not a nice smile. "New Spain or Cuba, indeed; I suspect your instincts are correct. You pique my interest, Lieutenant Smith. Please liaise with Slab regarding coordinating security measures and intelligence sharing. I will take steps to see to Dr. Martingale's aircrew. It shouldn't take more than three or four days. I suddenly feel the need for confession and I plan to light a candle or two to give thanks for Liam's recovery. I may also do something nice for your marines. I suspect they are bored as well."

I had questions regarding her motives. "Mrs. O'Shaughnessy, what's up with all the cooperation? I know as well as you do the English nobs have treated the Irish Catholics as subhuman scum since the Battle of the Boyne. Their attitudes have only hardened since the Revolt of '98. How come you're not crazy like a Fenian?"

"I rarely answer direct questions, Mr. Smith; even intelligent ones like the question you asked. I often answer questions with questions. For example, if the Fenians succeed beyond their wildest dreams and the Greater Britannic Empire collapses, will the Tsar or the Manchu Emperor suddenly stop playing their own Imperial Games? Or even King Louis XXIII? Do you think he would deal with the Irish any less firmly than he treats the Bretons?

"We Irish have been forced for centuries to learn how to corrupt and manipulate the current system, albeit around the edges. Objectively, we have made a lot of progress and I can't imagine any plausible, real world alternative to English hegemony would leave the Irish better off. We have to keep increasing the amount of influence we can bring to bear within the current political structures. Slow and steady wins the campaign, Mr. Smith. There are rarely any magic, silver bullets in real life."

Bridget seemed to have a lot of practice manipulating the system, and she had a lot of connections. Amazing enough, the Cardinal of New York City finds it easier to get on the schedule of the Chief of Navy Operations than does the average marine. The Cardinal arrived at the CNO's office, with the Chargé d'affaires from the Swiss Embassy in tow, only four days after Bridget left to buy some candles.

The Cardinal explained he had acquired through the sanctity of the confessional the knowledge there were believers who might need communion stuck in captivity near Sidney, Nova Scotia. Since his communicant thought the captives might be foreigners in need of diplomatic assistance, the Cardinal had asked the Swiss Embassy for its intercession.

The Cardinal suggested the navy move those folks down to Halifax, where the Swiss had a small consular office. The Swiss would check periodically to see the captives were being treated within diplomatic norms. The Bishop of Nova Scotia would arrange to provide communion for those who wished it. The "or else's" remained diplomatically implied, but they were very much there.

Our CNO did not make his rank because he was an idiot. Or blind. Actually, he made it because he was a political animal from his receding hairline down to his overweight toenails, though that's not the type of observation mere second lieutenants are supposed to make.

Anyhow, one week after Cardinal's visit, the WiG pilot Lycus, the sort of co-pilot Marcus, and Communications Technician Sergeant Julius, arrived in Newport. Lycus and Marcus were the only two commissioned officers in the crew and had signed their parole agreements in the presence of both a private solicitor and the Swiss Consul in Halifax. Paul had argued successfully that we needed to upgrade the sensor and communications systems on Melinda's estate, and Julius was the person to make it so.

Astrid grabbed the two officers the moment they walked into Melinda's cottage and said she was going to give them their overdue quarterly flight physicals. The three then disappeared into the basement medical facilities.

I glanced at Jules. He was sporting an enormous smile. He sighed and said, "My prayers have been answered. I mean that literally. I thought she was going to be the death of me."

The other aircrew members were transferred into a private resort complex near Halifax. There they met the Bishop of Halifax and a staffer from the Swiss Consulate. The Bishop's Latin proved adequate for communication, though he had to write words out on occasions.

He promised to arrange private, late Sunday afternoon religious services. He had also arranged for half of them to be granted thirty-hour leaves every Saturday morning. He emphasized they were not to travel over twenty miles from the Halifax city center and were not to talk about from whence they came. The Bishop left on other business and the aircrew talked at length with the Swiss consul.

Paul's folks were quite surprised when the Swiss Consulate staffer passed out not only some decent walking around money and but also some very-high denomination gift certificates to "*The Busty Mermaid: Halifax's Premier Gentlemen's Club*." At least they would all have something to confess during the Sunday services.

I asked Slab about that the next day when I was giving him my thoughts on his own physical security layout and how we could better coordinate a response to hostiles in the event something occurred.

He replied, "I spent a six-month tour as a bouncer there, back in my younger days with the outfit. I can sure think of worse places to be stuck.

"Mrs. O'Shaughnessy and all her kids each own eight and half-percent of the stock and thus control the corporation. She made sure those other-earth guys were comped at the Gold Membership Level. That means free transport to and from their lodgings and free meals at the club, including a great Sunday brunch. It just goes to prove that Mrs. O'Shaughnessy, down deep, is a total sweetheart."

Home, Home on the Range

Try as we could, neither Slab nor I could identify any hints that specific hostiles were planning action against us. Army and navy intelligence reported nothing unusual; the Rhode Island Colony Constabulary sources reported similarly. More worrisome, no one in Mrs. O'Shaughnessy's vast network of eyes and ears had learned anything either.

I figured at least two or three hundred researchers and support people at the Newport Naval Base and at JBWK were now aware of our research. Realistically, Bridget's folks couldn't possibly be the only outsiders who were aware of our other earth visitors.

Jennifer, now a brevet captain commanding the RIPPM/WASPs, and the rest of her Valkyries moved to the cottage to the east to provide security for the Sisters of healing. The Bishop of Providence came over to bless the priory's opening. Then we moved all the Sisters of Healing out of their Salve Sancto University quarters and into the massive cottage.

I could now adjust our security protocols for Melinda's own cottage and its eighty-acre grounds. We would now have near guaranteed warning if something went wrong at either our eastern or western flanks, so I wanted to beef up both the front and the back doors. Jennifer came over the day after the Sisters moved in, having talked with the Sisters about the proposed security arrangements. We worked some security protocols and then she shared a couple of other observations.

"I got some extra comments for you, Hotshot. I talked with Francine. She's pretty sharp when it comes to reading women. All those novitiates are cute and cuddly and eager, like a basket full of puppies. I guess they all got over losing their world pretty damn quick. Weird.

"The two senior sisters, Mary and Theodora; well, they don't give off the same vibrations. We Valkyries started off as the 1st Mounted Dragoons. We have all spent a lot of time around horses. Those two senior sisters have both been rode hard and put up wet, at least a couple of times in their lives. Well, Francine and I think so, anyhow. Maybe you should check them out."

Jennifer then demanded I bring in Dr. Astrid into the conversation. Once Astrid arrived, Jennifer spoke. "The Sisters saw our folding stock Wembley pistols and went nuts."

"What's the matter?" I asked, smugly. "Do loud noises scare them or something?"

Beside me, Dr. Martingale giggled. That was out of character.

Jennifer continued, "No, that's not it, Mr. All-knowing and All-seeing Marine. They all want one and they are demanding range time as well. Also, they all want full concealed carry getups."

"I thought they were nuns as well as nurses."

"They are," said Astrid. "They also were expected to be sent into the nastiest places on our earth under conditions where civil order is often near or beyond the breaking point. Sometimes their accompanying security can be overwhelmed.

"They have all had the equivalent of your basic infantry course. One cannot provide medical care when one is dead or being repeatedly raped, so they are expected to contribute to their own defense, in extremis. You should schedule me some range time as well. I am now quite overdue."

Melinda made some more calls to her godfather, Major General Bartholomew, Commander JBWK. The Sisters got kitted out with uniforms befitting the RIPPM/WASP medical service within the week. We also issued them a boatload of weapons and we set up a schedule for qualifications and range time over at the Joint Base.

I joined them, Astrid, and Kathy one session when they were plinking away on the fifty-yard range with six-inch barrel, folding stock Wembley .30-caliber pistols. Astrid was absolutely rock steady and as deadly accurate as the weapon and ammo allowed.

After her session Astrid complained to us our ammo sucked. "It has absolutely no target seeking capabilities whatsoever. I am forced to concentrate excessively since the stupid ammo only goes in the general direction of where I aim. Fortunately, I have exceptional concentration."

"Cry me a river, Dr. Martingale. It gets worse if folks are shooting back at you or trying to drop mortar shells on your head. It's tough having to be a Neanderthal. Your Sisters of Healing haven't complained about our ammo, though."

"That's one reason I left the Order after my short stint as a potential novitiate. I have never been the type to suffer in silence. Also, I thought they might have been more reasonable about granting periodic exceptions to the vows of celibacy. Given my great-grandmother set up the endowment which originally funded the Order, you might think the Mother Superior could have cut me some slack."

At least sometimes Astrid was self-aware of some things. Kathy even acknowledged, while on the firing range, that sometimes Astrid seemed nice, at least compared to other doctors Kathy had known.

Ruth and Paul spent most of their waking hours at the ever-expanding research facilities at the JBWK. They prioritized getting a dead virus polio vaccine up and ready for human testing. Ruth and Astrid had pursued the dead virus approach to minimize the risks of adverse reactions.

Mrs. O'Shaughnessy and Melinda worked out a deal with the Catholic Church and its charitable orphanages on the East Coast. Otherwise healthy orphans between seven and fourteen years-old would be the volunteers for the first phase of human testing, the Church serving in loco parentis and the Colony Governors discretely giving administrative approval. The Church and the colonies of New York, Connecticut, Rhode Island and Massachusetts would care for any children who developed adverse reactions to the extent our technology allowed.

Our two new officer guests, Lycus and Marcus, took different paths. Lycus, the sea-skimmer pilot, spent most of his time over at the aerodrome side of the Joint Base. I learned from Ruth that he hung out with his fellow pilots and was learning English and how to fly lighter-than-air craft. When he wasn't doing that, the dirigible pilots had great fun teaching him how to golf.

The other officer, Marcus, was both the spatial and temporal navigator, as well as an electronic warfare officer, whatever the latter job was. He spoke passible English, partly because he had spent almost a decade exploring the multiverse and his job included monitoring radio broadcasts.

Sometimes Marcus wandered around all by his lonesome, noodling around Melinda's estate. I came upon him after he was taking a break while helping Julius and some RFC navy communications technicians set up an improved surveillance system for the estate. Marcus' idea of a break was lifting weights in the garage complex alongside half-a-dozen of Scarbutt's marines.

I introduced myself at greater length than had been possible previously. Then I asked him the question which had been bugging me ever since Jules had brought up the subject many weeks ago.

"Dr. Martingale once mentioned in passing that Lycus was one of the few literate pilots she knew. What the heck was that crack supposed to be about?"

Marcus laughed. "It's a long tradition among the non-pilot aircrew to believe pilots are an illiterate sub-human species, differentiated by their eyesight, reflexes, arrogance and self-proclaimed sexual prowess. All military pilots in my Empire are male, of course. Do you have extra-duty assignments in your military?"

"Do we ever! It's always described as an opportunity to excel and it always turns out to be something like cleaning up after diarrheic elephants after a big parade."

"Maybe two years back, Dr. Martingale, who you would classify as a lieutenant colonel in the medical corps, drew the short straw and had to give the quarterly health and safety talk to our aircrews, most of whom wanted to do nothing more than catch up on their sleep. You know the drill; tell a joke to get the audience's attention, tell them what you have to tell them and then say I have time for only two questions. Answer those two questions succinctly and leave."

"So she starts off saying during her medical research she once discovered a literate pilot. That provoked a lot of laughter among the non-pilots in the group. She described the situation. She was leaving a research library, having been doing some research on the positive correlation between overall physical health and sexual abstinence.

"Then she spotted, emerging from the combination tavern and bordello across the street, a pilot well known to all in the lecture hall. The pilot exhibited typical signs of extreme inebriation. Everyone got in the spirit of things and agreed that was normal pilot behavior. She made swerving motions with one hand to illustrate how the pilot had walked. She followed said pilot for several blocks until he got to a construction site. The site displayed a large sign which read 'wet paint.' So the pilot did. She therefore concluded he must be literate."

I said, "That has to be near the top of the list for the worst joke in history."

"It got better," said Marcus. "Everybody laughed, but we laughed a lot louder when we all realized as the *'words to remember'* appeared on her lecture hall screen in a column. The leading letters for each of these keywords spelled out Lycus. They had ended one of their many intermittent flings, and she blamed him.

"The joke is funnier if you know Lycus. He needed an unprecedented dispensation to graduate from flight school. He had the highest reflex and spatial awareness scores the school had ever seen. He was also at the bottom of his class academically. He is hands down the least literate pilot in the history of pilots. Still, if you could only pick one pilot to fly you to Hades and back safely, he is the guy you would pick, as long as somebody else navigated."

"Nevertheless, they'll probably tire of each other again in another week or two. She's super smart, and will help you folks a lot, but you might want to set her up with some of the more in-shape dirigible pilots over at the joint base if you want her to stay focused on her work."

"How's your work here going?" I asked, "Or are you planning to go back to your world to see what happened and if anyone survived?"

"Nah; I already took one extra flight since I got here, though we did not hop to another earth or anything. Your navy insisted we prove our bona fides. We took a demonstration flight with the Deputy CNO, the chief scientist of your navy, and a couple of navy dirigible pilots.

"The navy called an exclusion zone off Nova Scotia for three days of military exercises and we went out the second night for a couple of hours. We flew around about fifteen feet above the water and your folks were more than excited enough to be doing two hundred knots per hour. Personally, I wouldn't want to risk taking the old girl out in the multiverse again without a couple thousand man-hours of preventive maintenance."

"Let me explain. Your folks already know how to distil fuel pure enough to fire the main engines, but we normally replace all the synthetic hydraulic fluids and many of our gaskets every hundred hours of flight time and not all of them had been replaced on schedule when we popped over here. All our gaskets are made of synthetic materials; your folks won't develop similar gaskets for decades. Even so, our gaskets tend to suck. The morons who designed them were from what you call England. It's a tradition there to build equipment which leaks transmission and brake fluid and the like. Don't get me going on English electronics; they suck worse."

I gaped at Marcus; there was such a thing as a universal constant and the name of the beast was English electronics.

Marcus continued, "Our power source for the chronos-hopping process is an on-board fusion generator. It feeds an array of lithium-cobalt-oxide batteries. We need the compact energy storage and buffering to maintain the perfect standing wave when we pop across to various other earths.

"Those batteries process a lot of energy pass-through, so they wear out quickly and should be replaced on a rigid schedule. They are quite dangerous if they explode. Since we left in a bit of a hurry, we don't have a full complement of spare batteries. The old girl is a bit of a hanger queen. As things stand, we would have to be desperate to set forth to cruise the multiverse again."

"What's a fusion generator?"

"That's right, you folks wouldn't know it if you sat on it, which, in fact, Vice Admiral Francis did, though we had powered it down once we arrived on your earth. We don't need it just to bounce around just above the waves. Think of it as a stove with a near-microscopic sun inside. The tricky part is the engineering. We have to capture the energy it produces and then transform it down to feed the batteries even as they are pumping out energy to maintain the standing wave for the trans-temporal device.

"The device itself is simple, once we discovered inadvertently the principles behind it. It's called theChronos-Matic Overthruster. I engage it to travel upstream in a temporal sense. If I want to travel in the other direction, then I reverse the polarity of the neutron flow."

I nodded sagely. Neutron particles had been mentioned in the more recent sciencey fiction literature. I often sort of skimmed those paragraphs, preferring to get to the chapters where scandalously underdressed, gorgeous young ladies from outer space attempted to take over our world. Marcus kept explaining about his WiG.

"We have another device to tell us where we are in relation to our own earth, the Distance and Relativistic Temporal Instinctive Synchronizer. I only know how it operates; I have no clue as to the theory behind it. No one who did could leave my earth."

"I have one last thing I would like to mention; perhaps you can help resolve it. I already told you we powered down the fusion generator. I also told your navy they need to let us strip down and disperse our battery arrays or else they risk the biggest explosion they have ever seen in Nova Scotia. They said they didn't have the secure storage places to house them. They need to listen to me.

"Your navy gave us a ride on a light cruiser when they brought Julius, Lycus, and me from Halifax to Newport. They showed off some of their secondary weaponry. If even a single battery explodes, it will do so with the explosive power of a three-inch shell. If our whole WiG torches, it could take out all of Sidney."

I flinched. That wouldn't be good. "I'll ask Kathy to arrange a call to Admiral Francis. That should set things in motion. Once you blow up just one from a safe distance, you'll have the navy's attention."

Now Master Doctor, Have You Brought Those Drugs?

Astrid spent a day taking the Rhode Island medical licensing board's written examination. As a notional foreigner of unspecified origin with a medical degree of unspecified providence, she applied for a license under a little used alternative procedure.

She first had three senior doctors vouch for her skills; one was an army colonel, one a navy captain, and the last was a senior surgeon in Massachusetts. The civilian surgeon had been Melinda's father's roommate for their junior and senior high school years at the incredibly exclusive "*Pompous Upper Class Nob School for Insufferable but Destined to Succeed in Spite of Lacking Any Discernable Talent*" boys' school in New York City.

Because the fix was in, it didn't matter one whit that not one of the three doctors had ever actually met Astrid. The day after Astrid took the test, I asked her how things had gone as I fixed her a late afternoon lemon tonic and I treated myself to a short draft beer.

"I spent all day yesterday correcting the Latin vocabulary and grammar on the test and explaining how various medical concepts implied by the questions on the test should be discarded into the dustbin of history.

"I couldn't believe your medical Neanderthals think red meat and sweetened frozen dairy products are bad for one's health. Too much water can kill you as well, of course. Moderation in most things is my motto. Naturally, I am quite certain I passed the stupid tests; if anything, they should be grateful I took the time to correct their primitive misconceptions."

"John," said Astrid. "Speaking of possible misconceptions, I have a few questions of my own. Your air service airship pilots are decent enough folks and I even met some navy dirigible pilots. Why are there not any marine air ship pilots? Don't give me any phony story about the marines not being smart enough to fly airships. I know better."

I realized Astrid would not have heard the marine version of how that policy came about. She might enjoy it, so I told her, "The official story is that it doesn't make economic sense because the RFC Marine Corps is too small to have such a specialized component. I believe it would be useful militarily, since littoral combat is different; I suspect any cost savings are minimal.

"The marine version of that decision is a bit risqué. About twenty years ago, the top brass in all the services authorized a test of concept. About two dozen young marine officers were selected for aircrew famil-iarization; they were all training at the big air service base in the middle of New Jersey Colony.

"On one practice flight, ten of them were flying over Trenton with a marine pilot in training at the controls of a big airship. The pilot put the training dirigible into a dive, the instructor pilot went nuts and was not paying attention when a different trainee snuck to the fantail, dropped trousers, and he launched a 'bomb' right as the dirigible hit the perigee of its dive directly over the Governor General of New Jersey Colony's palace. The Governor General's wife was giving a garden party at the time."

Astrid's eyes got wide. She opened her lips minutely as if to ask me something, but instead let me continue the joke.

"Things then got sporty. Marines don't rat out their colleagues over the odd, hilarious practical joke. The Governor General's wife, how-ever, insisted somebody should get the high drop. The Corps sent in a full colonel, about to retire, to take charge. The colonel already had a knighthood and had inherited a bundle and his family estates were in Kentucky Province, in the RCC. He made sure everything done was straight by the book.

"He assembled the nine potential perpetrators in dress uniforms in a line-up room. When the governor general's wife arrived, he shouted the following commands, 'About face. Drop trousers. Spread legs. Grab ankles.'

"Then he turned to the governor general's wife and asked, 'Can you identify the arse-hole responsible, Ma'am?'"

Astrid was incredulous. "I wasted my time listening to that? You have got to be kidding me!"

"Astrid, I bet it's as true as half the stories you told us."

Two weeks later I wandered over to the skeet range where I was hearing lots of 20-gauge boom sticks making bird shot noises. There was a pause in the cacophony and I saw Kathy and Melinda holding each other tightly because they were both giggling so much that if they didn't hold each other up, they would fall over.

Melinda shared the news, "We got the word from Jennifer, who answered a phone call from the Governor's wife. Astrid passed her medical boards with outstanding scores. And she did it almost entirely on her own efforts."

They both giggled again. "The head of the Rhode Island Colony Medical Certification and Licensing board was ordered to talk to the governor before he released this set of scores. He whined he had graded the strangest test; when the board checked with some Latin Professors at Yale and Harvard, they found out some lady would-be-doctor was linguistically correct. The test had indeed been using some Latin phrases incorrectly from what would have been the case back in Roman times. But her medical answers were the most arrogant and condescending collection of borderline plausible but medically questionable blather the board had ever seen.

"The governor acknowledged how the medical board head was an expert on arrogant and condescending, but said if his board did not give this lady doctor-to-be an outstanding grade, things would happen. He hoped it would not be necessary to investigate rumors about whether the Colony's delegations to the annual RFC medical conventions spent Provincial funds inappropriately on items such as French champagne and professional hostesses."

I briefly gritted my teeth in frustration. I didn't recall ever being provided champagne and hostesses when I got sent off on field deployments; perhaps I should have gone to med school or joined the air service. "Gee, Melinda, your dad must have given his favorite governor quite a talk to inspire so much backbone."

"Not a bit, crayon-eater. Dad didn't say a word. It's always good to cultivate an illusion of independence, at least occasionally. The governor is forty-five years-old. His wife is thirty years old. Did you meet her at the tea we held here two weeks ago? Or were you and Joseph swilling beer and playing pinball down in the basement rec-room yet again? We took the liberty of introducing the governor's wife to Astrid."

"I was not *swilling* beer with Tiny. I might admit to having quaffed just a sip or two."

Kathy and Melinda both sneered at me. Melinda continued.

"Once Julianne found out Astrid was a real lady doctor, they had quite the private conversation. Private until after the tea finished, of course, and Astrid talked to us. Anyway, after talking with the governor's wife, Astrid generously gave Julianne ten each of her special pills. 'Cut them in half dear, you're both probably out of shape. Crush half of this one to a powder and slip the powder into his sweetened iced tea or sweetened coffee or something. Take half of the other type of pill yourself and be ready to respond in about an hour.'

"Even now, Ruth and Astrid are working on a clandestine project at one of our super-secret labs. We envision these pills will be strictly controlled only by women throughout the entire distribution chain. Bwa hah-hah. Bwa hah-hah. Bwa hah-hah-hah-hah!"

Melinda mimed twirling the mustache she didn't have. Then she collapsed in giggles. Kathy joined her. I thought to myself our stupid politicians should have granted suffrage already to keep young ladies from resorting to more nefarious means of maintaining control.

Dr. Astrid Martingale received her official results two days later. She had passed the medical boards with outstanding marks and a citation for original thought. She was more insufferable than usual for the next week. Did I mention her arrogance? If not, I should have mentioned she was also extra arrogant.

We got some other interesting news a week after that. Out of the blue, I got a call from Warrant Officer First Class Glynda Smith from Brigadier Hamilton's office. She informed me the Rhode Island Constabulary had set up a temporary, portable weight station and licensing checkpoint on the main coastal highway about a mile from the Connecticut line. Selected commercial trucks and motor coaches were waved off into a portable weight station and fully checked.

A private motor coach ignored directions to pull over. It traveled another mile when it found the roadway blocked by a trio of RFC armored cars from one of the two 1st Armored Cavalry Brigade squadrons stationed at JBWK. A second trio of armored cars closed in on the motor coach from behind. Surrounded, and faced with six .50-caliber Maxim guns and a host of regular army types with battle rifles, the motor coach stopped.

After instructions from bullhorns, everyone in the coach eventually emerged and got to lie down on the pavement, hands behind their heads, the better to enjoy the Rhode Island sunshine. There were twenty-one folks in the motor coach, including the driver. They all spoke Spanish with Cuban accents, but had no identity papers of any sort. They had enough small arms on the bus to outfit an infantry platoon.

They didn't want to say squat except they demanded to see their solicitors. The Rhode Island Colony deputy crown prosecutor in attendance formally stated the coach had crossed from Connecticut into Rhode Island. The coach passengers, being of sufficient number to constitute an armed band, had violated the RFC Insurrection Act and thus it fell to the army to investigate and prosecute the passengers under military law.

The army ignored the demands for solicitors, heavily shackled all the alleged perpetrators and hauled them off to Ft. Amherst in the western wilds of Massachusetts Colony. The firm which owned the motor-coach reported it stolen about an hour after it was stopped.

There must have been a trailing car witnessing everything. I bet the boss bad guys were pissed.

Discovering the coach was full of Cuban thugs was a relief in one sense. I was not looking forward to going another round with a platoon or two of Imperial Spetsnaz. Knowing they were Cuban didn't help our authorities much. As much as they might have wanted to do so, they couldn't go around arresting everyone who speaks Spanish as a native language.

Puerto Rico was a crown territory; the Republic of Texico was an official ally. Old Spain had signed a twenty-year treaty of peace and friendship five years ago to let them focus more on their festering North Africa issues.

The People's Commonwealth of Alta California wasn't trusted by anybody with more than a grain of common sense, but our relations with them were officially cordial. Besides, their *Alcade Supremo* wouldn't have risked staging the motor-coach incident. He stomped ruthlessly on any folks whom he even imagined might put his revenues from the trans-continental railroad trade at risk.

I had often thought it would be a great idea to build a canal through either the Isthmus of Panama or use Lake Nicaragua. That was never going to happen, though. New Spain was never stable enough politically for such a deal to stick, and the RFC, the RCC and the Texican railroad corporations would use every political favor they could call to scupper such a deal.

Bridget O'Shaughnessy called me that evening to say how wonderful it was that both the constabulary and army could respond expeditiously to anonymous tips. She mentioned how fortunate it was the anonymous tipster could give the motor coach's license plate and its projected route and an estimated time when it would cross the Rhode Island border. She thoughtfully noted the criminal penalty for illegally transporting unregistered firearms across colony lines was up to ten years in prison.

Her suggestions as to how the authorities might conduct the forth-coming interrogations of the alleged perpetrators would have given blush to the delicate sensibilities of the Spanish Inquisition. She told me straight out, "You and I both know those bastards are working for the same scum who killed my husband. Tell the army to make them talk. I want their bosses' names."

She must have been thoroughly annoyed when the army failed to take her advice on how to conduct effective interrogations.

A Trifling Touch of Tummy Tribulations

Tiny, Astrid, and I tended to be the earliest risers, getting up a few minutes before the rooster crowed. I normally jogged about five miles' worth of laps around the estate. Tiny regularly pushed loads of weights over in the garage complex, doing his best to show Scarbutt's jarheads the army was the superior service. Astrid often headed to the smaller basement gymnasium to work on her yoga, whatever that was, and/or do her pole dancing routines.

Two mornings after the coach incident, after I finished running and had showered off, I headed to the breakfast dining room's buffet for coffee and noshes. I found Astrid already there. She sucked down some freshly percolated nectar of the gods and then carefully spread a thin layer of orange marmalade on a single slice of wheat toast. I couldn't help but observe she was wearing a white tennis dress with a hemline so high it was probably illegal. Astrid, even at age thirty-one, did have the legs for it, though.

She frowned at me as I walked in. No big deal; ladies often graced me with a lot of evil eyes. More in hope than expectation, I glanced behind me to see if someone was behind me who was the real recipient of Astrid's annoyance. There wasn't.

I turned again to Astrid. She definitely had been working out. She looked good. Unpleasant, arrogant and obnoxious, but she looked good, if underdressed, a fact I noted when she bent over slightly to refill her coffee cup.

"Uh, Doctor Toots, what's with the tennis outfit? I guess you're not heading over to the Joint Base today, to like, maybe, research, not with those threads. By the way, we have a couple of sayings on this earth: 'When in Rome, do as the Romans do' and 'Semper ubi sub ubi.'"

"To answer your questions, merely to work on polishing my already impeccable social skills, your cultural mores are such that I am always expected to wear something when I appear in public. Melinda even reminded me yesterday that I am required to wear one of those ridiculous garments which you primitives call bathing costumes whenever I go to a public beach. How does it make sense to sculpt a healthy, attractive body and then cover it up with unnecessary layers of clothing?

"I never wore clothes at the beaches or public baths or saunas back home. I guess it's a cultural thing. Those of us who grow up in actual northern latitudes always strive to maximize our exposure to sunlight and thus Vitamin D."

She took a bite of toast.

"As for the research, I set the ultimate goals. Like the customer who wishes to purchase a well-designed wardrobe for the storage of clothes, I can describe what the finished product should look like. Here, however, the carpenters are using stone axes and obsidian chip saws to build their piece of furniture.

"Ruth and Dr. Semmelweis and Paul are at the base doing the actual research and development work. I have no clue what intermediate steps they should take to complete their project, and I have no interest in learning medieval carpentry. Thus, I only need a couple of hours a week to review the interim results and guide the research back on track."

I was getting a definite vibe of her being born to the deepest purple.

"Astrid, are you sure you're not a general officer or a princess or something? You seem darn comfortable giving impossible orders and expecting your flunkies to make it so anyway."

She winced, minutely. I could sense her tongue pushing out her lower lip as if she had just bitten the latter. After a couple of seconds, she spoke again.

"Don't be so tedious, John. Anyway, Melinda says I will need to learn either tennis or horseback riding to become socially acceptable among your aristocracy. Initially, she neglected to mention I am supposed to wear special underwear with this tennis dress; something about having pockets large enough to carry spare tennis balls. I plan to purchase such later this week. Maybe.

"If am required to wear too many layers of clothing to play tennis, I may reconsider riding as on option. Though I loathe horses with a passion, I just learned that bare naked riding is an acceptable pursuit for ladies of quality."

I blinked a couple times while I wondered how I missed hearing about that bit of aristocratic behavior. You'd think most such incidents would have been reported by our ever-vigilant tabloids.

Astrid picked up on my confusion. She explained. "Melinda told me of your earth's story about Lady Godiva. I thought it was a strange story. I, personally, have yet to care about what tax rates my family's subjects face. Does your King set the tax rates in your country or for the Empire?"

"Nah, not since a couple of centuries ago. Our taxes are set by parliaments. His Majesty can sometimes give his parliaments a nudge, though. If it has been a year and a day since the last parliamentary election, His Majesty can dissolve any of our various parliaments and force a general election. That can keep the politicians more in-tune with public feelings.

"Mostly he leads by example. He can grant pardons. He must approve the annual honors list for promotions within or entry into the peerage. Conversely, he needs to sign off on capital punishment for peers, but the guilt and stupidity of anybody at that level who gets caught and recommended for a neck chop is almost always painfully obvious. Finally, and more theoretically, he can command our armies in the field."

"Oh, all that won't affect me then; those times I decide to do something technically criminal, I am far too smart to be caught."

Ah, Astrid; she was as cold and rational as always. She also apparently had forgotten yet again about the alleged loss of her entire world, as she had used the present tense to refer to her home world's tax rates.

I briefly pondered that last bit while I examined the breakfast options available to me: coffee, tea, juices, biscuits, toast, beignets, cheeses, scrambled eggs, bacon, sausage, ham, fruit, tomato slices, oatmeal and

Cajun breakfast slop. Jules had been working with the kitchen staff here at Chateau Melinda and they had expanded their repertoire a bit. There were some decent perks to working for the daughter of a billionaire.

I went for the Cajun breakfast slop. My stomach was getting tougher.

Twenty minutes later, I was finishing up my third cup of the nectar of the breakfast gods and the last bite of my first round of breakfast. I was cogitating about going back for seconds, and, if so, how I would burn off the surplus calories. Then Kathy, Vicki and Melinda all walked in. Amazingly, they all bee-lined for the sideboard featuring the breakfast tea blends.

"Hey ladies; you might try the chef's faux Cajun breakfast slop which Jules taught him to make a couple of weeks ago. I realize a couple of critters in the étouffée have more limbs than I am used to critters having, and those green slimy vegetables and greasy andouille sausages look a little weird, but it's amazingly tasty. Especially with all those onions and peppers and garlic."

As one, all three ladies turned the color of the okra, put their hands over their mouths, and fled the room.

"What did I say?" I shouted to their rapidly receding, but still highly attractive, backsides.

I turned back to the table. Dr. Astrid Martingale glanced up at me as she was slicing a beignet in two with surgical precision. Naturally enough, I guessed. She had precise down to a literal science. I returned her look and said, "It can't be my ruggedly handsome face or witty commentary which frightened those ladies. Did you just now scare them off with your beads and rattles, Doctor?"

Dr. Astrid must have taken an advanced course in ice cold stares of death; perhaps she had learned how to do so either from Brigadier Hamilton or the Widow O'Shaughnessy. Astrid gave me one of her A-plus efforts.

"I have examined all three ladies. Without revealing too many medical confidences, they each appear to enjoy a level of health well above the apparent average for your primitive civilization. I attribute their well-being primarily to a combination of a healthy diet, hygiene and exercise and, secondarily, to genetics.

"At this point, though, it behooves me to attempt to fill in some obvious gaps in your own, obviously limited biological education. Let me try to explain it using small words so your underdeveloped male mind can begin to grasp my meaning. Now, sometimes when a man and a woman love each other very, very much..."

I sort of zoned out about that point and her mouth kept moving, but I didn't process the words. When my brain reset and my ears turned back on, she was saying, "... so each young lady is fertile. I will check the medical resources available to me on this benighted version of earth to see if I can concoct some medication to reduce safely the impact of their morning sicknesses.

"If you were at all concerned about preventing pregnancies, why didn't you use birth control? By the way, what types are readily available? I only brought a three-year supply of such medication for myself. I didn't think I would need any more than that."

"Uh, rubberized or lambskin thingamabobs; I've read that some uber-rich women get fitted for diaphragms," I said with my mouth on autopilot.

She dropped her knife and beignet. The knife clattered on her plate. She drilled me with her eyes. "Contact Ruth Brittany at once. I, I mean all of us, have an incredible opportunity."

She paused, then said, "That is, if Tribune Paul does not veto this research because of its potential societal repercussions. That puffed-up princeling is already angry with me about revealing the sulfa drugs."

I stared querulously at Dr. Astrid, only for a moment, trying to interpret what she had said. I was about to speak when the attack alarms start screaming klaxon, klaxon, klaxon. I hate interruptions, especially when I feel I have missed something important.

Trouble by the Boatloads, Bullets by the Scores

I ran to the communications center. Technician Julius, the sea-skimmer communications expert, was tinkering with and sort of monitoring his make-shift sensor network.

"I had been tweaking the sensors so the damn skunks don't set them off so frequently. I realized the freighter is about seven miles southwest of us and is heading directly at us at, uh, fifteen knots. That's a stupid name for a measure of speed. I checked the sensor history; it's been on the same heading for about twenty miles since it abruptly left the closest shipping lane. I doubt the navy is aware of it yet. Should I call Newport Navy Base?"

"Damn straight," I replied. "Also, tell the Valkyries on duty at the Priory to go to alert. Then warn the Irish goons next door."

Scarbutt burst into the communications room. I explained what was up. I told him to deploy his marines for beach defense and call for backup.

"Find Tiny and tell him to stash all the girls in their safe room. Send the word out for all the non-combatants to shelter likewise. Astrid can explain why it's essential to secure the girls. Tell Tiny, whatever he does, don't take no for an answer."

I hit the general intercom. "Attention. Attack imminent. Primary attack will come from the ocean. First section of Burr household security will guard the non-combatants. Second section of Burr household security will watch out for a secondary attack from the north."

I gave those orders because I desperately wanted the civilian security types kept away from the initial attack to keep them from interfering with Scarbutt's marines.

I grabbed my field glasses and dashed up to the widow's walk to look for the freighter. There it was, closing fast. It would arrive here about ten to fifteen minutes before any possible reinforcements.

I swung my glasses to the east and saw a sight I never imagined I would see. The O'Shaughnessy mansion had hoisted a twelve by eighteen foot version of the flag used in the Irish Revolt of 1798-99. It was all gold and green with harps and shamrocks and crossed muskets and was absolutely rock-solid illegal in any territory within the greater Empire. I guess the gilded banner was our neighbor's way of signaling she was prepared to repel boarders.

Our plan to defend against a daylight sea-borne assault was straightforward, though we figured no one would be stupid enough to attempt such. Scarbutt's folks would assume their pre-surveyed positions at the clifftop, which would give them a gorgeous field of fire. If the enemy somehow made it to the rocky beach, Scarbutt's folks had plenty of grenades to drop on their heads.

Tiny was our second line of defense; he had picked out a spot near the house where we had put in a hardened firing position for his not-so-beloved WANCARs, or Wembley Arsenal New Concept Automatic Rifles. His first tour in the army, before he became a field medic, he had been assigned to a heavy weapons section.

Tiny had pre-positioned two WANCARs and two dozen drums, each loaded with forty-seven .303 rounds. He carried the key to his weapons locker on a chain around his neck 24/7. If the marines were forced to retreat from their positions at the clifftop, then he would provide cover fire for their retreat.

We figured the navy should be able to get its alert ship underway and sent down to us in an hour, about the same time it would take for the ready platoon of marines at the navy base to arrive. Our worries would be over when they showed. In the meantime, I would direct everything from up top or play rover as the situation demanded.

The freighter started slowing about a mile and a half offshore and came to rest three-quarters of a mile later. She was facing us bow on, but I could see she was lowering six boats, three each from both the port and starboard sides. The boats hit the water and figures started climbing rope ladders down into the boats. I took a closer look through my glasses.

The saying goes, "No plan ever survives contact with the enemy." Each of those boats seemed to sport what I would bet real money was a water-cooled, pintle-mounted .50-caliber Maxim gun. I couldn't see the guns themselves because their mounts included light armored fascia, so I judged their caliber from the size of the fascia. I picked up the phone and told Scarbutt to prepare for .50-caliber automatic weapons fire from the assaulting boats.

I presumed the hostiles were Cubans, based on the coach load of heavily armed Cubans the army had intercepted only two days ago. I wondered what they planned. Even if their initial attack was successful, they couldn't escape. Heck, a freighter with a top speed near fifteen knots couldn't make it as far as Long Island before being intercepted by our navy.

It had to be a kidnapping attempt. The only way the presumptive kidnappers would survive for more than an hour would be to grab a hostage who was important enough even the navy would think twice about writing her off. I would have to talk to Melinda about what she thought brought about the kidnapping attempt; the wench was a magnet for trouble.

I looked at the freighter again. I suspected the bad guys planned to use a couple of their boats to provide heavy automatic fire from three or four hundred yards out to drive us off the clifftops, while the other boats dropped off their infantry. Then they would attempt to overwhelm us with numbers, grab their hostages and scoot. If they used all six of their boats and concentrated on us, that plan might work. They sure had a lot of folks crammed into those boats.

I glanced back over to Bridget's estate to see what they were doing. I nearly choked on my surprise; Bridget, that scamp, had held out on me. Her estate had a pair of raised circular flower beds near the cliffs of her estate. Gorgeous flowers. Absolutely stunning. And now it was revealed the flower beds were planted on steel plates. I saw the plates swing out to expose obsolete inch-and-a-half guns on navy-style swivel mounts, which were being raised by hydraulics into firing positions. I was dumbfounded; God really had invented whiskey to keep the Irish from ruling the world.

Bridget's folks started firing their guns. The first shots did nothing except create some splashes a couple hundred yards away from the freighter. I guess gun crews don't practice much when their guns are planted under flower beds. Bridget's response was going to make it easier for Scarbutt's marines, though. The three boats on the freighter's port side started heading for the beach in front of Bridget's estate.

Two boats from each group of three headed for the rocky beaches in front of each estate, Maxim guns firing towards the clifftop all the time. The third boat in each group hung back about five hundred yards offshore and blasted the cliff tops at a better angle. I suspected the latter boat intended to dart in to drop off its own infantry once the other boats unloaded their troops and came back out to provide fire support.

It didn't look like any enemy boats were heading towards the Priory; maybe they didn't know or care what was located there. I got Jennifer on the phone and told her to send someone down to her cliff side and serve as a spotter and keep us informed. I also told her not to let her spotter call attention to herself.

I swung my field glasses back. I had another "Oh, drat!" moment. Two of the freighter's top side cargo containers dropped their sides to reveal pintle-mounted guns of their own, in this case what I judged to be six-pounders. The freighter slowly turned broadside and started firing her guns toward Bridget's mansion.

It turns out they weren't much better shots than were Bridget's folks. I guess Q-Ship gun crews also have issues maintaining their proficiency. The freighter's first broadside appeared to fly directly over Bridget's mansion. I hoped those two shells landed in a potato field somewhere. Suddenly I realized I was up in Melinda's widow's walk and my ass was sort of waving in the wind if the Q-ship fired a couple of six-pound shells in my direction. I clicked the phone to alert everyone.

"I am going down. Everybody listening, the enemy freighter is firing a pair of six-pound guns. Everybody find some place giving a little cover from shrapnel. Tell Melinda she's in charge of coordinating everything from the basement communications room. She knows the layout of her estate without having to see it."

I scooted. I grabbed my .50-caliber sniper rifle and a backpack filled with ammo on the way out the door and headed for the cliff edge, right at the southwest corner of Melinda's estate, to a spot I had long ago scoped out and readied. That spot gave me a nice flanking line of sight for half of the cliffs in front of Bridget's estate. Once I got there, I would be in an excellent position to nail bad guys attempting to climb up to Bridget's lawn.

I'll never know for certain why the bad guys split their forces, since none of their leaders survived to be questioned by the legal authorities. I can only surmise Bridget's inch-and-a-half pop-guns and the Irish Rebellion flag had the same effect on the attackers as a red flag does to a bull.

Even with their forces split, it was bad enough. All that automatic firepower meant Scarbutt and his marines would soon have to retreat to prepared positions next to the cottage to get out of the line of sight of those nasty .50-calibers. At that point, he would only be outnumbered, rather than seriously outgunned as well.

I arrived at my pre-surveyed firing position just as the first two boats directly in front of Bridget's place dropped off their assault troops. The third boat in that group closed to within three hundred yards offshore to provide cover fire. It was about five hundred yards from my position to its northeast.

The morning wind hadn't picked up yet, so that range was in my wheelhouse. I threw a spanner in their works when I nailed the boat's pilot and the Maxim gun operator. It floated around for a couple of minutes, not contributing anything to the fight. Then it darted in to drop off its troops. In the meantime, I started picking off exposed goons climbing the cliffs in front of Bridget's place.

I glanced to my left; Scarbutt and what I counted as eight other marines were heading to their fallback positions. Tiny was waiting for them, but he must not have had a target, since he was not firing at anything yet. As soon as the marines got back to the secondary positions, half of them started popping rifle grenades in an attempt to angle them just over the cliff wall. I picked up the pre-positioned phone and clicked it to get everybody's attention. "Any Valkyries who can see where Scarbutt's grenades land, try to serve as a spotter."

I caught a flash in my right eye. Two rooms in Bridget's mansion had gone blooey. To be fair, the bad guys were probably trying to take out Bridget's inch-and-a-half guns, but from their position on the freighter's deck, they had a rotten line of sight on those guns.

I caught a hint of motion out of my left eye. Since I was still holding the phone's speaker-receiver unit with my right hand, my left hand was rather naturally resting on my left hip holster. More on instinct than anything else, I popped three rounds from my Wembley .32-caliber into a rather swarthy looking dude I had never seen before. I figured it was time to beat feet from my current clifftop position.

As I scooted back from the cliffs, I heard a whing go past me. Great; more bad guys had reached the clifftop. I plopped into the next rifle sangar disguised as a flower bed and took a quick look around. Flashes were coming from the cliff tops all along the two estates. Marine return fire was getting sparse, but Tiny was keeping up sustained bursts from his WANCAR.

That shouldn't be right. My brain reviewed what it had processed unconsciously. Tiny had started out firing classic short bursts. About one minute after the marines retreated from the cliff-face, Tiny started firing with all the fire discipline of a hero in an action flicker.

The invaders wouldn't think about sticking their heads over the cliffs as long as he kept firing like that. Heck, they would hesitate to charge the house as long as he kept up traditional short bursts. And here I had been worried I should have insisted Tiny pre-position more ammo. I wondered where he got the extra stuff and why his guns' barrels hadn't melted yet.

I glanced back at Bridget's place and saw her two naval guns being lowered into their pits. The flower beds swung closed to once again hide the guns while the Irish Rebellion flag was hauled down. Some instinct told me these events did not presage Bridget was planning to surrender.

I spotted three new lines of smoke rising from the bay out in the west. Leading the smoke, about 2,000 feet up, was a dirigible from JBWK. I breathed a little easier.

Two minutes later, HMRFCS *Jaguar* got close enough to fire her two forward batteries of twin 4.5-inch guns at the freighter. This occurred about the same time the Cuban Q-ship fired her fourth and final volley at the O'Shaughnessy mansion. Bridget lost another couple of rooms.

The *Jaguar's* first volley was about a hundred yards short of the target. Her second volley, which roared out a half-minute later, was dead on target. The freighter flew to pieces. Must have hit her ammo locker. The Q-ship didn't have an armored ammo locker; she was just a freighter which had a couple hidden guns.

Our navy uses professional gun crews. They acquire a fair amount of practice and occasional real world experience. The freighter was doomed the moment she revealed she was a Q-ship and she had not yet acquired a valuable hostage. She couldn't outrun a destroyer like *Jaguar* and she certainly couldn't outgun her. The freighter's captain must have become irrationally annoyed the moment Bridget O'Shaughnessy's 1.5 -inch popguns started firing at him. Bridget paid quite a price, though. Those last three return volleys the freighter got off tore the stuffing out of her mansion.

The duty rifle platoon of marines arrived from the navy base about the same time the Q-ship got blown to splinters. They had been re-inforced with a heavy weapons section, so that brought two WANCAR crews and two three-inch mortars to go along with their thirty-two rifle-men. The platoon commander had detached two of his six rifle-squads to reinforce Bridget's folks. All our civilian folks were safe at that point, though there were still a couple dozen bad guys firing at us from the clifftop.

Jaguar was joined by HMRFC Torpedo Attack Ship *Whippet*, armed with two pintle mounts with .80-caliber light cannon and an enclosed turret mounting a single 3.5-inch gun. The latter chewed the six beach attack boats into splinters. She should have used the .80-calibers for that, but I bet the *Whippet*'s captain was itching for a chance to fire his main gun in earnest.

The *Whippet* closed to within about six hundred yards offshore and started firing at the base of the cliffs with its .80-caliber light cannons. It was a good thing the *Whippet* was aware if she fired at the Cubans at the clifftop, then many shells would overshoot and tear the heck out of Melinda's place. I learned later the *Whippet* was in direct radio contact with the lieutenant commanding the newly arrived marine platoon. He had his own objections to being torn to shreds by .80-caliber slugs.

It turned out the navy had also parked a four man marine sniper team on the *Whippet*. The Cubans hugging the cliff had cover from the direction of the mansion, but not from seaward. Cubans who shot at the *Whippet* were rewarded with return fire from her sniper team. That got one sided fairly quickly. The surviving Cubans started to surrender by taking off their shirts and hanging their white undershirts from their rifle barrels. I, briefly, felt surprised it took them so long to surrender, but I lost the thought.

I found the nearest phone position and told Jennifer to tell the Valkyries and the Sisters of Healing to split into two groups and start heading to Melinda's and Bridget's estates. I figured we were likely to have boatloads of casualties, what with having faced cannon and Maxim guns and all. Unfortunately, I was right.

The *Jaguar* sent out four boats loaded with another platoon of marines. The latter used bullhorns to bellow instructions in Spanish to let the bad guys know they only had two choices and one of them involved catching a lot of lead. Twenty-five bad guys survived, most had wounds. We found out later they were all common thugs who didn't admit to knowing anything, except if they didn't capture the blonde lady alive, their own lives were forfeit.

Half of the Sisters of Healing and some of their Valkyries arrived about five minutes after I called. They joined up with Tiny. He had already switched from WANCAR mode to field medic mode. Astrid joined them a moment later and finished the triage Tiny had started.

We wound up with four marines dead and three more had splinter wounds from when the cliff rocks shattered too close to them. We found Staff Sergeant Schultz in two pieces at the cliff side. A .50-caliber burst had literally separated his head from his shoulders.

Astrid grabbed me after about ten minutes and said, "John, your three wounded marines are stable and are on painkillers. Your navy doctors can handle their shrapnel wounds from this point on. Call Bridget and let her know I am on my way to check out her folks. Mary and Theodora will come with me."

I made the calls.

I gave the all clear to release the rest of our ladies from their safe room a quarter-hour later. I kissed Kathy and told her to stay safe for a couple hours while I processed the why's and how's of the attack. I had several possibly important, unanswered questions about why I couldn't get certain line items to add up.

Melinda emerged and began hugging and kissing Tiny while complaining he smelled like gunpowder. I hoped she was sort of listening to me while I explained to her the only thing I could think of that made sense was the attack was yet another kidnapping attempt on her.

I had doubts Melinda listened to my explanation. Eventually she processed the couple of thousand brass casings scattered around her lawn and she asked me to explain the bit about the kidnappings. Then she got really angry.

Serpents Hiding Under Innocent Flowers

The first thing I did after talking with the ladies was to corner Tiny. After I pried him away from his wife, he took in the spent casings littering Melinda's lawn, shrugged, grinned and said, "Talk to that thief, Scarbutt. His idea."

Two hours later, I tracked down Scarbutt at the Newport Navy Hospital, where his wounded were now ensconced. I added my thanks to his. After we were done talking to them, we found a vacant room. The door to the room was locked, but locks tended not to work well when Scarbutt was around. At least we had the room to ourselves.

"Let's talk about Tiny and the ammo fairy what sprinkled more ammo dust on him than any WANCAR-man ever dreamt of."

"Gee, Hotshot. It sure was lucky he stumbled into that. It all started when I talked to your best buddy, Paul. I don't trust him much; of course, I hardly trust anybody except for totally transparent Sir Galahads like you, but he is damn sharp.

"He knows an amazing amount about small unit tactics as well; far too intimately for somebody who's supposed to be a damn big-picture history professor. Once those off-shore machine gunners chewed the crap out of my guys at the cliff top, I figured it was time for Plan B. Fortunately, I had one.

"According to Paul, some other-earth militaries build their squads around their semi-portable automatic weapons. The WANCAR is not built for that job; the barrel overheats too quickly. Still, that's what Tiny trained on, so you go home with the girl you brung to the dance. Being a logistical genius, I had scrounged..."

"Stolen."

"Traded. I exchanged a full-case of twenty-one-year-old scotch for two extra WANCARs and forty extra forty-seven-round loaded drums of ammo. I stole the scotch. I told the supply sergeant at JBWK if I had a single misfire, then I would oversee his field expedient appendectomy, starting the incision around his toenails. I think Melinda's dad got off easy; a case of scotch is a small price to pay for saving a daughter. Anyhow, as soon as we left the cliff edge, I told Tiny to fire like there was no tomorrow. I sent my four healthiest guys to go grab the WANCARs where I had pre-positioned..."

"Secreted."

"... them and their ammo, and then my guys kept hauling ammo for the rest of the fight. I served as Tiny's assistant gunner. The other four guys provided cover fire and lobbed grenades. I didn't let Tiny know beforehand I had all that spare stuff because I might have needed the crap for some other escapade. Oh, and I forged your signature to make it look like you authorized it. And if you have a word of complaint, I have two words for you."

"They are?"

"*'Rubber scorpions,'* you rat bastard. You cost me my favorite shaving kit with your stupid practical joke."

Well, he had me there.

Being a sniper, I developed the knack for keeping track of potential targets and threats. I reviewed the official after action accounts and integrated those with what Bridget's folks had told me. I came up four hostiles short, and I hadn't seen any of them jump into the ocean.

The bad guys started with thirteen men per boat; a pilot, Maxim-gunner, loader, and ten infantry. They had six boats and thus had seventy-eight hostiles originally heading for the beach. I judged the four missing men were on the boat which landed at the cliff on the O'Shaughnessy estate's western-most edge.

I talked with Bridget O'Shaughnessy two days after the battle. She was now smiling most of the time. She was far calmer than I would have been had I just lost half my mansion.

"My people understand defending our own involves risk, Mr. Smith. Rest assured, the widows and children of the three of my men who died will be well cared for. We will also care for the families of those marines who gave their lives if the RFC refuses to provide them adequate support. We are noted for that.

"I also am grateful to Astrid and the Sisters of Healing for their help after the fighting died down. I understand it was on your initiative they arrived so swiftly. Their timely intercession saved at least three more of my people from losing their lives. I will find a way to thank the Sisters, as well."

I realized I had seen neither Slab nor Wires skulking around. It was not like I was going to miss them if they were nearby, since they did not do subtle one bit. I inquired as to their health. Bridget responded they were fine; they had been called away to settle some family business.

"Mrs. O'Shaughnessy, I feel I need to warn you about something, as you may not have dealt with the stresses of battle before. Some of those Cuban survivors might imagine having seen a couple of inch-and-a-half navy guns pop out of your flower beds two days ago. They might also imagine having seen a highly illegal Irish Revolt battle flag."

She fluttered a hand in an easterly direction. "Lady Melinda certainly can affirm, given her own skeet range, the relevant laws. Rhode Island does not prohibit owning shotguns or single-hot rifles or firing them for sporting purposes. Should you hire a solicitor to advise you on this law, he will tell you the controlling statutes contain no restriction as to the bore size of a single-shot rifle.

"It is, of course, illegal to use them for most purposes other than for personal recreation and competitions, although there are several limited hunting seasons for some game birds and nuisance animals. I think any neutral observer would agree the Cubans were a bit of a nuisance."

I nodded in agreement.

She continued, "By such time, if ever, the RFC authorities overcome my solicitors' best efforts and manufacture a legal reason to search this property, they will find naught but an overly complicated irrigation system under the petunias. Any visions involving Irish battle flags almost certainly should be investigated by the religious authorities as probable evidence of a divine intervention.

"Now, Mr. Smith, would you care to share with me how Mr. Sammartino acquired and used those Wembley Arsenal automatic rifles of his? I rather doubt Sir Charles Burr's solicitors currently are trying to fend off a similar horde of overly inquisitive Deputy Crown Prosecutors asking impertinent, weapons-related questions."

"Mrs. O'Shaughnessy, somehow, both the Burr Estate, and the Priory to the east, are classified as adjunct Rhode Island Militia facilities. I'll see what I can do."

She shook her head, unbelieving.

"If I may, Mrs. O'Shaughnessy, I have another question. It's sort of related to those inch-and-a-half pop-guns I hallucinated about. I saw the first salvo from the freighter miss high and I had hoped those shells landed in a potato field somewhere. Melinda first brought all those potato fields to my attention over a year ago, before the Spetsnaz attack. She was right; this island has all sorts of honking huge mansions located next to potato fields. How does that make financial sense? I once asked Melinda; she only stared at me."

Bridget smiled more broadly. "You continue to surprise, Mr. Smith. It makes no sense financially, only socially. A baker's dozen of incredibly wealthy families own almost all the land on Aquidneck Island, at least the acreage located outside the three municipalities. The Lady Burrs of the world are not worried about the wives of forelock-tugging leasehold farmers trying to rise above their stations, so these wealthy families lease most of their lands to farmers.

"Consider the alternative. Real estate speculators would kill their own mothers to develop such land; they would build much smaller versions of Melinda's family cottage. Imagine the horror! Lady Burr and her counterparts would have to deal with scores of grubby, upwardly climbing, nouveau riche as neighbors. These would not be the right sort of people at all, Mr. Smith. Let me assure you, Lady Burr already spends quite enough effort trying to pretend I don't exist."

"I guess that accounts for my own rare interactions with her. The last couple of times she deigned to speak with me, she seemingly had me confused with her deputy assistant gardener. I guess that's why she barked at me using Portuguese. At least I think she was trying to speak Portuguese."

Bridget grinned. "I think I keep better track of the Burr Estate staff than does Lady Burr; her gardener, *Senhor* Dom Pedro is from the Empire of Brazil. Speaking of foreigners, you may wish to remind Mrs. Sammartino to call her father's pet governor's attention to a point of law. Sailing private ships from international waters to attack the residents of Rhode Island Colony is considered piracy. The penalty for piracy is to be hanged by the neck until dead. No trial is necessary. The nearest commissioned navy or militia officer need only identify the perpetrators and affirm the act occurred."

Bridget surveyed the back of her fingernails; she had a superb manicurist. She sighed. "Personally, I would keep the Cuban scum alive until they gave up the names of those who hired them. I can suggest some theoretically effective interrogation techniques, but I suspect the authorities will again be too soft-hearted to use them. Alas, they are bound by the letter of the law. Double alas, I would never interfere in the administration of justice."

Bridget was remarkably placid as she said that; she did not resemble at all a vengeful widow who just happened to control the four East Coast Irish Mobs and who recently had half her house blown up. I don't think I had ever before been on the receiving end of such a steaming pile of obvious verbal horse hockey as the mess she gave me, either. At least not since boot camp.

Bridget continued, "You should share with Mrs. Sammartino and Mrs. Smith some additional information. I do not own this property, making its partial loss somewhat easier to take. The property belongs to the Emerald Eire Charitable Foundation for the Support of Widows and Orphans and it is well insured. I am merely the board chairman of this foundation.

"I usually only live here only during May and June. Come July and August, this estate normally is filled with orphans from New York and New England who will enjoy exercise, sun and sea. And soon, hopefully, they will also receive effective polio vaccines courtesy of this foundation."

"So your charity stuff is for real, Mrs. O'Shaughnessy?"

"Of course it is, Mr. Sherwood. Oh, sorry, did I let that slip?"

She smiled again. I grimaced.

"I am never directly involved in any sort of criminal activities. I merely offer to adjudicate the occasional disputes which arise periodically among select organizations. I offer advice to those who wish to receive such. Emerald Eire is one of many charitable organizations which I help direct. Two of my daughters are on its board of directors, as is an associate of a certain organization out of Boston, and is a representative from the Catholic Diocese of Rhode Island and Providence Plantations Colony.

"Now, for better or worse, we are going to be working together for the next several years, so I should instruct one of my own solicitors to explain, at least to Kathy, some peculiar territorial sensitivities which may affect the decisions of some of my colleagues and competitors."

I love solicitor type talk. "You mean you want Melinda and Kathy to know exactly which mob owns what so they won't do any too stupid and have some hard guy lash out at them because of some perceived disrespect? I mean, I already gave them the broad outlines of that, but I guess I would be grateful l if there was anything more specific you wish to share."

"Your Uncle Max taught you well, Mr. Smith. I hope his shoulder has fully recovered. Now, this is not the nut, nor even the vig, for my debt to you for your help two days ago. It's the type of small favor one does for one's neighbor, especially a thoughtful neighbor who plugged five hostiles with deadly and distinctive .50-caliber torso wounds while those now deceased hostiles were trying to kill me and mine.

"I believe the hitman who your Uncle Max wood-chipped and fed to his pigs was hired out of Montreal. I don't know the hitman's name. That is all I could learn."

I would pass the information on to Uncle Max the next time I talked to him. Maybe he would be inclined to follow up on the knowledge. I got ready to leave.

"One last thing, Mr. Smith. I know some professors with whom I sometimes consult on arcane subjects. Have you examined Astrid's unusual puffin broach?"

I nodded cautiously, not seeing where this was going.

"There is a fragmentary reference to puffins regarding naval warfare."

My eyes got wide. "You got me dead to rights, Mrs. O'Shaughnessy. Well, it was a bit more than fragmentary. It turned out some of those Danish sailors at the *Pie-Eyed Puffin* could pack quite a punch. Even Scarbutt was impressed enough that..."

Bridget harrumphed. "Don't be an idiot, Smith. I am not concerned with the tavern brawls of your relative youth. I asked my experts questions regarding some less-documented Norse myths.

"Odin, as is well known, had his two ravens, which he used for reconnaissance. I learned Freyja, the Goddess of War, had, in two Edda fragments, a connection with puffins. Also, Harald Fairhair, the first king of Norway, had a figurehead of a two-headed puffin on his personal longboat, according to another source. It's a bit of a stretch, based as it is only on tenuous clues, but the two-headed puffin motif may be closely tied to Nordic royalty, at least on Astrid's earth."

Well, Astrid certainly carried herself like a princess royal. I couldn't figure out what a snooty princess would be doing as bona fide field surgeon, though. Tiny swore that Astrid had handled the triage better than any army doctor could have.

"Thank you for sharing that, Mrs. O'Shaughnessy. I figure, on balance, I am still in your debt. The army interrogators at Ft. Amherst finally got a couple of those thugs from the coach the army intercepted to talk. They admitted they were heading to Fall River to await orders. I suspect their original plan was to have the thugs from the coach hit the front gate simultaneously with the seaborne assault.

"Your tip on intercepting the motor coach, and then running up the battle flag to provoke the Cubans into splitting their forces, probably saved our bacon. Let me know if there is any small favor which I can do for you. Please."

"I'll keep that in mind, Mr. Smith."

I returned to the Burr place, intending only to give Melinda, Tiny, and Kathy a warning about the mob stuff. Unexpectedly, Astrid intercepted me the moment I walked into the Burr cottage. She didn't want to talk about seabirds, though.

"May I kill Sergeant Oglethorpe, John? He insulted me."

"Huh? So what? Even I sometimes insult you, albeit constantly, but usually behind your back."

She glared at me. Women; no sense of humor. I might have to reduce the provocation level just a notch, though.

"I almost always discount your insults, John, but Sergeant Oglethorpe is not habitually such an idiot. It was immediately before the attack. He said I had five seconds to head for the safe room, otherwise he would thump me one on my head and then carry my bleached-blonde, limp, near-carcass to safety all by himself. I am a *natural* blonde, John. And he didn't even give me time to get dressed."

"Yeah, well, that's the point. We figured the Cubans were told to grab any good looking blondes, or else. Uh, what was that about getting dressed?"

"I had no idea what your stupid klaxon meant, John, so I had returned to my room and I was taking a shower."

She seemed to ponder what I told her about grabbing blondes.

"What would have happened to us, John, the women, I mean, if those thugs had burst through to the safe room before the reinforcements got here?"

"Well, they were pressed for time, so I doubt they would have raped you on the spot, but they would have grabbed you and Melinda, because you are both blonde. They might not have been able to tell auburn from blonde, so they might have grabbed Kathy, too. Vicki, well, they would have killed her out of hand; grudgingly, because she's a knock-out in terms of looks, but they hadn't been told to grab some babe with jet black hair.

"Now, once they got you back to their ship, they would have raped the lot of you in shifts before our navy reluctantly blew their boat out of the water. I doubt the thugs supposedly in charge would have been able to enforce any discipline, not after brutal combat with our marines and certainly not with your figure, even had they been inclined to do so. Not that I know much about pirate boot camps, but I doubt they spend as much time discussing the laws regarding armed conflict as our own armed forces do."

"How many of them did you kill, John?"

"Eight. But I shot five of them from the back or side while they were trying to climb the cliffs in front of Bridget's place, and I nailed two in a boat attacking Bridget's place. I only killed one guy attacking this place. Most of the credit for keeping your own delicate derriere safe goes to Scarbutt's marines, Tiny and his WANCARs, and Francine over at the priory. She was manning a field telephone and spotting for the rifle grenades which the marines were lobbing over the cliff edge."

Astrid studied me quizzically; I knew I needed to explain further.

"I had to make choices. Once the thugs split their forces, the odds shifted heavily in favor of our marines and Tiny holding out until reinforcements arrived.

"I wasn't as confident Mrs. O'Shaughnessy's folks could hold out. Bridget has some staff members at her place whose families live on the estate. She also has a couple of her grandkids and their playmates visiting. Besides, Melinda and most of her folks were armed, as was Kathy."

I paused and gave her a significant look. Astrid picked up on it and responded. "I was not wearing a holster, John; I was wearing soap bubbles. Your Sergeant Scarbutt lacked the nerve to thump me over the head, but he carried me down to the safe room straightaway."

"You might want to be more attentive to your personal safety in the future, Astrid. Anyhow, I figured you ladies had a better chance of defending yourself than did all those kids over at Bridget's place.

"It's my turn for questions, Astrid. Tell me, when you were growing up, were you shielded from the sordid realities of life? Treated like a spoiled princess, maybe?"

She sneered at me. "I will talk with Melinda and ensure I am never again unarmed if I have to endure a similarly interrupted shower. As to your specific questions, I grew up near the Arctic Circle, John. Every day was a struggle for survival. Speaking of survivors; have those Cubans been crucified yet?"

"Nah, they won't be crucified. Once our politicians figure out what to do with Cuba politically, those guys probably will be shot or hanged."

"Hanging's too good for those scum, John."

Astrid took a deep breath and tried to calm down.

"Thank you, John. There is a lot regarding your earth about which I need to learn. I guess I have to start taking more of an interest. Tomorrow I have to go clothes shopping with Mary and Theodora. Bridget and Elizabet are going to take us to meet Bridget's personal fashion consultant. The three of us will need new formal dresses and various lingerie items suitable for a High Irish Tea some two weeks from now. Astrid wants to thank us for the trivial gall bladder operation and also for the triage from two days ago."

"Is she taking care of security for this outing?"

"I gather so; she said we couldn't be safer if we were cuddled in the arms of Saint Michael."

Two weeks after the attack, while Astrid was enjoying her high tea, there was breaking news from Cuba about two absolutely massive sets of explosions. One explosion destroyed half of Lavoisier's most important precursor chemical facility. The other set of explosions and fires took out a huge private estate about forty miles from Havana.

To my mind, that answered the questions as to what happened to the four unaccounted-for bad guys and why Bridget exuded such calm. I figured the four goons her folks captured were fish food someplace, but only after they all talked and corroborated each other's stories. At which point, Slab and Wires probably volunteered to take a Cuban vacation with a couple of their more militarily savvy buddies. I suspected a couple of folks behind the death of David O'Shaughnessy, the late Grand Seamus of the Queens, New York, Fraternal Organization, got caught up in those explosions.

Two days later Melinda received in the mail a bright green envelope, of highest quality formal paper, containing equally expensive stationery. Edging the stationery's entire perimeter were cute little shamrocks. The note on the stationery consisted, in its entirety, "*Who the hell is Eduardo? B.*"

Maybe Wires and Slab had taken the time to engage in some field interrogation while working on their improvised demolition techniques. I realized I needed to go back to determining who the heck Eduardo was and how he fit in with the Lavoisier folks. With Ruth working twelve-hour days on vaccines, I didn't figure she was going to be too much help in bringing Eduardo out of his coma. Perhaps Astrid could help. In the meantime, however, it was time for the survivors to party.

Part Two

Romances

It's My Party but You'll Lie if You Want To

Chez Plonk, next door to Fiddlers Green Restaurant, Philadelphia

It was a raucous, pre-opening private party at the *Chez Plonk*. We still called it that. Melinda had yet to decide on a permanent name for her new place. Jules was working as the chef for the evening. Jennifer was serving as practice hostess. Top Sergeant Lucius Oglethorpe, aka Scarbutt, was looking at Jennifer like a love-sick puppy dog; boy was I going to rib him about that.

Anne, Beth, Connie, and Susan of the original Valkyries were working as waitresses. They were also practicing their cover and thus armed to the teeth, though not observably so, as Melinda had developed a flair for costume design. I doubted they would need their weaponry during the party. Kathy's extended family provided perimeter security. The word also had gone out from the leadership of both the Four Families and the three New York Fraternal Organizations that *Chez Plonk* and *Fiddlers Green* were on the permanent do not disturb list.

Other prominent ladies attended. Brigadier Hamilton and her husband, Lord Hamilton, the Foreign Secretary, were being introduced to Cajun hors d'oeuvres. Penelope Bartholomew Cabot and her husband came down from Boston. Lady-to-be-Ruth was on her third date with the dashing Captain Franks. Dr. Astrid had brought down her dirigible pilot du jour as well the two senior Sisters of Healing, Sister Mary Potter and Sister Theodora Karras.

The latter two both wore RIPPM/Medical Corps lady captains' mess dress gowns. They spent a lot of time with Kathy's mom, also a senior nurse, probably trash-talking doctors they had known. I wandered over to eavesdrop on the conversation. It turned out to be more of a monolog.

Kathy's mom, Sally, was saying, "So the wet behind the ears ER resident examines this guy's kneecap, swollen up like a grapefruit it was and the injured mutt was screaming in pain. Doctor has no clues whether it was broken; we don't have one of those experimental see-through machines, yet. He walks away saying he was going to prescribe some morphine while he thinks about what to do and the ice packs have reduced the swelling some more."

"So I examine the guy's kneecap while the doc is off doing something useless and I am replacing the ice packs around the kneecap. I could see at a glance his knee had a nasty bruise. Ya think I can't tell Kathy's second cousin Benny's work when I see it? I mean, Benny's been doing collections in Philly for a good ten years now and I see the results of his work maybe two, three times a month. There may be one better pro in his line of work than Benny, but ya can't tell me there's any more than that, at least not in this half of the Commonwealth.

"So I tell the dumb mutt he'll be up and sort of walking within a couple of weeks, but if he wants to keep using both legs for much longer then he better find a way to pay off his debts after he drops a bundle on the wrong nag at the races."

"So the clown stops his screaming and gives me a strange look. He says he fell down a flight of stairs. I tell him then and there I was actually the Queen of Bavaria and I had only been working the night shift at this crumby hospital for twenty-plus years 'cause I am a stinking humanitarian. I asked him whether he was going to believe me, or that handsome young doctor who had just started his residency. I tell the mutt what he got was basically a precisely controlled love tap; I say you don't want to see what happens to the kneecaps of those folks who try to skate on their legitimate gambling debts a second time.

"I told him if this had been the second time he got his kneecap whacked, even Dr. Babyface would have seen instantly how shattered it was. I tell the mutt I got better things to do than treat morons who should have known better, so if he has any brains at all, once he is back on his feet he better find a second job and start paying the vig. I tell ya; sometimes the patients are almost as stupid as the doctors, though in different ways, of course."

I backed out of listening range as I vowed to myself not to run up excessive gambling losses at unofficial off-track betting sites in the Philly area. Kathy's cousins took their professional responsibilities far too seriously.

I eased my way through the crowd to the massive bar. Barbara was working the gourmet plonk section and all of us who knew Barbara were glad to see her moving around so well. We were amazed to find out how knowledgeable Barbara had become regarding vintages.

Francine had bailed on the party. She had stayed behind in Rhode Island to serve as interim chief of security for the Sisters of Healing and to take charge, with the temporary brevet rank of Captain, of a new cohort of Valkyries for the RIPPM/WASPs. She was still miffed at Jennifer for being able to land Scarbutt.

The *Chez Plonk* blowout was unusual because of the absence of to-bacco smoke. This caused a fair amount of unease among some men folk. Astrid had been shocked to discover a part of Melinda's vision for the joint included a wine and cigar bar. Melinda had chosen the concept primarily because she had planned to impose an enormous mark-up on high-end, individually sold, cigars. She had expected to mint money, not that she needed any more. Still, I guess that is how the rich stay rich.

Once Astrid learned of Melinda's plans, Astrid screamed at her for a while about throat and lung cancer. Vicki overheard the screaming, wandered into the conversation, listened until she got the gist of it and broke into tears, thinking of her late uncle Jean Lafitte. The cigar bar concept got canned.

Lady-to-be Kathy, Dame-to-be Melinda, and Lady-to-be Vicki were all off to one side, comparing their still small baby bumps and showing them off to a dozen of Kathy's and Melinda's classmates from good ole Bala Cynwyd Women's College. The latter bunch's husbands, fiancés, or plus-ones for the evening were sensibly avoiding the pregnancy-related conversations and hitting the free bar.

That's what I planned to do, but only after I got something else off my chest. I waited until Paul was between conversations, darted in and guided him off to a side table to have a private conversation with him.

"You're still claiming you're never going back home, are you Paul? Are you sticking with your story that you can never manufacture the right blend of ultra-refined hydraulic fluids and lubricants to pop back safely, no matter how hard our experts try to help? Or will some critical part on the sea skimmer always go kaboom right before you would have made a trip?"

He stared at me. He said nothing for a moment. Then, "My home earth is destroyed. Why would we want to go back to a cooling, radioactive ball of dirt?"

"Maybe it's that way now," said I, "but I don't think it was that way when Astrid and the rest of your folks came over. Let me first get back to your lying lips."

I continued, "One clue is happenstance, two clues I get suspicious, but more clues than that all pointing the same way means someone is trying to blow smoke up my backside. My first observation, I guess, is I have learned a little about acting the past couple of years. Some of your folks are better at it than others. I have also seen up close and personal how combat and death affect young men, and how death and trauma affect the nurses who care for the dying and the badly wounded.

"Your people don't fit. Normal folks, and I think down deep all of your people are normal folks, well, a good third of you would still be catatonic if what you claimed happened had happened. All of you should still have a two-thousand-yard stare.

"We call it shell shock for the guys in the front lines; we don't have a phrase for the aftereffects of it for the guys who come back home. All of your senior folks seemed to have bounced back completely from the loss of your world after about two weeks of occasionally looking grief stricken."

I thought about what I said. "I have to correct myself, Paul; the two older Sisters of Healing each genuinely have worn the two thousand-yard stare. But it's been a long time since they first acquired it.

They have learned to hide it from civilians who don't know what they are looking for.

"But the rest of your folks don't look that way. That doesn't happen, Paul. Sociopaths wouldn't have the two weeks of grief to begin with and normal folks wouldn't have bounced back so quickly. So I figured your people are lying through your teeth about something important."

"I thought you kept insisting you were not a detective, John. You have thought about this fairly methodically."

"And you're acting like those navy intelligence weasels I used to work with. I'd tell you not to distract me, but that's my next point.

"I got distracted by the attack on Melinda's estate, but something kept gnawing at me, like rats chewing at the wainscoting in the night. It came to me right before the attack. Dr. Martingale said she only brought three years' worth of birth control medication, whatever the heck that is.

"Being a guy, and thus not having a clue how women actually think, it took me a while to figure out ladies normally would not be carrying three years' worth of such medication to a church vigil service. Especially in a military medical kit; that's not something you would prescribe when dealing with shrapnel wounds and such. Also, there were those performance pills she brought along and stuffed down Jules' throat and similarly gave away to the governor's wife. Again, not something one might ordinarily bring to a holy vigil.

"So Astrid, at least, planned to do a scamper. That means there had been a carefully planned plot. She had to be up to her eyeballs in it, because there is no way she can fly your monster bird all by herself. Also, she went through her period of grief so quickly you would have missed it if you blinked. Then she took to lording it over all us peasant types better than a duck takes to water.

"Astrid also let it slip during the gall bladder operation she was, legally, still under military discipline but not worried about it. Your folks still do the crucifixion bit? For fraternization? That seems a bit on the harsh side."

Paul finally smiled. "If you knew Astrid like I know Astrid, you wouldn't think it a bit harsh. It might be just a tad excessive for other folks."

"The final tip-off was your language ability. You claimed to be a trained linguist; still, I think you picked up our version of English too quickly. It was more obvious how quickly Astrid picked up our language. When I thought about it, I realized I could go to Australia and live there for five years and I would still screw up when I tried to use the local slang. And I grew up with and then married into an extended family filled with criminals, so I should fit in naturally with Australians.

"You, however, picked up most of our slang within a month. Astrid didn't learn at your rate, but she still made incredible progress with her language acquisition. It was almost like she had studied English beforehand because she knew her destination in advance."

Paul grabbed a couple of pretzels from a dish at the table. He ate a couple. He never took his eyes from me when he reached for them, though. Historian, my ass.

"For how long have you been planning this trip to our version of earth? Not that it matters much, I guess. You folks have more than earned your keep. And you have already been good for Vicki, though I think you manipulated her, rather than the other way around. Your whole '*I was so handsome* and *she was so in love*' routine also screamed to me you had sophisticated operational intelligence training.

"I don't want you to think because we are well behind you technologically, we are also stupid. There is a difference between primitive and stupid. So what type of intelligence officer are you, Tribune Paul?"

Paul stared at me a while longer. He took a sip of beer. "I guess you could say I am a senior operative for my Empire's military intelligence service. Our earth found your earth fifteen years ago. Chrono-hopping-wise, it's moderately difficult for us to travel to this earth. We recorded millions of hours of your radio broadcasts, acquired thousands of books, analyzed your technology for about a year and wrote your world off as an utter backwater. You had nothing to offer us in terms of either our competition with the Ming or anything else, for that matter.

"I came here looking for a missing WiG, one which disappeared after setting out for an earth dominated by some remarkably nasty Germans. It's difficult even for an advanced civilization to search an entire earth without help, so I needed assistance from one of your major governments.

"Even with your government's help, I have found neither the missing WiG nor rumors of its existence on this earth. I may have to report back that we need to search elsewhere. We know of a couple of other earths at your world's general technology level. We generally ignore them. Perhaps my empire is using its limited resources to search for the missing WiG on those earths rather than coming to retrieve us."

He ate some more shrimp. He shrugged. "Astrid still has not told me why she came to your earth. I am surprised she has remained silent because physicians are the same across every timeline we have visited so far. They tend to be arrogant beyond belief and oblivious to operational security issues. Llywelyn *claims* he doesn't know her reasons either, but he agreed with her stupid plan because he has never enjoyed having me going off on my own.

"Lycus and Marcus told me Astrid started acting more strangely than usual, even for her, about three months before they set out for your earth. I didn't bother to ask anything of Mary and Theodora. They will do anything Astrid tells them to do. Nor was there any benefit from asking Astrid's collection of younger nurses."

"Sounds sort of like the younger nurses on Sally's shift at Franklin Quaker. They are in awe of her."

Paul took advantage of my interjection and snarfed down three more boiled shrimp and washed those down with a sip of his pale ale. He responded to my original question.

"Naturally, I was furious when she arrived and I did go into shock that night. I can't force her and her entourage to go home and I can't leave her and her ladies here alone. Of course I have often been angry with her; she is quite skilled at grating on my nerves. She practices every chance she gets.

"Once Astrid's WiG arrived, I could and did inform my headquarters of that event. That is, I sent word home Astrid had arrived safely, but I didn't request an emergency rescue. I won't hear back from my colleagues until they send another WiG. I figure that has taken longer than normal because Astrid's idiot scheme threw things into a complete tizzy back home."

He took another sip of pale ale.

"I can wait here a while longer; it's not a bad earth as such things go. My folks will pick me up, eventually. Don't worry about Vicki; I will do right by her and my son- or daughter-to-be and give them both a chance to return to my world with me. Do you have anything else to say?"

"Yeah, I do, Paul. As I said earlier, 'Thanks, you lying weasel.' Even our dumbest senior politicians will soon realize there are other, far more hostile worlds, which might infiltrate us. At that point, even they might be forced to change their lazy, corrupt ways. Well, at least the lazy part. Heck, most of us were content to set here on our fat asses forever. Now we will all be dragged along with our politicians.

"You have single-handedly forced upon us another industrial revolution. Heck, we may travel to your world on our own in another two or three hundred years."

Then I got embarrassed. "Except for the polio vaccine. It's going to be a lifesaver. Ruth told me earlier tonight there have been nearly negligible side effects from the first round of vaccine testing, which is why all our ladies and Doctor Semmelweis are on the next honors list. You are not because I explained to Brigadier Hamilton I don't trust you much farther than I can throw you. She shared my thoughts with her husband."

He shrugged. "I was born a senator's son. I'm already in the nobility. Hell, I think you should thank me for giving you and your descendants a chance to avoid catching fatal but easily preventable diseases. The polio vaccine is the first of maybe five or six. After that, you're on your own, because these are the only vaccines for which I wrote academic case studies analyzing how they were discovered."

Paul drained his mug of beer. I picked up my own. It somehow was also empty. Intense talking is thirsty work. "Next round's on me, Paul. Now, what do you and Vicki want for a wedding gift? Think about it while I grab some more of Melinda's beer."

I grabbed two more free beers and returned. Paul stared at me for a good half a minute and said, "I have been focused on vaccines the last eight months and I don't have a good handle on what you folks were doing immediately prior to my arrival. According to Melinda, you have your own unfinished business. Every moment Melinda spares from talking about the wonders of impending motherhood, she complains about kidnapping attempts. Vicki caught a bunch of that. So I suspect our choice of a wedding gift depends on why this Eduardo guy Melinda mentioned was so important."

That stunned me. I realized I had never told Paul how I came to know Melinda, Ruth, Vicki, and Kathy. I spent twenty minutes reviewing the disgusting mess with him, from the comatose Eduardo, the institutionalized Delilah Honoré, to the deservedly deceased Wendell Honoré and Sidney Parker. I finished by telling him to talk to Ruth about the pharmaceutical details of all the drugs Eduardo, Sidney, and Wendell used on their victims.

His face hardened as he processed my back story.

"The pharmaceuticals you say Eduardo used have effects far too advanced to have been developed by your earth's science. This may have nothing to do with my original mission, but it's a near lock that those drugs were designed on some other version of earth. If Eduardo was based in Havana, then we need to investigate there. You had better inform the Brigadier she might live in more interesting times than she imagined."

He smiled. "Your Madeline is a piece of work, isn't she? I guess your Bard would have said, 'A rose's thorn by any other name would prick as sharply' had he met the Brigadier. If I had been precognizant, I guess I should have murdered the lot of you folks in your sleep down at *Chateau Pirates Paradise* and then tried to work with the French or the Russians instead."

Paul might have been joking, but I didn't let myself get distracted; my mind had already latched onto a thought. Heck, it happens. I knew I had missed something and I couldn't afford to let this go by.

Rosettes!

"Paul, grab a pencil or something. Use this napkin. Draw a picture of your WiG as if you were facing it head on and in a poorly lit hanger. I only saw that sucker up close from the side and it was dark as pitch and I was focused on driving my motorboat while trying to rescue your ladies. I have never seen your WiG in the light of day and head on."

Paul shrugged, made with the napkin and a pencil. I mentally kicked myself.

"Paul, I saw a picture of this type of craft in Wendell Honoré's flicker studio office about a full year before you showed up. From the dust on the picture, it could have been trapped between a desk and wall for six months to a couple of years before that.

"The lady in the picture, a Miss Eva Braun, supposedly lived in Havana, for what that's worth. Of course, she also claimed to be an actress, but I saw one of her flickers, so I know she lied about the actress part.

"She probably lied about everything, just like Wendell Honoré lied. Still, as he was dying, he implied Eva Braun was from another world. I thought he was speaking metaphorically because he, uh, also mentioned zombies, to be complete about stuff. At point Madeline and Melinda told me I was nuts for believing Wendell and told me, quite firmly, to shut up about it."

I groaned. "I bet the horse droppings hit the rotating blades a long time ago. I pinched the picture not quite a year ago, on a hunch. Right now it is lying in a drawer in Kathy's mom's townhouse, a couple miles away. You should look at it tomorrow."

Paul frowned; drained his beer and said, "Damn straight, Cassandra. No rest for the wicked. Did you say Eva Braun?"

I nodded a yes.

"Damn; we are so fracked. You will not believe how fracked we are."

I drained the rest of my beer. I realized it was the last one I was going to have this evening since it was clear tomorrow was going to be a very long day.

I talked to the Brigadier an hour later, and she agreed to stay over in Philadelphia for another day. We would all meet in a secure room at the Marine Corps Annex in Philadelphia the next afternoon.

Smoke Gets in Your Eyes

Philadelphia and Manhattan

Paul, Astrid, Ruth, Kathy, and I met with Brigadier Hamilton and came up with a list of things to investigate. Paul shared what he knew about the original Eva Braun and the Nazis who had existed on several other timelines. He terrified the lot of us.

The Brigadier decided our first task would be to re-investigate Eduardo and his alleged Cuban connections in light of these facts. Ruth was still too busy with the vaccines and Astrid was a surgeon. Astrid volunteered Sister Mary, her senior nurse anesthetist, to investigate Eduardo's pharmaceuticals. Madeline also decided to investigate the notoriously sleazy Lavoisier Corporation and its connections to the Cuban government.

Madeline would task Naval Intelligence to review their files of Cuban facilities, especially buildings near a seashore and capable of hiding something the size of a 130 by 300 foot WiG. She promised to talk to her husband about military and diplomatic support and ask his Foreign Office to review their classified files on the Cuban government. Vicki, Melinda and Kathy would scan the publicly available information about Lavoisier and its major subsidiaries and suppliers.

Our pregnant ladies finished their research first, naturally enough, as this sort of stuff was right in their wheelhouse. Lavoisier had an ownership upheaval six years ago, entailing massive changes to the board of directors. The fresh board brought in a gaggle of new senior researchers, most of whom had German-sounding names. Coincidentally, or not; we couldn't tell, that episode coincided with an upheaval in the precious gems' market when a lot of previously unknown gems came on the market.

Lord Hamilton briefed us in person, though we did not show up on his official calendar. He explained interlocking treaties prevented immediate military action against Cuba as such would be considered by Spain as an attack against Spain. Unfortunately, our Empire had fifteen years left on the latest treaty of friendship it had signed with Spain. Breaking the treaty would require His Majesty to request a declaration of war from Parliament. That would not happen.

The best he could do was to ask our Empire's various militaries to build up resources in the Caribbean, but until we had a casus belli, his hands were tied. He could not authorize the use of Royal Marine Corps Special Forces. I could go in on my own as a private citizen, but if I got caught, the Minister would disavow all knowledge of my existence.

Our first major break came when the RFC constabulary located Miss Annabelle Lee, aka Jasmine, Delilah Honoré's former secretary. The RFC authorities had kept the financial records of Honoré Studios as they existed at the time of Wendell's demise and they contained Jasmine's real name. She currently worked as a senior administrative assistant for a major import-export firm in Manhattan.

The Brigadier' folks reached out to the Brooklyn and Queens constabularies, who investigated Miss Lee's background. It did not make for pleasant reading. One set of Annabelle's great-grandparents was from Formosa. They were members of a moderately wealthy Han merchant family and were, fortunately for them, on a combined business trip and family vacation in Manila when the Chrysanthemum Empire invaded Formosa about a hundred years ago.

Those family members decided to stay in Manila, understandably. Back then, Manilla had a reasonably prosperous Han community. They spent two generations working like dogs to regain their former economic and social status.

Annabelle's mother subsequently lost most of her own family in the anti-Han pogroms, which occurred after the Mindanao revolt against the Spanish broke out and then spread to the greater Philippines. It's always tough being in a well-to-do minority group during violent times. Annabelle's mom somehow talked her way on board an English freighter and worked on her back the entire voyage to pay for her cruise to New York Harbor.

Annabelle wasn't illegitimate or anything; her widowed mom was two months pregnant with Annabelle when Mom boarded the freighter. Once her mom got to Brooklyn, she spent the next eighteen years working as a laundress. Annabelle was almost eighteen and had started secretarial college when her mom died of tuberculosis. I guess I would have had a chip on my shoulder if I had those tragedies in my rear-view mirror.

We made an appointment to see Annabelle's boss. A scummy dude from the Crown Customs Service and a smarmy New York Colony deputy crown prosecutor talked to her boss privately about nothing in particular. WOFC Glynda Smith, wearing a civilian outfit, and I talked to Annabelle in a separate conference room. Glynda and I sat across from her at a small table.

Annabelle was wearing a standard up-scale New York secretary's outfit. It consisted of a maroon short-cut blazer, a white, low-cut blouse and a pleated navy blue skirt coming to about one-half inch above the kneecap and low pumps with two-inch heels. She wore her long black hair in a tight bun and wore a triple-strand artificial pearl choker around her neck. To top it off, she wore eyeglasses which I didn't remember her needing to give herself the complete faux, semi-sexy librarian look.

Annabelle sat down; then she ostentatiously crossed her legs and adjusted her skirt to emphasize some expensive-looking silk tights. The current job must have paid well.

"Long time, no see, Jasmine. You appear to be wearing undergarments today. Those must feel constricting after your last job."

Glynda seemed startled by my rudeness, but snapped out of it quickly when Annabelle replied. "The name is Miss Lee, jarhead. It's about time you showed up. You got your five million yet? If so, I need to see it first; I don't take IOUs. I gather the ugly harpy beside you is to keep me from crying rape. Good planning, Smith. I might have considered doing that."

She lit up a cigarette and talked while smoking.

"You're here about Delilah or Eduardo; it can't be anything else. I have it all, of course, but with everyone dead or institutionalized, I've had no one to blackmail. That's changed, obviously. The government badly wants what they hope I have. Otherwise, you wouldn't be sitting here and they wouldn't have sent those two Confederation clowns to distract my boss.

"I know those buffoons are legit; I called their offices back to confirm the appointments. Besides being one heck of a good-looking lady and dynamite in bed, at least for some tastes, I am also a hell-on-wheels secretary."

She lit up another cigarette and blew some smoke towards my face.

"I was left in charge of winding down Delilah's business affairs after she got tossed into the rubber room. I know it's hard to imagine, Smith, but no one else at Honoré Studios wanted to know the details of what she had been doing."

She took a long drag on her cigarette and puffed an even larger cloud of smoke at me. She looked me up and down.

"I could be wrong, Muscles. I guess there's a chance you showed up to declare your undying love for me. Is that what you came for?"

"No, Miss Lee, you were correct the first time. We would like to know what you can tell us about Eduardo's drugs and experiments. It's potentially critical information relating to the Empire's well-being."

"Imperial entanglements, Smith? Well, you can count on me to co-operate; as soon as the Exchequer's check clears. Otherwise, no dice. Sure, I'm patriotic, but I'm also an underpaid, single girl with expensive hobbies and if I don't look after me, no one else will. I can give you some highlights up front, but the actual details are going to cost plenty.

She took another drag on her health-stick and relaxed a bit. She sighed.

"Ah, Eduardo; what a piece of scum. He had a lot of weird ideas. Towards the end, he brought Delilah some drugs so good those two could do anything they wanted with Delilah's co-stars. Those babes they used them on would literally beg for more."

She stubbed out her cigarette in an ashtray, grabbed another one out of her purse, held it out at me and said, "You gonna stay a jerk, or you gonna be polite and light this for a lady?"

"I'm, sorry, Miss Lee. I don't smoke; I can't light it."

She reached into her purse again and tossed me a lighter. I fired her up. She puffed; she continued.

"I have no clue what became of Eduardo. I mean, who was I going to go to? Anybody so evil had connections which would get me squashed like a bug if I started asking around. And of course Wendell and Sidney and Jean Lafitte are now all dead. What was a poor but borderline amoral girl to do? I figured my best bet was to keep things on ice and hope somebody came looking.

"You will have figured out by now that Wendell lied to you about almost everything; he often lied to his uncle as well. Wendell and Delilah, however, never realized I made carbon copies of all the notes she dictated for Eduardo.

"Delilah couldn't type worth a damn, so I had to transcribe everything; at least her cursive was legible. Eduardo came up from Havana every other month or so to review Delilah's experiments in person. Then he often traveled to Connecticut or Rhode Island for long weekends of fun with Sidney. I met the creep twice; he made my flesh crawl."

"Did you partake of in Delilah's experiments, Miss Lee?"

"I for sure didn't star in any of Delilah's stupid movies. As for your particular and very leading question; well gosh, farm-boy, I sure don't need my solicitor around to advise me on how to answer it. I'm not that type of girl."

She uncrossed her legs, unnecessarily adjusted her suspenders snaps, grabbed her lighter back and lit another cigarette. She took a few puffs and asked, "Now, I believe we were discussing how much my cooperation will cost the Royal Exchequer?"

"Why don't you talk a little more about Eduardo, Miss Lee?"

She took a long drag on the cigarette. She relaxed a little more.

"I think Eduardo also had some side projects going on up somewhere in New England, but I don't know much about that. When he came back from up north before sailing back to Havana, he would stop off at the studios and grab the typed version of his notes to take back with him. He usually also took along one or two of Delilah's more pliable co-stars; often the ones who Wendell had chosen for his own type of drugged-up, farewell attentions.

"I'm not as greedy as I pretended. All I want is half-a-million pounds sterling, a new identity, a full pardon and a town house in Victoria. I want the deal signed off in the presence of my choice of solicitors. There are a lot of ethnic Han in Victoria. I've never been there, but it's far away from here and sounds nice. Perhaps I'll meet some interesting people."

She lit another cigarette, took another long drag on it, and then blew some smoke in Glynda's face.

"Do that again, bitch, and you will find out what a lady learns while serving two tours as a matron in the Military Police," said Glynda, calmly. I flinched; I had known Glynda for two years and this was the first time she had used her voice in anger in my presence.

Annabelle sneered at us. "Not a chance, you dried up old hag. Not 'till you buy what I've got and by then it will be too late to lay a finger on me. I'll give you something more on account, though. Every one of Delilah's busty co-stars was ethnically German or Scandinavian, and they all had to be natural blondes.

"We were a flicker studio; we knew all about whether some dumb blonde dyed her roots. I can give you the names and originating address for all of Delilah's co-stars, as well as the drugs they were on and their reactions to various forms of stimuli.

"I also know what happened to most of them, at least up to the time some of them took a one-way cruise to Havana. The folks you have reading my notes, if we come to a deal, better have strong stomachs. No skin off my nose if they don't, though; just saying, is all."

"As long as you're talking, Miss Lee, do you have any thoughts about why Eduardo and his suppliers were doing what they did?"

I waved my right hand, taking in the general office area and the building. "You have been working for this hoity-toity firm for almost a year and a half. You would not have lasted so long unless you were both capable and intelligent."

She smiled, puffed, and smiled again.

"Okay, because you were polite, for once, I will give you something more. I don't know why Eduardo and his unknown backers insisted on the blonde, busty German or Nordic types. Well, any blonde Irish babes would have been right out because the FOs would have gone homicidally nuts had they caught wind of Eduardo drugging up Irish ladies.

"As for the rest; normal people hate pain and most normal people shy away from inflicting pain. Also, most young ladies in our society would never seriously consider getting it on with another lady. If somebody can develop drugs which make doing all those things at the same time seem both normal and intensely pleasurable, then that somebody can make other people do anything he wants. Hell, maybe somebody, somehow, wants to use those drugs to take over the world."

I was proud of myself. I kept a straight face. So did Glynda.

"Eduardo never told me squat about anything, though. I was Delilah Honoré's exotic, but very obedient, assistant. I typed exactly what I was given, and I never said a word about what I was typing.

"Two last things; I got to observe a lot about Eduardo. He was far worse than pond scum, so it wouldn't surprise me if he forgot to turn in all his notes to whomever he worked with. About a third of those notes were phony, anyway. He skimmed drugs for his own and Wendell's and Sydney's use and they had to make up fake experimental results to account for the use of those drugs."

She smiled. She puffed some more. "And I am the only person on earth who can tell you which results were phony and which ones were genuine.

"If Eduardo's suppliers ever discovered what he was doing, then those folks might want to find him and ask him a few questions. Including, maybe, like why the moment Wendell left on a two-week trip, Eduardo and Delilah grabbed Dorte Johansson and stuck her full of needles."

I was startled; Annabelle continued. "Wendell was not completely in-sane, at least not regarding the nobs. Wendell enjoyed manipulating and breaking naïve, blond farm girls and such, but he was careful with the risks he took. Once he discovered Dot came from a highly connected family, he told Delilah to keep her psycho mitts well away from Dot. Perhaps Eduardo was the one who started poking needles.

"I know Dot's mom's family was from the Norwegian part of the Dual Kingdom, but with a fair number of Danish ancestors; Dot's father's family was Swedish, with a lot of ancestors from their middling nobility. Dot was pure Scandinavian, going all the way back to the Vikings, and as blonde as they get.

"Delilah acted like a bitch in heat from the moment she laid eyes on Dot, but I don't think she would have had the nerve to disobey Wendell unless Eduardo manipulated Delilah somehow.

"I said two things. Eduardo never skimmed any drugs those times when he brought his German secretary Brunhilde along. Secretary my ass; I am one hell of a secretary and she was a worse secretary than she was an actress. She sucked as an actress."

Annabelle started shivering. Her cigarette went out; she lit yet anoth-er one. She calmed down after a couple more puffs.

"Brunhilde never explicitly insulted me, but she talked down to me and treated me like I was a cockroach. She only showed up those times when Eduardo or Wendell had taken a fancy to some busty blonde who was being a little too recalcitrant to take a one-way zombie cruise to Havana. Or she showed up when she wanted to act in one of Wendell's stupid mutt flickers.

"If it was the former, then Eduardo and Brunhilde would slip the dumb blonde something in a drink and stick the babe full of needles filled with happy juice; Brunhilde clearly had some medical training. She scared me spitless; I think she was more insane than was Delilah, but far more focused."

I showed Annabelle the picture of Miss Eva Braun and the weird craft. Annabelle shuddered again, took a last puff, pursed her lips, glanced at Glynda, thought better of it and blew a last whoosh of smoke in my face.

She stabbed her cigarette butt into the ashtray with a vengeance and let out a sigh.

"You sure her name was Brunhilde and not Miss Eva Braun?" I asked.

Annabelle thought for a moment, nodded, then replied. "Eva Braun was her stage name; she picked it out of thin air for all I know. At least I never heard Eduardo call her any other name other than Brunhilde and he was always respectful to her. It was clear why. Compared to Brunhilde, I am merely edgy and Delilah was eccentric. Brunhilde would make Satan crap his drawers. Wendell might have called her something else, though; he spoke German and I sure don't."

Suddenly Annabelle grinned. "Sometimes Eduardo would talk to Eva Braun or even to himself using Spanish. I never let him know I understood every word they said; that's part of why I learned so much about him. My mom's family spoke Spanish; three generations in Manila, they almost had to speak it there, just to get by. Heck, my mom never learned to speak English, not more than a couple words, anyhow.

"Anyhow, it took me six months to wrap up all the paperwork after Delilah got stuffed in the rubber room. I saw all three of the flickers Brunhilde was in as they were being filmed. Well, I only saw part of the third one. The only other fluent German speaker on the lot was Ron Cross, the actor who played Dr. Gruesome in the last two flickers. Brunhilde and Ron hung around together a lot, babbling in Deutsch."

"Ron, short for Ronald?"

"Nope, Ron is full for Ron, but Ron was his second name. His first initial was 'I.' I don't know what that initial stood for. Did you know those two hokey spaceman flickers still make money? They're considered cornball classics on the drive-in flicker circuit. Ron could chew the scenery like nobody's business. The law says Guild actors have to be paid their contracted percentage residuals, if any, whenever a flicker is shown, even if the original studio goes broke. If you want to find Mr. I. Ron Cross, or at least find out where the money he is owed goes, then ask the Guild.

"Frau Brunhilde was never on Wendell's payroll, at least not while I worked there, so I don't know you will find any records on her. You only have to join the guild if you want a pay-check. If she didn't want the cash, it's just more proof she was crazy."

She fingered her cigarette case again; then she stopped. She stared at me.

"The deal is I deliver the notes; I never typed my name on them, so I don't think they prove anything except somebody once typed some nasty fiction. I will identify which notes are phony and which are not. I will not answer questions clarifying anything else. I don't want to be involved any further in this crap; it's way out of my league.

"That's enough of the freebies, so it's time you cut to the chase, Smith. I'm also a busy girl and I'm scheduled to leave work a couple of hours early today. I have a hot date laid on for tonight. I can give you the details about it when if I see you again though they would probably shock you.

"Anyhow, I'm giving you three days to come through with the deal; otherwise I torch all the notes. I am sure you can find your own way out."

Annabelle got the deal. I wish I could have been there when she signed the papers. They gave her everything she asked in return for complete and total non-disclosure. I wasn't there, but Brigadier Hamilton was. The moment Annabelle signed the papers and had her solicitor witness them, Brigadier Hamilton pulled out another document.

"Miss Annabelle Lee, you are now under official caution. This warrant I am giving to your solicitor to review is signed personally by the Governor General. It allows me, as permitted under the national security laws, to hold you as a material witness in an ongoing investigation. You are to be held, in relative luxury, in a secure, non-disclosed location for the next eighty-nine days.

"You are not under technical arrest, but from this point on, you are not to say a word to anyone other than duly authorized government or military representatives. This prohibition also applies to your solicitor. Miss Lee, the next word you say aloud could put you in violation of multiple national security laws.

"Your solicitor will explain to you the applicable laws after he has read this document. You may nod or shake your head in answer to any of his yes or no questions. After that, you will be escorted from this room. After the aforementioned time has expired, you will be returned to this room, at which point the national security injunction ends, but you will still be held to the non-disclosure agreement's terms."

The Brigadier opened the door to the conference room. WOFC Glynda Smith, in her class-A uniform, and four tough-looking lady MPs entered the room.

WOFC Smith saluted the Brigadier and said, "The escort awaits your orders, Brigadier. I hand-selected the escort detail, Brigadier. Miss Lee will arrive safely at her destination."

WOFC Smith turned to Annabelle and said, "Hello, toots, long time, no see."

I learned from the Valkyries, the lady MPs and the Sisters of Healing that Annabelle loathed her initial days at the priory. The Sisters were all anti-smoking fanatics, so Annabelle had to go cold turkey. It sucked to be her.

The Brigadier's folks checked on I. Ron Cross' residuals from the Guild. They were delivered to a law office in the Netherlands Antilles. Her folks couldn't push the trail any farther.

True Spies

We had no pity at all for Annabelle's nicotine withdrawal once we, led by Sister Mary, started going through Annabelle's notes. The experiments were worse than we had possibly imagined. When Paul reviewed Mary's analysis, he came back almost in shock.

"It's a separate cross-time incursion; this completely confirms it. You saw how various formulas were notated as being from something like lot number 1234 or such and included the hoped-for result and the actual result. Several times they were listed as MIRTD batch such-and-such. Once Eduardo slipped up and mentioned the Mengele Institute. Annabelle dutifully transcribed that. We are so fracked."

I was clueless. "That sounds German, but we already know when the Lavoisier management coup happened six years ago, they hired a handful of German senior scientists. What makes this fresh news?"

Paul provided more details regarding a time line wherein a corporal named Hitler ascended to power, forcibly unified Germany, and plunged the world into a world war. Almost six years passed before he and Eva Braun committed suicide in his bunker in Berlin in 1945, just before hordes of vengeance-seeking Russians arrived. He next described some of Doctor Mengele's experiments and said no one from a sane world would ever name a research institute for the mad doctor.

"Those folks in Cuba have to be doctors or medical researchers from an earth where Hitler won. Those guys will be both dangerous and, by your standards, completely insane. If your diplomats won't budge on what it will take for them to commence military action now, then we need to acquire solid proof.

"So we need to send someone to Havana who knows what to look for in terms of cross-earth incursions. We also have to send folks who can identify people from my earth, if any remain alive, who were brought here against their will. It could be these lunatic Nazis are here because they captured my world's missing WiG. Melinda, Vicki and Kathy are all out, as they will all be five or six months pregnant by the time we get organized."

"Kathy's not going, Paul, because of her medical history. Astrid's not letting Kathy out of her sight. Besides, Kathy never had any military police or bodyguard training."

He responded with a nod. "You will take four of my people with you. Sergeant Llywelyn is a sneaky piece of work and is in the same business as you were. Don't bother denying anything. You also need Julius to ensure secure communications. He had our basic infantry course, but that's it. They will both need range time first."

"You can never get enough range time, Paul."

He waved off my insightful comment.

"Next, Mary and Theodora are going to volunteer to help."

"Why them?"

He shook his head in a manner which suggested I was acting like I was still eight years old. "Two reasons, genius. They had been stationed at our Bermuda base almost forever and can identify the missing crew members. You may not have considered my next reason."

I got wide-eyed. This should be good.

He scowled fractionally. "As I understand your culture, at least in the RFC and RCC, ladies who like ladies, if they are considering a commercial arrangement, have to travel to Cuba. Neither Bridget's places, nor other such east coast establishments, offer ladies such services.

"You and I both know that Bridget usually has plenty of cover from hypocritical, wife-cheating politicians. Heck, they're some of Bridget's establishments' most reliable clientele. She also bribes local constables when she has to do so. The constables would never raid her places unless they are under immense pressure. They would roust her bordellos in a heartbeat, though, if they heard so much as a rumor of babe-on-babe action."

I stood there, stunned. He was spot on. Somehow, I had never focused on that aspect of the mission. Paul kept talking at me.

"We don't know into which aspect of the Havana sex trade the kidnapped ladies might be trapped, so we have to look everywhere. Mary and Theodora will need appropriate cover to investigate places where men can't enter. I think the ladies will need beards. 'Pretend husbands' is how Vicki explained the term to me. If I have guessed correctly the modus operandi of the Lavoisier mad scientists, they may even still be looking for someone like Delilah to serve as a front for some experiments.

"There aren't too many natural blondes available in Havana and these madmen have certain views on ethnic purity. They may jump at the chance to engage Mary and Theodora as cutouts for future experiments. Those two can claim to be from Pennsylvania Colony. There are a lot of ladies of German descent there, including scads of natural blondes."

"What's the thing with the blondes, Paul? I can see being interested in good looking ladies, but why do they all have to be blonde? I much prefer redheads myself."

I said the last sentence loudly. I looked around to determine whether my auburn-haired wife was in the vicinity. I hadn't heard her sneak in, but it never hurts to express publicly my preference for a certain hair color.

Paul continued. "And German or Scandinavian, John. That earth went nuts about seventy years ago. I'll explain later. Most of their history doesn't matter for now, but early on, at least, Nazi doctors typically pursed whacko research projects to enhance their personal political influence. I still can't imagine how Delilah Honoré's and Eduardo's weird experiments would benefit the Nazi doctors politically.

"Anyway, maybe your party can rescue at least one of the missing ladies or grab some of the drugs which Lavoisier uses to control their behavior. Or you might get a solid lead on our missing WiG. Achieving any of these tasks should provide your government a sufficient reason to compel Havana to turn over the Nazi doctors.

"Now, I expect you and Llywelyn to keep Mary and Theodora safe. The actual tactics you use do to do are up to you and Llewelyn. You do plan on sailing to Cuba, don't you?"

"Sure, Paul. I'm going."

Of course I was going, but I intended to kill some carefully selected folks slowly and painfully rather than conduct a simple recon and rescue. I had decided to go the moment I realized the bastards in Cuba were responsible for the fact I would never know my first child. The drug-addicted and justly deceased Wendell Honoré was merely their catspaw.

Yeah, Paul could be right, though. I needed first to identify all the bad dudes; I might have to make two trips.

If Mary and Theodora needed beards, then I needed two more hard guys, best case in their early forties, to provide the ladies verisimilitude. Lord Hamilton forbade me to use any former colleagues who had served in my classified sniper outfit. That didn't bother me too much; most of them weren't skeevy enough to fit the mission profile. The right guys should be able to run some recon of their own in sleazy places where Mary and Theodora couldn't enter.

I had no leverage over the folks I knew out of Detroit, and I didn't want to involve Kathy's extended family in Philly in that type of stuff. I figured I could ask Bridget if she could spare Wires and Slab since they had already operated in Cuba. She turned me down cold. She feared they were too famous professionally and would be recognized if they visited downtown Havana. They had kept to the countryside on their one prior visit to Cuba.

She suggested looking for skilled help from an area not so heavily contested by the Cuban or New Spain organizations. I thought about it for a while and decided she was right, but I still needed some leverage on whomever I got. Then I think I got smart. I asked her if I could borrow either Slab or Wires for a quick trip to Ft. Pitt City.

She said sure; she also offered me the services of Fingers Malone, forty-eight-years-old. When he went in the jug three years ago, he was considered the best safe cracker in the business. She thought I might need such a skill set. Then, more reluctantly, she also offered the services of Elizabet.

"You will need to remember every detail from the pre-mission briefings when you arrive in Cuba. She is the only one who can do that. You must keep her safe or die trying."

I agreed to her conditions and asked, "If Fingers is so good, Bridget, why was he caught?"

"Stupid, dumb bad luck. I gave him permission to go independent some five years ago. The Railroad and Shippers Bank of Baltimore ran a practice security drill at two o'clock in the morning. Fingers almost talked his way out of his arrest by claiming the Bank had hired a fake safecracker to make the drill realistic. I want him and another dozen of my folks freed from prison. I don't want his release to stick out, so it has to be part of a broader amnesty. I intend to soak our government for all it's worth.

"Oh, and John, please be extra careful. Upon their return from Cuba, Slab and Wires reported something is outrageously wrong. They heard a rumor that some senior Church hierarchy members in Cuba have been completely compromised. That goes far beyond any sort of traditional criminality."

Fingers got sprung three days later and started his limbering up exercises. Elizabet started studying everything there was to know about Havana and Cuba. Elizabet would pretend to be a senior novitiate in the Merciful Sisters and would dress accordingly. Fingers would pretend to be her father, taking her on a grand vacation, just prior to Elizabet taking her final vows.

Two days after I talked with Bridget, I walked into an interview room at the *General Braddock Commonwealth of Pennsylvania Colony Medium Security Prison* plopped right smack in the middle of the notoriously sleazy Bradford Forest area north of Ft. Pitt City. Wires accompanied me. I bet the prison's head screw had a cow when he learned he could not so as much touch Wires. The guards brought in Ratso Jimmy, whom I had not seen for over a year. The guards left. I took out my stiletto from my shoe and cut the cord holding the overhead microphone. Then I smiled at Ratso.

"Hello, Ratso. Long time no see. Are you and your two Yinzer pals keeping busy? Gosh, it must be lonely for you, especially not having any visitors, what with you not having married that gal you had two kids with and her not wanting to see you again until you pay off your back child support."

"What's it to you, Hotshot? The name's Jimmy, by the way. I see you brought along a new set of muscles."

I faked looking hurt. "Gosh, Ratso, I'm sorry about forgetting your name, especially after I did so much research on you. My companion here goes by the name of Wires. He hangs around with a guy named Slab. Wires, you got a last name you go by or anything?"

"Not that I'm going to share with this dirtbag, I ain't. Anyhow, he's remembered who I am. I think you got his attention now."

Jimmy's eyes were now bouncing back and forth between Wires and me like pinballs gone crazy.

"Slab and Wires told me you and your pals had a reputation for being a lot better than the frack-ups you were on the last job you tried to pull. How'd you like a pardon, Jimmy? All you and one of your buddies from the failed kidnapping need to do is to take an all-expenses paid, tropical trip with me and a couple of my acquaintances.

"You will pretend to be a married man who cheats on his wife every waking second. That shouldn't be too hard for you. You may also need to kill somebody if I tell you to do so. You ever killed a man, Ratso?"

Jimmy stared at the cut wire dangling above his head. He turned back towards me. He did not say a word, but he opened his lip and scratched his top front teeth using his right pinky and ring fingers. I took that as a yes, meaning two stiffs.

"Okay Jimmy; so pick which pal is going along with you. If things go right, then you two will spend the entire trip shagging call girls. If things go south, well, then that's when you two earn your keep.

"Now, the reason you and your pal are getting this outstanding offer is a while back, some nasty dudes hired some expendable thugs to lob artillery shells at an Irish orphanage. A certain dear, sweet lady took personal offense. Slab and Wires can't yet go discuss the nasty dudes' bad behavior in person because they might be made. This is just a reconnaissance job. If it succeeds, then maybe Wires and Slab can do a follow up and they will know which doorbell to ring.

"If you can convince Wires you can be relied on to see this job through or die trying, then you will be invited to a party which the Widow intends to give. If you live through the Widow's party, then the Governor of Rhode Island and the RFC Governor General will sign your pardons.

"Then the Widow will pay off your back child support and offer legitimate jobs doing security at an East Coast gentlemen's club to all three of you mutts. Finally, if you are killed, the Widow promises your two kids will be well taken care of."

"How do I know you can swing all this, Jarhead?"

"Come on, Ratso. Use your brain. If I didn't have the juice, do you think the head screw would let Wires sit in on this conversation?

"Tell me which one of your buddies you trust to join you on this. We'll bring him in and make him the same offer. If you two decide you are in, you both leave these fine accommodations today. If you decline this offer, you'll be put on ice someplace isolated until the job is over. Then you'll be sent back here to finish your term. You have fifteen minutes to decide on how you want to play this."

Ten minutes later, we had Ratso Jimmy and Ferret Phil tentatively on board. I hadn't told them explicitly they were going to be beards. I sure hoped Mary and Theodora still agreed to being "married" to those Yinzers once they met them in person.

I returned to Philadelphia and talked with the Valkyries. Anne and Susan agreed to join the group. They each had private sector bodyguard experience. We all returned to Melinda's cottage to train for the mission. Once we arrived in Newport, Francine resigned her brevet commission in the RIPPM/WASPs and joined as well. Jennifer again took over as head of security for the priory. It gave her more time to be with Top Sergeant Scarbutt.

Most of my new team put in lots of range time, began to learn or brush up on Spanish, and spent a lot of time looking at maps and photographs we got from the navy intelligence folks.

Bridget hired a clean solicitor and six legitimate and licensed body-guards to escort Elizabet, Ratso, Jimmy, Mary and Theodora down to NYC. They spent a couple of weeks viewing the Wendell and Delilah Honoré flickers which the RFC constabulary had stashed in their evidence vaults. Normally Wires and or Slab would have escorted Elizabet down to New York, but because Elizabet and the gang would spend hours a day at the RFC Constabulary HQ building, Bridget was diplomatic.

While we were training and planning, our Foreign Office prepared the battlespace, so to speak, for either a diplomatic or a military confrontation with Cuba. Foreign Minister Hamilton let the Cuban consul and the Spanish Ambassador know the RFC was more than a little miffed that a ship which operated out of Cuban ports and had an all-Cuban crew had been lobbing shells at a Rhode Island estate. He asked the Cuban consul if his government was going to help track down the antecedents for those guys.

The Cuban Consul responded it was not his problem. He suggested we complain to Siam, under which flag the ship was registered. Hamilton authorized our plan to proceed as scheduled.

Our reconnaissance was based on the assumption any lady who Eduardo had carried off to Cuba remained trapped in the sex trade, at least if she was still alive. Once we finished our research, we had the names and pictures, well complete flickers in most cases, of seventeen young ladies who met five criteria. They had had roles in Wendell or Delilah Honoré's flickers, Annabelle Lee had confirmed they left with Eduardo on a ship sailing to Havana, their families or friends had filed a missing person report, the New York Constabulary had shared such a report with the Cubans and, last, the Cubans officially denied any such person had arrived in Cuba.

Ratso, Jimmy, Mary and Theodora would seek blonde babes trapped in the sex-trade once we got to Havana. Elizabet would determine definitively if any such were one of the seventeen we sought. Llywelyn and I would provide security, assisted by three of the original Valkyries. Julius would keep us securely in touch with Major Marcus back in Newport.

If we found a single such lady, Lord Hamilton would assume the Cubans had lied to his face. At that point, our diplomats and military would put the squeeze on Cuba. It seemed like a reasonable and straightforward plan. I mean, really; what could go seriously wrong?

For King and Country

With two weeks and two days to go before we began the long trip to Havana, things looked good. We would arrive in Havana as a hosted tour group escorted by a guide from St. Petersburg, Florida Colony. What type of group? Well, Melinda's original cunning plan had been for us to disguise ourselves as a troupe of flamenco dancers to better blend into Havana and Santiago de Cuba.

She had never been to Cuba and had some weird ideas about the place. I figured she must have taken her idea straight out of some radio farce. I diplomatically asked her if she had gone bug-nuts crazy as part of her pregnancy.

She explained the idea came from a stage comedy where a man and woman, both super-duper, tip-top secret agents, going by numbers instead of names and all that, disguised themselves as flamenco dancers. They then were sent to a South American country to keep the bad guys from seizing control of the world and causing utter chaos.

She said the bad guys would never see through this because they were German and she was distantly related to many Germans, all of whom completely lacked a sense of humor. Besides, this disguise worked marvelously on stage, primarily because the male super-spy was an oblivious moron. She said such a plan should fit me like a glove.

I calmly explained if the price of saving the world was me getting fitted into some overly tight silk pants and prancing around with a rose between my teeth, then the world would have to go hang. I could never show my face among marines again in my life.

Melinda, Vicki and Kathy reworked the idea. They decided we travelers would go as a tour group devoted to spending most of our evenings attending flamenco performances. I figured fine; whatever made them happy was okay, at least as long as *I* didn't have to wear tight silk trousers.

We made our cruise ship reservations and committed to three nights in Nassau, six nights in Havana, three nights in Santiago de Cuba before finishing up with three nights in Montego Bay. Then we would board an airship back to New York City. We would skip the leg of the cruise where the ship was scheduled to head east for two weeks, visiting various French-owned Caribbean islands before she returned to St. Petersburg.

Anne, Francine and Susan had been hoping to check out those French Caribbean resorts while on the government shilling. The Brigadier put paid to their fantasies when she shared with the others the news that I was still officially *persona non grata* with the French. The Brigadier mentioned although she had no personal issues with my butt being thrown onto Devil's Island for the rest of my life; she acknowledged it would unnecessarily complicate the mission debrief.

We had to choose the right tour escort, one selected for his intimate knowledge of Havana's notoriously seedy entertainment options. Vicki's contacts in Florida Colony identified a guy she thought would suit us. The tour director was reputed to have a boyfriend in every port, and he bailed on his tour group the moment the ship docked. The latter sounded absolutely perfect for our purposes.

I had focused on traditional preparations. Ratso, Ferret, Llywelyn, Julius, Francine, Mary, Theodora, Anne, Susan and I all put in a lot of range time, focusing on using our .30- or .32-caliber Wembleys. Elizabet watched and listened and recorded our thoughts. Fingers got more limber. So we were disguised as five married couples plus a late middle-aged man and his novitiate daughter.

The Valkyries had talked among themselves. I got Francine to be my fake wife; I figured it didn't matter much to me. Yeah, I once joined the marines and twice I had re-enlisted, so I had to have been born stupid.

Brigadier Hamilton phoned Kathy late one afternoon and had a long talk with her. Then Kathy talked to Francine. Then Francine and Kathy tracked me down and gave me an unexpected talk.

Kathy started. "Madeline called me and discussed some potential security issues you will face on your Cuban tour. Truthfully, they had not occurred to me. Nor, apparently, had they occurred to you."

Francine spoke next while Kathy stood frozen, as tears started glistening in her eyes.

"The Brigadier called to say the rooms we will stay in Havana and Santiago de Cuba may be wired for sound. She warned me the hotels' staffs in Havana and Santiago de Cuba may well check the bedsheets for evidence the beds got used for more than just sleeping.

"Jimmy and Phil will complain their hatchet-faced wives are totally frigid and weird. That will give them an excuse to find if the women we are looking for are still trapped in a different niche of the sex trade. Besides, Bridget told them if they so much as touch the Sisters, then they are fish food."

"I'm not worried about them either, Francine. If they screw up, they go back in the jug."

"Right, John. Fingers and Elizabet don't have to worry such perceptions; not with their cover stories. As for Llywelyn and Julius; well, Anne and Susan started making whoopee with their alleged husbands about two weeks ago, once Astrid got them fitted up with diaphragms.

"You, on the other hand, are the last Knight of the Round Table, so you won't be pounding the prostitutes like Ratso or Ferret. That leaves me, your alleged wife, on an alleged honeymoon, sleeping in the same bed with you. If nothing goes on, and things in Cuba are as bad as the Brigadier says they might be, then the lack of normal activity will be reported up the chain. You know it's true."

I was concerned that Francine was trying to circle in on an important point. I looked back at Kathy and tears were running down her cheeks.

Francine continued, "I can handle my end of the deal, John. Hell, I gave away my virginity when I was seventeen and I was already being laughed at by every other farm girl I knew for being so reluctant and waiting so long. You grow up watching a damn bull put it to damn stupid cows thirty times in a day and you don't have any illusions. Double hell; I only picked you when Anne and Susan and I were talking about who chooses whom 'cause you grew up on a farm, too, and I thought we might have something in common.

"It's not like I have been scheming to throw myself at you. Well, anyhow, not since two years ago when Dame Melinda told all us girls to knock it off back, right before those Spetsnaz attacked."

Kathy kept a neutral look on her tear-streaked face through sheer force of will.

Francine continued. "That said, I am going to be more than annoyed if you get us all killed because you can't live your cover. Or even get us worse than killed. Did you ever see either Mary or Theodora bare-assed naked?"

I shook my head no. Obviously. Duh!

"Astrid insisted Anne, Susan, Elizabet and I had to check them over. Bridget accompanied Elizabet. Mary and Theodora have scars you wouldn't believe. Astrid explained their injuries stemmed from half an hour or so of mindless violence and lust."

"What happened to them?"

"Astrid explained Mary and Theodora had been abused by Ming soldiers, though the soldiers in question were mercenaries working for local drug-growing warlords in a location near our earth's Siam. The Sisters were responding to massive devastation in the aftermath of a typhoon and half of their initial security folks were delayed for a couple of hours by an aircraft engine malfunction.

"After their follow-up forces rescued the few surviving Sisters of Healing, they deployed two brigades of their own marines. They spent the next six months tracking down the local warlord encampments and crucifying every male of military age they could find. And burning the drug crops and salting the earth. Paul and Astrid's folks may not be the type of folks who go looking for trouble, but you sure don't want to piss them off, John."

Francine had a far more positive view of Paul than I did. I gave Paul credit for not looking for trouble for which he might be blamed.

"Astrid told us the folks she thinks are running Cuba will be far more vicious than her world's Ming mercenaries, but also far more deliberate. We girls are all going anyhow, because that stuff needs to be stopped.

"So you got two choices, farm boy and former super-marine. You either commit to making me moan with pleasure a couple times a night while we live our cover or you find somebody else to be your fake wife. Along with two more ladies to replace Anne and Susan, 'cause I sure am not letting them be killed or worse because you can't see to do your damn job.

"That should be a simple decision. Hell, John, I'm two years younger than you are and I keep in damn fine shape. You make your choice. I've said what I need to say. Now you need to hear it from Lady Katherine."

Kathy spoke haltingly. "I never believed I would be asked to share you, John, but Francine is correct in her assessment, as was the Brigadier, as much as I hate the Brigadier for pointing this out. There is no way Astrid will let me go to Havana at this stage of my pregnancy. Nor would it be plausible for an ostensibly single man to join this tour group.

"By the time you arrive in Nassau in two weeks, you two need to act like you are madly in love with each other. That means not shying away from Francine when she touches you. You should start practicing tomorrow night. It should be safe; Astrid has fitted Francine for a diaphragm."

"Kathy, dear," I stammered.

"Damn it John, shut up and listen. I want you to identify those people who manipulated Wendell Honoré and Eduardo and who were responsible for the loss of my first pregnancy. Then I will have them brought to the RFC and I will see them hanged. I will not let them threaten the child I now carry."

Kathy took a deep breath. "You first need to talk it out with some guy friends. I told Tiny and Scarbutt to be ready. Then drink some beer; rage against all manipulating women and their scheming plans. Please."

I spent the evening commiserating with Tiny and Scarbutt. I may have had four beers. Scarbutt said I seemed woozy, so he called Astrid and she showed up to give me a headache pill. Not the type she gave Jules, though. I think I fell asleep on Tiny's sofa. I woke up in my own bed, but I had a headache even so; funny that.

The next evening, I buckled down to other activities. Francine did not lack for enthusiasm. I wished she had been the one to nail my old pal Scarbutt instead of Jennifer. The next morning, worn out and bruised, it finally came to me to what role Mary and Theodora needed to play. That meant I had to talk with both them and Astrid. We met that afternoon.

"Ladies," I said, then paused, looked at my shoes and looked up again. I started over. This was going to be tough. "We need to talk about living our cover lives. One reason we are going to Havana is to throw out some bait and see if anyone bites. That means you two will need to engage in Delilah Honoré-like behavior and make it look legitimate. Do you think this can work?"

Mary answered calmly. "We have reviewed all the notes which Miss Lee provided. Theodora and I are quite aware of what is required of us. We will help you cut off the serpent's head and we will use the weapons we need to use. Rationally, any lady with whom we will interact is assuredly lost until the serpent dies; their only chance of escaping entrapment depends on our success."

Theodora broke in. "That said, John, I suspect you will enjoy your time with Francine far more than we will enjoy any moments we spend with those poor, exploited women in Cuba. You have your understanding of your duties. We are quite aware of ours."

Astrid interrupted, "John, trust me. Mary and Theodora will do just fine as long as those two clowns from Ft. Pitt avoid any screw-ups."

Two weeks later, we flew on a commercial dirigible from New York City down to St. Petersburg. There we met our tour director, Ricardo, the day before the cruise ship sailed. He was a great deal smarmier than Vicki assured me he would be.

Nassau was pleasant since we were still in the greater Empire and we didn't have to worry so much about security. We spent a couple of afternoons on the beach. Anne, Susan and Francine pranced around in their new, French-style two piece bathing costumes, which left little to the imagination. Francine had a lot of fun pretending to be on her honeymoon.

Mary and Theodora complained, falsely, they were having problems adjusting to the heat. Heck, their previous tour had been in their world's version of Bermuda. Ratso and Ferret then used the ladies' fake ailments to establish their cover and asked Ricardo to round up some local professional women to keep them company during the Nassau leg. Ratso also told Ricardo that Mary and Theodora were expecting their own type of exotic entertainment once they left Empire territory, so he should call ahead to Havana and arrange things.

Ratso shelled out a substantial gratuity as he made his twin requests. Ricardo nodded sagely and said he would get right on it. Other than that, he excelled at being useless. Vicki had outdone herself on the research front.

Mary found Ricardo beyond obnoxious during our three days in Nassau; so much so she slipped him a debilitating overdose of long-acting laxatives immediately before we docked in Havana. I snippily asked her about medical oaths and doing no harm and all that. She told me that those did not apply to nurses, only doctors. She warned if I gave her any more grief, then I would learn more about the '*Green Apple Quick Step*' than I had ever dreamt possible.

I shut up. It's not like she was wrong about Ricardo. Besides, his absence would give us far more flexibility to investigate Havana appropriately than would his presence.

Dance Hot and Hasty; Like a Spanish Jig

Havana, the Spanish Protectorate of Cuba

We docked in Havana in the early afternoon and Ricardo was first off the ship; ambulanced to a hospital. We were left with going to a five-star hotel in Havana and having to cope. That first evening we attended a previously arranged, traditional and utterly boring flamenco exhibition at one of Havana's many fine clubs.

Upscale concierges can do almost anything, especially when sufficient funds are supplied. After an excellent breakfast on our first morning in Havana, Ratso and Ferret and their pretend wives, Mary and Theodora, showed up at the senior concierge's station. Ratso and Ferret went first. They explained that because Ricardo, who should be well known to the staff, was in hospital, they would depend on the services of the hotel staff during their time in wonderful Havana.

Ratso and Ferret asked the concierge to arrange for four ladies of flexible virtue to attend to their needs that afternoon at another hotel, if the location was going to be an issue. Mary whacked Ratso over the back of his head with her parasol and said, in English, "The word is prostitute. And tip the man. Here's ten pounds. Give it to him. Pretend to be a gentleman."

The concierge inquired what quality of escorts the gentlemen expected to receive. He suggested the super-premium, low-mileage models for a not terribly exorbitant cost. Ferret said that sounded great as long as they were blonde or red-headed. Theodora whacked him over the head with her parasol. "Premium is fine. You don't deserve any better."

The concierge quoted the price for premium escorts. Mary checked her purse, looked at Theodora, nodded, and gave the concierge that much money. Then they ostentatiously gave Ratso and Ferret twenty pounds each and told them to pretend to be gentlemen and be sure to tip the girls. Ratso and Ferret left.

Mary and Theodora approached the concierge and smiled. He smiled back broadly and inquired how he could help them enjoy the wonders of Havana. They held hands and said they would like to see a variety of young ladies do exciting things with one another. They explained that Ricardo, and we all hope the dear man gets better soon, assured us that such things would be available in Havana. If we judge the ladies to be suitable, then we will hire them for the next week.

The concierge checked his notes, nodded and quoted a price. Mary and Theodora didn't haggle. They informed the concierge they had previously established a line of credit with the local Grande Banca Royale Barcelona branch. The concierge assured them he had no doubts their credit was impeccable. Then Mary and Theodora asked for a limousine and two licensed lady bodyguards to take them to the viewing.

Mary and Theodora returned around four thirty in the afternoon. The concierge on duty was new, but they laid into him like drill sergeants going after the recruit they had decided had made their permanent shitbird list. They complained at length the girls they had viewed were listless and completely lacking in passion and imagination. They would give the hotel one day to come up with something much, much better or they would ensure not one of their rich lady friends from Ft. Pitt City would ever travel to Havana again. Or if they did, they would never stay in this hotel.

Then they told the concierge to move an extra bed into Theodora's room, and have Ratso's things moved into Theodora's room, and Theodora's luggage moved into Mary's room. They gave him an hour to make it so while they relaxed at the cocktail bar.

The rest of us had hired a tour coach and spent our day visiting legitimate historical sights and locations around Havana. We chose our sights not so much for their historical import, but because Llywelyn and

I wanted to develop a feel for how the view on the ground related to how stuff was portrayed on the maps we had spent weeks poring over. Moreover, we drove to locations chosen to ensure our hired coach had to go past three separate Lavoisier facilities of various sorts, to give us a ground eye view of potential targets.

Our coach returned to the hotel, whereupon Francine and I were surprised to discover we had been moved into a suite that was a corner room. The rooms next to our new rooms appeared vacant. I told Francine she had been overdoing the fake cries of passion the previous night. She smiled and said they were all genuine; she was a sensitive girl. I figured again that if I somehow survived this mission, Kathy was so going to kill me.

We spent that evening at another deadly dull flamenco club. At least the ladies dancing on the stage were all good looking. The next morning, we had an early tour of Ft. Havana, where we mingled and interacted and individually reported everything we had learned to Elizabet. I also got to talk to Ratso about his adventures the previous afternoon.

"I told my two girls to go paint their nails while Phil did his thing. So he gets undressed, hands me his two shoulder holsters and crawls into bed with his two broads. They were decent looking, but a couple of years older than the babes we are looking for. I guess we need to spring for super-premium to have a chance of finding one of those ladies. Ah well, live and learn. Besides, Mary was establishing her character and we had to play things by ear.

"Anyhow, the ill-fitting but expensive silk suits we wore were a nice touch. I am sure the girls told their bosses we are typical, classless thugs and obvious beards.

"If this hotel has the contacts we think it does, Mary and Theodora are going to see a much more interesting show this afternoon. This time Phil and I will go along with them for security."

Francine and I were waiting in the hotel's surprisingly uncrowded cocktail lounge for Phil to get back and report. It was early in the evening, a little before the normal dinner hour. Francine was wearing too much make-up and a scandalously short skirt. She was staying in character by giggling a lot and occasionally nibbling on my ear.

I had finished checking the table for obvious wires when it hit me that both the lounge and the hotel were way too empty.

"Hey, Francine; could you stop pawing at me long enough to tell me if you have any ideas why this hotel seems way too vacant?"

She leaned over and nibbled my ear again. In between nips she asked, "Do you know what horses are, farm boy?"

"Yeah, uh, the stuff that glues are made of. What's that got to do with anything?"

"Melinda or Madeline should have told you. I guess they thought you knew. It's racing fortnight in the RCC, culminating with the race for *The George Washington Cup*. The host city rotates among Charleston, Mobile, Sarasota and Savannah quadrennially. Right now, half the real nobs in the RCC and perhaps a tenth of the uber-nobs from the RFC are taking flutters on the gee-gees at Hildago Downs in Sarasota.

"Last week, this place would have been packed. It will be packed again in two weeks' time. That's why Madeline accelerated our training schedule; she wanted us to arrive when there was less competition for the ladies we seek."

Phil walked in and easily spotted us. He sat. He shook his head in amazement.

"Jimmy and I thought we were scum of the earth. That just goes to show how naïve we were. That show they put on for Mary and Theodora, I can't begin to describe it, but it involved eight different girls. Anyhow, Mary and Theodora thought a couple of them appeared familiar. They rented four of those ladies to interview as potential 'maids.'

"Tomorrow morning, Mary and Theodora will choose which two ladies will accompany them to Santiago de Cuba. They're supposed to turn them back in to somebody before we sail for Jamaica, though."

Phil squinched his eyes. "I'm not sure you needed Jimmy and me, at least for security. I never thought I might lack civic pride, but this town is way worse than Ft. Pitt City ever was, at least for having constables on the take. They had uniformed Havana constables providing security for that show, totally out in the open, like.

"Anyhow, as we walked back into this joint, Elizabet got a glance at the ladies' maids-to-be. She gave me a signal. Mary caught it as well. Jimmy and I will stay here tonight; we may be on to something."

Francine put one hand on my thigh and used her other hand to pull my left ear within a half inch of her heavily painted lips. She whispered into my ear, "Those Yinzers aren't as dumb as they look, John. I am feeling better about this job."

"What's on for tonight, by the way?" Phil interrupted.

"The Jai Lai games. Want me to place some bets for you?"

The next morning, we, except for Phil, Mary and Theodora, took a harbor cruise. Francine and I, holding hands, drifted over to stand next to Elizabet and Fingers, who were leaning against the rail at the bow of the boat.

Elizabet spoke into the wind. "The blond maid with the pearl earrings is Miss Linda Hoffbauer, of Portsmouth, Ohio Province. She was recruited by Wendell Honoré three years ago and was the second female lead in the flicker, '*Woof the Wonder Pooch Saves Guy Fawkes Day*.'

"She made two untitled films for Delilah Honoré. All three films were entirely formulaic within their respective genres, and Linda showed no discernable acting talent. She left with Eduardo on a ship to Havana two years, three months and fourteen days ago and her whereabouts were unknown until yesterday.

"Linda appeared to be in a semi-trance-like state when she arrived yesterday; in fact, all four ladies seemed that way, if to a lesser extent. Mary and Theodora kept Linda per my signal and chose Hilda, last name not given, at random, to stay in cover."

That night our group, now including the two newly acquired ladies' maids, attended another exhibition of flamenco dancing. We chose this dance club because it was in the same city block downtown as the Lavoisier Cuban headquarters building. We arrived at the show intentionally early.

Fingers and I took the opportunity to buy some top-rated Cuban cigars. We walked around the block, blasting smoke and casing the Lavoisier joint from the outside. He enjoyed his cigar; I was nearly publicly sick from pretending to smoke the darn thing. I was never into smoking. It was way too expensive a hobby, back in the days of my misspent, impoverished youth.

Between puffs, Fingers said, "The third floor, fourth from the left window facing the alleyway, is not fully closed. Odds are they wanted extra ventilation, forgot about it, and never locked up. I bet we come back in a week or two and it's still stuck in the same position. If you don't mind, tomorrow afternoon I will go off on my own and case a couple of other Lavoisier places, merely to keep in practice. I'll keep a low profile."

I gave Fingers a thumb up; the guy was clearly a pro, so I figured not much could go wrong. We ambled back to the nightclub.

The show was a bit less, so to speak, than we were used to viewing. The flamenco ladies started out wearing traditional costumes, but by the time of their last dance, they were down to nearly invisible G-strings and flashy jewelry.

Elizabet was the only nun in the audience, at least the only one wearing a habit and identifiable as such. She sat stolidly through the performance. Fingers spent his time looking suitably embarrassed. After what seemed to me like an embarrassing eternity, the performance ended. We climbed into our coach and our driver took us back to the hotel.

I wanted to go to sleep immediately; Francine insisted on staying in character and I got less sleep than unusual. I fervently hoped Kathy never grilled me on the details of this trip to Havana. The things one is forced to do for King and Country.

We showed up a bit late for breakfast, entering the breakfast dining room in time to walk past Mary and Theodora lambasting the concierge over their maids' lackluster performances last night. "They were both outstanding the night before. We want our money back."

The concierge assured Mary he would check into the situation. A half hour later, the concierge came over to Mary at her breakfast table. He whispered to her and explained the two maids each suffered from some minor tropical disease. He assured them a doctor would arrive within the hour to provide their maids with their once every other day injections of a proprietary Lavoisier B-vitamins compound.

The doctor showed. He injected each maid. Mary asked if he was coming along on the Santiago de Cuba part of the tour. The doctor said, no Senora. Mary demanded he provide her with two additional injections for each maid. How else would she be able to keep their symptoms under control through the tour group's last day in Cuba?

Mary told the doctor she had trained as a nurse before she married her incredibly wealthy first husband, who died tragically and accidentally, far too young. Would the doctor accept a substantial gratuity for arriving so promptly? The doctor said he would check with his office to see if he was permitted to provide the bespoke vitamins. A messenger service delivered four vials of a clear fluid to Mary later in the afternoon.

Ricardo showed up at the hotel that evening just before dinner, though he was still looking somewhat worse for the wear. I glanced at Mary's table; she gave me a surreptitious shrug. I figured Havana hospitals either were better than she had suspected or they had a lot of practice treating gastrointestinal issues.

Ricardo apologized to all of us, saying he truly would try his best to show us Havana at its most exciting. Ricardo explained he had already checked with the concierges and learned what types of entertainment we had enjoyed in his absence. He proudly announced he had booked us reservations for the next two evenings at incredible flamenco shows. He assured us these would make the previous night's entertainment look like a Presbyterian prom.

Elizabet begged off from attending those performances, so we dropped off Elizabet and Fingers at *Catedral de San Cristobal* on the way to the Flamenco shows. She told me they spent their evening hours in prayerful contemplation.

Parting is such Sweet Sorrow

Atlantic Ocean, East of Havana

We played straight tourists for the next two days until we boarded the Siam-flagged cruise ship *Bangkok Beauty* bound for Santiago de Cuba. Communications Technician Julius used his other-earth, miniature equipment to call Major Marcus about an hour after the cruise ship left Havana Harbor. Marcus told him the navy intelligence folks believed they had located the missing WiG. I considered whether we had accomplished what we needed to do. I pulled the plug on our mission.

Five hours later, the RFCN light cruiser *Emerald*, and two destroyers, the RFCN *Greyhound* and the RCCN *City of Charleston*, stopped *Bangkok Beauty* in international waters.

It took a warning shot, but the cruise ship captain slowed his ship and came to a dead stop in the middle of the ocean, under the guns of the three warships. The task force commodore radioed the *Bangkok Beauty*'s captain to tell him he could send his protests to the nearest consulate of the Kingdom of Siam. In the meantime, however, *Bangkok Beauty* would be boarded by two squads of marines and a navy legal officer.

The ship's stewards rounded up our tour group and our luggage and herded us into a dining room. Simultaneous with our arrival, the navy legal officer strutted into the dining room from another hatchway. He sneered at the lot of us and turned to face the *Bangkok Beauty*'s captain. When I returned to Rhode Island, I would have to congratulate Admiral Frazier, the head of the navy's legal service. I hadn't thought his executive officer, Commander Woodson, had a theatrical bone in his body. He had plenty of them, actually; all ham.

"Well, Captain, you are carrying a truly pathetic cargo of human scum. To wit, Ratso and Ferret from Ft. Pitt City, wanted on parole violations, bigamy, back child support and conspiracy to assist in human trafficking across international borders. Your new 'wives' are wanted for conspiracy to human traffic across international borders, as well as gross indecency.

"Fingers; it's been a while. I see you picked up a new partner for your con games and safe cracking schemes; Suzie Shamrock from Staten Island, I haven't had the pleasure. Nice nun outfit, by the way, you disgusting trollop."

At that point, Elizabet launched into a tirade spoken in a Staten Island Irish accent, "Youse abusing a lady of the cloth, you puffed up Pommie-loving bastard. Wait till my solicitor gets hold of you."

Next, she unleashed a parade of profanity so complete it would have left my old drill instructor in speechless awe. Elizabet only went quiet after a couple of marines put a gag in her mouth. It certainly put the captain of the *Bangkok Beauty* into a state.

Then Woodson had a marine open up Fingers' luggage. What emerged were not exactly the Crown Jewels, but the haul was within spitting distance.

"Fingers, I think you have some explaining to do. Not that I will believe a word." Woodson gestured to some marines to haul the stuff to the *Emerald*.

Fingers sneered back at him and said, "You got nothing on me; I was recovering some misplaced property. You get us back to New York; then you can check who really owns this stuff. That is, unless my solicitor gets your license stripped first."

I ogled the jewels. Gosh; Fingers and Elizabet must have cut some of their prayer sessions a bit short to ensure the Cubans helped finance remodeling Bridget's cottage. I would have to speak to Bridget when I got back.

Woodson turned to me next. "Your wife wants you back, for some reason."

Francine screamed at me. "What wife? You said you were divorced, you lying piece of crap. You said your ex-wife was frigid. Just so you know, I faked every one of those screams, you lying weasel. What about my ring?"

Francine waved her left hand, which sported a three-carat hunk of glass on her ring finger.

Fingers said, "Toots, I've seen better sparkles coming out a two-shilling carny operation. You got taken. Hope he was at least good in the sack."

Francine started screaming at me with language which made Elizabet look like the nun she was disguised as. I guess Francine had learned a lot from her drill instructor back in basic training. I briefly felt guilty for not giving the army enough credit for imagination. The marines quickly gagged her as well, but not before a corporal had begun to blush out of embarrassment. Well, we marines are noted for our refined social sensitivities.

Woodson told the captain our tour group consisted of criminals and material witnesses and would be escorted from the *Bangkok Beauty*. Then Woodson turned to Ricardo.

"Ah, Mr. Ricardo! The captain of *City of Charleston* informed me that since you are an honorable subject of the RCC, you may not be held as a material witness unless you volunteer for such. Would I be wrong in suspecting you are going to decline this honor?"

Ricardo bailed on us; it was too bad I couldn't put a bet down on that outcome. We all went to the *Emerald* shackled and under guard. The guards took off our cuffs the moment we disappeared below deck. The *Emerald* then headed at flank speed to Kingston.

Even before I got the cuffs off, I told Julius to call up Madeline in Newport and tell her I thought we had enough evidence to go with Plan Gamma. It wasn't my call, but I figured I could express my opinion. Plan Gamma was the best I figured we could hope for, considering our evidence consisted only of one identified, trafficked lady and four vials of unknown fluids.

The plan called for the RFC to implement a naval blockade and take control of the customs service facilities at a couple of Cuban ports. We could then squeeze Cuban finances until Cuba fessed up and returned or otherwise accounted for the other missing women. Foreign Secretary Hamilton had explained earlier there was not sufficient international political will to intervene more extensively into Cuba's domestic behavior.

Julius sent the message off and got a reply. He gave me a lopsided smile. "The brass told me to tell you that you and Llywelyn just volunteered to take part in the forthcoming Guantanamo-area military festivities."

He then explained the outline of our mission. I silently cursed for a bit and wandered to the wardroom to grab some coffee and consider my options.

I grabbed a mug of Java, turned around, and almost bounced off Fingers and Elizabet. "What's up, Miss O'Conner, Fingers? Glad all this is over?"

"You don't know the half of it, jarhead," said Fingers. "You did your job maintaining profile and getting us in and out. Now I don't have to kill Elizabet like I would have had to do if something had gone tits up."

Elizabet interrupted Fingers. "I would like to add my thanks as well, Mr. Smith. He would have been correct to kill me in extremis, as much as I would have missed not seeing Mrs. O'Shaughnessy again until the blessed day when St. Patrick called her home. Moreover, you have given me much to ponder regarding my life."

Fingers continued, "If you hadn't been so focused on your own mission, you would have realized Elizabet knows every detail of Bridget's operations. She also knew every contact or halfway trustworthy associate Bridget has left in Havana. Brigit sent Elizabet anyway, to give you a sliver of a chance to escape alive if we got made while in Havana or Santiago de Cuba.

"If had you thought about it, there was no way Bridget was going to let Elizabet be interrogated by those monsters, so I had my orders. Bridget didn't get where she was by being unwilling to take calculated risks. Hell, I started working for her late husband's dad when I was seventeen."

I stared at Elizabet. She was amazingly placid for somebody who had known for weeks one of her own would have killed her in a heartbeat to prevent her capture. Fingers kept talking.

"Before I discovered my talents with locks, I used to be a straight torpedo. Bridget wanted me out of the jug, not only to recover her jewels, but because she knew I would do what I had to do. She told me I could tell you this as soon as the mission was over. She didn't want you figuring it out for yourself later and holding a grudge.

"It would have broken my heart to have had to scrag Elizabet; hell, she's almost family. I spent two years driving Elizabet to her parochial girls' school when she was twelve and thirteen. I want to say I am personally glad you didn't frack up. I know Bridget will appreciate it."

Fingers glanced towards the hatchway; he turned back to me. "Joseph Sammartino gave me the background of your cozy group of horny lady soldiers. Francine, for example, worships the ground Lady Katherine walks on and now she fell for you like a ton of bricks. Try to be sensitive, jarhead. Francine is going to go through a rough patch; all the blather about mission first and doing it for King and country is so much bullshit."

Elizabet spoke again. "Mr. Smith, I also thank you for letting me spend those last two evenings in prayerful thought at the Cathedral. I remained there while Fingers went off on his other duties for Mrs. O'Shaughnessy. Truly, this journey has helped me expand my horizons in so many ways.

"I had vowed to myself after Mrs. O'Shaughnessy rescued me from the streets, I would never let another man touch me in a carnal way again. Now I sometimes wonder about my vow. Francine has been such a dear; she so deeply enjoyed her time with you. She told me every detail of every evening and those occasional mornings and afternoons.

"Then Mary and Theodora reminded me it is up to individuals, not groups, to choose between good or evil paths. I now realize not all men treat women as did my justly deceased step-father.

"Just before she spoke to you, Francine saw the two of us waiting for our chance to speak with you. She told me, 'Honey, it's time you found yourself a decent man. Not that I think John is ever going to be available, 'cause if Lady Katherine somehow dies, the way I feel right now is I would kill every other woman on the planet to grab him for myself. Still, if he ever is available, jump on that chance, 'cause you could do one hell of a lot worse.'"

I realized Fingers was dead on accurate in a lot of ways. First, I was a moron for not recognizing Bridget would have taken precautions to keep Elizabet from talking if captured. I must be getting stupid in my old age. I glanced back at Elizabet and remembered my impending military mission. Strangely, that cheered me up because I figured the chance of Kathy kicking the bucket before I did was darn close to zero. That meant I didn't need to worry about the prospects of enjoying matrimonial bliss with either a sex-crazed farm-girl or a fake nun with mental issues.

"Uh yeah, sure, Elizabet. I'm glad you got to sort all of that out and you're still in one piece."

She smiled at me. "Thanks again for keeping me alive."

She leaned in and kissed me, briefly, on my left cheek before she left for the cabin which she would share with Francine.

In all those two-for-a-half-crown novels I read in my youth a real hero would have managed to pull a breaking and entering job in the middle of the night, gone straight to the one safe in the world where Lavoisier kept all its incriminating documents, copy them, and escape without leaving a clue he had ever been there. All the while seducing Cleopatra and writing the complete symphonies of JS Bach.

I felt I should have accomplished more. We had, I thought, acquired barely enough evidence to give my government an excuse to let the professionals take over. Actually, I had been kicking myself for pulling the plug too soon. Now I grasped the extent to which we had been pressing our luck to accomplish even this. I would have been a nervous wreck had I realized the feminine half of our make-shift, undertrained commando had spent the entire mission gossiping like a group of Midwestern church ladies after the pastor left the room.

Now Francine was in love with me. Tiny and Scarbutt had even assured me I was far too obnoxious for such to happen. Tiny explained, confidential-like, how Kathy had only fallen for me because she spent a lot of time in her youth hitting herself on the head with a hammer. I had seized at his obvious lies regarding Francine like a drowning man would clutch for a straw.

At least things couldn't become any worse. I shook my head to emerge from my reverie, opened my eyes, and found Francine standing right in front of me.

"My job's over, so I guess that's it between us, John. I want to thank you for the best month of my life. Lady Katherine is one lucky woman."

Francine kissed me chastely on the cheek. She stepped away and said, "At least we will always have Havana. Julius told me you and Llywelyn are going to stay in-theater and hit the beach. Why'd you go and do a stupid thing like volunteering for that duty? How long's it been since you rappelled out of a dirigible, anyway?"

I nodded. "Five years. I only volunteered because I was about to be conscripted. Besides, it reads better on any posthumous awards if I pretend to volunteer. After we deal with some harbor defense guns, Llywelyn has to dash to that dirigible hanger and try to engage some safety features on the WiG. Otherwise, we could face the largest man-made explosion in the history of our planet. I was told I had to go along to ride herd on Llywelyn.

"I suspect Llywelyn knows what he's doing, but if something goes wrong and I don't come back, you owe me. Take care of Kathy. Keep her safe."

"All us Valkyries were going to do so anyway, John. You go back to your mission planning. Damn your eyes, stud; don't go getting yourself killed."

Francine left the wardroom. I think I saw a glint of tears in her eyes as she turned to walk away.

It was now the turn for some other servants of the crown to earn their miserable wages. Two hours after I recommended Plan Gamma, Foreign Minister Hamilton received permission from the Prime Minister and the Governor General to lay the diplomatic basis for the blockade. He had the two Delilah-made films starring Linda Hoffbauer pulled from an evidence locker at the RFC Constabulary HQ in New York City and delivered to the Foreign Ministry offices.

Hamilton called in representativesfrom the embassies or consulates of Britain, Cuba, Spain, Switzerland, France, the Papal States and the RCC. He asked them to view two films starring Linda Hoffbauer. Viewing was halted twice as representatives from first the Papal States and then the RCC had to excuse themselves to lose their lunches.

Lord Hamilton explained to the visiting diplomats about the missing persons' reports for Miss Linda Hoffbauer and sixteen other ladies. He used their payroll records to establish they had all been employed by Wendell Honoré's flicker studio. He provided copies of their missing persons' reports, which had been sent to Cuba's national constabulary over the previous three years. He provided the responses from the Havana constabulary, who had denied knowing anything about any of them.

He announced Miss Hoffbauer had been rescued after being entrapped in the Havana sex trade. She was now undergoing medical treatment in Jamaica. The RFC also had evidence that addictive, advanced drugs had been used to control Miss Hoffbauer.

Hamilton stated Cuba was in default of certain obligations regarding suppressing human trafficking, incurred by virtue of the treaty of friendship Spain signed with the Greater British Empire five years ago. In consequence, the RFC government demanded Cuba immediately and explicitly account for the other sixteen ladies who we knew had sailed to Havana.

Given the unusual effects of the drugs were involved, the RFC demanded six named senior scientists at Lavoisier facilities in Cuba be made available for questioning, either in the RFC or in a neutral location such as France, Switzerland, or the Papal States. Lord Hamilton told the Cuban representative if both these steps were not taken within twenty-four hours, the RFC would undertake unilateral actions to determine the whereabouts of the sixteen missing ladies and the six scientists.

The Cuban representative told Lord Hamilton, using diplo-speak, to frack off. That answered the question as to who was controlling Cuba.

Fine, said Lord Hamilton. Our naval blockade of Cuba starts now. The RFC Ambassador made it a joint blockade ten seconds later. The RCC Navy had long been eager to put the squeeze on Cuba to force Cuban authorities to deal with the Cuban gangs which ran drugs into Florida. They volunteered to lead the Havana and East Coast portion of the blockade. The Blokes also jumped on board, but explained it would take them four or five days to deploy naval assets into the theater of operations.

The French ambassador asked to see the pictures of the missing ladies again. Lord Hamilton obliged. The ambassador got in contact with the French Consul in Kinston, Jamaica, who, in turn, visited Linda Hoffbauer at the Rodney Royal Navy Hospital in Kingston.

That Consul reported back from Kinston half a day later. The French heavy cruiser *Fromage Grande* and her accompanying destroyer left their port call in Boston the next morning to join the RCC's blockade of Havana.

Night Moves

The RFC navy blockaded the ports on Cuba's western and southern shores because our navy intelligence wonder dudes believed the missing WiG was housed in a dirigible hanger at the Guantanamo Aerodrome. They had discovered one hanger on the west side of the Bay which had twin steel rails laid on a concrete bed leading from the hanger down past the bay's low tide line. We had built a similar system for the WiG parked in our hangar in Sidney, Nova Scotia.

The navy reviewed all its files on Guantanamo Bay and figured those rails were put in about seven years ago. Paul confirmed the construction occurred just after the time a WiG went missing from his earth. Lord Hamilton convinced the Prime Minister to authorize an attempt to capture or render safe what we hoped was the missing WiG from Paul's earth. Logically, if the WiG was sitting in the Cuban dirigible hanger, then the surviving crew folks could be imprisoned nearby. If so, we needed to plan for their rescue as well.

I thought we had a decent chance of accomplishing both objectives, but the timing was going to be tight.

The Bay itself was defended by four, single eight-inch gun emplacements, two on each side of the bay's entrance. The guns were obsolete Swedish Boofers manufactured forty-five years ago. The Cubans bought the guns cheaply twenty-two years ago when the Dual Kingdoms modernized Trondheim's coastal defenses. Cuba had never fired those eight-inch in anger and seldom fired them for practice. The Cubans also had a pair of Customs Service ships stationed at Guantanamo, but each had as her main armament only a single turret-mount-ed, three-inch gun.

Our Guantanamo flotilla had a lot more firepower than that. The flagship was the HMRFCN battlecruiser *Resolute*, formerly the HMS *Sir Humphrey*, originally named after Queen Victoria's Cabinet Secretary of twenty years. She was affectionately known to its RFC crew as the *Pommy Bastard*. She carried six eleven-inch guns as her main arma-ment. The flotilla also included the heavy cruiser *Coventry*, the light cruiser *Garnet*, the destroyers *Greyhound* and *Cheetah*, and the RCCNS destroyer, *City of Charleston*.

The pride of place in the task force was, of course, jointly held by the two marine assault ships, *Hector* and *Paris*, each carrying three companies of RFC Marines. All told, we had approximately twelve hundred marines for the forthcoming festivities.

The navy would have had more, though, but Navy HQ ordered the RFCN light cruiser *Beryl* and the RFCN destroyer *Antelope* detached to ferry ten civilians and four vials of suspicious drugs to Newport. The two ships' absence scarcely affected the local balance of forces.

Our navy brass figured the two capital ships in our southern task force could neutralize the four coastal defense guns in three or four hours, tops, given daylight and weather decent enough to enable navy dirigibles to spot shells for the two capital ships. That approach, though, would provide the Cubans time sufficient to destroy the WiG and kill or move any hostages in the area.

Special Forces, used intelligently and inserted at night, gave us a better chance to grab the WiG and rescue any hostages. Once our commandos knocked out the defending shore guns, our marines would invade at the break of dawn, rapidly overwhelm the local garrison and search the local jails.

That's where Llywelyn and I came into the picture. Have I ever mentioned how much I enjoy rappelling out of dirigibles in the dead of night?

We had four teams of six men each. One team was assigned to take out each specific gun. If you have the blueprints for an artillery piece, then you know exactly where a couple of pounds of thermite should be placed to render the guns inoperable. The light from the thermite doing its stuff might be visible from offshore, but in any event, we would fire signal flares once we got the job done.

Llywelyn and I were leading the six-man team tasked to take out the westernmost eight-inch gun. Once we set the thermite charges, our team would hoof it to the dirigible hanger about a mile away to the north. Well, that was the plan, anyhow. We all knew no plan ever survives intact upon contact with the enemy. Heck, we even got off to an unusual start.

Normally we would have flown directly north-east from Kingston to Guantanamo, but there were some minor storms north of Montego Bay. The mission controller didn't want to take any chances with the weather affecting our mission. He sent us way east towards Haiti first, thus our four dirigibles, my pair leading the other pair by about four miles, approached the targets from the east-south-east.

We were floating about twelve miles out and one mile up in the air from our target when the biggest explosion I had ever imagined ripped the through the sky from the dirigible aerodrome on the bay's western side.

I screamed at the pilot, "Prepare for collision!"

He hit a button. A klaxon sounded. The air-blast hit us not quite a minute later. I had kept my mouth open to equalize pressure; I was glad I did. Our dirigible was shaken like a rat a terrier had just acquired. We somehow stayed in the sky.

"Was that the frack what I think it was?" I screamed at Llywelyn. I hoped he could still hear me.

"I suspect that's what used to be one of our world-hoppers. I guess the bad guys were trying to ditch the evidence. I gather the crew for the world-hopper sort of forgot to tell whoever captured them how to minimize the risk of explosions.

"We can cancel this mission, Hotshot. From the simulations I have seen run for this class of disaster, the overpressure killed outright every-one within a half-mile of the airship hanger and scrambled the brains of everyone within one to three miles. That means anyone who was supposed to be manning those two guns on the bay's western side is dead or dying already."

The western side of the bay was now lit up like Guy Fawkes Night. Gas, electric and other fires were popping up all over the place; heck, fires were starting on the bay's eastern side as well.

I motioned to the co-pilot to hand me the radio mike. "This is *Hotshot One* calling *Broadsword*. *Hotshot One* calling *Broadsword*. Objectives *Gold One* and *Gold Two* have been completely neutralized. Repeat *Hotshot One* says objectives *Gold One* and *Gold Two* have been completely neutralized. Recommend all other *Gold* assets redeploy against Objective *Juno*. Assets targeted against *Sword* are still good to go. Over."

"*Broadsword* here. Message received, *Hotshot One*. *Broadsword* acknowledges. Over and out."

The pilot leaned over, tapped my shoulder and said, "With all those fires, I can't promise I can maneuver close enough to the ground to drop you off. You want me to take you to another target?"

"Belay that. The last thing we want to do is interfere with the folks already assigned against the two eastern targets. All we are going to do is drift right here way up in the air until the brass in charge of this mess tell us what to do. Better pass that on to *Hotshot Two*, though I bet they already figured that out as well. It's better to be safe than sorry."

Thirty minutes later, we got orders to return to Kingston. I never saw any actual combat that night.

Two days after that, for reasons the navy never explained to me, I floated into Guantanamo Bay on the RFCS *Hector*.She had returned to Kingston to pick up additional supplies. Waiting at Guantanamo for the *Hector* to arrive were three companies of marines which were being redeployed to join the cluster-frack that was the liberation of Havana.

Major Stuart greeted me pier-side. He would command the rump battalion of three companies which would remain at Guantanamo. We shook hands instead of saluting; Major Stuart was too good an officer for me to salute him in what was still officially a hot combat zone. Former enlisted scum like me saved that type of rat bastard behavior for those special 2nd Lieutenants we fervently wished would never, ever be promoted to 1st Lieutenant.

"I gather Havana is a real mess, Major Stuart."

Major Stuart nodded. "Sure is, uh... It's a little awkward, seeing as I don't know how to address you. I checked; they made you resign your commission before you left for Havana, and they haven't yet reinstated it. I don't know how they let you board the assault dirigible, but I am glad they did. The scuttlebutt is once the entire sky lit up over eastern Guantanamo, all the brass and top hats had to admit your warnings had been on target all along, so you may be in line for a knighthood."

"Scarbutt calls me '*Hotshot*.' I'm okay with answering to that. Scarbutt also tells me you're a damn fine officer, so you can call me whatever you want. Speaking of the devil, or more accurately, his absence, what's up with him?"

I made some overly dramatic, looking around gestures. Major Stuart picked up on that.

"We left him behind, uh, Hotshot. I guess I can call you Sir John once the knighthood comes through."

"How did that goldbrick weasel out of actual work this time around?"

"Uh, Hotshot, we staged out of Kingston. The statute of limitations had long since expired for most of the charges he had left behind before he enlisted, but the half dozen outstanding charges for which there is no statute of limitations were way beyond my ability to resolve. We couldn't take the risk. I detailed him to look after your various ladies. Now he owes me big time."

I must have looked like the ventriloquist's stupider dummy. "What do you mean, statutes of limitations? Scarbutt always claimed he was an altar boy and a philanthropist."

"Philanthropist? Hah! Have you ever heard of that Robin Hood guy? The original steal from the rich, give to the poor dude? Well, Scarbutt grew up so poor that poverty would have been an upgrade. Connect the dots."

"Yeah, Robin Hood. It rings a bell." I tried to keep from glaring at Major Stuart. It's not like he would have known about my childhood traumas.

"Back to Havana," said Stuart. "After that monster explosion here scared our all politicians silly, the big brass authorized a Havana landing. The RCC sent their lone offshore brigade in immediately, hoping all the firepower offshore would intimidate the Cuban government.

"The bad guys, though, almost immediately started taking hostages and killing them; deaths are into the thousands. There are always a lot of tourists visiting Havana. All the major powers are absolutely appalled at Cuban behavior.

"It has been hard to figure out who was giving orders on the other side, because hardly any senior bad guys we captured were telling us squat. That changed about twelve hours ago. An RFC and two additional RCC brigades and a Gurkha battalion have arrived in Havana, so we now have plenty of combat power. Also, our leadership has authorized the Gurkhas to conduct their field interrogations in their traditional manner."

I know I turned pale upon hearing that. I sensed my testicles tried to crawl up into my throat. Most marines, at least in enlisted-only bull sessions, agreed by far the better alternative to being rigorously interrogated by Gurkhas was to roll to your rifle and blow out your brains.

Major Stuart knew that, too, but he had to appear to be diplomatic. "Their English officers wander off for a spot of tea, and by the time teatime is finished, the senior Havildar usually has all sorts of interesting gossip. It sucks to be in the Cuban army or the Havana constabulary, but after all those dead tourists; nobody who counts has much sympathy for them.

"Also, Hotshot, this was the easiest assault I have ever been in; everyone who was supposed to be raining flaming death in our direction was in a daze or was staring at the fires across the bay. We had hardly any casualties, and it was a piece of cake to disarm the local constabulary and *Guardia Nacional* and find the four other-earth survivors locked up on this side of Guantanamo Bay.

"They were glad to see us; they were especially glad to see Sergeant Llywelyn and his three security folks who spoke their own lingo. Llywelyn's folks said the four survivors were the missing WiG's four-man security team. Those guys were in terrible shape and didn't know where the actual aircrew members were kept."

I was amazed. This had to be the cleanest operation in which I had ever participated.

"Any idea what come's next for me, Major? The navy never told me."

"Yeah, you're supposed to ride herd on Llywelyn. He, his own three guys, and the four guys he rescued will sail back to Kingston with you tomorrow.

"One last thing, Hotshot; Scarbutt tracked me down a couple of hours ago. All your folks back home are safe; Newport and the surrounding area are locked down so tight a mouse couldn't sneak in. The navy always has at least one torpedo attack ship practically parked offshore from Dame Melinda's cottage. The government also leased the house north of Dame Melinda's cottage and moved two platoons of marines onto the grounds. I doubt anything can go wrong."

A Princess of Venus

Llywelyn, his security crews, and I pulled into Newport Navy Base aboard *Emerald* a week after I sailed into Guantanamo. I reflected that after extensive practice and enormous worry, I had not fired a shot in anger, nor had I one fired at me. I was more than a little surprised when one of *Emerald*'s officers told me I would disembark first. Then I saw Brigadier Hamilton, looking tired and grim, waiting on the pier. Her staff car was idling at the shore end of the pier. She walked me to it, slowly; I noticed I had to adjust my pace so as not to leave her behind.

"We are going to the navy hospital, John. Kathy's alive, but she is in a bad way. Astrid will explain once we arrive."

Astrid met us at the hospital entrance. "I had to do an emergency C-section. Kathy is sedated and out to the world. She will remain so for at least a couple of days. She is in a private room. Hell, she has the wing to herself."

She took a deep breath. "There are some things you don't know until you open folks up. Your son was premature and basically brainless. He was dying even as I opened up Kathy's womb. If I hadn't done what I did, then his attempted birth would have killed Kathy."

Astrid looked like she was sick to her stomach. That's how I felt.

"I apologize, John. I can't yet figure out exactly what happened to Kathy's reproductive system after Wendell Honoré drugged her up something awful and then taped his damn electric wires right over her ovaries. Melinda should have shot the bastard a dozen more times. I made an instant decision and performed an emergency hysterectomy."

She stared at the floor for a moment and mumbled. "And some other stuff. The good news is Katherine is fortunate I am a surgical genius, otherwise she would be dead. The bad news is you two will never have any children.

"Katherine will be unavailable for sex of any type for at least a year, depending on my medical judgment. That's if she ever again has any desire for sex. I had to do a lot of emergency cutting under primitive conditions. And you folks are decades away from learning how to synthesize hormones."

I stared blankly at Astrid.

"Damnit, John. I did my best. Hell, I'd be proud to have her as a sister. I'm the only surgeon on your earth who could have saved her life. I'll do everything I can for her, and you, going forward."

Astrid took another deep breath. "Also, John, you need to go talk to Francine. She is serving as part of Kathy's guard detail."

I first checked on Kathy. She was clearly sedated, sleeping, and oblivious to the world. Astrid grabbed me after I stared a moment and led me to Francine. I should have spotted them all before, but I had tunnel vision. All six of original Valkyries were in uniform, armed to the teeth and keeping the riff-raff away from Kathy's wing. Francine took me aside and said, "John, I never wanted it this way. Lady Katherine's like the younger sister I never had."

I thanked her for her concern, a little too abruptly.

Francine ignored the slight and plowed on. "I have to tell you something else, because it's going to be apparent after a while. Astrid already confirmed it. The diaphragm didn't work so well."

She hugged me tightly and kissed me full on the lips. Then she pulled back her lips from mine, smiled, and said, "Daddy."

I sort of went into shock.

One week later, Astrid notified me Kathy was now available for a coherent conversation. I steeled myself and entered her room. She was lying prone, though the bed was slightly angled, and she had a couple of pillows.

"I can't sit up yet, John, and I am still on heavy duty pain killers. The pain flares up if I move in the slightest. The nurses still have to feed me by hand.

"You look worse than I do, John. Don't be worried. Things will work out. What's happening outside this hospital room? All they let me listen to is the classical music station on the radio."

I explained Cuba was now being run by an international coalition. A senior Spanish General had been appointed Interim President of Cuba until the rot had been cleared out. He would maintain martial law with the help of a full brigade of UK Marines and a battalion of Gurkhas, amongst others. The RCC sent their best regular army brigade, the French sent a Legion brigade, and the Spanish contributed two regular army brigades. Heck, the Poles and the Russians volunteered to send troops, but nobody else thought it was a good idea to have their troops on the same island, so their offers were declined, regretfully.

The French and Spanish governments had seized Lavoisier Chemicals and were systematically combing its records. We killed four of the six Lavoisier senior German scientists when we attacked their compounds. One Nazi died in a hail of bullets as he was running into the surf to escape to a waiting speedboat. Two other-earth Germans remain unaccounted for.

I also told Kathy that Paul and the four survivors from the original security guard detail from seven years ago were in London explaining to an international conference of high-ranking diplomats and military what they thought happened. That WiG traveled to the Nazi world to pick up an advance scout, like Paul. The scout had been made and tortured, though, and local bad guys were waiting at the pickup site. They shot off the WiG's wingtip and captured the retrieval crew, except for the WiG's navigator, who committed suicide.

The Caudillo of Cuba, who supposedly reported to a very authoritarian Spain, which had been a German ally in that world's last major war, was frustrated by his lack of upward mobility. He figured if he turned in the WiG, he would probably be disposed of for his efforts, because his superiors were not known for their gratitude. He turned conquistador and to set off for new worlds to conquer. Under torture, the surviving aircrew described the other worlds they knew of.

The Caudillo, not being a complete idiot, and seeing as how he could not fit over twenty of his most loyal folks into the WiG, used stealth over direct military force. He loaded up the WiG with every valuable jewel in Cuba, put a temporary wingtip on the WiG, grabbed six German medical doctors from the Mengele Institute for the Research of Tropical Diseases at gunpoint, took his twelve most loyal bodyguards, and set forth conquistadoring.

The German scientists were more ruthless than was the Caudillo. Within a week of arriving in our Cuba, the Caudillo was a mind controlled robot. A few weeks later, he died of a "heart attack." The scientists decided they were going to develop a master-race paradise on their own. Cuba lacked a reliable supply of genuine Germanic blondes, but otherwise was perfect. The Nazi Germans spoke Spanish, of a sort, and soon determined if they could control Lavoisier, headquartered in Havana for tax purposes, then they could use it to control the Cuban government.

There are always starry-eyed blondes heading for New York, hoping for stardom, so after the Germans achieved surreptitious control over Cuba, they tried to muscle in on the NYC mobs. That attempt ended badly, so they were forced to use scum like Wendell and Delilah as cut-outs to help with experimentation. That was one part of their plan; every field grade and above officer in the Cuba military or constabulary, and many senior politicians became controlled through extremely nasty addictions. The Nazis were on the verge of attempting to expand their control to the RCC when the various navies and marines showed up.

Finally, I told her our world now has to decide how to prepare if a new batch of Nazis showed up.

Kathy listened to me patiently and said. "That's all very interesting, John, but what about you? And us? You seem to have gotten yourself into a bit of a pregnancy pickle with Francine."

I sort of mumbled, "Hummana, hummana," for a while.

Kathy continued. "I had to make a lot of decisions before I talked to you again. Obviously, I had to talk to the Brigadier, Astrid, and Francine. I tried to talk to Melinda, but she is at the stage of her pregnancy where often it's difficult for her to focus. So I also talked with Tiny, my sister Rhonda and Penelope and my mother. Penelope is three months pregnant, by the way. We will need to send a suitable gift. To continue back on topic, I have made several decisions on the assumption I heal adequately."

She smiled at me. "I am a solicitor, so I need to point this out. Since I am no longer fertile, and we have no children, you can always demand a divorce, you know."

I shook my head no.

"Anyway, I asked Francine to describe to me every intimate detail of your trip. She did; she is an honest and forthcoming woman. She promised to show me some of those positions once Astrid gives me medical clearance. I was shocked that some of those were physically possible. Astrid said I should take up yoga, whatever that is, and pole dancing. Francine suggested I take up flamenco, though she hasn't yet explained why."

"It's because Francine is a flaming insane cheap-skate. Did she mention how abbreviated some flamenco costumes can be?"

"I am glad you mentioned money, dear. While we are only modest shareholders in Asclepius, we are now rather wealthy. The French, the Spanish, the Swiss and the entire Empire have now all acknowledged the legitimacy of our vaccine patents. More surprisingly, the Russians and the Austrians did so as well. Madeline estimates I am now worth on the order of six million pounds sterling.

"You are worth well over a million on your own. There are other vaccines in development; I think the one for Scarlett Fever is next, so our wealth will only increase. Also, I am now Lady Commander Katherine Green Smith, retired. The Brigadier convinced the CNO I was on active duty when Wendell inflicted his tortures, so I have been both promoted and medically retired from the navy reserves.

"Now, once I am discharged, we are going to need a security detail of our own, since we will be incredibly wealthy and you will be too busy being a father to your child to provide security for him all by your lonesome. Excuse me, I mean our child. I believe I will be his or her official godmother. We will discuss these issues with the solicitors specializing in such things. I think some original Valkyries may wish to join our security detail; Jennifer can hire new ones to take over security at the priory."

I realized Kathy was trying to work up to a point. For the life of me, though, I couldn't figure out where she was heading. She kept talking over my meditations.

"The Brigadier has explained the series of events you initiated from when we first met Paul literally saved our world. She said I could tell you will be promoted to major in the reserves and your own knighthood is in the mail. That means you are officially in the nobility, Sir Farm Boy, and you know the nobility can do anything they damn well please.

"Astrid has taken full responsibility for what happened; after first blaming our primitive technology, of course. And I was the one who demanded you did exactly what you had to do. John, dear, I know you can keep your pants buttoned when you need to. You don't have to do so for my sake; in fact, I order you not to. Though there are conditions."

Yeah, there are always conditions.

"Melinda often told me how miserable she was growing up as an only child. I was so fortunate to have a twin sister and so many nearby cousins. So Francine's child is going to have a brother or sister or both. Astrid assures me Francine can safely have children for another eight to ten years, at least if Francine remains under Astrid's medical supervision.

"When I am healed sufficiently to return to Philadelphia and establish a real household, Francine will move in with us. Vicki assured me this type of arrangement is considered practically normal over in France. Any other Valkyries who wish to join our staff can do so, though the harem deal does not apply to them, of course."

I think I stared at Kathy in abject disbelief while she talked.

"John, I will not second guess myself. Francine is a decent, honest, and loyal woman. I have liked her since I first saw her riding around, whooping and hollering while riding Melinda's horses. It is difficult to be angry with a woman who has thrice put her own life at risk to protect ours. It is not rational for me to be angry at either you or Francine for following orders to do your duty for King and country.

"Francine had a condition of her own. She described her farm and how they would rent a bull once a year to get the cows pregnant. She said she will not be treated like some damn cow. I agreed completely; that is no way to treat a lady, so you will share your affections with her regularly.

"Francine is in the next room over. You know firsthand how horny pregnant women get, at least early in their pregnancies. Now, go do something nice for Francine. She deserves it if she has to put up with your presence for the rest of her life.

"I have already warned the hospital staff and the other Valkyries to ignore any loud noises. Francine has admitted to being a tiny bit of a screamer."

Kathy said, "Come closer to the bed and kiss me, you idiot. Gently." I did.

"Now shoo. If I don't hear Francine screaming from the next room within thirty minutes or so, I will call up the Brigadier and have you arrested."

I stumbled into the next room. I closed the door behind me. There was a real, oversized bed in the room, instead of a hospital bed. Francine stepped out from behind a changing curtain. She was wearing silver knee-high boots with five-inch heels, silver tights, silver suspenders, and a wisp of a translucent silver loincloth. She wore a short silver cape over her shoulders. She wore no other garments except for a double strand pearl choker around her neck and a gun belt strapped around her waist.

The two holsters held .30-caliber Wembley Lady Defenders semi-automatics. She held a single rose between her teeth. She removed the gun belt and took the rose out of her mouth.

"Lady Katherine told me about Zeera, Queen of the Venusian Airship Pirates. She instructed Melinda's seamstresses and local merchants to make a realistic costume, but jeweler in Newport had ever heard of necklaces made from Spican fire gems. Also, Marcus told me his folks didn't bring any ray-guns with them. He probably lied; I think he lies a lot, but I can't prove any differently and so I had to make do with the Wembleys. Ah, hell, farm boy, had I known about your taste in teenage literature, I never would have picked you to shack up with during that Havana job.

"I must be crazy for signing up as your concubine, except you are the most honorable man with whom I have ever shared a bed and our kid-to-be deserves to have an on-call father. Also, you and Lady Katherine are the best damn people I ever met. And I can't believe I think that of you, even after Lady Katherine told me in gory detail about each and every one of your many flaws."

I shook my head to see if I was dreaming. I wasn't, but I was still speechless.

Francine continued. "So anyhow, Lady Katherine swiped your very own dog-eared copy of '*Captain Majestic versus the Love Slaves of Venus*' when you two last visited your Uncle Max. She had been hoping to pick up some ideas from it; she suggested I do the same thing. Tiny brought it over yesterday morning from Kathy's room at Melinda's cottage, and I read through it immediately. I never imagined anyone could write crap like that.

Francine paused. "Actually, my wearing this getup is almost entirely Lady Katherine's idea. I sort of got swept up in the proceedings; though it's not like I got to have much of a vote. I will give you another day or two to become used to the idea, but you have to be the one to tell Lady Katherine *you* bailed on *me* tonight. She's expecting a full report from me in the morning and I'm sure not going to lie to her; her bullshit meter is too damn good."

That cured my temporary laryngitis. "Are you insane, woman? If Kathy has put that much thought into this, I'm doomed. She would feed me to the sharks."

"What I figured, Jarhead. Also, you say one word about my boobs not being as big as the real Queen Zeera's or if I somehow sense you find this costume the slightest bit amusing, then I will shove this long stemmed rose so far up your butt you will think it's a tonsil massager."

I think I somehow survived the subsequent events; I remember waking up alone the next morning in the hospital room because the phone was ringing. It was a call from my Uncle Max. He had somehow tracked me down. He wanted me to go to Montreal with him. I went to Kathy's room to see if she thought that was okay.

A senior nurse was feeding Kathy breakfast. I did a double take, since I saw two Kathy's. I still must have been loony. Both of them ignored me while Francine waved around a long stemmed rose in a variety of complicated maneuvers. She still wearing her not terribly modest Queen Zeera costume and was apparently pantomiming the parts of last night's performance I had no memory of and suspected never happened.

Duplicate Kathy and the nurse were alternately grinning and laughing like hyenas. Kathy just smiled. My sluggish brain then informed me Duplicate Kathy was Kathy's twin sister Rhonda, who I hadn't seen in half a year. Rhonda must have found a babysitter.

Kathy interrupted Francine's choreography. "Francine, I think you should phone Mrs. O'Shaughnessy and see if she can spare Elizabet to come to the hospital to remember all this for us."

Kathy paused; she clearly was far from strong. "I fear my memory is not fully recovered and there a lot of interesting things I need to remember so I can try them out when I am healthy. If Bridget wants to come over as well, that's perfectly fine, too. She might get a kick out of meeting Queen Zeera. I know she always enjoys hearing about John.

"John, did you have something important to say, or are you going to be tedious? You are interrupting an important girls' chat and we haven't begun to get to the good parts."

I decided then and there I was far safer going to Montreal with my Uncle Max than I was hanging around demonstrably deranged women. It was time to man up and start making my own decisions again.

I said, "Hello, Rhonda, it's good to see you again. Kathy, Francine; I have nothing to say worth interrupting your important conversation."

I left the room and waited until the nurse left and the conversation died down. I steeled myself to go back in and ask Kathy and Francine if I had permission to go to Montreal. I might have been a fearless Major in the marine reserves, a knight of the realm-to-be, and a Wolfe-Montcalm medal bearer, but I wasn't insane.

I walked back into the room. Francine had put on a robe. She grinned at me and said, "See you this afternoon, Hotshot. Rhonda and I are heading off; first we go to my room so I can change out of this ridiculous outfit and then we are going to track down some breakfast. She is also going to give me a few pointers about motherhood."

Rhonda smiled at me, "You're looking good John, if a little tired."

Rhonda glanced back at Kathy and then spoke more softly. "I talked with mom; you just missed her. She left about an hour ago to catch some sleep. She needs it.

"Anyhow, Sally has seen more babies born than I can count. Sally also talked to Astrid. Mom agreed Astrid did what Astrid had to do. All of us have to go on from here."

They left; Kathy was now speaking on the phone. She spoke a while longer. She finished, turned towards me and said, "Real life is messy. I know the look. Why am I going to be upset this time?"

I explained about my uncle, but also how I wasn't ever going to leave her side.

Kathy answered, "Your planned trip with your Uncle Max may be providential. Madeline has informed me some other stuff has come up. We girls have a lot to talk about first, though. I will let you know within the week. In the meantime, start working out again, weights, running laps, not merely exercising with Francine. Nurse says you can visit briefly every day. I will discuss Montreal with you as soon as I am able."

Get Thee to a Nunnery

Kathy called six days later and told me to meet her at the Priory for an important meeting. Astrid had Kathy moved to a Priory recovery room where she got twenty-four seven oversight from the Sisters of Healing. I stayed at Melinda's cottage with Francine, who was demanding my affections constantly. Francine had left for the Priory earlier that morning to take advantage of its indoor pool.

Jennifer met me at the Priory gate. She told me not to stare too much when we entered the huge indoor pool area.

I looked at Jennifer curiously. We got to the indoor pool area and I immediately realized I was probably the only man on the grounds. The six ladies swimming laps were wearing only the traditional alternate earth bathing costume, which was to say, they were bare-assed naked, except for their bathing caps and swim goggles. I stopped, stared and started up again after Jennifer gave me an elbow hard to my ribs. She led me towards a large table at the far side of the pool.

I evaluated the group sitting around the table. I walked up to it, nevertheless. Had I been a lesser man, I would have fled in panic.

"Hello Brigadier, Bridget, Astrid, and beloved wife Kathy. Glynda, it's always a pleasure. Mary, Theodora, I see you are taking care of Kathy. How long has she been able to sit up?"

Astrid broke in. "We eased her into her wheelchair yesterday; it's where she will be in three months that counts, though."

Suddenly, I realized that Brigadier Hamilton was also using a wheelchair. I'm sure I looked confused. Well, I'm good at that.

Astrid continued, "Mary, go ask Francine and Elizabet to join us."

Mary did. Francine and Elizabet climbed out of the pool at the far
side, toweled off, and put on fluffy robes. Then the three of them walked
over.

The Brigadier told Jennifer to take Mary and Theodora and visit the
other end of the pool. They left.

The brigadier spoke. "Astrid has agreed all of our forthcoming discussions will be considered by her to be confidential, at least in the doc-
tor-patient sense. Four days ago, Astrid diagnosed me with inoperable
and inevitably fatal pancreatic cancer. She believes I will be dead or on
the verge of death no later than three months from now.

"My impending untimely death has consequences for all of you. First,
upon my recommendation, Prince Albert has asked Lady Katherine to
be recalled to the active rolls in order to assume my primary duties."

"I am sorry, Brigadier; Isn't Kathy a little young for that? I thought
Colonel what's her name, Jillian Brown, was going to inherit."

"Oh, Jillian will take over the actual army legal duties regarding the
women's reserve, but she can't possibly take over my primary duties. On
paper, Katherine will be Jillian's executive officer. Katherine will take
over my other, more important obligations."

Bridget interrupted. "This nasty old battle-ax, who has bested me
about one-third of the infrequent occasions when we have been at cross
purposes, is the Coordinator of Intelligence Activities for the RFC. You
will not find the position listed in any description of our over-staffed,
overpaid and under-worked bureaucracy, but it has existed ever since
General Benedict Arnold established it during a war with Spain.

"Amazingly, it is the one position in the government which tradition-
ally has been filled by a woman; usually by a prominent society woman
of independent means. The first lady to serve in this capacity was one
of Melinda's distant cousins, Elizabeth Schuyler Andre."

I remembered then that both Melinda and her ex-fiancé had
Schuylers in their family trees. Heck, Melinda's family tree was basically
an RFC history book.

Bridget continued. "After Colonel Sir John Andre died of some tropical disease while serving on General Washington's staff during the

Florida Campaign of 1785, General Arnold asked Andre's widow, Lady Elizabeth Schuyler Andre, if she would help the war effort. Lady Elizabeth agreed and continued to do so after that war ended.

"She spent the subsequent thirty years fluttering through society, meeting and corresponding and gossiping with ultra-important people. You might be surprised how much the wives of foreign dignitaries know about their husbands' official duties. The widow Andre reported everything she learned to senior army officials.

"Most of Lady Elizabeth's successors pretended to be total bubbleheads, but no one would have believed that of Madeline. That bit of history went by the wayside some twenty-three years ago. You may have observed how promptly Madeline's phone calls are returned when she wishes to speak to some admiral or general who outranks her in the military lists. Have you observed how easily she gets in contact with the Governor General and how casually she has thrown his name around?"

"For whom do you actually work, Brigadier?" I interrupted.

"I report, as will Colonel Dame Katherine Green, to the Governor General, our head of state. I consult with the Prime Minister, our head of government. I exist to provide them recommendations, independent from those offered by our sometimes parochial intelligence bureaucracies."

Bridget turned to Madeline, "Damn dear, I am going to miss you and our occasional skirmishes. It's going to be tough to go semi-legit. Does Heather know yet?"

"Heather?" I asked. "Am I missing something or someone?"

The Brigadier gave me one of her rare smiles. "Heather is my younger sister. She has two sons, one daughter and seven grandchildren. Bridget, here, was Heather's roommate for two years at good old Bala Cynwyd. I have known Bridget the better part of my life, though our paths diverged shortly after Bridget got married.

"I will tell Heather about my imminent passing soon, after I have settled my work affairs. I would prefer to turn over to Kathy all my unacknowledged responsibilities within a matter of weeks, depending on her own medical progress. Then Kathy and Glynda can have the pleasure of dealing with Bridget and all of her wheels-within-wheels schemes."

Something rang mental a bell. Ding dong, ding dong.

"Colonel Dame Kathy Green. Her last name is Smith."

"Not for a while, I'm afraid. Also, your knighthood is on hold, as is your promotion to major. I believe you will be estranged from Kathy for a bit for the safety of the realm. We still have two nasty Nazis to apprehend. Our armies lost track of them somehow. Well, the Havana area of operations in our intervention was utterly chaotic.

"If you are socially prominent, you can't go gutter crawling with your uncle to search for the two remaining German doctors, not and be believable anyway. You will pretend to be a philandering pig and will once again consort with those known criminals, Ratso and Ferret.

"I had them run in on sort of phony bigamy charges, just to keep track of them. My office will spring them once they agree to accompany you. Senior Sergeant Llywelyn will also join your party."

"Which Germans are we talking about? I haven't tried to keep track of who got caught or killed and nobody has told me who was still missing."

"Brunhilde, last name unknown; also known as Eva Braun. The other German, possibly her husband, went by the name of Johann Schmidt."

"Yeah, right! Pull the other one. Johann Schmidt. That's too stupid an alias to fool anyone."

My insightful comment elicited a host of laughs and giggles. I wondered why.

Bridget said, "Elizabet, take off your robe and pose for John."

"She really doesn't have to."

I got shushed by the women. Elizabet dropped her robe and took off her bathing cap. Naked, she was stunning, surprisingly fit, and had a much better figure than Francine. Certainly she had a more prominent set of lungs. When she took off her bathing cap and shook out her long, light brown hair, it fell down well past her shoulders; I had never seen her wear her hair in any way other than a hideously tight bun.

Kathy spoke first. "Elizabet, you're lovely. How could your wardrobe possibly have hidden your looks so thoroughly? And conceal your vast tracts of real estate, so to speak, as well?"

Elizabet answered, "My breasts are approximately the same size as yours, Lady Katherine. If you remember, I saw you in your hospital gown; such garments are not designed for concealment.

"To answer your question, though, Mrs. O'Shaughnessy has access to the best wardrobe designers and seamstresses. Even so, it was always quite uncomfortable walking around with my breasts bound so tightly. I also loathed wearing all of those plain colored, long-sleeve, ankle-length dresses, and eschewing makeup, but such camouflage was essential to keep me unnoticed in the background.

"I have agreed to work first for the Brigadier and then work for Dame Katherine upon the change of command. Mrs. O'Shaughnessy had a premonition several months back, so I will continue to pretend to be Suzie Shamrock for perhaps the next several months."

I was still processing Elizabet's words when she turned to me.

"I will be your companion for the forthcoming trip, John. You come highly recommend by Francine, if unintentionally so, and I have seen with my own eyes how Dame Katherine adores you. Mrs. O'Shaughnessy also thinks highly of you, John, for your code of honor.

"You respect her, but you do not fear her, and you have been as honest and forthcoming as you could; given, of course, your other obligations. I am uniquely qualified to evaluate the depths of human depravity; you are remarkable free of it. Besides, in your case, the precedent has already been set."

Bridget interrupted. "Madeline and I cut a deal, John. It's a question of Irish Catholic legitimacy. Elizabet and I want RFC officialdom to treat the Irish Catholics at least as well as they treat our Empire's German Catholics. They are generally respected because our Imperial family is related to eighty percent of the Catholic monarchs in the dozens of German Catholic mini-states. They even tolerate ethnic Italians, well, by and large.

"It's just the Saxon scum, sorry Madeline, never got over that damn bloody, bloody Irish revolt. Madeline has assured me His Imperial Highness will recognize all four of my daughters for their charitable works and take other steps to ameliorate the semi-official oppression of the Irish. However, we first must deal with the two remaining Nazis."

Bridget grimaced. "Well, His Highness may not recognize his own reflection in a mirror, but Madeline has assured me Prince Albert will make all this happen. If need be, recalcitrant elements within the Empire bureaucracy will be brought to heal. If push comes to shove, Sir Rupert will be made the RFC Cabinet Secretary. Madeline owns him now; she will give his leash to Dame Katherine.

"Until the Empire has internal peace with its Irish Catholic minority, some of us risk becoming pawns in the event of a broader cross world incursion. Indeed, I fear such may already have happened.

"I wield great influence among the RFC's Irish Catholic community's more pragmatic elements. Once the English dial back on the discrimination against the Irish, we will forego our more illegal activities and help Imperial Intelligence surveil for incursions from other earths. I promised Madeline we would strive to be neither more venal nor more criminal than the average politician or civil servant."

Madeline snorted. "At least it's a start."

Bridget smiled and continued, "I am involved because I sense something is ongoing with the Fenians, though I have only limited sources within their organizations. It's hard to infiltrate hereditary secret societies. Your Uncle Max must have mentioned they control much of the criminal underworld in Buffalo, Rochester, Toronto, and to a lesser extent, Montreal.

"The Fenians have always believed in violent revolution as a method to establish a free Irish state. They have, on occasions, worked with the French separatists of Quebec Province. If those two remaining Nazis are going to renew their malevolent schemes anywhere in North America, my gut tells me they are working with one or both organizations. Elizabet will accompany you, in part, because she knows everything I know about these oft-time rival, groups.

"Kathy plans to accept Madeline's position out of a sense of duty. Madeline has refused to confirm my analysis, but I judge Kathy and Melinda were the odds-on choices to succeed Madeline, as they have had the most interactions with our other-earth visitors. The choice was simplified when Melinda turned Madeline down cold; Melinda stated explicitly she will be focused on child-rearing for the next decade, so that left Kathy."

Brigadier Hamilton grunted, but was otherwise silent. Bridget continued.

Bridget continued. "Kathy is young, but she knows how the underbelly of our society works. She also has the backbone required to take over for Madeline, act decisively, and accept the consequences of her actions.

Bridget looked at Kathy. "Don't deny it, girl. I investigated the circumstances of the late Sidney Parker's death. That was nice shooting, Katherine."

Kathy sat serenely, not reacting to Bridget's unstated, but totally accurate, insinuation.

"Finally, I have army veterans in my employ. Kathy is a legend among and has the respect of the army's non-commissioned officer corps for her defense and acquittal of MSgt Mutton. These attributes will be useful, as many problems will fall into Kathy's lap shortly. I believe Kathy's job will be much easier and more productive if she has Elizabet at her side to remember and integrate the minutest bit of information. I, however, will insist we neutralize the Fenians before she assists Kathy. To do that, I must once again send Elizabet into the field with you."

I groaned. "You really insist on forcing me to do this?"

"You said yourself, in the wake of the attack on my estate, John, you owed me a favor. Fine, so be it; I'm calling in the nut. I think it might be wise for you to assist your Uncle Max; his desire to travel to Montreal to look for whoever hired the would-be assassin may be providential. No one who knows of him would suspect your Uncle Max of working with the government. Also, in the event he works with us, I will take steps to see to the complete safety of your Aunt Maude."

I looked down at Kathy. She radiated calmness. I couldn't figure that out. I sure as heck didn't feel calm. I turned to Madeline.

"Sorry, Madeline; no can do. I am sure the RFC Constabulary already has informers inside the Fenians, so there's no real legitimate, operational need for Elizabeth to put herself in danger again. I sure don't plan to acquire yet another mistress. Besides, it's probably a snipe hunt; the missing Nazis have an entire world in which to disappear."

Madeline glared up at me. "Think, John. The WiG is housed in a specially adapted airship hanger in Sydney, Nova Scotia; we lack a suitable, alternative shelter. We have reinforced its guard detail, but the missing Germans may have, as yet unrevealed, capabilities. We need to disrupt their plans before they attempt their strike."

"Sure, Madeline; now a Canada focus makes sense. The Nazis probably will try to work with the Fenians or French separatists. You still don't need me to help disrupt that cooperation, though. You have the entire RFC Constabulary."

Madeline shook her head. "Ethically, you're right, John, but I don't care. This is straight-up, put on your big-boy pants, in-your-face politics. Suck it up, farm-boy.

"John, I once pled with the military authorities to have your young worthless ass thrown into the brig until the next ice age. I was convinced you had subtly instigated the entire fight in *The Pickled Herring* for your own amusement. They said they could do better than throw you in the brig; they would ensure you were heroically killed off instead. You were better than they thought and you didn't get yourself killed. Hell, you got yourself a medal and a promotion.

"Nevertheless, a pair of otherwise innocent army privates spent an unnecessary month in the brig because of you. I pled, unofficially and in chambers, to spare them for what I suspected were your deliberate provocations. Perhaps you were merely young and stupid then. I can now sometimes persuade myself you have matured, at least to an extent. I believe you owe your country for your fomenting the fight which resulted in those army privates being screwed by the system."

"That was a long time ago, Brigadier. I have more than paid off any obligations I might have incurred regarding that episode."

"There is always the *Sozzled Sturgeon*, John. That extradition request has never been rescinded."

"Even you wouldn't stoop that low, Brigadier."

"Of course I would, John; I have often done far worse. Elizabet has her reasons, reasons which I consider valid. Bridget has persuaded me, given Elizabet's unique abilities and connections, Elizabet can never be intimately involved with anyone who would be tempted to manipulate or blackmail her. Besides, for some reason, Elizabet trusts and admires you.

"I can't imagine why she feels that way; not after I told her about your Danish tavern brawl. And yes, don't ask. You are still banned from returning to Copenhagen."

"I hadn't planned on it, Brigadier. I think the *Pie-Eyed Puffin* management even put a bounty on my head, though honestly it was that rat scum Scarbutt who started the fight and left me holding the bag."

I looked all around. I realized from the ladies' facial expressions that they didn't believe me or they didn't care. I turned back to Kathy. She shook her head. "Madeline has a few more words to say, John. Listen to her carefully. Then decide."

I faced the Brigadier.

"John, I have asked Katherine to take over for me, rather than choosing someone older and more experienced, for two reasons. I believe Bridget and Elizabet's enthusiastic cooperation is critical in improving our chances of tracking down the remaining two Nazi doctors. Subsequently, Bridget and Elizabet will work with Kathy; they may not work with anyone else.

"Also, both Penelope Cabot and Dame Melinda love Kathy like a sister, so she, through them, has access sufficient to interact with our most senior aristocracy."

The Brigadier frowned.

"Upon recent reflection, I realized I gradually have been losing my access among the social elite. I was not conscious of this at first, perhaps understandably, as I have concentrated on foreign threats these past decades. It was not my remit to involve myself in domestic affairs; other than counter-espionage, of course.

"I worry this indicates a larger, perhaps societal, problem. I think too many of our aristocracy may be far more corrupt and compromised than has been the case, historically. I am worried the rot goes deeper than I ever imagined. It's speculation; I have no actual proof. Bridget, for reasons of her own, feels similarly.

I looked at her, though I couldn't bring myself to speak. Madeline kept talking.

"I dare not entrust my duties to a self-promoting functionary. I know it will be difficult for Katherine to grow into my job, but it will not be impossible. Consider; Henry V was only a bit older than Katherine is now when he won the Battle of Agincourt. Lady Elizabeth Schuyler Andre was only twenty-eight years old when she became the first such lady to accept the position which I now fill."

Madeline paused; then grimaced. She didn't look at all well. She paused again, for much longer. She took a couple of deep breaths. Her voice weakened some.

"I shared my concerns with Prince Albert over the secure telephone three days ago. His Royal Highness regrets the need to ask any of his brother's subjects to make such personal sacrifices. He concurred with my reasoning, however.

"He offered Katherine her Colonelcy, effective immediately upon acceptance of this offer, followed by promotion to Brigadier in two years. Lady Katherine will also become Dame Katherine when she pins on Brigadier. These promotions are conditional on the two of you accepting the deal. Yes, it's a shameless bribe, but it's the best his Royal Highness could do on the spur of the moment. Now you, Katherine, and to an extent, Francine, are once again going to make unpleasant choices to help save the world."

Kathy looked up at me from her wheelchair. "Madeline can be callous in how she calls in her markers, John, but she has convinced me I may be the best person to fill her shoes. Sometimes, dear, the personal problems of three people like Francine, you and me, don't count for a hill of frijoles.

"When you left for Cuba, I viewed the extant Delilah Honoré flickers and read as many of Eduardo's experimental notes as I could stomach. They were all created as part and parcel of a series of demented experiments designed by proponents of utter evil. I, at the least, owe my sister Rhonda and her children my best efforts to fight existential evil. You have the same obligation to your own nieces and nephews and your child-to-be with Francine."

"Except for my niece, Cheryl. She's too much of a pill. You recall our wedding reception, don't you, Kathy?"

"She was going through puberty, John. It's tougher for girls. Stop your whining and trying to change the subject, John. Just listen. While I regret Elizabet's choice of a man, her reasoning is impeccable. She at least showed excellent judgment and I believe, for our earth's sake, I cannot deny her."

I turned to Francine. "Did they give you a vote, Francine?"

She shook her head no. "Nah, it just proves the old army adage, 'No good deed goes unpunished.' I said too many nice things about you, John, while I was down in Havana. Well, I sure learned my lesson."

She grinned. "From now on I am going to trash talk you worse than Scarbutt does. Besides, you already heard from these important ladies. It's power politics, John, and I'm a jumped-up staff sergeant. It's not my department and it's well above my paygrade. Sometimes you have to salute and obey. Anyhow, I don't want our children growing up in a world controlled by those monsters, either."

Kathy raised her voice enough to cut through the noise. "John, a part of me which is repelled at the thought of sharing you with yet another woman, even temporarily. Another part of me burns to extract my revenge from those Nazi savages. And it's more than personal revenge.

"I read the preliminary summaries of the military interrogations teams' interviews with survivors of some of the Nazi doctors' other experiments. Our world faces mortal risk unless we kill or capture them.

We must leave no stone unturned in our attempt to find the two missing Nazi doctors. Just make sure you are there for me when I am healed."

My eyes opened wide in amazement. I was so hosed. Elizabet, still naked, silently took my hand and pulled me towards the nearest doorway and the fate which awaited me. Meanwhile, the four naked Sisters of Healing paused amid swimming their laps and started whooping and whistling. Mary, Theodora and Jennifer did the same from the far side of the pool.

Scarbutt would never believe this. Not that I would ever tell him, but I was sure as heck Jennifer would. If Jules ever found out about my predicament, I would never hear the end of it; maybe I shouldn't have ribbed him so much about Astrid.

Still, the more I thought of it, the more convinced I was the entire world needed to know it was actually controlled by a secret cabal of crazy, ruthless women, most of whom graduated from the same darn girl's school outside Philadelphia. I decided to write a pseudonymous letter of warning to the RFC Royal Marine Corps newspaper of record, *The Jarhead Journal*.

"Dear *Jarhead Journal Forum*: You never are going to believe this, but there I was, surrounded by horny naked ladies, criminal ladies, and the spy ladies who actually control every aspect of our government via hidden levers, when suddenly... "

Poutine: It's What's for Breakfast

Montreal, Province of Quebec, Royal Federated Colonies

I woke up exhausted. It's a hazard of ever having been in the corps. Even when you stay up late at night, almost every morning at the same darn time around zero dark thirty, the body is convinced reveille is only moments away and you need to get your posterior up and out of bed.

Not that I was going anywhere this morning; Montreal was snowed in and it would be another two days, at least, before the tracks would be cleared and we could continue to Quebec. Madeline hadn't believed the Fenians had much of an organization here, but this was where my Uncle Max wished to begin his own researches. Now we were trapped by the unexpectedly nasty weather.

I gently disentangled myself from the grasp of my still sleeping and recently acquired second mistress, Suzie Shamrock, aka Elizabet O'Conner, aka Miss Elizabet O'Shaughnessy. Had I known Bridget O'Shaughnessy, the East Coast Irish Mobs' Dowager Empress, had formally, but covertly, adopted Elizabet over a decade ago, I might never have let myself be blackmailed into shacking up with Elizabet.

Elizabet had continued her impersonation of Suzie Shamrock for operational reasons. The actual Suzie, originally from Staten Island, was a top-of-the-line prostitute for the Queens, New York, Fraternal Organization. Two of my travel companions, Ratso and Ferret, even believed Elizabet was Suzie, as we had never told them otherwise.

First things first; I started making coffee using the cheap coffee-brewing machine sitting on the hotel room sideboard. I headed for the toilet. Next, I wiped down my teeth with some dental cream to remove my overnight breath. Finally, I ate a couple of crackers to mask the nasty dental cream taste. You do all that before you can drink coffee. Coffee is essential.

Greeks lied, you know. Prometheus was not slabbed and spread-eagled on that rock to have his liver munched every morning because he stole the secret of fire; he got lashed to that boulder to prevent humans from discovering coffee. Eventually Hercules came to rescue him and Prometheus unbound would discover the secret of the magic beans.

I argue coffee, not fire nor indoor plumbing, is the true foundation of modern civilization. I had a lot of arguments with my Uncle Max about this topic; he claimed the foundation of civilization is beer. We eventually agreed it had to be some type of breakfast drink, but he had insisted on the caveat beer was not just for breakfast anymore.

I splashed some more cold water on my face to shock my brain into awareness; I convinced myself the coffee machine had bleeped or sputtered, which probably indicated something important. I made one more face swipe with the hand towel and by that time, the coffee, such as it was, was ready. It was vile, but it would do for a jumpstart. I slugged it down and began exercising.

The carpet on the hotel room floor was thin, though it was thick enough to let me do stretches and sit-ups and such. After exercising for an hour, I would wake up Elizabet and see if she was ready for some breakfast. My Uncle Max, Senior Sergeant Llywelyn and the two thugs from Ft. Pitt City, Ratso Jimmy and Ferret Phil, should be waiting for us in the dining room. I would then try to pretend I didn't know any of them.

I had discovered I could wrap a towel around my ankles and hook my ankles under the clothes dresser and thus could do my left elbow to right knee and vice versa sit-ups. I didn't worry about hitting my head on the clothes dresser because I had done three tours in the marines and everyone I knew claimed my skull was too thick to worry about injuring it. After sit-ups, I started making with planks and push-ups and stretches.

I must have grunted too loudly; Elizabet got up and headed for the toilet. She emerged and saw the coffee. "How can you drink that vile stuff, John? I tried it yesterday and I will be stuck with that awful memory for the rest of my days."

Elizabet had a point about the coffee's quality. She also had a completely photographic memory, so I doubted she was exaggerating about the bad taste sticking with her. It was a good thing for her she had never been in the navy or marines; shipboard coffee was way worse.

"It's still dark outside; the dining room won't be open for breakfast for another fifty minutes. Why do you always wake up so early, John? I know I didn't let you sleep much sleep last night. You are quite remarkable, you know. Everything Dame Katherine and Francine said about you was correct. If anything, Dame Katherine makes too much of your very minor flaws."

"What flaws? I mean, other than being too humble."

"We have all learned to ignore your so-called sense of humor, John. Anyway, Francine says your only two real flaws are you are not flexible enough and you can't hold your liquor. Of course, she still worships you. I am glad you are working on your stretches and such. Doctor Astrid told me you need to do more stretching relative to pushing weights. She said if you keep trying to compete with Joseph Sammartino by pushing heavy weights, your spine will be locked up by the time you're fifty."

I processed what she said earlier. "Suzie," I whispered, "*Ix-nay on-yay athy-Kay*." I gestured the walls have ears. Here, I was probably being paranoid; not that there is anything wrong with that.

This hotel had been vetted by Brigadier Madeline Hamilton, the chief of the Royal Federated Colonies Army Reserve Women's Judge Advocate Corps and the secret Coordinator of RFC Intelligence Activities. Her staff had pulled the constabulary records of every non-fleabag hotel in Montreal. They found no evidence to suggest this hotel indulged in such listening activities, but it is always good to practice operational security.

Elizabet smiled at me; she was still naked as she didn't wear clothes in bed. "The room is somewhat cold, John. Be a dear and crawl back into bed with me. My feet got a little frozen just now, so I will first warm them up using the small of your back. Then you can warm up the rest of me. We can be a few minutes late for breakfast."

I vowed aloud and at length if I ever met His Royal Highness in person I was going to give him an earful for approving this scheme into which I got blackmailed into agreeing; protocol to be damned. I crawled back into bed. Elizabet's feet were ice cold.

My whole body shuddered, involuntarily. "Why me, Suzie? Really, why did you choose me?"

"Honestly, John? It wasn't my idea, and I got caught up in this rather suddenly. I learned, only recently, that I am destined to become a politician of sorts. Henceforth, John, political necessities will influence many of my formerly private decisions. All I can say at this time is that my options were constrained."

She sighed, noticeably. "Had you asked your question two weeks ago, and had everyone involved been working with a clean sheet of paper, on a personal level, I might have chosen Joseph. Melinda can be insufferably smug, sometimes, the way she has bragged about his sexual prowess. Joseph is quite the devout Catholic, though, which means as things stand, he would have refused me as a matter of principle."

"Religious principles, Suzie? Then what are you doing here?"

"At the moment, I am trying desperately to warm my frozen feet. You, however, keep arching your back, so stop that immediately.

"Returning to Joseph; there is no earthly reason for him to be stumbling around Quebec Province during a miserable early winter. Moreover, suicide is a mortal sin; well obviously, but it is also irredeemable.

"Melinda would have had me killed the moment I so much as batted an eyelash at Joseph. While Melinda respects my mother, Melinda is not afraid of her. Thus, had I provoked Melinda, it would have been no less suicidal than had I stepped off of a cliff."

"You're kidding me, right? I mean, Melinda wouldn't have you killed because you made goo-goo eyes at Tiny. Anyway, she can't have any real reason to be all that possessive of the over-muscled goof; she has never once called Tiny a Lothario while in my presence."

Elizabet snorted. "John, please; use your skull for something besides polishing the clothes dresser. Ladies do not gossip in the presence of other ladies' menfolk. On those rare occasions we deign to indulge in gossip, we keep those conversations to ourselves. Trust me, though. Melinda is potentially one of the most dangerous women on earth.

"I have a doctorate in history; I can read the signs. Melinda intends to start a dynasty, of sorts, of her own, and she will be its founding empress. She does not plan to let anyone or anything block her way.

"You, however, need to be here now; you need my help in the short-term and you need my mother's help in the long-term. Lady Katherine understands this. Francine accepts this. Don't blame either of them; neither is at fault. My decision to choose you was guided, in part, by informed consensus."

I was shocked. I sat up in bed. Elizabet started unbuttoning my pajama top buttons.

"Say what? I thought you said ladies rarely gossip; it sounds to me like every dame on the East Coast got involved in yacking about my personal life."

"Don't be thick, John. We didn't gossip, we merely discussed a few of your intimate foibles over the course of a week. I took part, obviously, but otherwise the select committee consisted solely of Kathy, Francine, Jennifer, Bridget, Melinda, Astrid, Ruth and Madeline. Oh, and Nurse Mary and Nurse Theodora assisted, for medical reasons. I suspect they shared our discussions with all the novices for training purposes. And of course we ran our choice and our reasons past Barbara and Penelope, to make sure we hadn't missed anything. I hadn't met them before. They are both utterly delightful.

"Well, I also had to consult with Slab and Wires, and some of their senior associates in the three New York City Fraternal Organizations and the Boston Mob. I am supposed to tell you that you have will brief, though painful, regrets if you treat me less than respectfully, but they didn't believe that is going to be an issue. We also had to inform Sally and Rhonda because if Sally thought you were cheating on her daughter again, other than for reasons of state, she would poison you while you slept.

"So the true story leading up to our early winter frolic is known only to a select handful of ladies and Slab and Wires and several of their colleagues. All of them are known for their total discretion. I am sure our analysis of your faults and virtues couldn't be safer if it was locked up in the Tower with the crown jewels."

I shook my head in disbelief. I contemplated running away to join the Foreign Legion. I figured that flock of harpies would track me down, anyway. I was certain Slab and Wires could. Instead, I asked, "Did you actually say you had a doctorate, Elizabet?"

"Yes. It's from Heidelberg. And no, I don't have any dueling scars to prove it. I will not use edged weapons or firearms to shed the blood of others. If the need arises, I plan to hand to you one or both of the two .25-caliber semiautomatics which Mother forced upon me for this trip."

Now I knew she was insane. I told her so. She calmly shook her head no.

"John, I am not defenseless. I always carry either a collapsible baton or, if my purse is sufficiently large, a custom collapsible quarterstaff. Slab has been training me on the quarterstaff since I was twelve years old.

"And regarding your initial question, I wrote my dissertation on the economic and cultural foundations of military power. I used academic-style German, about two sentences to every three printed pages, so our English overlords would not be tempted to translate it and use my insights to further oppress the Irish. Now, that's quite enough talk; my feet have warmed. You can now warm up the rest of me."

An hour later, Elizabet and I went down to breakfast. Elizabet looking every bit a call girl trying to half-ass disguise herself as a respectable woman. I didn't understand how she achieved that look, even though I watched her get dressed.

It wasn't a great a dining room under normal circumstances, much less after a blizzard. The hotel was barely one step up from mediocre, so it was exactly the type of place my Uncle Max, Ratso and Ferret would use.

We entered the dining area and the two pairs of moderately respectable matrons laying into their breakfast poutine all glanced up from their tables at Elizabet and all shuddered in disgust. Then they all somehow rearranged their seats so they would not have to look at Elizabet.

Our waiter arrived; Elizabet told him the poutine looked disgusting. I figured she was playing her Suzie Shamrock persona to the hilt. "Don't you have something healthy and tasty, like scrapple?"

The waiter looked nauseated in turn. Upon hearing there was no scrapple to be had, Elizabet ordered a fruit dish, a small cheese omelet, some wheat toast, and lots of coffee. Fruit was way out of season, so I was going to be paying through the nose. Oh well, that's the price of staying in cover.

Elizabet spoke using a nasal Staten Island, lower class Irish Catholic accent, which was dead on. Like I mentioned earlier, she not only had a photographic memory but owned a phonographic ear as well. I stuck with bacon, eggs, pancakes and more coffee. At least the maple syrup was acceptable. Too late, I realized it would have tasted better on French toast. I would try to remember to order French toast for breakfast tomorrow.

Ratso and Ferret walked into the dining area, accompanied by two local prostitutes. You didn't have to guess these ladies were pros since they were wearing exactly the same clothes they had worn last night at the Irish sports-themed tavern where Ratso and Ferret had negotiated for their temporary affections.

The unexpected, massive overnight snowfall must have kept the girls from getting home last night. I didn't blame the girls for not leaving, even if it meant staying with Ratso and Ferret. I suspect they came down instead of starving because room service currently was unavailable, again thanks to the snow.

Elizabet said, "I see our friends from last night are up. It's time for a visit."

Elizabet got up, walked over to their table, grabbed an empty chair from a nearby table, parked it next to Ratso and Ferret and said, "Mr. James; Mr. Phillip, we met last night at the tavern, *The Nine Hostages*. You gents don't mind if I asked your lady friends about local conditions, do you?"

Ratso Jimmy said, "Sure toots, I forgot your name, but whatever; knock yourself out; only these birds don't speak English so well."

Elizabet switched to some version of French, but one close enough to Montreal French to enable the two ladies to understand her, albeit with difficulty. After about five minutes, when Elizabet saw her breakfast had been served, she hugged each lady and rejoined me.

"I was solidifying our cover, John. I speak Parisian French. The real Suzie lived in New Orleans for a year; long story, most men are scum, details irrelevant. Suzie does not have my gift for languages, but it's plausible she could have picked up French while there. I explained I wasn't competing with them, but you and I recently had to leave New York City suddenly because of a major financial misunderstanding with my former employer.

"Ratso and Ferret don't understand a word of French, so I also explained to my new acquaintances how I was on track to blow through every last shilling of your hard-stolen money within a month. I asked what conditions were like up here in Montreal for a lady who intended to remain in the trade."

"They said they worked as licensed contractors for Connacht Commando; the gang which provides cover for the Irish sports tavern we went to last night. Both girls are Irish, of course. Well, most of their ancestors were.

"Many Irish emigrants in the 1800s left initially for Quebec Province, the only majority Catholic province other than Ireland itself in any Empire member country. Many of those families assimilated here rather than moving on to New York or the western provinces and their descendants speak French as their native tongue. Giselle said conditions are not so bad, but Marie said that if I wanted to stay in the trade, I had to work with one of the local gangs. Accidents happen to ladies who try to freelance.

"Did your Uncle Max make any progress in his own inquiries?"

My uncle Max is fifty-seven years old. He married my late mother's younger sister, Maude. Max retired over seven years ago from his then job of being the number two hitman for the Ft. Detroit City Purple Posse. The Purple Posse was the exclusive provider of several insurance-like and pest control-like services in southeast Michigan, northeast Indiana, and northwestern Ohio.

My Uncle Max walked around the corner of his barn on his ranch in the Michigan Territory Upper Peninsula several years ago and saw a hitman pointing a pistol at him. Uncle Max took a slug to his right shoulder, but used his left fist to coldcock the erstwhile assassin. Then, wounded and bloody, Uncle Max fed the would-be-assassin into a wood chipper.

Even after two operations, my uncle's right shoulder, though functional, is still sometimes tender. Max never knew who hired the hitman; it's not like Uncle Max did not have a surfeit of potential enemies. Earlier this year, though, Bridget O'Shaughnessy informed him the hitman had been hired out of Montreal. Uncle Max wanted me to come along and help with his investigations. The spy ladies thought having a cover story for my cover story would help, so they gave me the go-ahead.

"I haven't seen Uncle Max since last night at the tavern when he walked by on the way to the Gents' Room and whispered, 'I think I got a lead.' Llywelyn accompanied him. I suspect he is okay. Even if they had to stay out all night, this is tropical weather for someone who lives in the Michigan Upper Peninsula. Llywelyn is probably a frozen wimp-sickle in some snow-drift somewhere; his previous posting was in Bermuda, on the other version of earth. I guess the climate there's the same as it is on this version of earth; I never asked."

Uncle Max stomped into the dining room; Llywelyn was in tow. They had melting snow on their shoes. Uncle Max knew enough bad French to get by, at least if you knew enough profanity. He was industriously cursing lazy frogs who were way too indolent to clear a measly ten inches of snow from the freaking streets, darn their shiftless frog butts. I figured if I didn't act first, something serious might happen, so I stood up, waved my hands to include the scandalously dressed whores sitting with Ratso and Ferret and said, "I must protest; there are ladies present. Control your language, sirrah, or face my wrath."

"You insolent pup; damn your eyes. Well, I am a fair man. I outweigh you by at least four stone, so I give you your weapon of choice, as long as it might be fatal."

"Fine," I said, "Beer it is; last man standing wins and the loser pays all. Choose your tavern of choice."

"The nearest one," Uncle Max bellowed, "I will not go one step out of my way for the likes of you. Appoint your second to establish the rules of the bout."

Ratso and Ferret started discussing how to wager on the outcome. Their escorts suddenly became excited and claimed the nearest tavern was the one we were at last night. I bet myself the tavern would get a rake-off from any wagers placed. Ratso suddenly shouted, "I'll be his second, whoever he is. I'm putting a hundred pounds down on the younger guy."

"Seven tonight?" asked Max. "A real man cannot drink seriously on an empty stomach."

"Done," cried I. "Now behave, sir. I will see you on tonight on the field of honor. In the meantime, show these fine ladies all due respect." I waved to include Giselle and Marie. I thought they were much closer to tarty than fine, but Uncle Max was on a roll.

It was clear Uncle Max wanted an excuse to interact with me while burnishing his credentials with the local underworld. *The Nine Hostages* had had all the signs of being controlled by a criminal organization, though I had never heard of the Connacht Commando until about ten minutes ago.

I wondered what Uncle Max discovered. Also, I figured I needed a plan to weasel out of the contest before I had too many beers. Three pints in an evening would seriously affect my metabolism. Uncle Max could do three beers for a pre-breakfast pick-me-up and not notice much but a mild warm glow. Heck, he was retired and a guy needs a hobby.

Elizabet was sharp. She caught the attention of the two babes with Ratso and Ferret and said, too loudly, "Johnny, sweet-ums, if we are going out tonight, I will need a new outfit to look my best. I need to do some shopping as soon as they clear the streets. You want me to look my best when you win, don't you?"

She grabbed me and nibbled my ear. I reached into my wallet and ostentatiously pulled out a hundred pounds sterling. She stuffed it down her front, stood up and said, "I think it's time for some desert, Johnny. I know just what I want and you need." I caught her winking at the two local pros. They smiled back at her. I suspected Giselle and Marie knew more English than they let on. The respectable matrons stared more intently at their yummy poutine.

As we left, Elizabet babbled something in Frog to Giselle and Marie. They babbled back. We returned to our hotel room and I pleaded with her. "You can't be serious! Heck, woman; that would make you worse than Francine and she nearly killed me. I have to be able to think."

Elizabet told me to shut up and sleep; she had her own thinking to do. I counted sheep for three hours and when I woke up; she had a plan.

"I will signal Llywelyn to pull one of the tavern's fire alarms once you start on your third beer. We won't move because we will know it's a phony alarm, so we shouldn't be trampled if there is a rush for the exits. The tavern meets code regarding exits, so I doubt there will be too many fatalities."

I glared at her, wondering if Elizabet was afflicted by a previously undiagnosed mental disorder.

"Suzie, it will be safer for everyone if we hit the silent alarm to the local constable station. That way, a bunch of constables will come by and find Max and me yelling at each other and the contest will have to break up. All we want to do is give Max some publicity and local street cred. Also, I don't want to be remembered by some local thug who lost a thousand pounds betting on me because I couldn't pound my beers. If the constables break up the place, all bets will be off. You figure out where the silent alarm is hidden and have Llywelyn set it off during my third beer."

Elizabet smiled. "I was joking, John. I actually have a sense of humor. Anyway, the silent alarm is under the bar counter immediately to the left of the main cash register, from the tapster's perspective. There are two reasons for this. Most people are right-handed and the tavern places the pump handles for the most popular beers they sell on the right side of the main register. Thus, the tapster usually is working those taps if a threat walks through the door. The barkeep often has his left hand free and so can push the silent alarm button without attracting attention.

"Four times last evening while we were at the tavern, someone who met the barkeep's threat criteria walked through the door. One of those times was when your Uncle Max walked in. On each occurrence, the barkeep shifted slightly to his left, to be ready to press the alarm surreptitiously."

I was surprised by Elizabet's powers of observations. I seldom noticed such things, unless I was staring through a rifle scope. That explained why the Brigadier, at least, insisted Elizabet go along with me. Elizabet then popped my bubble.

"I knew what to look for because that is also where we put the silent alarm in most the establishments of this type over which Mrs. O'Shaughnessy enjoys ownership or control. We have such alarms because if we have a bar fight among drunks, it is often easier to let the constabulary deal with the cleanup; it gives them something to do rather than harassing us. Slab or Wires or their senior lieutenants deal with more serious matters.

"First time free-lance offenders against our businesses or people we let off with a stern warning and our version of parole. We offer this option if they have hurt no one too seriously. Of course, they must repay the amount of any theft or robbery and then go straight, with our help if need be. Also, we expect them to tithe a percentage of their legitimate earnings for the next five years to help care for the widows and orphans."

She smiled. "It all goes to Church charities; it makes Bridget popular with the common folk. Or malefactors could choose to face immediate justice from Slab or Wires. I know of no tales involving the existence of recidivists."

I thought to myself for at least the hundredth time I should always try my best to be extra polite anytime I dealt with Bridget O'Shaughnessy.

"It's almost noon, John. Let's go someplace else nearby and grab something for lunch. We have to meet Giselle and Marie in the lobby at two o'clock, by which time the downtown streets should be plowed. We girls are all going to the premier Montreal department store's intimate apparel section. They will advise me, for a fee, while you will ooh and ah over my choices of scanty clothing each time I emerge from the dressing room.

"By the time I am finished, that hundred pounds you gave me at breakfast is going to have vanished, and I plan to hit you up for more. Don't you dare complain about the money! If all this doesn't convince them I am a born-to-the-sisterhood, amoral, money-grubbing whore and you are a love struck sap, nothing will. We should be back by five; I will then have my way with you while wearing my new finery. We can next have a quick, light dinner and then you can drink your uncle under the table."

When she put it like that, it sounded so logical. I just hoped she had a way to hit the silent alarm button before I started my third beer. If she waited until I started on beer number four, it was going to be a night to remember.

"Do you have any more helpful advice for me, Suzie?"

She stared straight at me. "Yes, John. Don't get carried away and take tonight's contest too seriously. Other issues are in play, so please remain alert and be very careful. Remember, beer is the mind-killer."

A Man Walks Into a Bar

Elizabet and I arrived at *The Nine Hostages* about 6:45. Ratso and Ferret had preceded us to reserve a table and establish the rules, set the betting protocols, and clear any last moment things with the barkeep. Giselle and Marie were already there as well, explaining to the barkeep what a fine gentleman I was to defend the honor and ears of decent girls like them. Elizabet spotted her two new bosom friends and went over to chat with them. Elizabet took them to a somewhat private corner where she could sort of surreptitiously show off which of her many new and incredibly expensive undergarments she had worn for the evening.

Max barged in and bellowed, "Where's the mark?"

We got together and agreed to the rules of the bout. The barkeep would draw one pint for each of us every ten minutes. The moment one of us fell at least one full pint behind the other, he, and that would be me, would be declared the loser.

All bets would be cleared through the barkeep's assistant, who would keep five percent of the handle. Toilet breaks would be permitted once an hour, for five minutes. I didn't expect it to last that long.

We got started about 7:20; it had taken a while to get the bets down and the odds set. Sure, I looked athletic enough, but Uncle Max was the clear favorite, since he outweighed me by fifty pounds and he had the glowing nose of a veteran beer drinker. The book was declared closed; there must have been a couple thousand pounds on the line. What can I say? A lot of folks had heard of Detroit Max.

We started sipping our beers. Watching folks drink beer is a lot like watching paint dry; except Uncle Max and I at least got to trash talk each other. After a couple minutes Max asked me, "Yooper or Troll?"

A decade ago, once they built the bridge connecting the two parts of Michigan province, the folks living in the Michigan mitten, the part below the bridge, became known as trolls. I told Max troll, to which he responded this was going to be easy, since trolls were known throughout the Upper Peninsula as being utter wimps. We sipped some more. The beer was okay, but nothing special, and I was not looking forward to drinking three or four of them. I reconsidered the brilliance of my plan.

Given both my Uncle Max and I had some experience with the hazards of life, we were sitting so we each could see the front door. Thus, when the man with a double-barreled 12-gauge shotgun entered the tavern in the middle of our first beer, neither of us was taken unawares.

There were three intruders. The leading dude fired a single blast from the shotgun into the ceiling to announce his presence. The results were probably not what he expected, though I would never know what he thought because I was already reaching into my left shoulder underarm holster. I lined up my .32-caliber Wembley Defender before the buckshot in the shotgun had hit the ceiling. A second later, the shotgun dude had three .32-caliber holes in the front of his forehead.

I could not aim any shots at his companions because a table top was now in the way. It would have been tough anyhow; I had thrown myself back in my chair the moment I saw the shotgun and I was now bouncing off the floor.

The table top blocked my aim because Uncle Max had picked up the table we were sitting at. It must have weighed well over a hundred pounds. It was made of pressed wood, covered with linoleum, and would not have stopped any round larger than an underpowered .22-caliber. Max charged the door with it, using it as a shield, which at least made it darned near impossible for the two remaining bad guys to target him accurately.

They were also hindered by the blood and brain fragments which had splashed from the shotgun wielding dead guy's forehead and into their eyes. They weren't hindered for long. Max was still fast for a big man and crushed the two follow-up guys into a wall before they had decided what to do. By the time the two would-be robbers got their breath back, two of the tavern's bouncers had them face down on the floor and had grabbed their pistols.

Max bellowed that since I had spilled his damn beer, we would have to start the contest over from scratch. Instead, I put both my .32-caliber shoulder-holstered pistols and the .30-caliber holdout Wembley from its holster in the small of my back down on the floor and waited, briefly, for the constables to arrive.

The constables had only begun to sort things out when my solicitor appeared. Elizabet was a darn fast thinker. She figured her new girl pals had solicitors on call. She told them if they got one of their solicitors here on the double quick, then she could guarantee Giselle and Marie a substantial bonus.

Once my solicitor arrived, the constables had to do things by the book. The solicitor explained it was clearly a matter of self-defense and pointed to the shotgun and the fresh holes in the ceiling. All the witnesses confirmed that. By that time, the tavern's own solicitor had shown up, as had someone from the city morgue.

I guess the local constables had to make their quota of arrests. They noticed I did not have a Montreal license to carry, so they hauled me to the nearest precinct where they would at least book me as a material witness.

This was not the way I wanted to be remembered by the local thugs and constabulary, but stuff happens. The solicitor accompanied me to the precinct house and insisted he had the right to talk to me first.

We went off alone and he asked, "What was that about?"

I explained I had never seen the three dudes before in my life and had no clue why they had shown up, other than they might have learned about perhaps a couple thousand extra pounds floating around the tavern because of the drinking contest. I told him my erstwhile opponent, Detroit Max, was not unknown in some select circles.

My solicitor asked me what I was doing in town. I figured honesty was the best policy, so I told him I was on a secret mission for His Royal Highness, Prince Albert, who wanted me to track down aliens from outer space.

The solicitor gave me a glare any drill sergeant would have envied.

"That type of story will not help you beat the weapon's charge, Mr. Smith. Also, that was pretty damn good shooting. Even I can recognize exceptional marksmanship and I am merely an amoral solicitor making a living keeping the local working girls out on the streets and earning their wherewithal. The Montreal constables are going to figure you are a professional of some sort and they will use the weapons charge to hold you for a long time until they decide who and what you are."

"I did three tours in the marines. I have knocked around since. The locals found my Pennsylvania Colony bodyguard license; that should be good enough. If you think it's not, well, they may have missed something when they searched me. I need to beat the weapons charge. I can't hang around here; I need to be in Quebec City in a couple of days."

I reached down and flipped open the heel of my left shoe. I took out a piece of laminated heavy stock paper signed by the RFC Constabulary Deputy Chief, which authorized me to carry any weapons I could physically lug.

"You can have the Montreal constables call the telephone number on the back. It may take a couple of hours, but the local RFC constabulary office will validate this. This is solicitor-client privilege stuff, so don't go blabbing it to folks who don't need to know."

The solicitor examined the carry permit; then he sighed. "I hate dealing with political stuff like this because that raises another complication. Even if this checks out, then you don't want to stay in Montreal any longer than you have to.

"The Montreal City Constables loathe the RFC constables with a passion. So, the first time they have an excuse to arrest you for spitting on the sidewalk or jaywalking they will throw you in the drunk tank and misfile the paperwork.

"Better have the RFC goons escort you from the precinct-house; otherwise, you might trip down the stairs on your way out. Just saying, is all. You will be better off if I stay in your presence until the RFC comes to rescue you. I will include those hours in my invoice, naturally."

I took his advice; it was his town. It took a lot less time than I expected. An RFC constabulary lieutenant had come to the precinct station for other reasons, but was available to take charge of my case. Three hours later, the RFC lieutenant escorted me from the precinct house and drove me back to my hotel. He didn't say a word to me the whole time.

It was almost midnight when I got back to the hotel. Uncle Max had shared all his discoveries with Elizabet earlier. She took one look at my sad, exhausted carcass and told me she would wait until morning to tell me what he had found out.

Thanks for the Memories

For once, my body let me sleep in, but life didn't. We got a wake-up call from the front desk at 7:30; somebody wanted to meet us for breakfast. We met Giselle and Marie in the lobby, and they escorted us to a decent diner a couple of blocks away from the hotel.

Two obviously hard guys were standing outside the diner; they nodded to Giselle and Marie and ushered the four of us in. The two local pros escorted me to a table where sat a flashily dressed man of about forty. Giselle and Marie took Elizabet to a different table, a couple of booths removed. No one else sat near us.

"The name's Blaney, Mr. Smith." He pronounced it Blay-neigh, emphasis on the last syllable. "Patrique Blaney. If that's too much, you can call me Paddy. My organization provides the insurance and security services for *The Nine Provinces*. The man you killed last night was a notorious independent operator. The local flatfeet have been trying to nail Gentleman Johnny and his two moronic cousins for months."

"Are you packing still, Mr. Smith?"

"Barely, Mr. Blaney. At the moment, I'm only carrying Suzie's spare weapon; a ladies' model .25-caliber. It's way too underpowered, but it's what I got. The locals didn't me let have my own pistols back yet; they want to run them through some checks to see if they are clean. They will be. I have a legitimate bodyguard license out of Pennsylvania Colony. That solicitor your girls called for me last night says the constables will have to return them by tomorrow."

"Well, they shouldn't be able to prosecute you effectively for getting rid of a guy who was on their most wanted list. So, what were you doing in my tavern last night staging a drinking contest with Detroit Max? You didn't honestly expect to win, did you, Mr. Smith?"

"No, Mr. Blaney, you are partially correct. I did not intend to win honestly; if something is worth having, it's worth cheating for. I didn't know for sure he was Detroit Max, though; I thought he could have been another random blowhard. Still, the posted odds were long against me, so with that seemingly dumb yinzer betting for me as my cutout, I would have cleaned up big once Suzie slipped something into Max's third or fourth beer. She has been blowing through my money a little faster than I had hoped."

"So Giselle and Marie told me; it takes a lot to trigger their professional admiration. Why'd you need the money?"

"It was a bit of a misunderstanding. I thought I was hocking the jewels which Suzie had received as a vacation gift. It turns out she had to take a vacation because she grabbed the jewels. I need to clear some dough to redeem the jewels, or at least some of them."

I stared at the ceiling and cleared my throat. Hopefully, I was pulling off my act.

"The actual owner is more than a little possessive. You know how some ladies can be overly sentimental about some things. I have been awful polite answering your queries. What do all of these personal questions have to do with the price of maple syrup?"

"I wanted to take your measure, Mr. Smith. I suspect some of what you told me is at least partially true. Tell me, have you ever studied military history?"

I didn't like where this had turned; so much for my planned alternative, a career in show business. "I did a couple of tours in the corps. I guess I picked up a little about the history of the world. I guess it never hurts to learn a little more."

"Wonderful; then when you visit Quebec City, take in its world-class military museum, the Wolfe-Montcalm Museum. They have a display featuring photographs or paintings of all the bearers of the eponymous decoration. Did you realize the most recent picture in the display features a handsome young man who looks remarkably like you, after accounting for perhaps five years' worth of aging?

"The picture itself is five years old, though they only added it to the display last year. The other four living bearers of that medal are all over sixty years old. There is no man native to Montreal who could have made such a tight, three-shot cluster into the late Gentleman Johnny's under-endowed cranial cavity. I suspect claiming to have done merely a couple of tours in the marines is overdoing the false modesty."

I grinned, albeit wanly.

"I, myself, have studied a lot of history, Mr. Smith. My senses tell me there is a shakeout coming. I intend to wind up on the winning side of that shakeout. The next time you, or Suzie Shamrock or Detroit Max, see the Widow O'Shaughnessy in person, you may relay to her that I, at least, will be on her side. Since you are strapped for funds, please let me pick up the check both for your breakfast and for Suzie's. Bon appétit. I heartily recommend the breakfast poutine. The cheese curds here have an exquisite texture."

I chose the bacon, eggs and pancakes again, and a couple of extra cups of coffee. I remembered the French toast too late. Well, at least Elizabet's cover had stood up. I hadn't yet talked to her about what she learned from my Uncle Max. After she finished breakfast with her two new best gal pals for life, Elizabet and I walked back to our hotel. On the way there, she told me it was better if I talked to my Uncle Max in person.

We stopped at a newsstand and she purchased some cigarettes. She told me to learn to smoke; it would give me an excuse to be outside and to strike up a casual conversation with Uncle Max.

Neither Max nor I smoked, but we both stood outside our hotel and pretended to chain smoke while Max brought me up to speed.

"Yeah, kid. A couple of weeks ago, I got a call. He said it was from a pay phone from a tavern outside Lansing. I knew the voice. 'Max, it's Bill. I know you're retired, but you may be the only one who can help. She called me in a moment of lucidity. They got hold of Cynthia; she was always a little nuts. They made her worse. She said they said if I started looking for her, they would kill her. And me. They may already have tracked me down. She needs help, Max. Could you rescue my little girl? I gotta go.' I haven't heard from him since."

"That's when you called me, Max?"

"Yeah, kid; I had already done some preliminary work, though. Back when you passed the word from Bridget, I phoned some of my old contacts here in Montreal. I tracked down that lead a month ago, at least for the hit on me. The cut-out's cut-out said he heard the customer was some gorgeous, stacked young blonde babe with a nasty attitude. The word went out she wanted a pro for a job in Michigan Province.

"She gave her name as Jane Smith. She offered big money; an out-of-town hard guy took her up on it. Nobody knows what happened to him, he never came back. I think my well-fed pigs know why the guy who attacked me disappeared, but I can't be sure yet it is the same guy. So I drove down to the Mitten to do some more research."

"You must have found something, Max."

"I hope so. Tell me what you think. I first went through your local newspaper's back files from around the time of your parents' deaths. I found squat.

"I played a hunch and drove to the other side of the state and did the same for the newspapers near the up-scale suburb of Ft. Detroit City where Bill Valentine used to live. I also checked Cynthia Valentine's high school yearbooks. A kid in the class ahead of her died tragically in the middle of his senior year. He was a handsome young dude, but he would never be a world-class scientist teaching at Oxford or Cambridge or Hull or someplace like that; he had planned to be an auto and truck mechanic."

"He died while doing some illegal deer hunting in the middle of winter. Someone, unknown, had mistaken him for a deer. His death came four days after your parents and Rachel died in their auto accident. Another yearbook mentioned he had escorted Miss Cynthia Valentine to his Junior Prom when she was a sophomore. That's a lot of coincidences and a lot of dead ends."

Max's meanderings brought back some memories. I thought I had buried them forever.

I was a twenty-one-year-old marine, and I had just been promoted to Lance Corporal. Damn, I was so proud. I wore that uniform everywhere, including when I proposed to my high school sweetheart, Rachel.

About a week after we got engaged, I was still at my parents' home near the western shore of Michigan Province and was about halfway through my three weeks' leave. Uncle Max had driven up the night before. He thought Rachel and I might enjoy attending a picnic which his employers where were hosting at a huge provincial park north of Ft. Detroit. The Purple Posse took great pains to be family friendly within their organization; they wanted to be known as "The Mob with a Heart."

I was in my uniform sitting down at a picnic table under a shade tree, waiting for Rachel to come back with some lemonade, when this nearly flat chested blond girl of maybe fourteen comes up to me. She said, "You look chiseled, soldier boy. I bet a big brave hero like you shouldn't be scared of my dad, right?"

Rachel had returned with the lemonade, and as she was approaching the mouthy blonde from behind, Rachel caught most of the brief, but one-sided conversation. She tried to defuse the situation in her own diplomatic way. She yelled, "Shut your whore mouth, you teenage tart. My fiancé wants nothing to do with trash like you. You don't even have a real set of boobs yet, you skinny blonde tramp."

Rachel had a fine set of lungs in more than one sense; she could project her voice like an opera diva. Rachel threw both glasses of lemonade in the blonde's face when the blonde turned around to see who was calling her out. The hair pulling and the rolling around on the grass had only barely started when the more muscular folks arrived. That's when I first met "Wild Willy" Valentine, who was then the number three ranking hitman for the Purple Posse.

Wild Willy and my Uncle Max came rushing up to break up the cat fight. Well, Max stood back while I disentangled Rachel from the young blond tramp-to-be. Willy wound up holding back the little blond who was still screaming at Rachel.

Willy scrutinized me. I was holding Racheal tightly to keep her from rejoining the scrum. Then he shifted his to look at Uncle Max, who was standing behind me.

"I didn't know you had a kid, Max," said Willy.

"I don't, Bill," said Max. "He's my wife's sister's youngest kid. Made Lance in the marines a couple weeks back. Rachel here is his fiancée."

Willy said, "Cynthia here is going through a stage. It's been tough since her mom died. She picked up some strange ideas. Cynthia, apologize."

Cynthia glared at us with hate-filled eyes, but gave us a lame-ass apology, which we sort of graciously accepted.

I returned to the present. That had been the first and only time I had ever met Cynthia Valentine. I was suspecting she hadn't mellowed with age.

I coughed from the unfamiliar cigarette smoke and continued, "Tell me about Bill Valentine, Max. That sounds like an English name."

"Nah, kid, it's German. Same spelling, only it's pronounced a little differently in German. Actually, his first name is Wilhelm. His family all came over in the 1870s. He married another sort of German girl; his wife's folks came out of Alsace. That place bounced back and forth between France and the nearby German states so often nobody knows what they are, but his wife's parents spoke German at home.

"Cynthia came by her blondeness honestly. And a couple of years after the picnic, I met her again; it was at the Posse's annual '*Take Your Daughter to Work Day.*' Whooie, had Cynthia filled out her bustenhalter!"

I thought to myself, "*German, check. Blond, check. Probably a pyscho killer, check. Female, very prominently, so check. Gosh, what pair of Space Nazi evil doctors still at large might find that combination of attributes more than a little irresistible?*"

I came back to the present and stared at my uncle.

"Why are you going to Quebec City, Max? For the rest of us, it's a job. You don't have to go with us."

"I finally confirmed something yesterday. The hitman the blonde hired was originally from Quebec City. I am going there to track down his background. I finally got a name."

That worked for me.

The Near Fatal Glass of Beer

Quebec City, Quebec Province, Royal Federated Colonies

Hey, at least we stayed out of trouble at the Quebec War Museum. I tried to find my picture; there was a blank space on the wall where it should have been hanging and a small sign said, "Under Repair." The picture's absence set off my finely tuned paranoia alarms. As far as I knew, that was the last photograph anyone had taken of me since I joined that elite unit on my third tour. Heck, I hadn't let the wedding photographer take any pictures of me when Kathy and I got married. That was something else to discuss with Madeline and Kathy when I got home.

I still had some investigating to do, so we used Uncle Max as an excuse to test the beers on tap at a variety of French-speaking taverns, all of which the Brigadier's sources had claimed were sympathetic to or controlled by the illegal French liberation folks. Elizabet begged off the third night when we were scheduled to go to a massive sports-themed tavern, the *Bibulous Beaver*. The walls were absolutely covered with photographs of famous local ice-lacrosse players. She told us she would spend the afternoon shopping with Llywelyn and would meet me back at the hotel.

That evening's tavern brawl was epic. It ended way too early because I think half a battalion of the local constabulary quickly showed up and put the habeus grabbus on everyone within a couple of city blocks of the place. Various frog types bonded with us as we were crammed into constabulary vans and carted off to jail. They were thrilled to have been caught up in such an epic bar fight. They didn't seem to care that Max and I were of English descent, while Ratso and Ferret had predominately Polish and Lithuanian ancestry.

Once we got to know each other, they had a lot to say. They complained bitterly about the Irish Fenians, saying how the rat bastards had stabbed them in the back a couple of years ago. They were adamant the local French gangs wanted nothing to the do with the loathsome Fenians.

Two hours later, I became more suspicious. Some high-priced solicitors showed up way too quickly and bailed the four of us from the lockup. Then the local constabulary practically bowed and scraped to me as they escorted me from the jail to the waiting taxi, which took me back to my hotel. They didn't give Max, Ratso, and Ferret the same royal treatment, but they didn't trip them on their way down the precinct house steps, either.

The solicitors got back me safely back to my suite at the five-star hotel with a splendid view of the Plains of Abraham. Elizabet was waiting for me there.

"I listened to Max practice his French, John; it's execrable. When he kept trying to say ice-lacrosse players are tough bastards on skates, he was saying they are ballerinas on skates. How many times did he repeat himself before the fight broke out?"

I shrugged. Some muscles protested being exercised. "He sent me off to the bar to pick up a couple of beers and the fight was starting before I could return."

"John, though this one was Max's fault, you have taken part in an impressive number of tavern brawls. Why is that?"

I figured honesty was the best policy, though I had never admitted this to anyone before. "It's because I was poor and thrifty."

Elizabet furrowed her eyebrows. She examined me for a long moment. "Explain please, John. Even I can't understand that particular connection."

"During most of my three hitches in the marines, I was engaged to Rachael or planning to be, so I was trying to save up some money. The first thing a horde of marines wants to do when they wash ashore after a couple of months bouncing around on the ocean waves is hit the bars and the bordellos. That blows through a lot of coin."

"I understand the concept. Certain of Mother's subsidiaries make substantial profits from those particular impulses. Her establishments don't roll the drunken marines or sailors, though; that's bad for repeat business."

"I appreciate that, Suzie. Anyway, I didn't want to look like a wimp in the eyes of my buddies, so initially I always went along, but only to the first tavern on the circuit. I realized if I always subtly instigated a fight in the first place we went, after drinking only a couple of beers, my mates would soon view me as too toxic to take along on such outings. That meant I could spend the bulk of my shore leaves reading sciencey fiction or working through my college correspondence courses.

"My buddies never figured it out. None of them ever thought I was a wimp. I got to save my coin and do a lot of reading. Tonight was an actual surprise; I had thought that stuff was behind me. You arranged for the solicitors, Suzie?"

"Yes, and Llywelyn made an anonymous tip to the constabulary regarding a possible illegal bare knuckles match at the tavern you visited. He claimed there was going to be massive betting. Enough talk. Right now, you need to shower off the stench of eau du lock-up. Then I have some plans for you."

I analyzed our conversation later that evening. It accounted for a lot, but not the bowing and scrapping by the local constables. Most of them behave like petty tyrants the moment they think they have ditched their oversight.

I strongly suspected a couple of guardian angels were involved, somehow, above and beyond what Elizabet was doing. For the life of me, though, I could not figure out how they were keeping tabs on me, but I was sure they were. The only explanation other than magic which made any sense was they were using advanced technology from Paul's world.

It took Max a couple of days in Montreal to confirm to his satisfaction the late hitman's closest family members had moved to Rochester. We spent five days in Rochester. Max finally found someone who knew for sure the late guy's brother was working as a machinist in Buffalo. He gave Max the brother's last known work address. We also knocked around some places Bridget and Madeline had recommended we check out. We tried to pick up any leads regarding the Fenians. We failed miserably; nothing seemed out of the ordinary.

Meanwhile, Elizabet was relaxing me at a pace that made Francine look like a talented amateur. Eventually, it came time to part ways. Elizabet explained, "Bridget told me I could not travel to Buffalo, John. Too many people there know the real Suzie Shamrock. I thank you for our weeks together; I will always treasure them. You were wonderful. I am sure Bridget will try to do something nice for you when you finish your mission. I hope you enjoy surprises."

We took Elizabet to the Rochester train station. I checked out the crowd. I had worried about Elizabet's safety on the trip back since I couldn't spare anyone. Then, about halfway across the train station, I saw a familiar face.

I thought about waving to Wires or asking him "How are they hanging?" or something, but that would be unprofessional. I identified a couple of other guys who seemed to be with him. At least Elizabet would have a reliable escort to return to Newport or New York City or wherever. I needed to shuffle off to Buffalo.

I could sense we were getting close to the finale.

We did the usual stuff in Buffalo; I was picking up squat. After four days there, we were getting way down the list of taverns and other dives we were supposed to visit. Max was off doing his own thing; the folks he talked to said the guy Max was looking for was off ice-fishing that week.

I found myself in a rental coupe with Llywelyn, Ratso and Ferret outside a dump of a pub called *The Gilded Harp*. I told my guys we would do this a little differently. I planned to go in alone and order a draft beer. Llywelyn would wander in after a couple of minutes.

I bellied up to the bar. I ordered a beer. I took a couple of sips. Apparently, time passed, but I sure as heck was not in any condition to notice its passing.

The Mutant Menace

Quebec and Maritime Provinces

I woke up. I was naked and spread-eagled on a large, comfortable bed. The shackles keeping me there seemed quite solid. I noticed an intravenous drip in my left arm. There was a wall to my left, so I turned my head to my right and found myself staring at a blond guy in a lab coat. He was about forty years old. He was sporting a monocle.

"*Holy stereotypes!*" I thought to myself.

"Hello, Robin," said the stranger. He had a vaguely Germanic accent.

"My Fenian hirelings identified Detroit Max as the person who was making like a bull in a porcelain shop, so we investigated his background. Subsequently, we discovered an underling who knew of both him and you. We learned which high school you attended and we got your picture from your senior yearbook. I don't think our minions would have identified you absent that picture."

"The pleasure's all mine. You wouldn't be a kindly tavern-keep who rescued me from a snowdrift or something? If you are, I feel great now, so you can go ahead and release me and pour me a beer or something."

"You need to work on your alleged witticisms, Sergeant Sherwood. Clearly, I am a medical doctor."

"Well, doc; it seems to me you are as mad as a hatter. I mean, you're straight out of central casting under low-budget flicker needs whacko scientist. Also, my name was legally changed to John Smith in case you want to update your medical records. You know, your voice sounds familiar, somehow, though I swear we have never met."

He grinned. That was unusual. My snark usually grates on folks' nerves more effectively.

"We have never met. I am Herr Doctor Carl von Clausewitz. You have, though, already met my beloved spouse, Frau Doctor Brunhilde von Clausewitz. Indeed, she was ecstatic once she saw your high school senior class picture and realized she might once again have the pleasure of seeing you in the flesh, so to speak.

"We are both medical doctors. I specialize in pharmaceuticals and tropical diseases; her specialty is galvanic response to external stimuli. If you think that sounds unpleasant, I can assure you the actuality for most of her test subjects is far worse than your grimmest nightmares. Naturally, we have also studied racial genetics; the basis of all real medical and racial sciences."

"We seem to traveling, Doc, unless this is one of those cheesy hotel beds where you drop a shilling coin into a slot and the bed vibrates for a while?"

"We are in an eighteen-wheel, cab and trailer combination. There are two others like it in our little convoy. We are six hours out of Buffalo, on our way to Sidney, Nova Scotia. It's cold, but the weather is expected to be clear for the next week. It's a long way by road, say three or four days, as we wish neither to tire our drivers excessively nor call attention to our vehicles. Also, we will avoid the major cities.

"I suspect you know there is more of interest in Sidney than clapped out iron mines. Once there, we will steal a certain craft from your navy and leave this degenerate world. My Reich's forces will return to this earth at a time of their choosing."

"I heard some vague rumors, Doc, but that has nothing to do with me. I was traveling around the Great White North only because I had promised to help my uncle pay back an old debt."

"While it's proper to take familial obligations seriously, Sergeant Sherwood, your Uncle Max does not deserve such consideration. For one thing, he drinks like a fish. Fortunately for you, and for your forthcoming chemical interactions, you are far more abstentious.

"Also, as long as I brought up the topic of families, while you have an English last name, the other twenty percent of your genetic makeup comes from Norwegian and Danish stock. I found no statistically disqualifying percentages of inferior ancestry in my analysis of your DNA. That means that, quite unlike my sub-human Fenian hirelings, I can use you as part of my current research. That is the reason you remain alive. Had you been unsuitable, I would have disposed of you already; scientific rigor is a harsh mistress."

I wondered what the heck DNA was. I didn't seem like the time to ask.

The Doc chuckled, sort of. "You must have been mocked unmercifully as a child for wearing a silly feathered hat, wearing green leggings, and carrying a bow and arrows; Robin Fletcher Sherwood, indeed. That would have been fun to watch; we Germans are notorious for our finely developed sense of humor, especially when laughing at the travails of the lesser classes and races."

"Yeah, Doc; hah-hah! If you want me to dress up in green leggings and prance around in a feathered hat, though, you need to remove my chains."

"No, Sergeant Sherwood. You will remain shackled until it's time to kill you; perhaps just before I return to my home earth. I miss it so, but arriving here was a gift direct from Wotan. Every true German medical scientist wants to research genetics and eugenics. My own chosen area of study, discovering how various drugs and external stimuli affect beautiful young ethnically German ladies, requires a plentiful supply of the latter. Alas, few such ladies volunteer for what are often painful and humiliating experiments.

"The dearth of suitable test subjects is one reason I wound up researching mosquito-borne diseases in our version of Cuba instead of doing genuine science. The six of us were excited to arrive on your earth; an entire world full of potential experimental subjects was now ours for the taking."

"Cuba, eh? I guess that invasion of Cuba thing sort of knocked you folks tuckus over teakettle, Doc. Pity."

"I began taking private precautions before that event, Sergeant. Once our colleagues' misguided and premature direct efforts to take over the New York City drug trade failed, my dear Frau and I pursued a more indirect approach. We used Delilah Honoré as a cut-out in one of our several efforts to collect useful data. I concede we acted more out of duty than rationality. We hoped more of those fake Romans would come looking for their missing world-hopping craft. It now appears our efforts were not in vain.

"It's difficult to improve the overall quality of an entire race, Sergeant Sherwood, nor is the process without stress, even in my Reich. Lower- and middle-class German girls in my world are culled when they reach eighteen. The exceptionally beautiful and the outstandingly bright girls are taken from their families for the personal use of top Party or scientific officials. The overly stupid or ugly ones are sent to breeding hostels to become host mothers. They are not permitted to pass on their own inferior genes.

"What we have learned from our experiments will do wonders to help many of those young ladies who are torn from their families to become enthralled with their new circumstances. Frau Doctor Brunhilde and I will return to the Reich as highly decorated heroes."

"Medals are usually overrated, Doc. I got a bunch of them, once, and it costs more to earn them than you might think. So now I'm just a mercenary for hire, so to speak, who was trying to help my uncle tramp around in the hip-deep snow."

"There is no need for such false modesty and self-deprecation, Sergeant Sherwood. Your hometown newspaper's archives chronicled some of your exploits. Speaking of Michiganders, there is a young lady in the next room who has waited many years to meet you again.

"She had powerful memories of the one time she met you. Once we discovered your identity, we modified her pharmaceutical dosages and increased the amplitude of her external stimuli conditioning regime. We transformed her anger over your past behavior into what is now a passionate desire for you. It is a shame her conditioning now prevents us from using her sharpshooting skills in an assassin's role. There are so many people in your decadent society who need to be killed."

"I gotta agree with you on that one, Doc. Have you looked in a mirror lately?"

His left eye twitched a couple times, but otherwise he ignored my bon mot. It took him a while to respond.

"I will destroy your pathetic world."

That clicked a memory; I almost remembered a tag line used in a flicker; I couldn't place the flicker.

"I read about that whole Cuba thing in the news rags, Doc. I doubt conquering this world will be as easy as you believe."

He relaxed a bit and then smiled, thinly.

"You would be right, of course, from a purely military perspective. I am not a military man, so I have pursued non-military means. Several days after we leave your earth, my trusting Fenian underlings will unleash a plague of unprecedented virulence. Those Gaelic dupes seriously believe I could create a plague toxin designed to spare the ethnic Irish. As if I would even bother!

"When German settlers from my earth arrive to conquer your world in ten or fifteen years, I doubt over five percent of your existing population will remain alive. Those few will be reduced to utter barbarism. It's a pity about the Germanic peoples who live here now, but the Reich has always demanded sacrifices from her volk."

"That's nice Doc; why are you telling me all of this? Aren't you worried I will somehow reveal your cunning plans to the authorities?"

He chuckled. "You are quite naked and completely shackled. Also, when we kidnapped you, we distributed the clothes you were wearing to the alcoholics hanging around the tavern's back door. If you think Woof the Wonder Mutt is going to dash in and save you, you are barking up the wrong tree.

"You thought I didn't notice, Sergeant Sherwood; you called me mad. Mad you say? Then Hippocrates was mad, Chauliac was mad, and surely William Harvey was the maddest of the lot. Ever since time began, they've called mad all the great doctors in this world. I am quite sane by the standards of my civilization."

His left eye, the one without the monocle, blinked uncontrollably. He used his left forefinger to stop the blinking. Then he smiled, quite evilly.

"You realize, of course, the rules of the mad scientist game now require me to punish you for that insult. Do you have any suggestions?"

"Uh, Doc, you forgot to say, 'Bwa-hah-hah!'"

The doc said, "Bwa-hah-hah!"

He puffed up with pride, seemingly sensing my belated recognition. He reminisced. "Yes, I was the incredibly talented actor behind the rubber mask. I am still hurt I was not nominated by the Guild for an award of some sort; that alone is sufficient reason to conquer your world.

"Wendell Honoré was an underappreciated cinematic genius. Had he not been cut down in his prime, I might have taken him with us to my earth. Did you kill him, Mr. Sherwood?"

"No, Doc. I was slow off the mark and there was a long line in front of me."

The Doc started reminiscing. "I understand an artist must make compromises if he is to be successful commercially. Still, I wish he had let me play Dr. Gruesome the Mutant Menace in a more sympathetic light. Dr. Gruesome's research was for the cause of science, after all. It's an eggs and omelets thing. I loathed those stupid golden retrievers, though. I urged Wendell to use German shepherds, but he always faced the grim financial reality of his fans' expectations.

"Dr. Gruesome was going to appear to succeed, temporarily at least, in his tragically unmade third outer space flicker, '*The Revenge of the Martian Mutant.*' In the fourth and final flicker of the series, Commander Honoré and his Last Planet Spacemen and some damn stupid, slobbering golden retriever with the inevitable bladder control issues would vanquish forever that noble, misunderstood, truth-seeking scientist."

If that's how he saw himself, then the Doc was loonier than I suspected. I kept quiet and let him rant. I had little choice. My shackles were awfully sturdy.

"It would have been ambiguous, of course; depending on the outcome at the box office, we would have pushed that franchise until it fell off a cliff. Artistic integrity can be damned. Even scientists have their weakness. But we learn from our mistakes.

"Look around, Sergeant Sherwood. In this lab, you will see no golf bags containing Wembley Automatic Rifles. There is no escape for you this time. Bwa-hah-hah! Bwa-hah-hah! Bwa-hah-hah-hah! I was made for the role of Dr. Gruesome."

The Doc's fruit plate was clearly missing a full pineapple and couple of melon balls. I figured I might as well play along. I wasn't going anywhere, so I had nothing better to do.

"Since you are clearly a fan of cheesy flickers, Doc, I guess you're going to use an energy beam or acetylene torch to cleave me from crotch to crown. Or inflict upon me an agonizing death from the spore-filled pustules of the Venusian swamp mange."

"You almost read my mind, Sergeant Sherwood. I am impressed. If my beloved Frau does not kill you out of spite, I can offer you a choice of potential deaths. You might be lucky and die from the enervating, direct effects of excessive bunga-bunga. Alternatively, you may succumb to the deleterious consequences of massive overdoses of debilitating and highly addictive drugs. I will inject the first such dose into your system momentarily."

He took a soft cloth out of his lab coat breast pocket. He gently cleaned his monocle, looked through it at a ceiling light, and cleaned it again. "Had I been born a gambler, Sergeant Sherwood, I would wager it will be the cumulative effects of my drugs which kill you."

The Name of the Rosettes

He hit a buzzer. Two women walked in. One woman was now closing in on forty years old. She had a lot of blond hair which was woven into twin rosettes, one covering each ear. She had maintained her more than decent figure, at least as far as I could discern, given the short, but tight, lab coat she was wearing.

I had seen her in person once before. She had gone by the stage name of Eva Braun when she played Nurse Strudel, a supporting actress in the mangy mutt from outer space flicker which Kathy and I had seen during our honeymoon. Subsequently, I swiped a photograph of her which I had found trapped between Wendell Honoré's desk and his office wall a couple of years back.

She still had utterly cold eyes; no, she had absolutely insane eyes. They were now bright blue, rather than green, but they were the type of eyes Delilah Honoré would have had if Delilah had been over-the-top bug-nuts crazy, rather than run-of-the-mill criminally insane. I guess that was the real reason she had worn contacts previously. She was still carrying a riding crop in one hand and a lit cigarette in the other.

The second woman was also blond, built like a brick kremlin and was almost as good looking as Melinda Burr Sammartino. She had long, meticulously braided pig tails. She was absolutely naked and oblivious to her nakedness.

I had also met her once before, eleven years ago. She had been an almost fourteen-year-old-girl when she had propositioned me in front of my first fiancé. The grainy, black and white newsprint photo I had seen of her from a couple of years back did not do her beauty justice.

"Hi, Cindy, long time, no see. You're looking good; you look like you've been working out. What type of meds do they have you on?"

That was the last snappy line I got off because Dr. Whacko stuffed a gag in my mouth.

"Say hello to Sergeant Sherwood, Cynthia," said the older woman.

"Yes, Frau Dr. Brunhilde. Hello, Robin. Frau Dr. Brunhilde helped me remember I am still angry at you; you publicly rejected me at the Purple Posse picnic. Then she helped me realize you killed Freddy. He took me to his junior prom. He was the only boy in my high school who didn't fear my father. Frau Dr. Brunhilde explained Freddy died because you didn't want anyone else to ever love me. Frau Dr. Brunhilde made sure you will love me this time and I can have you as many times as I want until the hurt goes away. I want the hurt to go away."

Cynthia paused. She looked confused. Deservedly so, as the story she related made no sense at all.

Dr. Bug-Nuts Crazy Eyes said, "Tell Mr. Sherwood what is going to happen now, Cynthia."

"Yes, Frau Dr. Brunhilde. Robin, Frau Dr. Brunhilde told me loving you as many times as I am able will help me feel much better. Frau Dr. Brunhilde also told me unless I have a lot of sex with you, she will punish me. I don't like being punished, though Frau Dr. Brunhilde tells me it's for my own good. She is such a dedicated and brilliant scientist, so I try to do what she tells me to do. She hardly has to punish me at all, anymore, and I promised her I would never again make any more telephone calls. I want to make Frau Dr. Brunhilde happy."

"You've become a very good girl, Cynthia. We are both so very proud of you," said Dr. Bug-Nuts. "Now step over here and then stand perfectly still while I wire you up so I can monitor your vital signs and galvanic reactions. This will take a few minutes. I know you are eager to make Robin love you like he should."

"Yes, Frau Brunhilde. You are so good to me."

Dr. Bug-Nuts instantly whacked Cynthia on the butt with the riding crop.

Cynthia briefly clenched her teeth, but said, "Thank you, Frau Dr. Brunhilde. You are so good to me, Frau Dr. Brunhilde. I apologize for my disrespect, Frau Dr. Brunhilde. I had no intent to forget your title, Frau Dr. Brunhilde. Shall I assume the punishment position, Frau Dr. Brunhilde?"

"No, Cynthia, not for now. Your punishment will be suspended until I evaluate how well you conduct yourself during the forthcoming experiments. You must not disappoint me, Cynthia. Do not backslide now; you have come too far. Now, step over there and then stand perfectly still for your wiring up process."

"Thank you, Frau Dr. Brunhilde. You are so good to me, Frau Dr. Brunhilde. I will do as you direct, Frau Dr. Brunhilde."

Cynthia didn't even try to rub her ass; I bet that riding crop stung like a nest full of hornets.

"I am sure you agree that proper deference to one's social betters is the true basis of civilization," interjected the monocled, but also clearly mad, doctor.

"Frauline Valentine has made wonderful progress with her behavioral conditioning program, but we still need to smooth some rough edges. It's so good of you to help. I will now administer your own invigorating medications through your I.V. so you will be unable to disappoint Frauline Valentine. She had the female counterpart of your injections fifteen minutes ago. It's a proprietary formulation which I spent years to develop. She should be quite ready when your own drugs kick in."

I had sort of wondered how that was going to work. Not that the topic ever came up during any of my enlisted bull sessions while sailing pointless donuts in the Atlantic, but I suspected most guys in my situation would have shrinkage issues. I sure was. Things wouldn't have been worse even if I had just crawled out of an ice-cold swimming pool.

Dr. Whacko opened a small valve on a tube leading to the drip bag attached to my I.V. and gave me a half-smile.

"As a gentleman, I apologize in advance. We have to use physical wires to hook onto the sensors my Frau is gluing to Frauline Valentine's body. These wires will restrict her athleticism. It's unavoidable, given the limits of your world's pitiable technology.

"You, of course, are and will remain thoroughly shackled. I need not attach any sensors to you; the toxic effects of the medications which are now flowing into you are well understood. Your initial, massive dose will turbo-charge your metabolism at the cost of even more rapidly depleting your energy reserves.

"Oh, and Sergeant Sherwood, my strict medical ethics compel me to warn you, yet again, the chemical cocktail now coursing merrily through your system is highly addictive. Moreover, its long-term abuse inevitably leads to a fatal outcome."

He removed my gag. "I didn't want your attempted witticisms to distract Fraulein Valentine. If the forthcoming process becomes too painful, feel free to scream in agony. Her medications have taken full effect, so your screams can no longer divert Fraulein Valentine's focus."

"I'm sure glad you take your Hippocratic Oath so seriously, Doc."

"The Party's needs take precedence, sergeant. My Reich no longer uses the Hippocratic Oath. Indeed, you may discover for yourself how little the old oath constrains us should my beloved Frau decide to incorporate you into her personal research efforts. Enough talk, Sergeant Sherwood, and bon appétit! Oh, and just one last thing..."

The doc paused.

"Okay, I'll bite. What's up, Doc?"

"If your condition lasts over four hours, you should definitely seek the help of a physician. Bwa-hah-hah! Bwa-hah-hah!"

That must have been a joke. I didn't get it. Yet.

Cynthia, eventually, reached her limits and Dr. Whacko took her away so she could grab some shuteye. Frau Doctor von Clausewitz, who had been monitoring a panel full of dials whose functions meant nothing to me, lit up yet another cigarette. She sucked down a lung-full of smoke, stood up, leaned over me and exhaled it all into my face. I guessed she was upset with me for some inexplicable reason. I smiled at her.

"To what do I owe the honor, Miss Braun? Or is it Nurse Strudel?"

She took another drag from her cigarette and exhaled languidly. "What do you think of Frauline Valentine?"

"She's extraordinarily beautiful and obedient, but she lacks passion. It's almost as if she was on autopilot."

She took a couple more puffs off her cigarette. "Yes, our female test subjects always embraced unquestioning obedience, eventually. Indeed, Delilah and Wendell Honoré helped expand considerably our understanding of what behaviors can be demanded of them. However, you were astute to have noticed Frauline Valentine's lack of passion, Sergeant Sherwood."

She finished her cigarette and flicked the butt unerringly into a large ashtray some five feet away. She lit up another one and started puffing away. "My husband and I remain frustrated by our test subjects' erratic enthusiasm levels."

She shrugged. "Perhaps it is merely because most of the young ladies we conditioned were peasants. Even German peasants, such as Frauline Valentine, are often too placid to savor life to its fullest."

She stared at me for half a minute. I sure wasn't going anywhere. She licked her lips and lit yet another cigarette.

"My husband is a rigidly principled researcher, Sergeant Sherwood. He had become rather frustrated by his inability to find a genetically acceptable research partner for Frauline Valentine. He would have killed her rather than permit her to be defiled by one of the lesser races. Your ancestors, however, were Angles, Saxons, and Norse; cadet branches of the core Germanic peoples.

"You have several faded scars, Sergeant Sherwood. I do not find them unattractive. Indeed, they testify to your military prowess. Genuine warriors always excite me, at a deeply feminine level."

She inhaled another lungful and blew more smoke in my face. "Perhaps we got off on the wrong foot when we met at Wendell Honoré's flicker studios. I was quite peeved with you for having rebuffed my advances. I had planned, if ever we met again, to amuse myself by inflicting excruciating punishments upon you.

"Serendipitously for you, Sergeant, I sometimes enjoy other types of amusements. Even now, you could apologize abjectly to me and mitigate the severity of your forthcoming tortures. Actions speak louder than words, so choose the nature of your apology wisely, Sergeant Sherwood."

She took off her lab coat.

"Gosh, Frau Doctor Fruitcake! Were you in such a rush that you have to leave all your dresses behind when you fled Havana?"

"Always you are making with the attempted humor. We maintain a precisely elevated temperature in this room to reduce environmental fluctuations during our experiments on Frauline Valentine. I simply had no desire to perspire unnecessarily and so wore only minimal lingerie, tights and suspenders underneath my lab coat today."

She leaned over me again and kissed me on the lips. She stood up and slowly twirled around. "Still, I may have chosen my wardrobe fortuitously. I have quite the remarkable figure, do I not? Besides being a striking beauty, I have a near fatal attraction to younger, muscular, lower class, and *obviously* virile warriors."

I mentally kicked myself for my life's choices. I was regretting not having joined the airship service so I could have enjoyed an uncomplicated, peaceful, and extremely lonely life, utterly bereft of any female companionship.

She kissed me again. "You could discover I am far more passionate than Miss Valentine. I never lack for enthusiasm."

"Ah, but sweetie, not to put too fine a point on things, but the last time I checked, you were still a *married*, albeit passionate, woman."

"My husband is driven by his research and his political ambitions, Sergeant Sherwood. He has never denied me my occasional, innocuous dalliances. Should you agree to become my most recent conquest, all I will require of you is unwavering devotion and instantaneous obedience. In return, I will spare your life for as long as you keep me amused.

"If you apply yourself, you may live long enough for me to exhibit you to all my lady friends upon my triumphant return to my Reich. They will be so jealous when I demonstrate how perfectly I have tamed and trained you to embrace your role as my devoted pet.

"So, do you regret spurning my affections? Answer quickly, Sergeant Sherwood. My supply of patience is limited."

I thought frantically. All that exercise with Cynthia had scrambled my brains. So far on this trip I had been shot at, ensnared in a tavern brawl, and kidnapped. The two times I had been tossed into Quebec lockups, though, not only had I been sprung abnormally quickly, I was treated respectfully. That meant someone important had to have been tracking me and intervening; I guess the how of it didn't matter.

I checked; yup, I was still shackled to the bed. I was going to need some help. I wondered what was keeping my guardian angel this time. Oh, yeah. The delay probably had something to do with that virulent plague Dr. Whacko had been yammering about. Maybe somebody needed some extra time to locate the plague toxins.

The metaphorical light bulb that always appears when you get an idea just popped on, right above my head. I realized I now knew how to buy a little extra time for my guardian angels. I wished it could have been a *good* idea, but hey; once a marine, always a marine.

"Sorry Sweet Cheeks; you're not my type. Yeah, your looks are tolerable, that is, for a mature woman, but you need to work on your attitude. Heck, if I wanted to be ordered around, I could have stayed in the marines. Speaking of which, Sweet Cheeks, I've kept in contact with some of my old buddies in the RFC Marine Corps. They couldn't keep their mouths shut about how the authorities disabled that weird, earth-hopping craft in Sidney.

"So, Toots, if you expect me to share this information, you had better learn your place and earn your keep. The first thing you need to do is you cut me loose. When you've done that, go fetch me an ice cold beer. I take my beer shaken, not stirred."

I mimicked blowing some cigarette smoke into her face. "So, no, Nurse Strudel, I have no regrets, because we'll always have Bratislava.

She calmly finished her cigarette. She flicked the butt into the ashtray while she exhaled smoke into my face yet again.

"You chose... poorly, Sergeant Sherwood. I now will teach you the painful consequences of false pride. Be of good cheer, though; I will not ruin you for Fraulein Valentine. I would never sabotage my beloved husband's critical research."

She lit up yet another cigarette and started smoking it with her left hand, holding it between her ring and middle fingers. She picked up her riding crop in her right hand. She swished it several times. Her face lit up with joy. Her eyes got even crazier. She rediscovered her long-departed German accent.

"Varrior zo you be, Sergeant Shervud, rest azhured, I still haf vays uff making you talk."

I'll never understand dames. I had just made Frau Dr. Bug-Nuts smile; she treated me just plain rotten in return. I passed out after a while.

The Return of Dr. Gruesome

Eventually I woke. The other mad doctor was playing with his monocle.

"You have incredible stamina and toughness, Sergeant Sherwood. Your new bruises should heal. Even Brunhilde was moderately impressed by your tolerance for pain. You should have shared your knowledge sooner, though. Your overweening stubbornness caused you to suffer a great deal of unnecessary discomfort."

"I've always been the strong, silent type of guy, Doc. In fact, I was so silent I almost ran away to join the circus to become a mime rather than enlist in the marines. Folks told me I had more than enough talent to be a mime, but I was way too erratic. You might even say I was the best of mimes; I was the worst of mimes."

"Wotan forbid you take up comedy, Sergeant Sherwood. Anyway, we now believe the Fatherland can use you in our elite warrior breeding program. Indeed, your male offspring, properly educated, might qualify to become senior sergeants or perhaps warrant officers. All actual officers, of course, must descend from pure German stock of appropriate pedigree.

"Naturally, your existence remains conditional on your good behavior, so it behooves you to comport yourself as a gentleman for the next several weeks. After that, in four weeks at the most, you will be so utterly dependent upon addictive drugs the focus of your life will be reduced to begging Brunhilde to administer them. I am sure she will be delighted to agree to your entreaties, for a price. She so enjoys her harmless hobbies."

"How long was I out?"

"About six hours; it's an unavoidable aftereffect of overdosing on these noxious drugs. I will administer your next dose shortly. The drugs will do nothing to ease your remaining pain, but your body will not care. You should be ready for additional sessions with Frauline Valentine within the quarter hour. Oh, and try not to annoy Brunhilde with your banter. The risk to reward ratio is unfavorable."

He played with his monocle.

"Science never rests, you know. I will continue to run tests on Frauline Valentine until we leave Sidney for my earth."

He stared through his monocle at a ceiling light, pulled out a soft cloth from his desk drawer, and cleaned his monocle yet again.

"I was delighted to meet Frauline Valentine. In my Reich, a young lady with her obvious charms and pure, albeit peasant, Aryan bloodlines, would have been selected to join the household of a top Party official the instant she turned eighteen. It would be inconceivable for her to have been available to be used in scientific experiments."

"Right, Doc, inconceivable; it sucks to be her. And Doc, while I was born, I wasn't born yesterday. Your earlier spiel, about doing this for your world's version of humanitarianism, is so much hogwash. It's inconceivable hogwash, to coin a phrase."

"You are backsliding, Sergeant Sherwood, and your manners are slipping. Though I acknowledge you are completely correct."

Dr. Whacko pushed a button and Dr. Bug-Nuts and Cynthia reentered the lab room. Cynthia, per previously, was wearing nothing but a vacant look.

Dr. Whacko said, "Darling, please ask Frauline Valentine to do something unpleasant to Sergeant Sherwood."

Dr. Bug-Nuts then flashed a smile. I had a brief vision involving starving sharks and wounded seals.

"Cynthia, Robin no longer loves you. On the shelf is a small serrated knife. I wish you to take it, walk over to Robin and then very slowly carve off his left testicle. I believe it may be defective, so I wish to examine it for flaws. Ignore his screams."

"Yes, Frau Dr. Brunhilde, of course. You are so good to me, Frau Dr. Brunhilde."

Cynthia picked up the small knife and turned around. Dr. Whacko signaled Dr. Bug-Nuts. She said, "Stop, Cynthia. Robin has begged you to forgive him. He loves you again and you love him. Put the knife back where you found it. Now, chew two of your breath mints and give him a deep, passionate kiss."

"Yes, Frau Dr. Brunhilde, of course. You are so good to me, Frau Dr. Brunhilde."

Cynthia chomped a couple candy-things and then explored my tonsils for half a minute. She reeked of peppermint.

Brunhilde snapped her fingers and Cynthia backed off. I got to breathe clear air again. My eyes stopped watering. Cynthia and Dr. Bug-Nuts went back to the adjacent room.

"Heck, Doc. I understand everything now. That little trick with the breath mints will sure as heck earn you the *Reich Prize for Pointless Medicine, First Class*, if you ever return home."

"No, it won't, Mr. Sherwood. I won't be publicizing some aspects of my experiments, in part because knife-work lacks plausible deniability. However, had those been a different version of *breath mints*, the colorless, odorless chemicals in the mints would have interacted with the powerful performance-enhancing drugs soon to be coursing through your system. Ninety-eight percent of the time this drug interaction occurs, it causes the male participant to suffer a massive, though delayed, heart attack.

"The delay ranges from three to five hours. The female partner is unaffected and the precursor drug, which is harmless by itself, is quickly flushed through her system, well before the victim suffers his heart attack. Consequently, there is no indication whatsoever the male's tragic death is because of anything other than his dissipated lifestyle."

He smiled. "Several hundred expendable Cubans died to validate these medical findings. Naturally, I strive to use statistically valid samples for all of my research projects. My test subjects' involuntary, but painful, sacrifices will not be in vain.

"On my earth, as on your earth, political and bureaucratic advancement is often determined by the selection of one's parents, rather than the originality and merit of one's research. It's quite sad, but many of my earth's overweight, out-of-shape, and narrow-minded senior scientific officials eschew structured research entirely.

"Instead, they use less-powerful and less addictive versions of the drugs which I am injecting into you to assist with their, ahem, more personalized efforts to perfect the Aryan race. Alas, even they are at risk of dying should they *accidentally* ingest my *special* breath mints."

Something still didn't add up. Then it hit me. "Doc; killing off bunches of your senior folks sounds like a great idea, but that doesn't explain why boatloads of Cubans attacked that Rhode Island estate. Yeah, I heard about that incident through the jarhead grapevine. Had the Cubans not attacked, you guys could have stayed in the shadows a while longer. Now you are doing stuff on the fly and on the run."

He sighed. "We had recently deciphered that idiot Caudillo's diary. He had left clues behind on my earth. He had intended to impress his relatives or something similar. My earth may now be aware travel to alternate earths is possible. My colleagues wanted to return home immediately. They believed if they captured the wife or daughter of the wealthiest man in the RFC, they could exchange her for the WiG hidden in Sidney.

"If we had returned with a stolen world-hopping device, we would have been heroes. Had we sat on our asses waiting to be rescued and somehow were, we faced the prospect of firing squads for dereliction of our duty to warn the Fatherland. My foolish colleagues talked themselves into a panic. I warned them if a Spetsnaz platoon could not penetrate Sir Charles Burr's security cordon, no amount of Cuban thugs would stand a chance."

The Cubans came closer to kidnapping Melinda than he thought, but I didn't feel like correcting him.

He shook his head slightly and continued. "Top Party officials often have similarly effective physical security procedures; neither kidnappings nor assassination attempts typically succeed. Few such men are celibate, though; quite the contrary. A beautiful, sexually insatiable young lady always has a chance of being physically intimate with such men. At which point, if properly conditioned, she can administer the complementary drug to deadly effect without ever realizing she has done so.

"I doubt more than ten or twelve carefully selected senior scientists and bureaucrats need die before my path is cleared to become the Reich Minister of Health and Medicine. Perhaps you have heard of the aphorism, '*Whether it's milk or cream, the scum also rises to the top.*'"

"I'm not sure that rings a bell, Doc. Though I bet it sounds really profound in the original German."

"Oh, indeed it does, Sergeant Sherwood. There may be hope for you yet. Anyway, once installed as Minister, I plan to appoint my lovely and brilliant Frau as the Reich's Director of Human Experimentation. She has many theories which she wishes to test using rigorous, laboratory conditions. It will be a glorious era for science, if not for her test subjects."

Growing up on that Michigan cherry farm I had never imagined that the embodiment of absolute evil would be sporting a monocle and wearing a lab coat. I figured I might as well confirm it.

"So Doc, everything you two have done since you arrived, all the drugs and torture, all the shattered lives and painful deaths, came about because you and your wife wanted to advance your political careers a couple of steps if you ever returned home?"

"Precisely correct, Sergeant Sherwood; your intuition continues to surprise me. To coin a phrase, 'All your world's my stage and all of you are merely players.' Any Party member from my Reich would have acted similarly."

If there ever was a guy who missed seeing the massive beam in his own eye, it had to be Herr Dr. Whacko. I figured it was time to shift deftly the topic of conversation away from his raging cuckoo-somiasis.

"Is that why you are taking Cynthia with you? As an assassin?"

"No, she wouldn't pass. She speaks only limited German. She is coming solely to ensure my research is complete. I will need to condition other young ladies to serve as my unwitting assassins."

"Uh doc, you'll need a crew. And if you already had a crew, why didn't you use the craft which got you here originally?"

"The Cuban earth-hopper had been sabotaged by one of its now deceased crew members. If the Sidney craft is intact, it can be operated, barely, by six crewmen. Six survivors from the original aircrew are in the third rig, being carefully chaperoned by some expendable Fenian scum.

"The aircrew has been conditioned to cooperate; my dear spouse is quite the expert in such matters. It was so thoughtful of you to tell Brunhilde about how the WiG's batteries probably have been dispersed."

"Yeah, doc, it's clear you two are meant for each other; she's a total sweetheart."

"I quite agree, Sergeant Sherwood. We complement each other wonderfully. It's such a pleasure to be married to a woman who so enjoys her work. Speaking of work, our plan to capture the craft in Sidney entails thousands of innocents dying horrible deaths. Neurotoxin aerosols are remarkably effective when dispersed correctly. I foresee no issues which will prevent us from returning to my earth once I gain control of the world hopping craft."

I was beginning to understand why Wendell Honoré cast Herr Clausewitz as Dr. Gruesome in those flickers. He really was born for the role.

"What's your plan if my folks *have* dispersed the bird's special, explosively unstable batteries for safety reasons? Just suppose it's going to take you two or three days past the scheduled plague release date to collect the batteries. Do you want to commit suicide if all you needed was to wait two or three extra days? Or do you have a backup plan for global conquest, like targeted earthquakes, controlling the weather, or death beams from space?"

The Doc thoughtfully played with his monocle.

"You're correct about the back-up plan; if it proves impossible to make the world-hopper operational, then we will decamp to another location. I will proceed to conquer your earth slowly, but inexorably, using a different type of biological weapon.

"My Frau and I will condition a cadre of gorgeous young ladies, similar to Frauline Valentine. They will spread a deadly, debilitating, and painful disease amongst your senior politicians and military officers. I will offer to cure your world's leaders, albeit temporarily, as long as they obey my every order. You, personally, will either assist us or you will die.

"I feel conquest is my humanitarian duty. My many years in Cuba gave me unparalleled insight into the decadence, deviancy and corruption of many of your vacationing aristocrats. They truly offended me. Those who I cannot control, I will eradicate and replace with my choice of far more moral and obedient minions."

"That's a bushel-load of public-spiritedness, Doc, though your plan reminds me of the plots of some awfully cheesy flickers. Well, come to think of it, that would be right up your alley. Still, I have to ask, given the nature of your experiments on me thus far, what the heck do you consider deviant and decadent?"

"You are a test subject, Mr. Smith. You fall under the category of research. Pain is sometimes an unavoidable consequence of the scientific method. My Frau and I worked selflessly, and indeed, have sacrificed much to advance the Fatherland's eugenic ideals.

"Conversely, many in your aristocracy indulge the worst sort of lusts and manias in an egotistical pursuit of purely personal, hedonistic pleasures. They often traveled to Cuba to enjoy such. The names I could name; the stories I could tell."

An overhead light blinked a few times. The doc reached for a valve amongst the mess of tubes and bags leading into my arm.

"Science never rests, Sergeant Sherwood. Brunhilde has just administered Frauline Valentine's drugs. She will return in a few moments, so you need to be ready as well."

Cynthia appeared; her eyes as vacant as ever. In time, she gave out, and Brunhilde led her away for a quick nap. I closed my eyes and was on the verge of sleep myself when Brunhilde returned.

Doctor Monocle said, "Brunhilde, I have decided the barbarian is right; his navy probably has separated the batteries for safety. Even if we gas the entire island and there is no one alive to stop us, it may take us several days to collect the batteries and install them in the craft. I must use the radio telephone in the other trailer to call Muldoon and Seamus and instruct them to delay the plague toxins' scheduled release for at least a week."

I think I passed out about that point. Time did its thing.

Dawns and Departures of a Jarhead's Life

Nova Scotia

Some Fenian thugs shook me awake, dressed me in winter clothes, re-shackled my arms behind by back, and gagged me. I felt unsteady when I stood up. Even so, the Fenians guided me outside into what turned out to be the early morning cold. I took in the view; we had stopped by the roadside, near the crest of a decently sized hill.

Doctor Whacko and his wife Doctor Bug-Nuts were some ten yards away on a bit of an outcrop from which they could see Sidney harbor off in the distance. The two doctors were looking back and forth between some maps they were holding and the view of Sidney Harbor. The Fenians departed; they probably wanted to get out of the cold. Dr. Whacko turned towards me and walked over.

"Don't try to walk yet, Sergeant Sherwood. Your legs will probably collapse. Consider this breath of fresh air your reward for warning me about the batteries. Thanks to you, I should be able to return to my beloved Reich within three or four days.

"My advance scouts tell me your navy recently constructed three dispersed and guarded bunkers in this area. The weather reports project a frontal system is expected to arrive in twenty-six hours. Once the winds are right, I will release some rather nasty neuro-toxins. They will blanket Sydney and vicinity and tens of thousands of people will die excruciating deaths. We will be fine; I plan to administer neuro-toxin antidotes to our party midday tomorrow."

I opened my eyelids wide at that. The Doc smiled.

"Don't worry a bit, Sergeant. The antidotes are quite effective."

He shrugged. "Still, the craft may not be flyable. Thus, I will reveal to you the names and hobbies of several of your more perverted aristocrats. Once you comprehend the enormity of their crimes, perhaps you will realize what my Frau and I aim to accomplish regarding your earth is more akin to pruning diseased branches to save the rest of a tree. If you acknowledge the necessity of our work, your own conditioning process need not be so stressful. We could use competent help.

"Shall we play charades? You can nod yes or no, initially."

He held up five fingers. I surmised the first person he was going to name had either five letters or syllables in his. I doubted I would have to play along with his stupid game for long; I planned to share a couple of self-improvement suggestions with him if he ever removed my gag.

I was looking right at Doctor Whacko when his head exploded. A half a second later, out of my peripheral vision, I saw Doctor Bug-Nuts' head explode. Then I heard the noises from the twin shock waves from .50-caliber rifle shots. Someone must have owned a beautiful custom job to nail two perfect head shots so close together. Someone was also an egotistical showoff not to aim for center mass.

I started running for the oblique tree line the moment I saw Dr. Whacko's head disintegrate. I got about twenty yards before my legs gave out or I tripped on something. I rolled to take the fall on the frozen ground with my left shoulder. I had heard mortar rounds incoming; as I fell and twisted, I saw the initial rounds were smoke, for some reason. I hoped that was planned to give me cover to escape.

A few moments later, I sort of duck-waddled and inch-wormed out of a tendril of the smoke and slipped into a shallow ditch. I realized I was hearing a lot of shots. Most of them sounded like standard Battle Enfields. I looked up and saw Paul Drake, PhD, PhD, and occasional rat scum, smiling at me while a couple of marines went past me towards the convoy. Paul was uniformed as an RFC Royal Marine Corps major with staff officer tabs. I was glad to see him, for once.

Paul grabbed me and helped me from the ditch. He guided me past the other side of a small stone wall and we sat down on the frozen ground. Meanwhile, a full platoon of marines wearing gas masks headed past us towards the smoke. I didn't think the Buffalo Fenian goons the Doc said he kept in the other two trailers were going to last too long. Paul sliced off my gag, took out his canteen, and held it for me while I swallowed some water.

Paul lit up a cigarette and started sucking smoke.

"I sometimes sneak these when Astrid is not around. I took up smoking, in part, to annoy her into trying to catch me at it. It's payback. She often intentionally grates on my nerves. She has been nagging me for almost two decades about any vices of mine which she doesn't share. Damn all doctors and their stupid god-complexes."

He took another puff.

"Someone will be along with a hacksaw or wire cutters shortly. That was Llywelyn who took out the two nutty professors. I told you he was a hell of a shot. Also, he used target seeking ammunition."

"Paul, why the heck are you here? Aren't you valuable? And what's with your lack of a gas mask?"

"Your powers-that-be wanted someone familiar with the totality of cross-world travel up here. Lycus is an idiot savant with incredible reflexes and piloting skills. Marcus is back in Newport, helping to run communications. That left me. I'm not wearing a stupid gas mask, because it wouldn't do squat to keep me from getting killed if those Nazi doctors had used neurotoxins. So I explained I didn't have time to train on the stupid gas masks.

"That's the reason they sent marines, instead of constabulary folks. Marines train to use gas masks. I didn't have the heart to tell your senior folks it was pointless to wear gas masks. It would have ruined your marines' illusion of safety."

Stuff still didn't add up. "I figured you were listening in, but I still have no idea how."

Paul flipped his cigarette butt into a snowbank. "To cut to the chase, you have a combined locator beacon and microphone inserted in your right ear. The slight scars are usually hidden by earwax. Astrid is a surgical genius; she says so herself. Hell, she never quits saying so. Madeline and Kathy gave us permission to operate on you before you sailed to Cuba. Astrid implanted the device the night you were drinking beer and playing pool with Tiny and Scarbutt.

"Astrid had one of Melinda's serving staff slip something into your beer on that occasion. That's why you had a headache when you woke up the next morning.

"What you don't know happened, you can't tell. We tracked you from the moment you left Newport. We could do this because when my craft dropped me off on this earth, my folks launched a small satellite into geo-stationary orbit focused on the North American east coast. Once it's in orbit and calibrated, it can monitor the signals from those implants. I have the same type of ear implants, though I'm able to turn my implants off and on."

"Say what, Paul?"

"Okay, tell yourself we waved a magic wand and chanted a magic phrase or two to keep track of you. Anyhow, when the Caudillo on that other earth captured the other WiG off the coast of that alternate Cuba, that navigator/electronic warfare officer committed suicide. He was the only one on that WiG who knew about these capabilities.

"Marcus knew about them, of course; sometimes the navigator/EWO needs to track down scouts like me. My folks were always going to find me once they got to this earth and communicated with our satellites."

He smiled. "Anyhow, Astrid brought a couple of spare sets of implants with her for emergencies. You don't have to hide these things in an ear canal to track folks, but it makes it easier to listen in on nearby sounds."

"What? Every scream, every grunt and groan?"

"And every awful word of your D-list flicker dialog. You really should have been born a mime. Trust me, if you ever have to make speeches for a living, be sure to get a scriptwriter.

"Yeah, we listened in on your hammed-up conversations with the crazy doctors. Our communications technology is way better than what they had; besides, they were medical doctors, of a sort, and knew jack about secrecy. Their security awareness sucked.

"Double damn, dude. Those Nazis were more than nuts; when I return to my home world I will have to insist our scientists research such drug interactions. Using naked women as undetectable assassins; what a way to go. Hey, and speaking of trying to kill folks, why the heck did you goad Brunhilde into almost killing you? You had to know she would drop a wagonload of hurt on you the second you called her a mature woman with only tolerable looks."

"Gosh, Paul, and you claimed to be intelligence professional. What do you do when folks come in off the streets and spill their guts to you about your opponent's deepest secret plans? Do you immediately trust them implicitly or do you check them out six ways to Sunday?"

"But if you first had to torture the info out of them, would you be a little more inclined to believe what they said? I *had* to get them to delay the release of their plague toxins. I *hoped* Brunhilde wouldn't kill or cripple me too soon, because she told me she planned to humiliate me first and I figured she would prefer to humiliate a healthy boy-toy. I *really hoped* Astrid could fix any major damage."

His eyes widened. "Son-of-a-gun, Hotshot! You played those wackos like a Stradivarius accordion. Your country may just have to give you yet another medal. Or three."

He seemed to space out, just for a moment. He lit up another cigarette.

"Your instincts were correct. The nutty Nazis weren't going anywhere; the Sidney WiG is temporarily disabled in multiple ways. Physically, we could have hit their little convoy nearly anytime, but the moment Carl mentioned a world-wide plague, we couldn't risk it. We had to wait until they got to Sidney and forced our hand or they slipped up and said something to reveal where the plague toxins were stored.

"Once Carl mentioned Muldoon and Seamus, we got with Bridget and the Brigadier and they identified the likely collaborators. Then we listened to those radio telephone calls you tricked them into making and confirmed the identities of their top collaborators. You pain was our gain; we used the extra time to plan the assaults on their facilities in greater detail. Your buddy Captain Franks is leading the team which should be taking out their hitherto hidden facility in Buffalo even as we speak.

"It's also a good thing this world has not developed a world-wide web yet, though."

"Why, and what the heck is a world-wide web, Paul?"

"Let's say that if you had one, you and Cynthia would be rock stars. Hell, you and Elizabet would be rock stars."

"What's a rock star?"

"This is getting old, John. Shall we go back to the basics? When a man and a woman love each other very, very much or when they are both under the influence of enormous quantities of illegal yet powerful drugs, sometimes amazing things happen."

I was stunned. The totality of the implications finally hit me. "You mean you listened in to every hour of my life since before Havana?

"Not all of it, good buddy. Marcus swears he turned off the listening apparatus once you got back from your missions. And for this trip, Kathy's still in a wheelchair so she could only read the transcripts of your most recent adventures. Besides, Prince Albert told me I can't release any mission recordings to your tabloids or such without his personal approval."

Paul grinned. "Hotshot, why did you have to blame Prince Albert for getting you in your recent difficulties? Hell, I learned some new curse words while you were lying around, complaining about your prowess with women. You might want to be more forgiving of His Highness if you ever have to go out on another mission. The word back from him is he is only going to forgive you for your intemperate language this one mission.

"Also, Elizabet and Francine were practically living in our secure communications room, at least from the moment they learned about your ear implant. Elizabet claimed she was there to listen in on anything the crazy doctors said, but I think she just wanted to hear your manly groans. I bet she is listening in right now. 'Hi, Elizabet.' I have no clue why you are such a popular dude."

"Paul, I am sort of burnt out on that front; give me a couple of decades or so to recover."

He smiled. "Well, you should have listened to your Top Sergeant way back when during your many pre-shore-leave briefings about sticking your rifle in crazy. I guess you're not going to be up for a tag team with the two of them?"

"It's 'gun,' Paul, not 'rifle.' 'This is my rifle, this is my gun; et cetera.' Anyhow, you disgusting rat; you've got to be making all that stuff up. What was that about Elizabet? She told me she was finished with me. Also, I made a rude gesture at you, though with my hands still shackled behind my back, you couldn't have seen it."

"Fortunes of war, Hotshot.

"Hey, that reminds me, Elizabet asked me to download a copy of a different von Clausewitz's book, *On War*. We borrowed that from Timeline McClellan. It's loaded on the Sidney WiG's computer, though it's in its original German. She said she was fine with that. I never knew she was fluent in German. She has other surprising, hidden depths.

"Did you know she normally keeps in shape by practicing with a quarterstaff for two hours a day? You remember, like the stick that dude Littlejohn used in the tales of Robin Hood? Elizabet doesn't believe in edged weapons or firearms."

I glared at him in disgust; what a cheap blow to mention Robin Hood. "I won't ask you what downloading is. You sure you should mention all this stuff, Paul? Who else knows about my ear radio? If you do, then so does Llywelyn."

Paul nodded. Then he said, "As of right now? I need to count; Astrid, Mary, and Theodora. They performed the operation. Then there is Marcus, Julius, and Julius' assistant communications technician; Kathy, Francine, Bridget, Tiny and Scarbutt. From the government side, there is the Brigadier, her husband, Admiral Francis, the governor general and Prince Albert. I don't know if anyone else knows. Bridget swore she didn't tell Elizabet about your earpiece before you two set out; Bridget did not want Elizabet to act strangely. Well, considering it's Elizabet, let's just say, to act too strangely."

He cupped his hands and leaned into my right ear. "Just kidding!" he said.

"That's way too many folks already, Paul. Having an ace in the hole doesn't work too well if it's actually a show card. When do I get this sucker hacked out of my ear?"

"No need for that; it has an embedded self-destruct sequence. It melts. It won't hurt for long because it's a fatal process."

I mentally flipped him another one-digit salute. I could hear in the background the gunfire was dying down. I felt no urge to go help the marines. Also, it's hard to shoot or make rude gestures effectively when your hands are shackled behind your back.

So I glared at Paul, wondering if he was pulling my leg or not about the fatal process bit. He smiled and said, "Don't be such a total wuss. I guess you are going to love the good news I have for you, then."

I looked askance at him. "You have that 'I am such a bastard that I am going to enjoy telling you about the wagonload of manure about to fall on your head' look. I saw the look too many times in the marines. What's the news?"

Paul continued, "Well, Joseph and Melinda had a nine-and-a-half-pound baby boy. You owe their kid a gift of some sort. And Vicki will deliver in another two or three weeks. That's not the best news, though.

"Astrid says the good news is Elizabet's diaphragm would have worked perfectly. The bad news for you is Elizabet never used it. Naturally, being a guy, you never noticed. Elizabet was confident she was pregnant when she left you at Rochester. Astrid has confirmed her status.

"Dame Katherine, amazingly enough, appears resigned to having such things happen. At least I only have to deal with one woman on this earth.

"Anyhow, after you return to Rhode Island, consider treating Elizabet nicely. Of course, you know better than I do about what could go wrong if you piss off seriously your new, sort of adoptive mother-in-law, Bridget O'Shaughnessy."

Paul took great pleasure in watching my eyes glaze over in shock as I processed that thought. The gun fire ended. A marine corporal showed up with some wire cutters and snapped the chain connecting my wrist shackles. I grabbed some nasty tasting field rations from a passing marine and starting nibbling them cautiously as Paul and I walked over to review the situation. Llywelyn was waiting for us. He was wearing the uniform of a marine master sergeant and also wore a set of general staff tabs.

Paul said, "Let's see how many of my people survived. Your marines had orders not to shoot anyone who was not shooting at them. Still, who knows what your yahoos did. 'Take arms upon a sea of troubles, and by attacking, end them.' Indeed."

I glared at him briefly. I was too tired and hungry to do more. Obviously, the rat also had been reading up on his Shakespeare.

We found five original aircrew survivors, two of whom had been wounded. The other crewman had been killed during the brief firefight. I guess it didn't matter who fired that particular bullet; ultimately, the Fenians and the two mad doctors were responsible for his death. Navy corpsmen were evaluating the survivors.

Paul and I went up to his folks, and he said something rapidly to them in his version of Latin. The two healthiest ones jumped to their feet, and each gave him a Roman-style salute. He waved them off, said something else, and they relaxed. Llywelyn barked out a quick phrase of his own. We waited there until a marine captain arrived and we could be assured the rescued crewmen were going to receive VIP treatment.

Ambulances arrived. One of them carried nurse anesthetist Mary, who had been conscripted to identify and take charge of any chemicals or biologicals. Folks started stuffing the bodies of Fenian thugs into body bags. Several Fenians had surrendered, but I doubted any would qualify for a life insurance policy, given the laws regarding treason and rebellion and murder and such.

The marines found Cynthia naked and unconscious in the trailer room where she used to have her way with me. She had an enormous lump on her forehead. An ambulance crew covered her up in sheets and blankets, put her on a stretcher and hauled her off to Sidney Hospital.

Llywelyn let out a low whistle as the stretcher crew carried her past us. "I saw her before they wrapped her up. That's one healthy looking lady with some impressive flying buttresses, Majors." Then he grinned at me. "I sure hope you didn't ruin her for other men, Major Smith."

Paul eyeballed Llywelyn. "I thought you took a pledge of geographic celibacy while deployed after your last wild affair; the one before I left Bermuda. Excepting, of course, the call of duty down in Havana. I had planned on neglecting to mention that little escapade to your wife."

"It was all those Saturday nights chaperoning our guys at *The Busty Mermaid*, Major. I came to my senses. I mean, I had to go with the other guys to make sure they stayed out of trouble. Speaking of trouble, Major Hotshot, Max didn't run into anything. He and the Yinzers got back safely. Max never found who he was looking for, though."

That wasn't the only trouble Llywelyn should have discussed; given his obvious skills, Llywelyn should have been able to knock both mad doctors out of action without killing them so they could be interrogated. Not that Llywelyn would tell me diddly if I asked him anything. Still, it never hurts to ask.

"Hey, Paul, old bosom buddy and greatest pal ever; why did you have Llywelyn shoot the two crazy doctors? They died instantly. That was way too quick and much too painless. The way I figure it, their schemes were the root cause for Kathy's inability to have kids of her own."

Paul pointed his index finger at my ear. Then he touched his own ear with the same finger. Then he shook his head in a silent "no."

"Llywelyn had reason to believe the two insane doctors were about to hack you to death with scalpels. He shot only to stop the threat against you. Unfortunately, the two doctors wound up deceased."

Paul clearly didn't want to tell me squat as long as other folks were listening in on his answer. I would ponder that.

Over the next several days other RFC Marine units, aided by intelligence from Bridget's sources in Rochester and Paddy Blaney's gang in Montreal, successfully attacked major Fenian locations at the same time marines attacked the convoy. An RFC constabulary special tactics team found Bill Valentine's badly shot up and decomposed body in Buffalo. Certain captured Fenian leaders listened to recordings of Doctor Whacko talking about how he was using the moronically subhuman Irish as pawns in his plan for world domination.

It didn't take the remaining Fenian leaders long to rat out other potential locations where von Clausewitz might have been conducting his research. Some Fenian leaders avoided the hangman because of their enthusiastic cooperation.

We are confident we located all the fatal toxins. Ruth and Astrid set up field expedient containment facilities, put them under guard, and left them in situ. They hoped folks from Astrid's world would arrive to take charge of removing the toxins; Astrid judged it too dangerous for us to try, except as a last resort. After we located the toxins, our Empire politicians considered themselves to be in a state of war with that Nazi-dominated earth.

We learned from the surviving Fenians that Carl and Brunhilde were the only Nazis with whom they had ever dealt. We concluded their RFC research program with the Fenians was a personal secondary project for the Clausewitz's in the event something went wrong in Cuba. Our best surmise was their colleagues in Cuba did not know Carl and Brunhilde were conducting independent research, which could have killed them all.

Sleeping Beauty Awakes

Newport

Paul, Llywelyn, Cynthia and I traveled post haste on the RFC light cruiser *Diamond* to Newport. Cynthia didn't complain a bit about the seas being a little rough; she was still in a coma. We hit Newport and ambulanced Cynthia to the priory, which by now had the most modern small clinic in Rhode Island. I accompanied her to the priory, but only because that was where Kathy was staying. Kathy was still in her wheelchair.

"Astrid says I can practice walking again in two weeks. She has mapped out an initial therapy program where I will walk in the pool's lap lanes."

Kathy paused; then said, "I think we can talk openly, John. I told Marcus to shut down the monitoring equipment the moment you boarded the *Diamond*. In any event, he needed the rest. Marcus and Julius had been working rotating twelve-hour shifts ever since you left. No one is listening in now and the communications room is locked and under marine guard.

"Oh, John, ignore what Elizabet told you in Rochester. You must not neglect her during this stage of her pregnancy; she has both physical and emotional needs. Francine understands and agrees.

"However, I positively forbid you to impregnate any other ladies when we attend Madeline's funeral. That would be the height of bad manners. Madeline is not doing well at all and I have already had to take over for her. While I am on medical convalescence, I will stay here in Newport. I will use the communications room in Melinda's cottage to maintain contact with Glynda in New York. We will decide where to settle permanently once I have fully recovered."

"Rhode Island is fine, Kathy, for as long as you wish to stay. But I am fine with Philly if you wish to live close to your family."

"Maybe we'll move to Philadelphia once the vaccine program is fully up and running. In the meantime, Elizabet will serve as my executive officer; it turns out she has a legitimate, if unusual PhD in European History from a major German University. Madeline has already had Elizabet commissioned as a major in the army reserves. Elizabet will also serve as our liaison to the irregular intelligence collection activities conducted on our behalf by the East Coast mobs."

"Yeah, Kathy, Elizabet mentioned her degree, in passing."

"She took most of her course work by correspondence, but Bridget paid for the professors to sail over from the Palatinate once a semester. They administered Elizabet's exams and sat as her dissertation committee."

Kathy tired. We held hands and stared at each other for several minutes. I forced myself to talk, as much as the next subject pained me. I had to try.

"Kathy, I wanted to kill those two Nazis. Slowly and painfully. For you and for the children we can't have."

Kathy shook her head, smiled sadly, and sighed. "I know you did, John. I wanted to kill them also until I thought more about it. I am realizing how easy it might be, especially for us now, to conflate personal revenge with actual justice. It's probably better for your soul that Llywelyn denied you the chance to exact your revenge upon them. Besides, you will still have the chance to father more children, only not with me."

Her smile faded somewhat. "Ultimately, though, the mad doctors were Paul's responsibility. His Empire's carelessness enabled them to travel to our world. I am still pondering the whys and wherefores of Llywelyn shooting them in the manner he did, though."

She rested some more. We stared at each other for what seemed forever. Kathy spoke again.

"Life goes on, John, as do duties. The Governor General has already assigned me my first major task. Cynthia has been moved to a double room. I will be transferred to that room and be the other patient. I am to recommend whether Cynthia Valentine be hanged for multiple murders or shot for treason."

"Uh, Kathy, that doesn't sound totally legal."

"It's not, though I will insist the process be ethical. If Cynthia is pregnant, that will complicate things immensely. Yes, I know you were literally in no position to help yourself. I reviewed the transcripts of every audio recording of your sessions with the insane Nazis.

"It is my duty to evaluate Cynthia, and I will not shirk it. Apparently, being named a Dame of the Empire comes with attendant costs. Now, kiss me, you fertile fool. Then go pay your respects to Francine and Elizabet."

I kissed her and left. Francine and Elizabet were waiting outside.

A week after we got back from Sidney, Astrid and Mary decided Cynthia's body had flushed as many surplus hormones and other such chemicals from her system as it was going to flush. More importantly, they thought the lump on her skull had gone down sufficiently and they could bring her back to the land of wide awake without her suffering too much pain. They took steps to help her wake up. I was there at her bedside when Cynthia came out of her slumber.

Cynthia's eyes opened. She saw me. Mary gave her some water from a small cup. Cynthia flexed her jaw and slowly spoke. It was a sort of stream of consciousness.

"Hello Robin; you look a lot older out of uniform. I didn't expect to see you. Is Rachel nearby? Daddy told me I should make a genuine apology to both of you; not just that phony, half-assed apology I gave yesterday. I admit I was a real bitch yesterday; I guess it was yesterday. I remember Daddy driving me home after the picnic where I had been an absolute monster. My PMS was awful; Daddy had grounded me for two weeks because I told him yet again I wanted to be a call girl. I had to lash out at the world.

"No boy my age at the picnic would look at me because my breasts were too flat and because they feared Daddy. I shouldn't have taken it out on you. But you looked so manly and handsome in your uniform; I could have sworn we were meant for each other.

"Where is Rachel? She seemed sweet, I mean, when she was not pulling my hair. I could tell she loves you. You sense that when you are rolling around in the grass trying to claw the eyes out of another girl. When are you getting married? I didn't know you were engaged to Rachel. I guess I overreacted when she threw the lemonade in my face. It's cane sugar and water; it washes out. What am I wearing now?"

She glanced down at her body, covered only by her thin hospital gown and thin blankets. They kept the recovery rooms on the toasty side of warm. "Oh gosh, what happened? My breasts are huge! Something's not right."

Cynthia paused and blushed again. She turned her head and focused on Astrid. "You are dressed like a doctor. Why are my breasts so huge?"

Astrid answered using hitherto undemonstrated diplomatic skills. "There is a time and a place for everything, Cynthia. Yes, I am a doctor. I may be the best doctor on this planet. At the moment, you are lying in bed because you have suffered a terrible concussion of some type and you should not be engaging in any physical exertion of any sort until I give you medical clearance. I need to run some more medical tests before I answer questions about your breasts."

Cynthia blinked at Astrid's answer and focused on Mary. "You're a nun of some sort. I can't tell which order, though. Lust is a sin, isn't it, Sister? I have never confessed to actual lust before; I mean, I went to confession last week, but it was the same as every week for the past year since my mom died. I was a brat at home and I disobeyed my daddy and I told him I wanted to be a prostitute, but only to make him angry, not because I wanted to turn tricks. Yuck! The good father always told me to do better, but I couldn't help myself. So I guess I have one new sin to confess this week; I think I lust for Robin. I can't think of any other sins."

This was not exactly the conversation which I was expecting from Cynthia Valentine, possibly the Blonde Widow, killer of dozens and accomplice to Nazis from another earth.

I finally had a chance to speak. "It's good to see you, Cynthia. You are in a private hospital in Rhode Island Colony. You had a nasty bump on the head; that may account for the dreams and those other odd feelings. This lady beside you is Doctor Astrid. She and the other lady, Sister Mary, are going to talk to you for a while and check out that awful lump. The final lady in the room is Dame Katherine; she is recovering from her own surgery. After the doctor and the nurse have talked with you, I will try to come back and do the same. In the meantime, I am going to wheel Dame Katherine around the grounds so she may enjoy some fresh air."

I didn't want to tell her that her father was dead. Or what we thought she had been doing the past several years. It turned out what I wanted didn't matter at all; Kathy took that decision out of my hands. Kathy refused to let anyone say anything to Cynthia about what we thought Cynthia had been up to.

"It would affect the potential legal charges. Her solicitors would claim we implanted the memories by talking about events about which we had no firsthand knowledge and Cynthia was only confessing to our suspicions. Any decent legal defense would also claim, possibly with merit, that Cynthia was a drug-controlled puppet of those insane Nazi doctors and thus was not responsible for her alleged actions.

"We have no way to establish when the Nazis first met Cynthia, or how long ago they had injected Cynthia with mind-control and emotion affecting drugs. Senior Sergeant Llywelyn made certain those Nazis would never testify. And as to that, I have been told his decision to shoot them is beyond my purview. Indeed!"

Kathy lifted an eyebrow at that one. I suspected Herr Doctor Carl von Clausewitz had not been lying when he hinted to me that a lot of aristocratic roads led back to Cuba. I was also confident Kathy, Melinda, Elizabet, and Bridget would investigate such things the moment they could do so.

Kathy continued. "Besides, a public prosecution of Cynthia in her current state would be a fiasco. I will not be a party to extra-judicial prosecutions of possible innocents; His Royal Highness and the Governor General understood that when I accepted my position."

Kathy was right. Cynthia could never be brought to trial, even for murders, if any, which she might have committed before she got caught up with the two Nazi nimrods. Also, while I thought the circumstantial evidence against Cynthia was strong, the sad fact is there are numerous murderous blondes in the world. I couldn't prove a darn thing other than Cynthia used to be a successful hunting guide and had been a crack shot. Heck, she had been convinced to think I had killed her high school boyfriend and I know for a fact I was sailing across the Atlantic when he died.

I wondered what we would do with Miss Valentine.

A Pregnant Pause

Astrid finally got around to confirming Cynthia's pregnancy three days after Cynthia woke up. Astrid observed that in the absence of any ability to evaluate DNA evidence, whatever that was, we did not know for sure I was the father. Heck, Dr. Whacko could have been the father for all I knew. Damn all space Nazis and their fertility drugs.

Cynthia had not given the slightest sign she had remembered a thing about her life since the day of that picnic, back when she was almost fourteen, so we couldn't exactly ask her if there were other potential fathers of her kid-to-be.

We, of course, had her room wired, and Elizabet reviewed Cynthia's ramblings. Elizabet processed everything and said there were no inconsistencies to suggest Cynthia was faking her memory lapse. Kathy sent the file on Cynthia via an army courier directly to the Governor General along with Kathy's evaluation that Cynthia could not be charged successfully for any crimes. She also wrote the Governor General, warning him, if he ignored Kathy's recommendation, that she, Kathy, would resign all of her official posts as a matter of conscience and join Cynthia's legal defense team.

After that, Kathy and I had to have another one-on-one conversation. She spoke first. "Well, it's another fine mess you got me in. Someone will have to tell Cynthia she is pregnant, because that's the type of thing a girl notices, eventually. Then someone will have to tell her who the father might be and how she got that way.

"Astrid told me Cynthia is almost ready to walk again; her dizziness is almost gone. Since we will not be charging Cynthia, we have no legal reason to hold her, but in her present state, she is incapable of independent living. In the absence of other identifiable suspects that leaves you with another couple of impending kids to support. At least you can afford it. As of this morning, you, alone, were worth 2.2 million pounds sterling. It's fortunate you had such an excellent solicitor who made sure you got at least a minor share of those vaccine profits."

Yeah, lucky me.

"We have to do this ethically, John, or at least appear to do so, in part because I don't want anyone mucking around with national security issues. We first must deal with Cynthia's indigence. The mad doctors drained her financial resources and Bill Valentine used all his funds trying to track down his daughter.

"According to church records, Cynthia stopped going to confession the day she turned eighteen years-old, but she is still listed as a communicant of the Catholic Church. They can step in to act initially in loco parentis until we sort things out. I talked with Bridget and she will ensure the local diocese does so. She and the diocese also will hire a top-notch solicitor to represent Cynthia. I will, unofficially, be able to approve or disapprove her choice of solicitor."

"You won't leave anything to chance, will you, Kathy?"

She shook her head, no.

"Once we have agreed upon a solicitor, he will be given the background on the affair and he will work with Cynthia to determine how Cynthia wishes to proceed. She is, after all, almost twenty-five years old and legally an adult, even if she remembers nothing after that picnic before she turned fourteen.

"After Cynthia has had long talks with her solicitor, she may ask to join our cozy little extended family. It's clear she is yet another lady madly in love with you. It must be a marine thing, being able to charm so many young ladies so quickly. Though as I recall, I practically had to beat you over the head to get you to bed me, or at least have Cousin Tiny threaten to beat you senseless on my behalf.

"If Cynthia joins our happy little group, I will make sure His Royal Highness has no doubts as to the enormity of the debt He owes all of us. For Cynthia's sake, it might be best if she joins us. I think Astrid and

Mary and possibly Ruth, if she becomes available, are the best people on the planet to monitor Cynthia and help her manage and adjust to all those still unknown drugs to which those monsters subjected her. Then again, she may not join us. Sergeant Llywelyn keeps inquiring when she will be well enough to receive visitors.

"I understand some of Cynthia's issues regarding her father; I have a couple of cousins who have been alleged to be torpedoes in the Four Families, but my late father was a chef. It's not quite the same. It must have been tough for Cynthia after she lost her mother. I wonder when she went off the rails.

"John, I feel myself getting a little chilled. Could you push my chair over near the fireplace at the far wall?"

I did. She pulled out a large envelope out from under her wrap and gave it to me. I pulled a sheet of paper from the envelope. It was densely written in Kathy's precise script. It read:

John, say nothing aloud. Burn this after you read it. Elizabet was listening in on you in person when you were rescued. She memorized the brief conversation, much of it crosstalk, among Paul and the survivors of captured aircraft. Elizabet translated the conversation with the help of Bridget's pet professors. They took a lot of long walks along the coast. This is the critical part of your rescue.

One aircrew member cried out in the background, "Legatus Augusti." Paul replied, "No titles. I have come to bring you home; it may be awhile." Another voice cried, "Thank you, my prince." Then Llywelyn said, "Shut up, moron; his brother Britannicus is the stinking prince. He works for a living. Wait until we are alone."

The crewman thanking the prince was the rescued pilot, a major. Senior Sergeant Llywelyn called him a moron. The major shut up and took it. Recall that during Liam O'Shaughnessy's gall bladder operation, Astrid called Llywelyn an assassin and revealed Llywelyn and Paul and Astrid have known each other at least since Paul was eighteen years-old. I suspect Llywelyn is a family retainer and Paul's personal bodyguard and possibly his personal assassin as well.

Our visitors have been lying to us about Paul and Astrid's positions. Elizabet was listening on separate occasions when Mary and Theodora addressed Astrid using a term which another one of Bridget's pet professors believes is probably an ancient Norse word for princess. Our best guess, based on disparate conversations, is Astrid's sister is named Sigrun and Sigrun is married to Paul's older brother, a Prince Britannicus. Prince and Princess of what, we can't guess, except they are important.

Astrid appears confident she will see Sigrun again. They seem to have had cover stories for their cover stories, though we don't think they started out with the same cover stories. That led to some of their conflict. We do not know whether they are hiding their identities and the true circumstances of their world out of caution or out of malice.

On a personal note, I believe Madeline and her husband used you. In retrospect, I believe your investigations of the Fenians were useful, but not critical. I think you were used primarily as a goat; as in being the bait for a tiger hunt. You were staked out in the middle of a field while Madeline waited for the tiger to sense his prey and pounce.

I talked privately to Bridget and Elizabet. Bridget has known Madeline, albeit generally at a distance, for thirty-five years and has seen firsthand how focused and ruthless Madeline could be when pursuing her duties. Bridget believes Madeline had long planned for Melinda to take over as the Coordinator of Intelligence Activities.

Bridget noted Madeline is Cornelius' fourth cousin, once removed; Madeline's mother was a De Witt. Bridget believes Madeline knew all about Cornelius van Ruse de Veldt's preference for men. Had the Governor General requested Melinda take the position of Intelligence Coordinator after Melinda's arranged marriage turned to ashes, Melinda might well have accepted.

Bridget speculated Madeline only offered me an army commission and my initial position at Joint Base West Kingston in order for Madeline to have an excuse to interact more frequently with Melinda. Once you revealed the truth about Cornelius to Melinda and Melinda converted to Catholicism and married Joseph, Melinda was out of the question as a replacement.

When our visitors arrived, they became the most important issues of our time. Madeline then learned she was dying. She had to recommend a successor. I knew our visitors intimately and was both qualified and available, though not her first choice.

Bridget also now believes, and she explained this to me before your trip to Quebec, that our largely English aristocracy is more corrupt and degenerate than even she had imagined. She came to this conclusion based upon her extensive interviews with the four Cubans, one of whom was an officer, whom her folks captured during the attack on her estate. Bridget is an honorable woman, John; she kept her word to them. She kept them on ice and smuggled them to Argentina after Havana was captured.

Bridget also had some of her folks run an initial analysis to determine how many of our RFC aristocrats have spent an abnormal amount of time in Cuba over the last five years. The number is shockingly large. Mary and Theodora's subsequent conversations with ladies who had been entrapped in the Havana sex trade provided additional evidence to support this thesis. Herr Doctor Carl von Clausewitz likely was correct in his estimate of how depraved a portion of our upper aristocracy has become.

I plan to ask Penelope and Melinda to inquire discretely which folks in their circles seemed to have spent a lot of time in Cuba. I need a better handle as to whom in our own government we can trust.

Bridget admires you; she observed even the most cold-blooded antagonist might hesitate to strike at you if he knew you were the father of Bridget's latest grandchild. Bridget was the one who insisted Elizabet accompany you; Bridget made a lot of concessions to Madeline to make that happen.

Bridget has far more resources in Montreal, Quebec, Rochester and Buffalo than she had admitted publicly and Elizabet knew exactly how to call for help if needed. Elizabet left you before you went to Buffalo only because she thought it was likely she was pregnant.

I am almost certain the von Clausewitz's were killed to prevent them from revealing certain names; names too numerous or embarrassing for our government to make public. On balance, I suspect Madeline suggested that course to either our Governor General or perhaps directly to Prince Albert. I doubt I will ever know the truth of the matter.

Paul undoubtedly extracted his own concessions from our government to get them to accept such a plan. I now agree with Bridget that there may be more hyenas roaming around our little world than I had ever imagined.

I will do my duties for crown and country, at least for a few years, though our politicians may not appreciate who or what my inquiries may expose. I do not believe our world was meant to be merely a playground for a jaded and corrupt aristocracy. We will need every ally we can trust. I think we can trust Bridget more than we can trust many senior men in our government. I also think we can trust Astrid more than we can trust Paul.

John, please be nice to Elizabet; guard her with your life. She may be indispensable, not only to identify the more corrupt and depraved members of our aristocracy, but also to create a sustainable modus vivendi between the Irish Catholics and the Empire. Burn this now and watch what you say both around our guests and around Madeline.

I love you.

Kathy gestured in the fireplace's direction. I tossed the paper into it and watched it burn. Not that I planned to watch what I said, at least not for long.

Life never quit coming at you. I turned back to Kathy, and she smiled weakly. I looked at the bright side. At least I would not be the one to have the initial talk with Cynthia. I hoped I could stay out of trouble in the future while I kept tabs on our cross time guests. The only event where I was likely to screw up was Madeline's forthcoming funeral. Of course, the way things had been going, I was probably going to attend the funeral and wind up killing bunches of folks for a lot of stupid and idiotic reasons.

Wrassling with New Information

Brigadier Madeline Hamilton's somber and uneventful funeral service was held two weeks later in Westchester County, New York Colony. It was a huge of C-of-E service and had both army and navy honor guards. Half the RFC cabinet attended, which entailed a massive presence from both the RFC and the New York Colony constabularies.

Kathy was depressed the entire time and said she would not work in New York City. She would spend her next three years in Rhode Island and reconsider her options after the vaccine research program was fully spun up.

Recently we had stayed at the leased thirty-room cottage across the road from Melinda's cottage, just inland. After Kathy chose to stay in the area, the navy purchased the cottage outright and contracted for it to be fully rehabbed over the next three months. Once rehabbed, it would become an RFC Navy Annex with a full communications suite along with VIP living quarters for our unusual extended family.

At least the construction workmanship would be top-notch. Bridget O'Shaughnessy had vetted the local construction crews after the navy had selected its contractors. She had her enforcers, Slab and Wires, give a pep talk to the local construction guilds heads before the projects started. We weren't expecting any problems with shoddy workmanship.

Speaking of Bridget, I may have mentioned the RFC has almost always accommodated successful criminals; after all, our politicians all worship the memory of Aaron Burr. The RFC parliament voted to give Bridget O'Shaughnessy an official "Thanks of Parliament" for her multiple philanthropic works. Her daughters received similar, though lesser, awards.

Bridget had completely solidified her position as the most powerful and respected Irish Catholic in North America, possibly in the world. She was certainly the most ruthless and I would be the father of one of her grandkids. Some folks hit the lottery. At least I was undoubtedly luckier than the next set of cross-world Nazis who showed up if they found themselves guests of Bridget's folks.

She had reviewed the recordings of Dr. Whacko expressing his opinions as to the sub-human nature of Gaelic scum. I thought I had seen Bridget's angry look in the aftermath of her estate being shelled; it turns out that was her "I am a trifle annoyed" look. Kathy was going to get plenty of help from Bridget's folks when it came to looking for signs of cross-world infiltrations.

Melinda invited us back to her family's place during the interim while remodeling chaos reigned next door. Melinda's estate, huge as it was, was getting crowded once her parents returned.

About a week after we had moved back over to Melinda's cottage, Kathy gave me some good news.

"We found Cynthia's custom rifle, John; the one the German whacko doctors hocked, the .48-caliber Creedmore. It was sold to a collector who is the owner of twelve Zephyr dealerships in the Indiana and Illinois Territories. We blackmailed and pressured him shamelessly. He turned over the rifle and the Provincial Business Licensing Inspectors agreed to forget to investigate complaints involving previously owned sedans. His dealerships sometimes had sold cars which, miraculously, had fewer miles on their odometers when he sold them than when he purchased them.

"Llywelyn is taking Cynthia over to the rifle ranges at JBWK this afternoon. Astrid will go along to monitor the medical aspects of her reactions. Llywelyn believes Cynthia must have spent hundreds, more likely thousands, of hours doing maintenance and modifications of this very rifle, so range time will bring something familiar back into her life."

"It probably will," said Elizabet as she walked into the room. "I have made quite the study of human memories, to better understand my own. The more time Cynthia spends on the range, the better, as shooting will help her learned reflexes push her lost memories to the foreground. Oh, and John, what's a tag team?"

"It's a type of wrassling match. Teams of wrasslers fight one-on-one, but at any time a wrassler can try to go to his corner, slap his partner's hand, and they switch places in the squared circle. These matches have more action and provide the participants more opportunities to cheat than do one-on-one matches."

"Well, I was indeed listening in when Paul rescued you near Sidney and he mentioned Francine and I might be interested in seeing a tag team match. I asked Francine about that and she responded with an earthy version of no. She said that she, instead, was going to cultivate a more refined appreciation of aristocratic culture. What do you think, Kathy?"

Kathy rolled her eyes and said, "I think I married a complete and utter moron."

"Obviously, it would be impolite to contradict you, Kathy. I also asked Bridget. She said I could attend a wrassling event with John, as long as I had proper security. Her relationship with the Providence City Constabulary is delicate, so neither Slab nor Wires will be available to escort me.

"The next major match is going to be at the Providence Civic Arena tomorrow night. The local constabulary will be in charge of arena security. Bridget will arrange for a couple of licensed bodyguards to make carrying weapons legal, but she suggested that you, John, also might want to invite some of your pals from the corps. It's Bridget's treat."

"I think we are going to be a little too busy for that, Elizabet."

"The North Atlantic Tag Team Championship is on the line, whatever that means. The championship belts are currently held by the team of Boris Medved and Nature Boy Jean Rousseau. They will be challenged by War Chief Tomahawk Tecumseh and Flying Freddy Falcon."

I thought about it briefly. "That doesn't make any sense, Elizabet; three heels and one face. Being Russian and French, Medved and Rousseau understandably are two of the most vicious, conniving, underhanded, cheating skunks in the game. The strange thing is Tomahawk Tecumseh is even worse. Freddy Falcon is one of the cleanest faces in all of wrassling. I'll give Scarbutt a call and see if he can round up a couple of buddies."

Scarbutt brought along Jennifer and a couple of his buddies from the Newport Navy Base. Pro wrassling fans can get rowdy, so the local constables were supposed to search all bags, containers and purses for things like brass knuckles, zip guns and mountain howitzers. Don't ask. It happened. Once. The licensed bodyguards Bridget had hired, a guy and a gal, had already made their arrangements to carry concealed. As had Jennifer.

There was a moment of tension when the uniformed Providence City constables handling security wanted to search Jennifer's massive purse. She smiled and flashed her Rhode Island Constabulary Reserve captain's badge. They checked their list of authorized officials and waved her through without checking either her person or her purse. She was carrying two .25-caliber semi-autos in her garter holsters and three .32-caliber Webleys in her purse. We all settled in five rows back from ringside, ready to enjoy a couple of hours of athletic excellence.

It didn't take me too long into the matches to realize it was a bad idea to have taken Elizabet; she kept asking the wrong type of questions.

"Why does that lady wear her hair in such a long ponytail when she knows the other lady is going to pull on it whenever the referee is distracted? Slab and Wires told me every time they have seen ladies wrassle there is mud involved; where's the mud? Why does he keep stamping his foot when he almost, but not quite, hits his opponent? Can you see his leg muscles flex? It's almost as if he is helping his opponent flip himself into the air. Is the referee giving them signals about what to do next?"

Elizabet stopped trying to disrupt my suspension of disbelief after a couple more matches. The main event was everything I expected of a headline match. The War Chief initially played it straight as the Falcon's tag-team partner and the two of them gave as good as they got for a full twenty minutes. Then the Falcon suddenly missed connecting with a leap off the middle rope and wound up getting the snot beat out of him.

He managed to crawl to his corner to tag the War Chief, who sort of stared at him without tagging.

The War Chief then walked away from the ring to the ringside announcer's table. Tecumseh grabbed the announcer's microphone and told the audience that he was tired of having to carry Freddy Falcon, who wasn't a decent enough wrassler to deserve to lick the War Chief's diamond-embroidered moccasins. Meanwhile, Medved and Rousseau were going to work on Freddy Falcon. The War Chief reentered the ring to help stomp on Freddy.

Suddenly Wolverine Smith and The Iron Ox flew into the ring, jumped Medved and Rousseau from behind, and knocked them into the War Chief. Then all six wrasslers fought for a couple of minutes before Medved and Rousseau decided that discretion was the better part of valor and beat feet. With a little three-on-one help, Freddy pinned the War Chief and was declared the winner.

Alas, under the rules of wrassling, the title belt couldn't change hands as Medved and Rousseau had lost by disqualification. The War Chief was carted from the ring on a stretcher. I figured he would be okay as he was had a wrassling match scheduled in Boston two nights hence and pro wrasslers usually had miraculous powers of self-healing.

Elizabet and I rode by ourselves in the massive passenger compartment of our armored limo during the ride back to Newport. Our chauffer and the lady bodyguard rode up front on the other side of the thick, closed, smoked-glass interior window.

After a couple of minutes, Elizabet sighed and said, "Kathy was right about the wrassling; she mentioned you had dragged her to a couple of such events. I think Francine also would have enjoyed watching the wrassling matches. It's almost as stylized as Flamenco dancing, but far more exciting, especially once I let my imagination roam free."

Elizabet slid across the big bench seat and snuggled close to me. She sighed again. "I need to talk with you about two things, John. Make that three. It's quite safe to do so because Astrid loaned me a gadget which blocks your ear implant's transmissions. Kathy and I explained to her I needed assured privacy, so it's in my purse right now. Also, this passenger compartment is quite soundproof, and Bridget vetted both the chauffeur and bodyguard. We can talk in absolute privacy."

I snorted. "Astrid would have wanted something in return."

"Naturally, John. She wanted my mother to develop a means to make pizza. That's a food which took her earth by storm some fifteen years ago. Astrid misses it. It takes a bespoke oven to make correctly. Mother controls a couple of underperforming restaurants in New Haven. She ordered them to build such ovens and learn to make pizza. Supposedly, it pairs well with beer."

I laughed. "I doubt it can ever replace stuff like plowman's lunches or steak and kidney pies or Cornish pasties as pub food. I'll eat my weight of that pizza stuff if it ever takes off. So what did you want to yack about?"

"First, John, I worry about Francine. As does Kathy."

"Huh?" I grunted, perceptively.

"Francine needs to work things out in her own mind; John. It's not about sharing you; it's her having to interact with society nobs, probably for the rest of her life. All Francine knows how to do well is run a farm, ride, shoot and bodyguard. Encourage her to focus on the latter two; there will always be some circumstances when Kathy will need a loyal bodyguard and it won't be appropriate to use marines."

"Kathy has proven she can take care of herself, Elizabet."

"Don't be an idiot, John. Since she met you, Kathy has been subject to a half dozen murder or kidnapping attempts. She has become the Crown's RFC intelligence advisor. She is quite competent and consequently will excel at her duties. People whose secrets are exposed often lash out; Kathy will face a life filled with peril. You have limitations as a guardian, John. I doubt you can be relied upon to protect her from female assassins."

I flinched. "What? Are you crazy? Of course I'll protect Kathy."

"Perhaps you will, John, but we can't take the chance you will do so without hesitation. We have all observed how you interact with ladies. You joust verbally, but you shy away from physical contact.

"Madeline noticed your body language during the party at *Chez Plonk*, John. When ladies conversed with you, you always responded by inching away from them. Then, while you were away in Cuba, Madeline reviewed your military files and discovered an anomaly. She concluded you had killed the English Catholic lady who went missing during the last stage of the Moroccan hostage rescue operation.

"I reviewed her analysis and concurred. Your handwriting is distinctive. You should have used a typewriter to compose the note you sent the lady's brother; the one assuring him she died a quick and painless death.

"The lady must have been immobilized, somehow, while wracked by pain and the fear of being recaptured. Simultaneously, she faced the sure and certain truth suicide is an irredeemable sin. You did what you had to do to prevent her recapture into slavery, but Kathy and I both sense reflections, even now, of how you agonized about your action. That's why we need Francine."

"Come on, Elizabet, Francine will be fine. She always wanted to have kids and now she won't have to settle for marrying some insensitive clodhopper."

Elizabet harrumphed. I made a mental note; I had never heard her harrumph at me before, but she mimicked her adoptive mother's intonations.

"That's not the point, John. If Francine does not have a clear role, Kathy and I fear Francine will try too hard to fit in with society ladies, a path which will cause her tremendous frustration. After all, the only actual nob she knows now is Melinda; since Madeline's passing, and Melinda is such a dear.

"Oh, and I guess Paul and Astrid hold high ranks within their earth's aristocracy, though Paul hides it much better. I think he outranks Astrid, but it's close. I wish I had more information. Paul is extraordinarily good at hiding important information. Unlike dear Astrid; she has shared many truly amazing ideas and other things with me."

I grunted again. "You are circling around whatever point you are trying to make, Elizabet."

"Let me say it bluntly. If Kathy is threatened, Francine will not hesitate for an instant before attempting to stop a threat to Kathy, even if the would-be assassin is female. Acknowledge your limitations, John, and let Francine complement your skills."

Elizabet stared at me for a while; then she giggled. That, too, was rare; I gave her a look.

"Don't worry, John; we all agreed that we won't dream about trying to change you. Astrid talked with all of us. She has had several psychology courses. She explained how in many cultures, such as our own upper Midwest, males are conditioned from early boyhood to radiate publicly all the emotional nuance of a bag of rocks."

"That's ridiculous, Elizabet. I may be sedentary, but I am not sedimentary."

"John," Elizabet said sharply. "Pay attention; don't go making jokes. This is serious and affects all of us. My second concern is that I cannot devote as much time being a companion, mother and friend to the rest of you as I might wish. It involves Irish politics.

"I was seventeen when David O'Shaughnessy, the only real father I ever knew, was tortured and killed during the New York City drug-trade war with the Cuban mobs. Bridget, who previously had been primarily a loving wife and mother, became the widow of a martyr. Bridget quickly married off the two of my older sisters, who had remained single. Mother now has a daughter married into each of the four East Coast Irish Mobs. Mother then became, as Joseph Sammartino would say, the 'Capo di tutti Capi.'"

"Loving wife and mother?" I was stunned. "Bridget?"

"Very much so, John, but like you, Mother does not shirk what she sees as her duty. The Irish Catholic community on the Eastern Seaboard rests on a three-legged stool; the legs being the local pub, the parish church, and the Irish Mobs. Left to his own devices, too often Paddy will drink to excess and fall away from the church.

"Simultaneously, the four mobs will squabble amongst themselves unless someone serves as the 'Capo di tutti Capi.' Such behavior only enables our English and Anglicized rulers to continue to treat the Catholic Irish as dangerous savages.

She scowled. "When the Fenians threw their lot in with the Nazi doctors, they almost ensured our rulers would continue to view all Irish Catholics as such. Had the Empire prevailed after a bloody conflict, London would have used the Fenians' revolt as an excuse to oppress us for yet another two hundred years."

I nodded. "Wars are like that, at the least the big ones. Not that the little ones are wonderful, either. So how does Bridget plan to change things?"

"She plans to use her charitable organizations to address the alcoholism and such. She also plans to nudge the mobs into pursuing legitimate, rather than criminal, pursuits. Mother believes that if we Irish Catholics cannot reconcile with the English, we risk becoming a cancerous pawn inside the Empire in the event our earth is again infiltrated by a hostile timeline."

"So, what's this got to do with me? Or us?"

"Bridget is fifty-six years old. The shocking news Madeline had a fatal disease caused Mother to address the generational consequences of her own mortality. When Mother passes, I will inherit her duties as the '*Capo di tutti Capi.*' That is the political complication to which I referred while we were in Montreal."

I blinked in shock, processed, and decided Elizabet was being serious.

"You, Elizabet? You don't seem the type."

"I am the only person the senior hard guys, such as Wires and Slab, will trust to remember the ledger of who owes what to whom and to adjudicate fairly any disputes among the mobs. It should be self-evident information of this sort can never be put to paper. I expect to work myself out of a job during my lifetime, so I hope it will not be necessary for one of our sons or daughters to replace me in my turn."

Elizabet, before she continued, first unbuttoned her gloves and slipped off her shoes.

"Still, my forecast may prove too optimistic. If it takes too long to go legitimate, then one of our children may need to succeed me as

'*Capo di tutti Capi.*' In consequence, all of your children, including those with Francine, will need to be exceptionally well versed in the arts of self-defense. That is essential, even; no, I mean especially, for your daughters, if any."

"I thought little girls played with dolls and such, not guns?"

"John, I spent more than a year without a doll because when I was ten, my late, loathsome step-father sold my last original doll for whiskey. Don't change the subject. It will make my tasks much easier if all our children are aware of and fully prepared for the threats they may face."

She smiled at me. "Not that Bridget envisions much opposition, at least within the mobs. Bridget convened an emergency congress of the mob heads and senior hard guys, the week before the two of us left for Montreal. The Congress forbade me from marrying into an Irish mob. They did not want my impartiality compromised.

"After a day of discussion, they agreed you would be an acceptable sire of my children and requested of Bridget that she arrange that. That was why she was so adamant about sending me with you on your last mission. That also explains why she made so many concessions to Madeline.

"You have earned a great deal of respect from those who count, John. Bloodlines are important in our world; if you have any doubts about that, you have only to ask Melinda her views on the subject."

I couldn't tell if Elizabet blushed; the light was a little dim. She continued, "Wires nominated you to be the father of our children, John. He thinks the world of you; he had a young niece and nephew visiting Bridget's estate during the Cuban amphibious assault. Never admit you know that of him, though. The wrong folks might think that Wires has gone soft."

I grunted again. Yeah, soft like the steel they use to build battlecruiser armor. I figured I could either take that secret to my grave or else make an earlier than necessary visit to the same.

"I guess I can do that; Elizabet, I understand the concept of living one's cover. You said you have something else you wanted to yak about?"

"Yes I do, after I conclude my remarks on this topic. I have not yet informed Kathy about either Mother's or Madeline's motivations. With your permission, I will ask Mother to explain this background to Kathy. You should not be the one to do that until the listening device is removed from your ear canal."

I nodded and grunted my affirmation.

Elizabet stared at me again. She sighed. "Astrid was correct about her bag of rocks metaphor. Oh well, on to topic number three.

"You remember the Cuban assault on my estate? You likely saved my life, and more, on that occasion. I analyzed Bridget's defenses, ex post. Had you not thinned the attacking Cubans' numbers, they would have begun killing the children and raping the women before the marines from the navy base arrived. I doubt I will ever be able to repay you sufficiently for saving me from that fate."

She kissed me on the cheek. "Kathy is going to be quite insufferable after she wins our private wager regarding the aftermath of tonight's wrassling match. Astrid explained it all has to do with pheromones. And hormonal surges during pregnancy, of course."

"Huh?" I grunted, yet again, as I was now understandably confused how the bouncing pinball that was the female thought process managed to function.

Elizabet kissed me, yet again, on the lips. "Two months ago, I had to steel myself to do my duty for my mother and my people. Francine even had assured me you are the most decent and caring man she has ever known. Still, I doubted I could give myself to a man, even one as remarkable as you.

"Mother and I then discussed my childhood traumas with Astrid, the day after the Mob Congress adjourned. Astrid provided me with fertility and other special pills the day before we all gathered at the Priory's indoor pool. I did not need to use Astrid's pills for long; I was shocked to discover how deeply and quickly I had fallen in love with you. I hope you grow to accept me as part of your life; I promise I will never knowingly act to embarrass either Lady Katherine or you."

Elizabet turned her back to me. "Be a dear and undo the hook and buttons of my dress. I don't want it too wrinkled. Dear Astrid shared with me some fascinating intimate recommendations when she loaned me her gadget. Initially, I only intended to use her gadget to ensure our privacy while I explained some things to you. Still, since we have complete privacy, I will not waste the opportunity."

I bowed to force majeure and started fiddling with the teensy metal hook and eye at the back of her dress collar, all the while plotting appropriate revenge. Yeah, Elizabet was spot on about Paul, but I had no leverage on him. I decided the time was ripe to winkle some information out of who I hoped was the weak link of that other earth chain. I figured I owed Astrid a lot of payback.

To Thy Own Self Be True

I saw Astrid at the breakfast buffet table early in the morning two days after the wrassling match. I had just finished my five-mile run. Astrid had slipped into a tennis outfit after she had finished her early morning yoga and pole dancing exercises. I figured I could engage in some small talk and see if I could find an opening. If nothing else, I might work up the nerve to ask what outfit she wore while doing her yoga and other exercises down in the small basement gymnasium.

"Hey, Doctor Toots. Those gams of yours are looking fine. Aren't you glad that Kathy made sure you patented that design for a stair-stepper? Now you are extra rich *and* you have great looking legs. And now that I have your attention, would you like to do a little explaining about all those tall tales Elizabeth told me? She claimed you said I reminded you of a box full of rocks."

Dr. Astrid Martingale glanced at me as she was getting some coffee from the urn in the breakfast room. After she filled her cup, she turned and smiled at me. That was one for the memory books; she had no reason to stay on my good side.

Astrid reached into her purse and pulled out a flat, box-like thing about the size of a cigarette case. She flicked her fingers over it, looked back at me, and said, "We now can talk completely freely. Actually, John, I mentioned nothing about geologic rubble. I merely told Elizabet you were extraordinarily unencumbered by exceptional emotional emissions; blissfully barren of bombastic or bashful brainwave broadcasts; surprisingly stoic in certain social situations..."

I figured if I tried to unpack all her alliteration, I would be insulted. I changed the subject and interjected, "What's up with the gadget, Astrid? Paul said that you folks turned my earpiece off, unless I was on a mission."

Astrid smiled again. "He simplified. It's always on; we automatically delete other-than-mission data after a day. He was correct in the sense that no one was actively listening in on you unless you were deployed. Still, better safe than sorry.

"We still have those recordings from when the von Clausewitz's held you captive, including from when you were asleep. You're very good at annoying people, John. Indeed, Frau von Clausewitz planned to addict you to her drugs and then condition you to be utterly subservient. Once she tired of humiliating you, she planned to castrate you and send you to the uranium mines for the short remainder of your pain-filled life."

She sipped some coffee as I stood there in shock. "You are quite fortunate that I am far too understanding and even-tempered to consider doing such a thing, although you provoke me constantly. Should you annoy me sufficiently, I will merely kill you painlessly, instantaneously, and undetectably."

I transitioned from shock to slack-jawed. Then I realized Astrid had to be joking. It must be her dry sense of humor and all that. Riiiiight.

She continued, "And damn straight I'm rich, though, even on this primitive earth. But just you wait, Jarhead, you're going to see super rich. During her copious spare time, Kathy is going over the laws on patents, medications and liability with a legal eagle eye. She says with my knowledge and flexible scruples we are going to make mega-zillions in pounds sterling once I seriously introduce the patented herbal supplement market to this world."

"That's already been tried, Astrid. About a hundred years ago, some patent medicine salesman showed up in a hot-air balloon west of St. Louis. He was a month-long marvel; then he disappeared. He kept asking questions about good and bad witches."

"I'm a skilled surgeon; it only seems like witchcraft to the sufficiently primitive. Anyway, I will make sure any substances we sell won't actually kill you. Kathy will craft the claims as to their effectiveness, so people will read them and think they might do some good, though we will make no such explicit claim.

"Kathy genuinely has many marvelous qualities, other than her taste in marines, though that goes without saying. Surprisingly, you, for once, are correct. My leg musculature and silhouette are incredible."

Astrid's tennis outfit barely hid anything, so the effectiveness of her workout regime was obvious. Astrid had turned to look at her sculpted silhouette as reflected in the almost mirror-quality surface of a breakfast room refrigerator. I took advantage of her self-absorption to ask a sneaky question, while she was not focused on me.

"By the way, how are Siggy's twins?"

"I am sure they are absolute hellions."

Astrid went to the sideboard and grabbed a small pitcher of cream from an ice-filled tray and poured another dollop into her coffee. While she stirred it, she reminisced. "When I left my earth, they had turned thirteen years old. I bet right now they are trying to discover boys and attempting trying to bribe or threaten the guards and their servants into looking the other way.

"Siggy is probably going crazy, and she didn't like it a bit a couple of years ago when I sweetly recalled what an absolute menace to incipient manhood she was attempting to be back when she was almost fourteen and I was eleven. Siggy was never smart enough to evade her guardians the way I did when I reached that age. Still, she got most of her looks completely effortlessly and I was left having to whip my every curve into shape via painful struggles. Of course I have an absolutely incredible brain. I guess it evens out, even if she was the one to marry Prince Charming."

Astrid paused, took a sip of coffee, paused again and said, "Damn it, John, I'm a doctor, not a fracking diplomat. You are a conniving, underhanded, rat, scum bastard. I bet your navy rejected your enlistment because of your utter absence of morals, and Scarbutt told me all about the barely existent moral standards in your navy. Paul is so going to want to kill me."

"Yeah, about that. I think it's time had ourselves a frank and wide-ranging conversation. Who and what are you folks?"

She furrowed her eyebrows.

I continued. "Your older sister married his older brother, right? Also, your sister and his brother are both serious nob-types back on your earth. And you and Paul are both at least highly ranked, decently serious nob-types. He once mentioned he was a senator's son. As I recall, before the Cubans hit this place, you mentioned you couldn't care less what tax rates your family's subjects faced. I try to remember such things; it's my job. I figure you're minor royalty of some sort. Are you?"

"Neb out, yunz bum. I ain't saying a word till my solicitor arrives."

"And I thought you claimed you didn't eavesdrop on me, ya lying fake yinzer. Besides, you don't have a solicitor, Astrid, other than Kathy and I know darn well she would love to be here to hear you come clean. Welcome to the real world, Dr. Toots.

"Just because all of us folks here on this world are primitives, it doesn't mean we are completely stupid. Heck, a couple of decades ago, we even figured out the world had to be round, because if it was flat, all the Australians would have fallen off."

Astrid sneered at me. Some folks have no sense of humor. I persevered.

"I wouldn't worry about Paul too much; if only because he knows I owe him for those jerk moves he pulled on me. For example, I was wearing Herr and Frau Doctors Completely Whacko and Gruesome's blood and guts for a good six hours. I was standing downwind of them when Paul's private assassin, Llywelyn, blew out their brains. It took that long to find a shower and some clean clothes."

I gave her a half-smile. "I bet Llywelyn doesn't even break wind in the line of duty unless Paul gives him permission. You wouldn't like to comment about why Llywelyn killed them, would you? That happened immediately before Dr. Whacko was going to tell me the names of some of the total sickos infesting our top aristocracy. I sure hope Paul collected his thirty pieces of silver for that favor to somebody."

Astrid grimaced. I finally hit a sore spot.

"Also, Astrid, what the heck do you mean by losing a bet? I thought he was angry about being scourged with birch branches or risking a frostbitten ass?"

"You don't know the half of it," said Astrid. "Fine; I'm tired of lying. You folks have been more than decent to me and to all my ladies. You deserve better, but I did not know when I came to this earth the extent to which I could trust anyone. Paul trusts no one on principle. Well, with him it's also an avocation. So we each lied, shamelessly, about lots of things.

"Once my party arrived on your earth, we played on both your sympathy and your avarice to gain your government's assistance. Paul and I had different ideas, so our lies were a trifle incoherent. He can be annoyingly headstrong."

Yeah, I thought. Mr. Pot, meet Dr. Kettle.

"I am the eighth in line of succession for the throne of what in your world would be the Kingdom of Scandinavia. My obviously senile grandfather is currently king; his oldest son is next in line, though my uncle has no heirs. My father is the second son and serves as the chairman of my grandfather's advisory council. Sigrun is the oldest of my four siblings and Sigrun has four children of her own, though she had wanted at least one more child before she becomes too old to have any more. I am my parents' second child and the Princess Minor. I have several lesser titles.

"My Kingdom of Scandinavia is a generally autonomous member of the Greater Britannic Roman Empire. The GBRE controls most of the worthwhile areas of our earth which the Ming Empire does not control. I believe Paul was something like seventeenth in the line of succession to become the Emperor if his Empire did things the way your folks operate on this world, which they don't. Paul, realistically, was the eleventh or twelfth in the line of succession when I left. His civilian rank is equivalent to a vice-admiral or a lieutenant general in your armed services."

"He's that high up, Astrid? What's he doing here, conducting field operations?"

"I'll get to that, John. Anyway, when we were children, we spent a lot of summers visiting each other; our elder siblings' marriage had been long planned. When I was thirteen, Paul claimed, inexplicably, I would not last for over two weeks as a novitiate. He volunteered to be the scrubber of the Royal Princesses of the Kingdom of Scandinavia's toilets for one day for every day over two weeks which I lasted as a novitiate.

"He may have forgotten that boast, but I surely did not. I joined the Sisters of Healing's novitiates-in-training program the day I turned eighteen, in part because they had always been so nice to me. Then again, one of my maternal great-grandmothers had endowed most of the original funding to establish the Sisters of Healing."

Astrid shuddered visibly. "Your own experience may have differed, but both Francine and Lucius claim their drill instructors were sadistic, inhuman monsters from the deepest depths of Hell. They got off lucky. They never experienced the Sister instructors of potential novitiates. I guess they figured once we were tempered by their fires, we would laugh at more mundane challenges. I lasted three weeks.

"That meant Paul, at age twenty-two, had to take a week out of his schooling to become our royal toilet scrubber. I gave him lots of cheerful suggestions about doing his job better, because during my three weeks as a novitiate, I had, albeit reluctantly, developed expertise in exactly that task.

"Did you study the Battle of Culloden, John?"

"*Say what?*" I thought.

"Sure I did, Astrid. It turns out you never want to fight a battle using muzzle-loading flintlock muskets and claymores while the rain is driving into your face and when your choice of which units is positioned where is constrained by which clans did what to whom a couple of hundred years ago."

"Not the tactics, jarhead, the leadership. The King's youngest son, the Duke of Cumberland, trained and then commanded the English forces on that battlefield. Our own Empire expects its own male junior royalty also to lead, if not from the front, to be at least within spitting distance. That often justifies their otherwise useless existence and helps cull the herd. Paul has been through a lot more military action than he admits to."

"I sort of figured that out all by myself, Astrid. Well, Scarbutt had to whack me across the head to get my attention, but I would have figured it out, eventually."

"Of course you would have, John. Let me answer further your earlier question about his rank. There are senators and then there are important senators. Paul's family name does not translate best as Drake, though that's close. It's actually Pendragon. I expect you understand the reference. He may sign legally binding treaties with your Imperial government, or other governments, if needed.

"His father is perhaps the third most senior senator in Paul's empire, having served as an Imperial co-consul for five separate, non-consecutive annual terms. His father is also the Prince of the Province of Hibernia, Dumnonii, and Breton. Separately, his father is Prince of New Breton, which partially overlaps the RFC. New Breton is bounded by the Atlantic to the east, the James River to the south, the Wabash River to the west, and everything south and east of the eastern and northern-most shores of Hudson Bay."

Astrid paused, then grinned. "I just realized that Elizabet was not the only listener to be offended when the two Drs. von Clausewitz disparaged the Gaels. Paul takes personal offense when others denigrate his family's Gaelic subjects. He comes by his excessive arrogance honestly."

I sensed a tragic backstory, bathed in jealousy or pathos or both, behind her last comment, but I would gnaw that bone later. She was on a roll. I did not interrupt her.

"As an aside, I did not know it was possible to travel to alternate earths until I arrived at Bermuda Station and was briefed forcibly into the program. As part of my briefings, I learned it took our Imperial Intelligence Service years to suspect the missing WiG might be on your earth. The stealthy surveillance satellite we had placed in your earth's orbit some fifteen years ago had not detected the missing WiG, though it was not programmed to look for such. Of course, our missing WiG's emergency signaling devices could have been damaged or intentionally destroyed.

"Paul came here to investigate those latter possibilities. To do that, he needed a government's help. He expected initially he would work with the RCC government, since the missing WiG had set out originally for a destination near the Cuba of that Nazi timeline. Anyway, Paul told that cock and bull story about traveling to the wrong version of earth so as not to appear to represent too much of a threat."

Astrid smiled. "You asked about our satellites. It's complicated. Our satellites can send stealthy message capsules on a trans-temporal journey back to our home earth, but only to pre-determined, secure locations like Bermuda or Ascension. Communications are purely one-way until our home earth sends a manned earth-hopper to respond.

"You know from the after-action reports, the Cubans kept the hijacked world-hopper in a dirigible hanger that included almost wafer-thin layers of copper both under the shingles and behind the drywalls. The copper was original to the hanger, installed to keep rain and sea spray from getting into the hanger, but the copper also blocked the craft's intermittent emergency electronic signals."

"Yeah, we have copper-sheathed rooms in places like the Newport Navy Base and at the late Brigadier's New York offices."

"So you're not an utter primitive, then, John. Anyhow, Marcus had launched another surveillance satellite upon our arrival to your world. After you showed Paul the photograph and mentioned Cuba, Marcus carefully re-calibrated our satellites' sensors.

"One day the Cubans left the hangar door open during an orbital window when a satellite was in position to detect the intermittent emergency signal broadcast by the missing WiG. We had a good read on the longitude, but somehow could only establish its latitude as south of the Carolinas. Nevertheless, we then sent another message drone back home."

She frowned. "That's all I can tell you about satellites and Paul's lies and such. Right now I am tired of being shot at and getting caught up in your earth's political issues. I want to go home; I hope they let me. I had to leave, but I would like to see my sister and the rest of my family again."

"What do you mean you had to leave, Astrid? It sure sounded like you were a top flight doctor while stationed at your version of Bermuda."

"Two months after Paul left for your earth, Sigrun secretly warned me my idiot grandfather intended to ship me to Italy. Grandfather wanted to marry me off. It was totally political. My intended is the eldest son of an Italian senator who leads a faction making up about one-twelfth of the Imperial Senate. My erstwhile fiancé is a vile beast of a human being and the only reason his two more loathsome younger brothers have not killed him is they risked being blamed.

"I would have been the perfect fall girl for his brothers' crimes because I would have had method, opportunity and more than sufficient motive. My new husband likely would have died within months of our marriage. Even if I had not killed him, I would have been convicted of his death. It would have been worse than marrying into the Borgia family of your earth's history."

"Yeah, I can see why you might want to avoid that."

"After Sigrun's warning, I talked to Llywelyn, Paul's personal bodyguard of almost two decades. He was already uncomfortable about Paul's solo mission. I extracted certain promises of secrecy from Llywelyn. Then, with his skills and my political clout, we managed to, uh, borrow a WiG. Llywelyn told me he left messages behind, telling the right people where we intended to go."

She looked pensive.

"What's the problem, Astrid?"

"I've had fun here on your earth, but it's wearing on me. I am becoming increasingly concerned that my earth has not followed up and contacted us. I'm quite certain my earth didn't suffer an actual nuclear war or some catastrophe of that ilk."

"Yeah, Astrid, I noted all your ladies all got over the shock of nuclear conflict, toe-to-toe with the Ming Empire, pretty darn quick."

Astrid sniffed testily. "Have I mentioned my mother is a granddaughter of a previous King of Iberia? I was also the twenty-third in line for the

Iberian throne when I left my earth. My ancestry means I'm sufficiently royal to be valuable, but not royal enough to have any important political duties. I had the skills to become a surgeon, so I became one. *Noblesse oblige* and all that, or perhaps I just didn't want to be another useless drone-ette."

I gave her a quizzical look.

"Perhaps in English the word is drone-ess as in stewardess rather than drone-ette as in suffragette?"

"It's just drone, Astrid. All drones are male."

"Of course they are, John. We ladies expect to have to work for a living." She beamed in triumph.

Ouch! She got me there; I had stepped right into her linguistically cunning trap. Anyway, the royalty part sure explained how Astrid carried her own mien of arrogance so effortlessly.

"That still sounds like horse hockey to me, Astrid. If you tell me the entire story, I may help. When I am not killing people, I'm a decent guy. Just ask those ladies in my life, including those pregnant babes to whom I am not married. And since the subject's come up, perhaps you have a couple of words you would like to say about all my impending kids."

"Fine, jarhead. Francine was an accident. It happens. Elizabet needed her own heirs, pronto, so I gave her some fertility and extra-powerful libido-enhancing pills. Given Elizabet's tragic personal history, I felt it was the least I could do for the darling child.

"I still can't believe Elizabet picked you, of all people, to be the father of her children. Well, at least you're not as disagreeable as Paul. Anyhow, Bridget explained you are suitable because you understand the mob ethos, can defend yourself, and are well-connected politically. She also mentioned that you are the luckiest sinner on the face of the planet."

"Lucky, Astrid? I am a marine, so I admit to being skilled, cunning, incredibly handsome, exceptionally intelligent, and modest beyond reproach, but lucky?"

"Both Bridget and I talked to Madeline before she passed. You faced four separate Captain's Masts, John. They gave you a verbal reprimand and recommended you for yet another medal at every one of them."

Maybe she had a point about my luck. Still, I couldn't let her have the last word.

"But I'm certainly not politically connected, Astrid. I just am a jumped-up, would-be cherry farmer out of Michigan Province."

"No, Major Sir John, OWM. You are more than that. Your children with Elizabet and Francine will be born on the wrong side of the mattress, but they will swim in an elite political sea. Heck, even His Royal Highness now owes you big time. Be sure to collect."

Astrid was right; His Highness owed me. I thought about how to leverage that, but Astrid continued talking.

"Consider your good fortune, John. Did you realize Elizabet will inherit nearly a dozen public houses? Talk about living the Australian ideal. Don't cry to me about aristocratic burdens; I was being forced to marry a psychopathic sadist.

"To complete the circle of our discussion, I had never realized your earth, like mine, might have a problem with an aristocracy infested with sadists. As I recall, Herr Doctor von Clausewitz named no names."

"You missed something regarding Doc Whacko, Astrid. He was about to play charades."

"Charades, John?"

I held up five fingers and wiggled the same.

"Hand gestures; it's a guessing game, so of course you wouldn't have heard anything, not at first. Oh, sure he wanted to toy with me, but I also suspect the vicious bastard knew whereof he spoke. I imagine somebody high up in New York or London made an emergency deal with Paul to make sure that no important names got mentioned.

"I can only imagine the political blowback if Dr. Whacko had named too many high-ranking nobs at once. I guess His Highness did not wish to deal both with the risk of a Nazi invasion and a domestic political crisis as well."

Astrid grimaced. "I was not privy to any such deal; nor am I bound to any agreements regarding aristocratic sadists, which Paul may or may not have made. Officially, the German doctors were to be killed nearly simultaneously at the first opportunity to do so. This was to prevent the survivor from unleashing the plague toxins. Had the decision been mine alone, I would have had them captured and then tortured until they gave up every secret.

"What bothers me, now that we found the missing WiG and rescued its surviving crew, is I can't imagine what your world has that Paul might value and why we remain here. Initially, Paul didn't want to leave your earth until this earth's Nazi-related issues were investigated and resolved, but that's now over and done."

"You are not thinking strategically, Astrid. I can guess the delay. While we killed the six whacko Nazis who had been forcibly decamped to this world, there is still a world where the Nazis are the top dog. Von Clausewitz mentioned those Nazis may now know cross-earth travel is possible.

"It's not merely a question of getting your own little group of folks back; it's what your folks in charge back on your home earth now plan to do about a potential threat from an entire world of technologically advanced hostiles. That threat exhibited the willingness to kill the three to three-and-a-half billion inhabitants of this earth. It would certainly worry me if those folks might ever make it into the multiverse. I suspect your leaders are likewise worried."

I had another thought; hey, it happens. Sometimes.

"As long as you are answering questions honestly, I've got to ask. Are you folks well and truly stuck here until you get rescued, Astrid?"

"Well, we sort of lied to you about that, John. We lied a lot. Our craft does require specialized maintenance, not all of which had been completed when we absconded with it. Our aircrew would prefer skilled help from home, in order to give our WiG an expert examination before we risk returning. Still, we probably have a ninety-nine percent chance of returning home safely.

"I remain here because I refuse to go home until I receive notice confirming my intended husband's tragic death. Before I left, I sent word to Siggy asking her to arrange something along those lines for me; she truly is such a sweetheart. By now she should have had more than enough time to deep-six that abomination of an arranged marriage. I hope she messages me soon."

I had the feeling high-level politics on Astrid's earth were not all ice-cream sundaes and fluffy bunnies. I felt somewhat relieved to realize Astrid would never be a political power on this earth. She was far too comfortable with the concept of taking direct action.

"Thanks for all the honest answers, Astrid."

"Not so fast; it's my turn to be annoying, John. Kathy told me she wanted me to talk to you. Let's discuss in more detail the bull in your proverbial porcelain shop."

I sensed where this was headed. I stared at the tips of my shoes for a few seconds and looked up at Astrid. "What am I going to do about Cynthia Valentine? She's pregnant and I may be the father. I never liked her; much less loved her. But if I am the father of her children, I have an obligation to her kid or kids, if you are right about the possibility of twins from those fertility drugs she was on."

Astrid gave me a look. I had seen that type of look on a doctor's face once before. There was that time I had wandered back to the field hospital to see how a buddy was making out. I saw how the surgeon looked at Corporal Hannigan as the doctor explained to Hannigan he could choose between getting his arm sawn-off at the elbow within the hour or he could choose to be dying in agony within a couple of days. That choice would suck, big-time. It was his shooting arm.

Astrid spoke. "What I hope you do is the right thing. I already talked with Mary and Theodora; they agree the risks are enormous if Cynthia stays here. Cynthia was filled to the eyeballs with many drugs and synthetic hormones, most of which I could not identify. Those damn Germans used a code for all their written medical notes. We cannot decipher them until we send their notes to my home earth. You were also subjected to a variety of chemicals."

I stared at my shoe tips for a moment more. I mumbled, "Yeah, Astrid. I know. Any idea what all that stuff was and did? I mean, besides the obvious."

She shook her head. "I am primarily a surgeon; I do not know what those particular drugs were or how all those drugs might have affected Cynthia's pregnancy. Your doctors on this world have less.

"If our rescue arrives in time, Cynthia should go to our earth with Llywelyn. Llywelyn's intrigued by her; a world-class figure and world-class marksmanship combined into one package. I can guarantee she will be treated as an Imperial ward and her child or children will have access to the best medical care we can provide. I will insist on this as a physician; I will not risk having what happened to Kathy to reoccur with Cynthia."

"Isn't he old enough to be her father, Astrid? And already married?"

"Damn, John; you're as sharp as a bowling ball. Of course he is; don't be absurd. Llywelyn has two unmarried sons and three unmarried nephews; all of them were of an appropriate age to marry her. At least they were available when we left for your earth. I am sure she will find a loving husband from one of that lot."

"That's good to hear. I don't think there's room for yet another lady in my life. What about the diseases of your world?"

"It's nothing to worry about. We all took precautions before we came here. If we can convince Cynthia to go back with Llywelyn, she will need to spend a month in quarantine and take some broad spectrum antivirals. No big deal."

I thought. I panicked. "What about the folks the Cuban Caudillo brought over? Shouldn't we all be dead by now?"

"Those Nazi doctors all worked with tropical viral and bacterial diseases. They were crazy, in our terms, but they understood diseases. That is why they killed and cremated all their erstwhile kidnappers in short order. Then they kept track of each other like hawks eyeing field mice."

She shrugged. "Their precautions must have succeeded; otherwise, we would all be dead right now. Their threat to depopulate this earth was not an idle one, however. They did not want to do so inadvertently until they returned to their home earth first.

"I have one last medically related topic to discuss with you, John. Once I hear from my earth, I promise you I will start Kathy on estrogen therapy as soon as humanly possible. It's critical that she do so."

"Thanks, I guess, Astrid. I have no idea what you're talking about."

"That's alright, John. I'm quite used to dealing with oblivious menfolk; my older sister married into a family which is positively overflowing with them."

By the Light of the Flickering Screen

Visitors from Paul's version of earth arrived three weeks later. A craft bounced over in the middle of Western Atlantic and sent word via radio they had a delivery. An RFC destroyer, the RFCN *Ocelot*, set forth at flank speed to meet them. The visitors floated over a couple of large rafts worth stuff; mostly mysterious equipment and lots of books, the latter predominately medical and engineering texts. They dropped off orders and suggestions for Paul and a private letter from Sigrun to Astrid.

We, in turn, informed our visitors about the toxins the Doctors Whacko had developed, at which point they decided not to take any of their compatriots back home just yet.

Astrid disappeared from sight for a couple of days and when she emerged she seemed, to me at least, to be artificially chipper.

The next WiG arrived a week later and came equipped to haul the von Clausewitz toxins back to Paul's earth where they could analyze and dispose of them safely. That WiG also swapped out Dafydd ap Owain, Llywelyn's younger cousin, and in his same line of work, in exchange for Llywelyn and Cynthia Valentine. The latter two got to ride back in a hermetically isolated retrieval cabin.

In the meantime, Julius and Marcus spent the next several days putting together a flicker theater in the second largest of Melinda's estate's stables. They finished getting their stuff set up as Melinda's staff whipped the stable into shape so it didn't smell so aromatic. Then we had flicker nights.

I learned about *D-Day*, *Desert Rats*, blitzkrieg, phony wars and Lyudmila Pavlichenko. Darn, that babe could shoot. Paul explained his folks got these flickers from an earth in which the Nazis lost the big war. It was a near run thing. Our War College, up at the navy base, teaches operational excellence, absent coherent strategy, is ultimately sterile. They may be correct in that, but it turns out sufficient operational excellence, like that exhibited by the Wehrmacht, can still give you one heck of a long ride.

Anyhow, Paul's folks sent these flickers to provide us insight into how the Nazis and their pals operated. Most of the flickers we got were made by countries which spoke some version of English so we would have a better chance of picking up language nuances and such, but they were all also subtitled to the limit of Paul's earth's ability.

It was the best Paul's world could do to demonstrate what Nazis are like because they didn't yet feel they could risk returning to the Nazi-dominated earth to find out how the Nazis viewed themselves. It was clear the late Drs. Gruesome and Whacko had not fallen far from the old glockenspiel.

I think my favorite flicker was the one where the Nazis had a secret base on the far side of the moon but came back to try to conquer earth. I mentioned too loudly in the presence of my beloved wife and the two mothers-to-be of my impending children that if the real Nazis only had an elite force of Valkyrie babes dressed only in scanty leather straps and carrying five-foot atomic death rifles, then their attack would have succeeded. It turns out it is remarkably hard to remove greasy popped corn butter from one's hair.

I also had a couple of unexpected visitors over the next couple of days. Jennifer called from the Priory to warn me about the first visitor.

"It's yet another gorgeous lady from your misspent past, John. We searched her. She's unarmed. You should remember her; she's a total knockout."

Jennifer drove the visitor over using a Priory limo. An East Asian lady just a hair over five-feet tall, wearing a couture robin blue skirt suit, stepped from the limo. It took me a moment to recognize Miss Annabelle Lee, aka Jasmine, but by that time, Elizabet had already run up to Annabelle and was giving her a hug.

Annabelle pointed at Elizabet's barely discernable baby bump. Elizabet pointed at me.

"Smith, you dog. And I was going to ask you if you had accumulated your five million pounds yet. I mean, I knew you were married, but I never dreamt you had good taste. Congratulations, Elizabet, I guess. I figured you were the last one in our high school class who would ever get married."

Kathy sniffed noticeably, but otherwise gave no sign of jumping into the conversation.

Annabelle shook her head, sadly. "Elizabet, sweetie; you are the smartest girl I ever met. I guess you must have had some good reason for shacking up with this hayseed."

"Anyhow, I have been listening to the radio and reading the papers for the last couple of months and trying to figure out what was going on in the world. I came looking to meet the person who whacked Eva Braun. I want to thank him in person. I realized that you, Smith, should know who the person was. I figured the Sisters would know where to find you. If it was you who bumped her off, Smith, I won't charge you the five million pounds I quoted you last time. You can have me for free, if Elizabet says it's okay."

"It would take more than that, toots," growled Francine. "Who do you think you are, lady?"

"Annabelle was the salutatorian of my class at my parochial high school, Fran," said Elizabet. "She was the only Han in an Irish Catholic parochial girls' school and all the other girls in school also considered her to be unusual. We got along well, except for her smoking habit."

"Yeah, my mom worked like a dog to earn enough money to send me to parochial schools all my life. They were safer than public schools. Mom was big on safety."

I answered Annabelle's original question.

"You're too late, Miss Lee," I said. "The actual sniper has already returned to his version of earth."

Elizabeth interrupted again. "The last I knew, Annabelle, you had gone to secretarial school, then you moved into the same boarding house as Suzie Shamrock, in Queens, working theater administrative stuff somewhere."

"Yeah, I was too embarrassed to tell anyone in the boarding house where I actually worked, but the money was too damn good for me to think of quitting. I didn't think anyone at Wendell's flicker studio knew my background; Wendell didn't knowingly hire any Irish Catholics. He sure didn't want to risk the FOs discovering Delilah's hobbies' sordid details.

"I didn't want to risk being booted from the boarding house. That was the safest neighborhood for a single lady in New York, especially if you usually wear clothes with Saint Brigid Parochial School colors and sport a legitimate Saint Brigid class ring. It was the safest boarding house as well. Elizabet sure knows why that is. Of course, my constant talking about sex with the girls living in that boarding house helped sort of mess up my understanding of normal guy and gal relationships."

Annabelle sighed. "Also, it sure wasn't the same after I gave up smoking."

Elizabet took Annabelle's right hand in both of hers and gave it a squeeze.

Annabelle continued. "Most girls at that boarding house enjoyed what they were doing. Heck, if they didn't, they could quit and the Dowager Empress would find them another job. It wouldn't pay nearly as well, but it was their choice. Still, I had always wondered why more of their customers didn't behave like pond scum, in contrast to most guys I ever met."

Elizabet smiled. "Not all men are scum, Annabelle, though often they have to be housebroken."

Francine snorted and nodded assent.

Annabelle continued. "Some men sure are. Early one morning, I was leaving for work. Just then, another resident returned, clearly having been out all night. She sported a nasty set of lumps. When I returned that evening, she was sitting in the front parlor talking with two of the biggest, meanest looking bruisers imaginable. I walked past slowly enough to get the drift of what was going to happen to her last customer, after the bruisers caught up with him.

"Once I got to my room, though, I remembered I had seen those bruisers previously, years before. I never saw them together before, but each had sometimes escorted Elizabet to or from Saint Brigid's School. I hadn't ever realized why the other girls never picked on Elizabet; not much, anyhow. With her being both super smart and seriously weird, you think she would have attracted tons of grief. I guess my St. Brigid's classmates didn't have a death wish.

"Ah well, good times. The real world's not like that, at least for me. I sure didn't have any bruisers looking after my ass, not in Victoria anyhow, though I could have used the help. So, Smith, did you at least help track down Eva Braun and help somebody else take her out?"

"Yeah; darn straight I did. I was the bait. The sniper got Ron Cross with his first shot. I was covered with both his and Brunhilde's bloody brains for at least six hours."

"Poor baby. Did those two torture you before they died? I bet you must have suffered."

"Yeah, they worked me over pretty thoroughly. It was pretty exhausting."

"Bull feathers, Hotshot. I have *three* older sisters, so I've been beat up way worse than you were. Heck, *your* bruises healed, so don't even think about putting in for yet another oak leaf on your combat wounded ribbon."

I glared at Fran. Way to ruin my heroic public persona. Besides, I had two older sisters, and she knew it. What they lacked in numbers they made up for with vindictiveness. Well, that's what I felt when I was eight or nine years old.

She had a point about the awards and decorations. I was still working on how to write up my adventures, official like, to receive an appropriate medal. So far I had written up both being captured because I was an inattentive moron and the subsequent adventures where I nearly died from the amorous attentions of a gorgeous, but drug-addled, young lady.

Scarbutt had suggested I make up something more heroic, like me saving the world from a plague of deadly giant, radioactively mutated locusts or scorpions. He had a point; an awards and decorations board might perceive my recent actions in an unflattering light.

Elizabet jumped in. "Jennifer, I plan to dine at the Priory this evening. Annabelle, let's return there and we will have a long talk and catch up with old times."

Heavy is the Head that Will Bear the Crown

We weren't finished receiving visitors. Prime Minister Hamilton, newly installed, invited himself up to visit with Sir Charles Burr. What was weird about the visit was one day after the Prime Minister arrived, Melinda's mom and dad basically got booted out of their own house and had to go visit the Bartholomew estate, yet again. Melinda's mother was surprisingly gracious about being booted, at least once Prime Minister Hamilton promised her, with rock solid guarantees, a bump in the next honor's list.

Prime Minister Hamilton told Paul, on behalf of his Majesty and Prince Albert, that London wanted our own eyes on the ground on the Nazi-dominated earth before our Empire could commit to help Paul's world. He was not willing to commit based only on media representations of any sort, no matter how intriguing.

Prime Minister Hamilton insisted a team from our earth undertake a recce of the Nazi-dominated world. Paul said he would send that request back home, but it might be as much as six months before his world could modify a craft to carry a full combat commando into a hostile and technologically advanced world.

Paul countered with his own request. He asked London for a treaty to enable Paul's earth to test some very unusual atomic weapons on this world. Paul explained his folks couldn't risk testing them on his earth, since the Ming of his world would go bonkers when they detected the explosions.

Paul's folks figured testing those types of weapons on this world should be fine, since this world hadn't invented even transistors yet and we still used far more robust vacuum tubes. Paul's scientists assured us folks on this earth would scarcely notice a thing if they conducted a couple of bomb tests on some remote islands in the middle of the Pacific Ocean.

Surprisingly, Astrid was utterly uninvolved in these discussions. I was suspicious; usually she stuck her nose into everything involving Paul.

Several days passed before Nurse Mary told some of us why Astrid had been acting so strangely. Paul had relayed to Astrid the news that Astrid's odious intended had arranged tragic, fatal, and officially unsolved aircraft accidents for his two younger brothers. Astrid was concerned it might not now be safe for her to return to her own earth.

A British naval task force, the battlecruiser HMS *Anson*, the heavy cruiser HMS *Hawke* and the three screening destroyers *Sailfish*, *Swordfish* and *Marlin*, came over for joint maneuvers two weeks after flicker week. The task force first stopped at Nova Scotia; I suspected yet another batch of senior Pommies wanted to take a personal look at the time-line hopping WiG parked up in Sydney.

Lycus and Marcus got to take another destroyer ride up to Halifax, where they picked up some additional crew members before they sailed up to Sidney to be the Pommie visitors' guides. They did their thing and were returning with the task force. The task force was destined for Newport but stopped at sea, for reasons unknown, due south of Melinda's Aquidneck Island estate.

I got my field glasses and went to the widow's walk on top of Melinda's cottage. I could see HMS *Anson* about fifteen miles offshore. HMS *Hawke* was somewhat closer. I shrugged and headed down to breakfast.

Suddenly, the navy signalman on duty in our temporary communications room came down and found Kathy while we were starting breakfast. He saluted and said, "Ma'am. Signals from HMS *Hawke*. Senior Rear Admiral Nelson requests the pleasure of your company along with Major Smith, Dame Melinda, Lady Ruth, Dr. Martingale and Dr. Drake; whoever is available. The Hawke has dropped a launch and Admiral Nelson will be here within the hour."

Kathy cursed. I thought about getting jealous; from the variety of her curses she apparently had been spending a lot of time with some exceptionally foul-mouthed squids indeed. It had to be squids, of course; marines are famous for their gentlemanly vocabulary and their impeccably polite behavior.

I also exuded confusion. She picked up on the latter and explained. "Admiral Nelson is the head of the Royal Navy Intelligence Service. The senior Royal Navy. The one HQ'd in Whitehall."

She turned back to the signalman. "Did you confirm this with Newport?"

"Yes ma'am. They could confirm Admiral Nelson was aboard the Royal Navy task force, though they cannot account for his actions."

"Right. Ring up the marine detachment commander housed at the annex-to-be next door. Have him send a detail of eight marines suitable to pipe aboard an admiral. Current rules apply regarding kit and fatigues. I will not force my marines into their dress uniforms merely to stroke some admiral's oversized ego. I will contact everyone else."

Kathy could slip into her "I am a full colonel with a guaranteed promotion to brigadier" persona almost effortlessly by now.

An hour later, Melinda, Tiny, Elizabet, Jules, Kathy and my own sweet self were waiting in the main living room. The marine captain from next door and Melinda's senior butler showed our visitors into the living room. Our guests were Admiral Nelson, a Lieutenant Commander, and two civilians in dark glasses. One civilian was built on the same lines as Tiny. Tiny locked his eyes on that guy.

"Admiral Nelson," said Kathy. "To what do we owe the honor?" Her tone reflected temperature lows from the last ice age. She got miffed when senior officers tried to pull rank on her and barge into her personal space.

"Admiral, this is Dame Melinda and her husband, Mr. Sammartino. They are your hosts in the absence of Dame Melinda's parents. Next to me is my private secretary and Senior Research Assistant, Dr. Elizabet O'Shaughnessy. Standing next to her is my husband, RFC Marine Reserve Major John Smith. Dr. O'Shaughnessy is also my husband's number two concubine, for reasons of state. Elizabet is also obviously about five months into the family way.

"Next to her is Mr. Jules Thibodeaux, the brother of Miss Victoria Thibodeaux. Jules has been involved with us since our off world visitors arrived. My husband's number one concubine, Miss Francine Miller, is currently swimming laps in the indoor pool at the Sisters of Healing Priory next door; there was no reason for her to attend this meeting. Now, what is the reason for your unexpected presence?"

"Lady Katherine, I apologize profusely for the short notice. I am operating under quite strict operational security constraints. I couldn't help but observe the marine honor guard detail were dressed in battle fatigues and carrying battle-rifles and were wearing two bandoliers positively festooned with eight-round clips.

"I also notice Lady Ruth, and Doctors Martingale and Drake are not here. Will they be arriving soon?"

"Admiral Nelson. My friends and I have been the targets of four kidnapping or assassination attempts, one of which involved a shipload of Cuban thugs and another which involved a platoon of Imperial Russian Spetsnaz. Any marines on this estate understand damn well while I am here I set the rules, one of which is if they are on duty, they are armed to the teeth.

"If their officers don't understand this, then I will ring Vice Admiral Francis and he will straighten them out. If that doesn't work, then I will ring Prime Minister Hamilton and he will either fix things immediately or I will give him my resignation. My current wealth far exceeds the pittance the RFC sets as my official remuneration.

"Dr. Drake and Victoria Thibodeaux will arrive after Vicki finishes providing a second breakfast for Paul Junior, who is almost four months old. Lady Ruth is over at Joint Base West Kingston and has been there since six this morning overseeing some delicate research procedures. She will not attend us today. Dr. Martingale is playing tennis at the priory; we have sent for her.

"May I ask to what I owe this visit and will you stop beating around the damn bush?"

Elizabet interrupted Kathy. "Lady Katherine, when in civilian clothes, etiquette requires you to curtsy in the presence of His Royal Highness."

Elizabet looked straight at the smaller of the two civilians and curtsied.

The latter took off their dark glasses and even I could see the smaller one was Prince Albert.

Admiral Nelson ostentatiously took out a ten pound sterling note from his dress blouse's left front pocket and handed it to Prince Albert.

Kathy and Melinda both curtsied as well. Tiny and I both saluted instinctively. Jules looked stunned. Civilian. Albert waved us off.

"I am here purely in the persona of the Count of St. Pierre and Miquelon."

Kathy said, "Excuse me, Your Highness. I mean Count. I need to change our security status." She stepped out and had a brief conversation with the marine captain.

She came back into the room accompanied by both Vicki and Paul. Paul nodded at Prince Albert. "Prince, we meet again." Vicki curtsied, found out she was dealing with a mere count and found a comfortable chair.

Kathy explained. "The marines will run a security drill. We still have two platoons of them across the road. They will close off Melinda's estate to visitors, excepting only Marine Master Sergeant Oglethorpe and Dr. Martingale, who should come from the Priory through the side gate shortly. The marines based at this estate will go to a heightened security posture."

His Royal Highness said, "Thank you, Dame Katherine. Let me begin. I sailed over to meet the people who have created a political crisis for the Empire. Well, that, and I will attend a private memorial ceremony for the late Vice-Admiral Dame Madeline Hamilton."

Kathy and Elizabet both flinched, at least they did if you knew them well enough. I am sure I flinched, too. No wonder Madeline got her way so easily most of the time. Wheels within wheels; secrets within secrets. I guess no one was going to chastise His Royal Highness for expanding the number of folks who now knew of Madeline's formerly double-secret identity.

His Royal Highness paid no attention to our reactions.

"Parliament will shortly enact a law removing my brother's only child from the line of succession to inherit the throne of the United Kingdom and Ireland, the Greater Britannic Empire and the Protector of odds and ends, etc. My nephew Prince Charles is even less of an intellectual than is his father.

"Immediately after that, my brother will renounce his throne to spend more time with his beloved Welsh corgis. He was perfectly acceptable as a figurehead during an era where we faced absolutely no existential threats. Now the situation has changed and I will have to work for a living. And get married.

"Have I ever mentioned how much I loathe German princesses? She will have to be eighteen or nineteen years-old at most in order not to have a history. Also, did I mention how I truly, truly loathe empty, bubble-headed German Princesses, many of whom are my fourth or fifth cousins and were only tutored in how to simper stupidly?"

He looked around; I guessed he did so to see if he had elicited any sympathy from anyone. He sure as heck didn't get any from me.

Paul, though, smiled. "Perhaps I can help with that. I've had some thoughts along those lines since the first time we met."

His Highness continued, "Anyhow, I came to the RFC to hear from the horse's mouth, unofficially so to speak, as well as to see the elephant up close or whatever expression you military types use. My scientific advisors tried to explain to me in simple words what Dr. Drake's earth wishes to accomplish. The best I could understand was it was akin to replicating a massive solar flare of the type which sometimes interferes with radio reception.

"That is an impressive craft parked up there in Sidney. My advisors have also explained it would be easier for Prince Paul's folks to do the tests they need to do on this world, using our help, as they would only need a couple of trips to transport their equipment. If they had to do something bare-base on an uninhabited version of earth, it would take them hundreds of flights to move infrastructure and they think time is of the essence.

"I, however, need also need clear and convincing proof of an existential threat of civilizational evil to enter an alliance. All we have so far is your word, a strange-looking air/sea-craft, and the half insane ramblings of two wacko German doctors, currently tragically deceased because of, of..."

He paused. Admiral Nelson whispered something in his ear. The prince continued. "... because of Doctor Paul Drake's evaluation there was an immediate threat to Major Smith's life. And some absolutely ripping flickers."

Well, it was clear the true powers that be had a story, and they were going to stick to it, no matter how stupid it sounded.

"I accept that Paul Drake's folks are who you say you are because of all those medical advances, technological hints, and the enormous air-sea craft in which you arrived. If We confirm to Our satisfaction such an existential threat exists, We will undertake political measures to provide all possible help."

The count's incognito was slipping. His last sentence was definitely said using the royal voice.

Paul smiled. "Count, sometimes multiple problems can be worked so they solve each other. Might I suggest your personal options would be different if you were the one who had to sacrifice yourself to secure a diplomatic alliance? If you were on the wrong end of the beggars can't be choosers' spectrum?

"Say, perhaps, if a larger and more powerful empire demanded as the price of an alliance, you must marry the most obstreperous and headstrong unmarried princess they could unload upon you, though one almost as brilliant as she is arrogant. One with an admittedly sculpted figure, an impressive libido and who is still young enough to bear three or four children if she starts the process soon enough."

Prince Albert gave Paul a puzzled look.

"I will explain in a moment, Count. I believe I hear the princess in question approaching, even as we speak."

Paul was right; we could all hear a storm front of vitriol approaching from the east.

When April Showers Come Your Way

We listened to Astrid lambasting some of Melinda's staff on the way in. "What's this about some damn important meeting? I was this close to beating Mary and Theodora in a one-on-two tennis match when that moron Scarbutt said I had to crank my ass in gear and get over here. I haven't even changed or showered yet. Fine, somebody find me about a gallon of iced tea. Unsweetened."

Astrid burst into the room.

Everyone was now standing. Paul said, "Astrid, dearest sister of my brother's wife, this gentleman is Albert, the Count of St. Pierre and Miquelon. He is a distant cousin of Melinda's. They share a great-to-the-seventh grandmother."

"You dragged me off the tennis court merely to meet the fracking Count of some pathetic flyspeck islands in the North Atlantic? Paul, you have pulled a lot of crap on me over the decades, but this is near the top. Have I mentioned lately how loathsome you can be when you try?"

She glared at Albert. "Don't try any of Paul's type of 'I'm high nobility la-de-da crap' on me, Count whoever you are. I am the Baroness of Barcelona, the Marchioness of Mallorca, the Duchess of Sjaelland, and the Princess Minor of the Kingdom of Scandinavia, though I am not exactly in the good graces of my family at this moment. Unless, of course, my idiot grandfather was thoughtful enough to have dropped dead recently."

She gave him a longer look. "I am also the best damn medical doctor on this ball of dirt. You are thirty-six or thirty-seven years old. You dress exceptionally well, but you drink a little too much. Your teeth are yellowing, probably from too many cigars. Give those up and the odds are you will live ten years longer. You have additional staining from the tea and coffee, but that is expected on this earth. I don't know how you folks process all the booze and caffeine. I grant you work hard to maintain your muscle tone.

"You need to dismiss your current dentist and engage one who knows his ass from his elbow, but Count, you are in no danger of falling over dead soon. If this is not a medical emergency, then can someone please tell me why the frack am I here and not victoriously trash-talking those pathetic almost losers, Mary and Theodora?

"Why are all you morons smiling at me?"

Albert smiled at Astrid. "Princess Minor Astrid; my advisors told me you are the best surgeon on the planet. I do not doubt that anymore. I smoke too many cigars and I push the limits on consuming my whiskey. I guess I could reasonably expect you to tone down your language during more public occasions. I suppose it is too much to hope for you to have led a chaste and virtuous life, at least on this earth?"

I caught something out of the corner of my eye and saw Jules choking, slightly, on a prawn canape. He quickly poured and slugged down a glass of mineral water.

Astrid glared daggers at Paul; then looked carefully at the Count of St. Pierre and Miquelon. "I broke up with that last dirigible pilot over three weeks ago. What a damp squib he turned out to be. I have been utterly virtuous since. Anyway, if an officer I have met socially starts any rumors, I am sure I can ask Sir John to shoot them or something. I know he used to kill people for a living, and he owes me a couple of favors. I don't think there was anyone else, at least no one of consequence. Has Paul been suggesting I am a loose woman?"

Most of the old gang stared at Astrid, amazed she had said any of that with a straight face. None of us turned to look at Jules, but every one of our eyeballs gave him a quick glance. If we had searched in a dictionary for the phrase "deer in headlights" the accompanying picture would have shown his current expression.

Astrid plowed on. "This is pointless; I have no time for Paul's petty grudges. I need to go shower and change clothes because this tennis outfit gets damn uncomfortable when it is soaked by sweat and I can see Melinda will die of apoplexy if I take it off right now.

"I still don't know why Melinda insists I wear the stupid thing outdoors in the summer heat, especially over at the Priory where it's almost always only women. All this outfit is suitable for is to interfere with my body's absorption of Vitamin D. And that damn G-string she absolutely insists is the minimum I can wear under the tennis dress, even when I play at the priory, is chafing."

According to the calendar, we were enjoying mid-spring. It still felt a little cool to me and I grew up in the middle of the mitten three miles from the eastern shore of Lake Michigan. I guess Astrid had grown up close to the Arctic Circle.

Paul interjected. "Astrid, I am continually amazed by your instinctive grasp of every nuance of delicate diplomacy. The Count also has a few other titles. Melinda, since the Count is your cousin, albeit distant, could you do the honors?"

Melinda, looking completely glazed, still rattled off a couple of paragraphs' worth of titles, starting with "His Royal Highness" and ending with, "and Lord Deputy Protector of the Realm."

Paul looked at Albert, the King in waiting. "I can assure you she hardly ever simpers. My Empire might even throw in a bit of a dowry, since I cannot hide the fact she is getting a little long in the tooth to be a brood mare. On the other hand, if she gives you any grief, I believe she can be brought to heel by swatting her naked butt with bundles of fresh cut birch branches. No charge for that last advice, by the way."

Astrid swiveled her head back and forth. She was understandably confused.

Albert said, "My brother will abdicate soon and I will become His Imperial Majesty, whereupon I will need a royal spouse. Prince Paul has suggested We should marry you as a condition for Us to receive his Empire's aid. We can envision situations in which Our world will need aid from your Earth urgently."

Paul finally broke cover. "Damnit, Astrid. You're annoying, but I don't want to see you dead for real. Britannicus sent me his own message relating to your grandfather's idiocy. If you go home, you'll likely soon be killed for real, or worse, disappeared."

"Think, Astrid. It's not only your dotty granddad or psycho fiancé. I always eschewed the limelight, because of my job, but you're far too prominent socially to go home. If you do so, you risk causing the Ming Empire to find out about cross-earth travel before we are ready to tell them about it. Hell, here, at least, you can be a live queen."

Astrid initially glared at Paul, then frowned and said icily, "What do you mean, dead for real?"

"I can't blame them, Astrid; we also had lied to you about how many folks realize it is possible to travel to alternate earths. That knowledge had been tightly compartmentalized within the Imperial Military Intelligence Service. We never told our politicians we could do this. We funded the program out of our black budgets and used surplus and obsolete equipment to keep it going."

"You have got to be kidding me, Paul. Did you just now say that our political leaders don't yet know about trans-temporal travel?"

He nodded, yes. "You were much too prominent to disappear inexplicably. Thus, the folks running the alternate earths program could choose to reveal they had kept the program hidden for twenty years or they could fake your death. Officially, your clothes and Marcus's were found drifting in a small sailboat, two hundred miles from Bermuda, a week after you arrived in this world. You were both declared missing, presumably dead by drowning, during a tryst. Both your reputations have been thoroughly scorched. Marcus can't go home, either.

"After the crazy doctors revealed there was a possibility the Nazis on that other earth might know about cross-earths travel, I informed our ranking military intelligence folks. They had a cow. Only then did they reluctantly inform a furious, select group of senior politicians about our program.

"As of a week ago, six senior politicians had been briefed on the program. Originally, it seemed like a good idea to keep them in the dark. Really, Astrid, who amongst the current lot would you trust? Heck, I didn't even share this secret with my father or brother. Britannicus would have told Dad, and Dad's a tactician, rather than a strategist. He would have used the knowledge too soon, for too little effect. He knows now, though, and he's probably furious with me."

She paused, thought, almost spoke, and paused again. Astrid sighed and said, "You're correct about Britannicus; he would have told your father. I might have informed my father. Certainly I would not have told Sigrun; she gossips too much. I guess your colleagues had to tell the Emperor."

"Yeah, they did, but they had a lot of reservations. Our political leaders weren't any more competent twenty years ago when our intelligence service accidentally discovered travel to other earths was possible. Since then, every year or two, we found yet other excuses to delay telling our political masters.

"Anyhow, stuff is getting messy back home. They want me back ASAP to take control of the process. If you return home too soon, you will be up to your neck in the politics of it all. You're not prepared for that and there will be folks who will find it convenient to have you assassinated or disappeared for real.

"When I go back, I can inform your father and Siggy in person, so the right people in your family won't worry too much more about you. Immediately prior to when you came to this world, Llywelyn sent a message to them via one of Siggy's bodyguards, explaining you planned to go into hiding; he just hadn't said where."

Paul grimaced again. "Work with me, Astrid, for once. Heck, if you give me a couple of years, I bet I can clean things up enough so you can go home and visit your family. It's just going to be a long, delicate slog."

Astrid pondered things for a moment. Then she nodded, slowly.

"I was so angry with Grandfather I never thought of the secrecy aspect of my actions. I suspect your colleagues thought they had legitimate reasons for some of their decisions."

She looked around at all of us.

"It's not an awful world; and it is inhabited by some decent individuals. Nevertheless, I believe my next decision depends on the King in question."

She scrutinized His Highness thoroughly. "I sometimes read the tabloids, Albert. You have a nearly libelous reputation for being a world-class womanizer."

"The House of Hanover has had many rooms crowded with womanizers, Dr. Martingale. Many of my late relatives were quite good at it, with reason. I had sometimes hoped to follow joyfully in their footsteps, but alas, my older brother never grew into his job nor provided an adequate heir. Now we are going to need a head of state, who, in your vernacular, knows his ass from his elbow. It's one thing for the third in line to the throne to play the field; a king, though, needs to put statecraft first.

"I had been lamenting to your sister's husband's brother how much I loathed simpering, bubble-headed German princesses in their late teens, who were the only types my advisors were considering. Paul implied you were neither simpering nor bubble-headed and were sufficiently royal and had never married."

Astrid glared again at Paul, but then shrugged.

She finally spoke. "I still need a shower. Bertie, you can come along and sponge my back. We'll see how things go. I will know within the week at most whether this is going to work out or whether I am going to poison the lot of you surreptitiously, starting with Paul. Except for Jules; I would not deprive the world of a world class chef and a decent human being. The rest of you bastards can go hang if this doesn't pan out."

She looked around the room again. "The big-shouldered guy over there eyeing me is your personal bodyguard, is he not? You should tell him squinting so hard is bad for his eyes. It's pointless, anyhow. My dress is tight enough he can't be worried about hidden artillery.

"Besides, frisking me wouldn't do any good; I know where most of Melinda's emergency pistols are concealed. There is at least one hidden behind cunningly marked tiles in every shower-room in this cottage. Of course, if we get married, and he still turns puce-colored, I will give him a medical examination he will never forget."

Prince Albert said, "Stand down, William. We should know in a few hours whether I will extend my visit to Rhode Island. Talk to my weasel in charge of publicity. Prepare a story about my being treated for indigestion or something while I accept the gracious hospitality of Sir Charles and Lady Burr for a week."

Astrid returned her gaze to Melinda. "Are your parents still staying with Penny's folks on Long Island?"

Melinda nodded silently. She was still in shock.

Astrid continued, "Not that it matters much, Melinda, except I needed to know whether I might have to switch to physician mode if I sent your mother into shock. Please have some pastries, hot and iced tea and coffee sent to the Blue Suite. No alcohol. We are going to ween Bertie from that, as well as the cigars. It's the least I can try to do for an allied head of state, even if he turns out to be worthless in bed."

I had a friend in high school and I was looking at him when he watched his dog get hit by timber truck. The mutt died instantly, but the look of shock on my friend's face lasted for months. It was exactly the same look that William, the Prince's bodyguard, was wearing now. Admiral Nelson wore a similar look. The Admiral's aide had turned around and was staring at the ceiling, so I couldn't gauge his expression.

I could only imagine the look on my face when Prince Albert and Astrid left the room.

We waited. Then we waited some more. Melinda and Vicki excused themselves in order to provide their sons either third breakfast or early first lunch. When Melinda came back, she had arranged for her staff to bring in a lunch for us. We all picked at our food, too tense to eat. Most of us kept glancing at Paul, thinking *what type of monster have you unleased?*

Astrid and his Royal Highness returned. Astrid now lived at the Priory next door, but maintained a substantial wardrobe at Melinda's cottage. She didn't want the bother of flitting back and forth for special occasions, such as dressing for dinner when Jules was in town and whipping up one of his classic Cajun meals.

Astrid had changed into one of her skirt suit outfits and looked like she had stepped from society page photographs of the Royal Box at the Ascot Races. We all jumped to our feet. Astrid and his Royal Highness were as expressionless as it was possible to be.

Astrid stuck her nose up in the air and said, "Aren't you all supposed to tug your forelocks or something?"

I yelled before I could think. "Damn it, Astrid. That's the sort of arrogant behavior that sparks revolutions."

Everyone else stared at me, slack jawed.

Astrid stuck out her hand at Prince Albert. He pulled out the distinctively rumpled ten pounds sterling note he had lifted off Admiral Nelson earlier and ostentatiously gave it to her. Then Astrid stuck out her tongue at me.

His Royal Highness guffawed. Loudly.

"Damn straight, Lieutenant Colonel Smith. Dr. Astrid wanted to demonstrate her political acumen, which Prince Paul had disparaged. The bet was you would mouth off first. Even odds against the rest of the room, and I still lost."

Gosh, somehow I had dodged a metaphorical royal bullet.

"It's still Major Smith, your Highness."

"It was Major Smith. We cannot make you a full colonel until you complete a real college degree. It's still a reserve commission and We may have to have a few more conversations before We can say whether it's an RFC or a UK Royal Marine Corps commission. It will take a few months to arrange a royal wedding; in the meantime, We expect you to help keep Our future queen safe."

Kathy let out a big whoosh. I don't think I had heard her breathe for over an hour.

Prince Albert turned towards toward his bodyguard. "William, We will need to add some lady bodyguards to the security detail. Please talk to Colonel Smith and Mr. Sammartino about that; they have some experience along those lines. Astrid has assured Us she is already a capable markswoman."

Prince Albert turned to Kathy, "Dame Brigadier Katherine, We thank you. You have sacrificed much and been the soul of courtesy and professionalism under stressful circumstances. We will ensure adjustments are made to the military and honors lists, effective immediately."

Kathy only nodded; she was still in shock. Well, so were we all.

Counter Attack and Fallout

The next world hopper to arrive brought along Astrid's dowry, a vast set of electronic files. Julius started looking through the data and discovered Astrid's dowry was a detailed geological survey of earth. Among other data, it showed all deposits of oil, coal, and natural gas and gold known to Astrid's earth.

Julius told Paul, who talked to Astrid, who talked to Kathy. Kathy talked to Elizabet. They both talked to Melinda and Astrid. The four ladies determined if the information was to be released all at once, then the global economy would collapse after a brief economic explosion.

Astrid gave Kathy operational control over the data. Kathy made a command decision and classified the lot at the "Royal Fuzzbin" level. She appointed Elizabet and Melinda as the committee allowed to release dribs and drabs of information when economically beneficial. Data releases would be attributed to successful efforts of hard working intelligence folks.

I told the girls "hard working intelligence folks" was an oxymoron and no one would believe the cover story. They all called me a dumb jarhead. Ultimately, Astrid blessed the approach, saying it was her damn dowry and she could do with it what she wished to maximize its value.

Because of all the other information coming from Paul's Empire, our own Empire was already about to embark upon an economic boom like this world had never seen. Of course, there was still a theoretical Nazi menace putting our world's incipient economic takeoff at risk.

Dafydd ap Owain and Captain Tim Franks were chosen as joint commanders of a team to go over on a recce of Nazi-earth Cuba. Initially they planned to return to Havana, in that other timeline, rather than surveying the other world's New York City on the grounds the Spanish, culturally, are less exacting in their enforcement of regulations than are Germans. Still, the potential for disaster was enormous. I was worried.

Paul had dashed off to London, but I tracked down Astrid and asked her why her world had so little information about the Nazi-dominated earth. She said she didn't know why all they had were recordings of radio and video broadcasts the first WiG to have visited the Nazi earth had recorded. She said her folks should have heard, but hadn't, from the satellite the first world-hopper had launched upon its arrival. Her folks figured the satellite must have malfunctioned as it had sent no messages.

I asked her to describe in more detail how the satellite works. She said fine, today my yoga routine is scheduled for mid-morning, we can talk then. It turns out she wore some type of clingy pants and a sleeveless top while doing yoga.

Astrid explained between deep breaths, "First, John, the world hopper does its usual trip to another world in the dead of night. Then they lift the satellite into orbit. Most of the work is done by a hydrogen-filled balloon. The balloon goes up to about twenty miles high. Ten minutes after the sensors on the balloon detect sunlight, things happen. The satellite is shaped roughly like a manta ray and is intrinsically stealthy.

"It slowly accelerates into orbit, helped by the lift inherent in its design. It is powered by incredibly concentrated onboard fuel. Our technicians would have liked to have used fusion, but our engineers were still working on how to hide a fusion ion trail."

I nodded, pretending I had some idea what a fusion ion trail actually was.

"While this is happening, the balloon starts its self-destruct sequences. The balloon destruction sequence has lots of redundancies. Our folks tested this process on an unpopulated version of earth we call Timeline Primitive. It's surprisingly difficult to spot an inherently undetectable balloon gently burning itself to ashes when the balloon is twenty miles up on the edge of the daytime/nighttime line.

"Even with powerful telescopes looking right at it, the balloon looks like a pint-size meteor hitting the upper atmosphere when it burns.

Once the satellite gets into its programmed orbit, a process which takes three or four days to complete, the WiG which launched it usually has returned home."

"That seems inefficient, Astrid. And it's potentially dangerous if you leave a guy on the ground on your first trip."

"Just like life, John, it's a matter of trade-offs. For the scout on the ground to initiate contact, he would need an inexplicably advanced radar and transmitter device. He would have to retain this equipment for several days while he waited for the satellite to attain its final orbit. Next, he would have to locate and communicate with the satellite. Any time you pump energy into space, you risk being detected.

"So instead, we always initiate communications from the satellite. It sequentially sends an ultra-tight beam to a limited set of specific, predetermined locations on the surface. If the scout is there, his implant acknowledges with a micro-burst reply and establishes the permanent link.

"Anyhow, on our first trip to the Nazi-controlled world, we launched a stupid satellite to whiz around. It was supposed to send stealthy data drones home every ten days until it exhausted its on-board supply. It did nothing. Then seven years ago we sent another WiG to that earth and it never came back. We hadn't planned to risk another WiG on that earth until we made some serious upgrades to our stealth technology."

I shared Astrid's thoughts at dinner with Kathy, Francine, and Elizabet. Elizabet processed things and said, "If they have upgraded their stealth, even a bit, they might risk a quick pop in and out, somewhere in the deserted middle of the far South Atlantic. Paul said his folks have a base on Ascension Island. That's far more isolated than is Bermuda. You already know the satellite's intended orbit, so it shouldn't take more than a couple of hours of passive observation to locate the satellite and determine if it will respond to new instructions to turn itself on.

"Also, send one or two of our folks along with Paul's folks when they pop over into the Nazi-controlled earth. That could be enough to convince his Majesty. Don't send a larger reconnaissance team until you have explored the other possibilities."

I told Paul of her suggestion. I watched him pound his head on the desk in front of him and repeat the process. He sent a suggestion back to his home world.

They got back to us rapidly. We sent two officers; one was Captain Franks. The other was the best German linguist currently serving in the UK Royal Navy Signal Corps. They took separate light cruisers down to Ascension Island. There they boarded a WiG world-hopper which had popped over from Paul's earth. It transited to the Nazi-run earth and lay doggo in the deserted middle of the South Atlantic for two nights and one day. They came back to Ascension and dropped off our folks.

A couple of weeks later, we got word from Paul's world. They evaluated the WiG's signals collection and decided the Nazi-dominated world was worse than anything our most appalling nightmares could have imagined.

Captain Franks and the Royal Navy lieutenant commander briefed His Majesty in person. King Albert examined pictures and read briefings. He spoke. "They cannot get loose into the multiverse. God have mercy on their souls. And ours."

Shortly thereafter, two WiGs popped into our world near Bermuda; they carried two atomic devices. A navy transport sailed the devices to Quebec City. They were transported by rail to Victoria on the other coast. A navy task force transported them to two former Royal Navy coaling stations on now uninhabited islands in the remote Southeast Pacific.

The two Pacific island test devices were code-named Little Boy and Fat Man. I wondered about the names until Paul told me about wartime events on yet another timeline. That was when Paul admitted to me that the nuclear bomb tests, conducted on our world so as not to concern his earth's Ming Empire, constituted the quid pro quo for killing Carl and Brunhilde von Clausewitz.

The tests two worked perfectly. As apparently so did the subsequent, nearly simultaneous massive EMP bursts over Berlin, New York, and Tokyo in the Nazi-dominated earth courtesy of EMP-generating devices named El Alamein, Stalingrad, and Midway.

Franks and the Royal Navy boffin sailed back to Ascension. Three weeks after the EMPs popped they took another trip to the Nazi earth. Again the WiG hung out doggo in the middle of the South Atlantic and listened.

The ultra-centralized governance on that earth had fallen apart quickly. Besides the electromagnetic pulses, both the Nazis and the Imperial Japanese had each popped off a half dozen nukes at the other country. Ain't trust among supposed allies grand?

Paul's intelligence professionals had hoped that any scientists on the Nazi-dominated earth who got wind of the possibility of cross-earth travels had kept it secret squirrel. It appeared they had.

Whether they kept it secret wouldn't matter for much longer. The surviving pockets of governance were being sent back post-haste to a horse and buggy age for which they were ill-prepared. All the subject nations and races were in revolt, except for some fascist nations of South America.

The latter were not economically autarchic and Paul's intelligence analysts judged they were burning through their supplies of advanced technology at a rapid clip. From those few advanced electronic signals still in operation, we judged the surviving centers of fascist governance, to the extent they still controlled anything, blamed the other nations of that earth for what had happened to them.

Neither our world nor Paul's world expected to face a Nazi threat any time in the next couple of centuries, unless, of course, that there was another Nazi world out there similar to that first one.

Our earth would have to prepare itself for such an eventuality. I figured interesting times were ahead because the French, the Austrians, the Ottomans, the Russians, the Manchu's and the Chrysanthemum Empire governments knew travel to alternate earths was possible. All their leaders and intelligence folks had all seen the flickers Paul and Astrid's folks had brought over and were now cognizant of what an existential threat might look like.

Most major nations sent senior representatives to a world congress in Vienna, where they would try to hash out some new diplomatic ground rules to cover our new circumstances. I figured there was at least some hope the threat would lead to some positive changes on that front. I was utterly confident the assembled cookie-pushers would do massive damage to Vienna's world-class pastry shops, brew-pubs and wine bars.

Meanwhile, back at home, Melinda appointed herself the head of Astrid's bachelorette party committee. She arranged a massive sendoff for Astrid at the Priory late one afternoon, several days before Astrid and her bodyguards left for England. Melinda contracted with one of Bridget O'Shaughnessy's wholly owned subsidiaries to provide the nibbles and such.

Kathy wouldn't say a word about the party. Elizabet told me this was the one time in her life she wished she did not have a photographic memory. Francine said she was shocked and appalled by the depth of aristocratic debauchery and she reminded me she had seen those shows in Havana.

I asked Kathy if she planned to use this knowledge to bring Astrid to heel if Astrid got out of line.

"Gosh, Hotshot. That would be tough. I wish I had thought of a way to take compromising pictures of Astrid. Maybe I should have become the secret head of RFC Intelligence. Melinda has both the originals and the negatives."

I finally worked up enough nerve to talk to Melinda. She showed me pictures of familiar female faces, though Melinda had to point out to me the RIPP Governor's wife. They were all dressed to the nines in formal gowns and elbow-length gloves. She said the bachelorette party was the finest Irish high tea in the history of our planet, and Astrid spent most of her time nibbling sugar biscuits and tearing up while hugging the novitiates goodbye.

King Albert sent the HMS *Anson* over to Newport to transport Astrid to England. Jennifer Oglethorpe and three other Valkyries escorted Astrid on the *Anson* back to England. They served as Astrid's personal bodyguards for a couple of weeks. The next WiG which popped over brought four other-earth Scandinavian lady bodyguards. They carried advanced weaponry and communications gear. Astrid's sister Sigrun personally selected them to protect Astrid, though she had done so on the down low.

Eight novitiates returned to their home earth's Bermuda base, taking the comatose Eduardo with them. If the docs on the other earth ever woke Eduardo, those folks would interrogate him thoroughly. Paul, Vicki and Paul Jr. boarded the same flight which carried Eduardo. I figured Paul had lied about going back to play power politics; I thought it far more like he wanted to skip out on Astrid's wedding.

Mary and Theodora and two novitiates stayed here to establish a permanent chapter of The Sisters of Healing. Bridget O'Shaughnessy, Melinda and Astrid co-sponsored it. They all had reasons to approve of the nuns with guns concept.

The world was enthralled by the news-flickers chronicling the wedding of Princess Astrid to King Albert. Our Empire was quite taken with the gracious, fashionable, elegant, couth, selfless, yet still mysterious Queen Astrid.

Astrid now spends two days per week serving as a surgeon at various London charity hospitals. She is nearly universally beloved. Word on the women's grapevine, via Mary and Theodora, was Astrid is already expecting.

My own new daughters, Mary, named after Elizabet's actual mother and Maxine, who got her portmanteau name from my Uncle Max and Francine, are both cute as little buttons. Somehow, Kathy, Elizabet, and Francine all got along together under the same roof. Francine has been the primary care-giver because both Kathy and Elizabet are working like dogs in their official duties.

Prime Minister Hamilton has promised to introduce some legislation to plus up the army and navy intelligence services and modernize the RFC constabulary intelligence office, but it looks like that is going to take a least a couple of more months to figure out how they wanted to structure things. It is sensible to measure twice and cut once, but in the meantime Kathy and Elizabet are flailing around like one-armed jugglers, each with seven balls in the air.

Our estate now has a platoon of marines as the primary security force. Joseph Sammartino recruited a full complement of the most formidable ex-RFC army types on earth to provide security for Melinda's estate. The Priory is guarded by the expanded Valkyries, Captain Jennifer Oglethorpe, RIPP Militia/WASP, commanding. All the Sisters are armed as well. There are two companies of marines now permanently stationed at the navy base eight miles north of us, and the navy usually parks a patrol ship offshore from Melinda's estate.

Jennifer's husband, that slug of a retired marine, Lucius Oglethorpe, bamboozled his way into an important position. He serves as the civilian consultant to liaise among the Valkyries, the marines, the navy, and select local neighbors. Bridget does not share with me what her current security arrangements are, but she said if another ship filled with Cuban thugs ever again attacked her estate, they would enjoy the surprise of their suddenly shortened lives.

I suspect Scarbutt has an idea what Bridget has in the works in terms of estate defense. He meets with either Wires or Slab to toss stilettos about once a week. Scarbutt took twenty-five pounds sterling off Wires at their first contest. Bridget O'Shaughnessy then offered him a job as one of her own security consultants if Scarbutt steps off the government contracting gravy train.

Lady Ruth and her husband, RFC Marine Corps Major Franks, now live on Colonel's Row at JBWK. Lady Ruth accepted a navy captaincy in the medical service. Then they gave her an extra swoosh on her dress gold braids, which proclaimed her a commodore. She found it useful indeed in her efforts to keep navy medical doctors in line. I hope she has a good backup for when she goes on maternity leave in a couple of months.

Jules went down to Philly to run *Chez Plonk*. Kathy wanted everything in expert hands since Melinda had given Kathy *Chez Plonk*. Kathy figured in another couple of years, she was going to step back from the current madness and decide if she was going to return to the restaurant business for good. As far as security arrangements went, since there was no more call for me to help save the world, I was now a fifth wheel.

I got bored. As in I will go bang my head against the wall because it's a change of pace bored. Then I heard my Uncle Max was trying to get hold of me, yet again.

About Blaine McCants

Blaine McCants is an Ohio native, earning a BA from Denison University in Mathematical Economics as well as Soviet and Eastern Studies in 1972, following up with a PhD in Economics from Duke. He retired from the Air Force as a Lt. Colonel after four years of active service and sixteen years in the reserves. Active duty was followed by a thirty year career at the CIA as an economist specializing in Soviet and then Russian and International Economics, including a year at the Navy War College in Newport, Rhode Island. After retirement he spent two years with the US Treasury Financial Crimes Enforcement Network. During his many years crunching numbers and battling bureaucracy he maintained his sanity with a steady diet of science fiction, fantasy, and cheesy movies, dreaming of a retiring to write novels.

Other works by Blaine McCants:

The Hands That Rock the Triggers (Volume I of The Clash of Timelines)

Super Spy Dawn and the Extra-Galactic Shoggoth

The Adventure Continues...

The Scum Also Rises: The Clash of Timelines Trilogy (Volume III)
Forthcoming

Former Royal Marine Sniper Sergeant John Smith, his wife, his politically mandated mistresses and a handful of visitors from a Roman-Britain timeline have disrupted the perfidious plots of some rather nasty, and now deceased, physicians from a Nazi timeline. Now comes the tough part—preparing Smith's own earth for a massive technological surge and the ensuing societal changes. Smith, his family, and his colleagues suspect that even deadlier threats may lurk in the multiverse and no one thinks that bolt-action Enfield battle rifles will cut the mustard the next time round.

On Smith's earth, where George III choked to death on an oyster back in 1767, high-level politics aren't beanbag. A lot of important folks will play hardball rather than relinquish their own hereditary, and often extra-legal, privileges and hobbies. Can Smith and his ever-expanding family make enough of a difference to give their earth a fighting chance? Would things have been any different if only Smith hadn't punched out the Tsar's youngest son in that tavern brawl at the *Sozzled Sturgeon* back in the day? These and other questions will be answered in the final volume of *The Clash of Timelines Trilogy*.